# THE TOWER AND THE HIVE

# THE TOWER
# AND THE HIVE
## Anne McCaffrey

## BANTAM PRESS

LONDON · NEW YORK · TORONTO · SYDNEY · AUCKLAND

TRANSWORLD PUBLISHERS LTD
61–63 Uxbridge Road, London W5 5SA

TRANSWORLD PUBLISHERS
c/o RANDOM HOUSE (AUSTRALIA) PTY LTD
20 Alfred Street, Milsons Point, NSW 2061, Australia

TRANSWORLD PUBLISHERS
c/o RANDOM HOUSE NEW ZEALAND
18 Poland Road, Glenfield, Auckland, New Zealand

TRANSWORLD PUBLISHERS
c/o RANDOM HOUSE (Pty) LTD
Endulini, 5a Jubilee Road, Parktown 2193, South Africa

Published 1999 by Bantam Press
a division of Transworld Publishers Ltd

Typeset in 11 on 12 Times
by Hewer Text Ltd, Edinburgh
Printed in Great Britain by
Mackays of Chatham plc, Chatham, Kent.

This book is affectionately and gratefully dedicated to

Graham Hamilton

For blue Jaguars and Eddie Stobbart Hauliers

# Acknowledgements

I have excellent reason to be particularly grateful to four experts in writing this conclusion of the Talent (aka *The Tower and the Hive*) series. Dr Jack Cohen of the University of Warwick and I discussed how I could solve the problem of colonizing Hivers. So I had a structure to begin with. I was dumbfounded to discover that my dictionary had only five lines about the very complex subject of 'pheromones'. The Web came to my assistance and I asked for help, which was quick in coming from Jonathan Brecher and Louis Culot of CambridgeSoft on their especial expertise, both as generalists and for specific knowledge about pheromones. We had some lively email exchanges since Jonathan knew of *Lyon's Pride* when I approached him for assistance. His colleague, Louis Culot, supplied additional details. I wish also to thank Bibb Graves from Hewlett Packard Houston for a description of gas chromatographs, which register the strength and composition of pheromones. We extrapolated – as is the function of science fiction – that the future would miniaturize what are actually large and cumbersome instruments. But then most current gas chromatographs (GC) have altered considerably from their original forms and no doubt will have altered even more by the time of *The Tower and The Hive*.

I am also grateful to my readers – Mary Jean Holmes, Lea Day, and my daughter, Georgeanne Kennedy – who try to spot any inconsistencies, typos and errors in the grammar which might occur in the fifth of a series that was first started in 1990. I am indebted to my editor, Susan Allison, and her staff of copy editors, for their valuable comments and assistance overall.

# WHAT HAS
# GONE ON BEFORE . . .

When an unknown enemy threatened all human life on Deneb, Jeff Raven shouted – telepathically – for help and reached the Rowan[1], the lonely Lady in the Tower at the Callisto Tower of the Federated Telepath and Teleport. With her help as Callisto Prime Talent, Jeff freed his planet of invasion. He also became the next Earth Prime.

The Rowan and Jeff Raven had five children. The precocious Damia, the second daughter of their marriage, emerges as a Prime Talent, too, and is sent to occupy the Tower at Iota Aurigae's new mining planet.[2] There she encounters an intelligence on a distant spaceship borne, known as Sodan, who tries to lure her into giving him directions to her planet. Her family become suspicious of her enchantment with this 'mind' and send her brother, Larak, and Afra, to divert her. In the ensuing meeting of minds, Larak is killed by a brutal telepathic bolt from Sodan who IS only a mind. Damia and Afra are seriously injured, too. While recuperating on Deneb,

1 *The Rowan*, 1990
2 *Damia*, 1991

Damia and Afra are contacted by the 'dreams' of the Mrdini. An alien race, they have been fighting the dread Spheres of the Hiver Queens who were the invaders which Jeff and the Rowan had thwarted.

The Mrdini are exceedingly impressed by the fact that Deneb was able to defeat the attacking Hiver Sphere without loss of life. They have been fighting the Hivers for two centuries and only suicide squadrons are able to penetrate and destroy the Spheres.

In order to cement relationships between the two species, Mrdini young are placed with Human young and grow up learning each other's language and culture. Damia's children[3], starting with young Laria, each have a pair of Mrdini young.

When Laria becomes sixteen, she is sent to Clarf, one of the five Mrdini worlds. On Clarf, Laria teaches Basic to Mrdinis and learns their 'adult' language, accompanied by her two 'Dinis, Tip and Huf. At eighteen, she takes over as FT&T Prime at Clarf Tower as the Star League Alliance of Human and Mrdini continues to track down or resist the Hiver incursions.

Then three Hive Spheres penetrate League Space and three pursuit squadrons of mixed Human and Mrdini ships are sent after each of the Hive ships, to track them to their separate destinations. Another group is sent to trace their ion trails back to their planet of origin. In order to continue these searches most effectively, FT&T is asked to supply the flagship of each group with a Prime, or sufficient lesser Talents, to keep in touch with the League Base and to 'receive' additional supplies of food and material on what could be long voyages.

Young Thian Raven, Laria's brother, is sent to the *Vadim*, under the command of Captain Ashiant as he and the ships backtrack the fleeing Hiver Spheres. Thian himself comes under threat when the nova-blasted, derelict Great Sphere of the Hivers is found in space. A jealous latent Talent attacks him while he is part of a team exploring the dead Sphere and he is nearly killed. Damia assists him in identifying his assailant.

Meanwhile one of the queens fleeing the Great Sphere has

3 *Damia's Children*, 1992

2

been captured and is incarcerated in an unused facility on Heinlein Moon Base where she can be studied from a viewing station, carefully stationed safely out of connection to her 'prison'. Mrdini and Humans alike await her exit from the pod. Attempts to contact the huge, mantis-like queen are futile, as she does not recognize any other species. All hopes to establish negotiations and thus curtail Hiver incursions in the Star League are thwarted.

The Mrdini are not convinced that the nova, which had devastated the Great Sphere, has destroyed the Hiver home world and wish to have proof. Thian, bravely recovering from the attack, agrees to accompany the Mrdini ship the *KLTL* in its search, thus making sure of supplies and contact during what is possibly a year-long trek. By doing so, he will prevent any young Mrdinis 'going on the line' – a Mrdini euphemism for self-sacrifice to feed their crewmates.

The League decides to try to salvage what it can of the Great Sphere to learn more about Hiver space-engineering.

Afra accompanies his second-born son, Rojer, to the *Genessee* under Captain Etienne Osullivan, for special duty when a Sphere is tracked to a Hiver-occupied system, identified on Mrdini maps as 'Xh-33'. Despite being of the same species, the Sphere is fired upon from the planet and its queens destroyed as they try to escape the bombardment of their ship in pods.

Back on Iota Aurigae, Zara Lyon, sister of Laria, Thian and Rojer, becomes quite upset about the condition of the queen in Heinlein Base and determines to assist the captive. She manages to sneak a ride to Earth's Moon. Her interference results in saving the life of the captive queen who has been slowly freezing. Even before this incident, Damia and Afra have worried about Zara's potential as a Tower Prime. Jeff and Rowan Raven agree that Zara might be better suited in another profession and Zara is training with Elizara Reidinger, a dedicated medical T-1.

Despite orders from the High Council to maintain a watching brief[4], a Mrdini ship captain attempts to coerce Rojer into

4 *Lyon's Pride,* 1994

teleporting the ship's missiles to destroy Hiver settlements on the Xh-33. Rojer's two 'Dini friends, Kat and Gil, are killed defending him from the Mrdini captain. Rojer barely escapes with his life. His mother, Damia, arrives to succour him and removes him to his grandmother's quiet home on Deneb Five to recuperate from the loss of his dear friends.

The Rowan, arriving on the *Genessee* in the Xh-33 system, helps Captain Etienne Osullivan execute a daring plan to 'steal' the refugee Sphere, and to destroy the two Hiver vehicles in orbit about the Xh-33. She requires the assistance of Thian, returned from his post on the Mrdini ship, and Flavia, a T-1 from the Rowan's native planet, Altair. With the use of Talent, the Sphere is purloined from the system and sent on its way to the League, thus giving the Alliance a relatively undamaged Hiver spaceship for Mrdini and Human engineers to examine. Teleported explosives blow up any chance for the Xh-33 Hiver population to leave the surface. The smaller Hiver scout-ships that emerge from an underground hangar to fight back are also destroyed. The Alliance sets up on one of the Xh-33 moons to monitor the surface.

Once the intact sphere ship is moored off Phobos Moon Base, teams are set up to examine it in detail. That is best accomplished with the help of Talents. To avoid the aggravating 'sting-pzzt' emanating from Hiver artefacts, the Talents control the exploration from a distance. Thian heads the team which includes the newest engineering graduate, his brother Rojer, Flavia and other assorted Talents, including several latent ones (for instance, Commander Semirame Kloo) who discover that they are 'bothered' by the sting-pzzt emanations of Hiver artefacts. (Only Talents are affected by this phenomenon.)

While the Talented team is able to search the intricate labyrinth of a Hiver ship, including the 'bridge' apparently staffed by twelve queens, they are unable to power it up. The Talents decide that the only recourse is to teleport the Heinlein Base Queen into the 'bridge' and see how she activates the ship. Ever watchful of his grandchildren, Jeff Raven, Earth Prime, approves of this ploy and comes along to be sure the queen does not escape. She shows the watching Primes how to power up the Sphere and is then deftly 'ported back to her prison.

Meanwhile, other squadrons are following a Sphere, which seems uninterested in many likely M-5 worlds that it passes. These are briefly investigated by Talents: in one instance, by T-2 Kincaid Dano whose capacity is overtaxed by the scope of the mission. Before he is burned out, both by his duties and the unfortunate struggle for his attentions by officers on his ship, he is relieved of that duty and transferred to Laria's Tower on Clarf with his 'Dinis, Nil and Plus. He insists, despite his fatigue, on contacting Earth Prime with a report that there are more Hiver-occupied worlds than previously suspected: Hivers now occupy four of the twenty likely planets he has probed. He recommends that these worlds should be examined by the League as possible colonial worlds to relieve the pressure on overpopulated Mrdini planets.

Consequently, while the main squadron under Captain Ashiant continues to follow the Sphere so obviously headed in a special direction, another group, under the command of Captain Vestapia Soligen on the *Columbia,* is staffed to explore the four M-type worlds: Talavera, Waterloo, Marengo and Ciudad Rodrigo. Prime Talent Flavia, Zara Lyon, Lt Rhodri Eagles, T-3 and incidentally cousin to the Lyon children, are part of that contingent.

Suddenly more Spheres are identified, some uncomfortably close to the *Columbia* while others speed to join or assist the Hiver that Captain Ashiant is tracking. This unexpected development suggests that the Hivers do have some form of communication. It would appear that this Sphere is searching for a star as near to their home world's primary as possible. But what are the parameters? Searching records of earlier star maps in the general area of the nova, the signature of the primary, before it was destroyed, is verified. Thus the searchers are able to discover exactly what sort of primary the Hivers are looking for.

Following the Sphere, the astrogators spot a primary with the requisite signature and Captain Ashiant engages some of the enemy in a space battle. At first the Human/Mrdini ships are overwhelmed until Thian realizes that Talents can end the battle by teleporting explosives to detonate the fuel tanks of the Hiver ships. As Talents are not supposed to engage in defensive, or offensive, manoeuvres, there is some criticism of Thian's actions. However, the explosives do destroy the Spheres. Captain Soligen's squadron, also being pursued by Spheres, is able to use this method, too, to destroy them. In contrast to a direct confrontation, the Hivers DO recognize other spaceships as threats. So the Hivers are prevented from establishing a new home world.

While that threat is eliminated, many more Hiver worlds have been located. All of them must be identified, and, since the ethics of the Human/Mrdini Alliance do not include species genocide, how can the Hivers be prevented from following their cyclic behaviour of overpopulating their planets and looking for new worlds to inhabit? How can FT&T under Jeff Raven's capable management find enough suitable Talents to keep up with the ever-expanding demands for Primes?

# CHAPTER ONE

By noon of the day after the destruction of the Number Three Hiver Sphere, the newly promoted Admiral Ashiant was already giving orders to elements of his Fleet to implement the second phase of their five-year mission. They could now begin to identify and reconnoitre all Hiver-occupied worlds in this quadrant of space. They were to initiate in-depth probes of such planets, disable any orbiting spheres and establish monitoring satellites to warn the Alliance of any further suspicious surface activity.

As the *Vadim* and *KLTL* were already within the system targeted by Number Three as possessing a primary similar to their original one, Admiral Ashiant ordered Captains Pat Shepherd and Prlm to do a thorough environmental exploration of the viable planets in the M-5 and M-6 positions.

'They might as well,' Admiral Ashiant told his captain, Ailsah Vandermeer, 'since the chase to destroy the two remaining scouts has already taken them halfway there. Rather far out to consider an immediate colonization of those worlds but who knows how fast the Alliance will spread once the threat of Hivers is reduced? The Mrdini certainly need more space.'

'So they do,' Ailsah agreed sympathetically.

'I suspect those habitable worlds closer in to our home systems, 'Dini and Human, will receive the first mandates. However,' and he slapped his desk top decisively, 'no need for us to hang about. Captain Vandermeer, if you will please initiate a three-hundred-and-sixty-degree turn of the *Washington*, we'll begin the long journey home.'

'Aye, sir,' Vandermeer said, giving him a crisp salute and a wry grin. 'It will, as you know, take us five full ship days to slow enough to execute the manoeuvre.'

'Long enough for Shepherd and Prlm to do their probes and be halfway back to us,' Ashiant murmured.

'Should be an interesting cruise, sir.'

'Indeed,' Admiral Ashiant said, lightly fingering the circle of tiny stars that was his new rank. Hastily withdrawing his hand, he cleared his throat.

'Anything else, sir?' Vandermeer asked, pretending not to see that gesture.

'No, Captain, that'll be all. Good day.'

When news of those orders reached the Primes relaxing in the FT&T lounge, there was both excitement and regret.

'I wish one of us had been able to go with Captain Shepherd,' said the recently promoted Lieutenant T-2 Clancy Sparrow in a wistful tone. 'It'd be interesting to see what Hivers consider "perfect worlds".'

'They seem to have found sixteen planets near enough perfect to eliminate any other life-forms, including Deneb,' Prime Talent Thian remarked in a droll tone. 'And seemingly about one in five of other M-type worlds we marked on our way while pursuing Number Three.'

He still couldn't believe that he and his fellow Talents had managed to defeat the Hiver Sphere: a process in which, after the first skirmish, only the enemy had died. It had been incumbent on the Alliance – somehow – to keep the Hivers from establishing a new home system to replace the original world that had been consumed by their sun's nova. If Prime Talent Thian had thought of a way to reduce loss of life among

Human and Mrdini, surely he should not be criticized for devising what was now known as the *Genessee* ploy. The fact that he *was* Talent was the point of dispute, for Talent should not be involved in combat, however tenuous the connection. The pacifist element of Humankind had been appalled and the Federated Teleport and Telepath organization had received considerable criticism, despite the success of the *Genessee* ploy. The success was almost irrelevant in the storm of dismay and rebuke. However, the majority of the Alliance had been relieved that the problem had resulted in few losses. After all, the Prime Talents had only *delivered* what the Navy explosive experts had prepared. 'Teleportation' was certainly a main FT&T function. The explosive packages, placed so carefully on the Hiver fuel tanks, had been actually detonated by naval personnel with the sanction of the High Council and on the orders of Admiral Ashiant, so the Talent involvement had been a quite legitimate duty.

The old argument about a gun not being dangerous until it was loaded and aimed at a target was revised and adjusted to the FT&T. So, as the delivery agent, like a gun delivering a bullet, were the Talents guilty because they had sent a lethal package where it could destroy the acknowledged enemy of the Alliance? Or were those who gave the command for the substance to explode the guilty ones? That the resultant combination of 'Talents' and 'naval specialists' had caused the enemy ships to disintegrate offered much fuel to the point where the satisfactory outcome was nearly irrelevant.

A good night's sleep had restored energy to the Primes and the rest of their team on the *Washington* and they'd wound up the last details of their controversial participation in the battle to their own satisfaction. They were definitely looking forward to the exploration phase of their current assignment, studying the scanty probe reports of the first Hiver-occupied planet on the Fleet's return heading.

'Will we have to wait until the other ships rejoin the Fleet before we actually get to probe or land on the up-coming world?' Clancy asked, pacing up and down the lounge cabin.

'Don't see why we'd need to wait for Shepherd and Prlm,'

9

Thian said. He was himself beginning to get restless, though the respite from frantic activity and precision teleportations had been welcome.

'Speaking of getting ANYwhere, just when do I get transferred to the *Columbia?*' asked Prime Rojer, cocking his head and making his urgency plain to his older brother and team leader. 'That was the deal for me, remember? I help demolish the Hiver Spheres and then I get transferred to the *Columbia* . . .'

'And Cousin Asia,' Clancy put in, his expression carefully bland. Rojer shot him another dire look that Clancy ignored.

'When you've helped me reprovision this Squadron,' Thian answered, linking his fingers behind his head as he leaned back and stretched out his long legs.

'Then you don't think the conservatives are going to insist that FT&T stop assisting the Fleet?' Roj asked.

Clancy's scoffing laugh echoed Thian's dismissal of that possibility.

'Look, bro,' Thian said, sitting forward, elbows on his knees, 'the FT&T was very carefully,' and he emphasized the syllables, 'nurtured as an autonomous public service . . .'

'And who can argue that getting rid of an implacable enemy isn't a public service,' Clancy put in.

'Back in the twenty-first century, when the first Peter Reidinger was the manager of our budding organization, he determined to split it from any political group and to remain legally separate from any governmental agency until Earth became a united world. His successors studiously kept FT&T apolitical and also made certain that the facilities of the Towers were on a first-come-first-served basis. It's impossible to bribe a Talent, remember, not with Primes who can "read" anyone's mind. The guilty always give themselves away, anyhow.' He grinned. 'Of course, the present emergency with the greedy Hivers required FT&T to do a lot of kinetic transfers that would make the founders of our élite band spin in their graves. Nevertheless, it is still in our precious Charter that we Talents are required to teleport a lot of people and things that are repellent to our sensitive souls, though not illegal. Meanwhile we preserve the entity AND integrity of FT&T . . .'

'And suborn Primes whenever they could be found . . .' Clancy added. 'Like your grandmother on Altair.'

'Grandad was the one who was really suborned. He had had no intention of leaving Deneb . . . before he met Grandmother.' Thian's grin was broad. 'Had the Hivers but known they had met their match in Jeff Raven and Angharad Gwyn aka the Rowan as partners, they might have quit while they were ahead.'

'Not while there were Hiver queens needing planets to colonize,' Clancy put in.

'And that, of course, brought the entire FT&T organization in at the time of the Deneb Penetration with the Rowan as the focus for the Mind Merge that helped Jeff Raven despatch the Hiver Scouts trying to depopulate his home world.

'And why the Mrdinis decided to ask us, through Mother and Dad, to join forces and defeat the Hivers,' Thian said, 'since we could take out a Hiver Sphere without having to resort to suicide missions.' He leaned back again, pleased with his summation of the events leading up to recent developments: denying the Hivers a new base from which to continue their unique form of colonization.

'I wonder how many of the bleeding hearts and conservatives have bothered to see the Hiver queen at Heinlein base,' Rojer said. 'The sight of her would be instructive.'

'We could ask Cousin Roddie Eagles,' and Thian gave his brother a sly look.

Rojer's anxiety to get to the *Columbia* had much to do with his courtship of Roddie's youngest sister, Asia, an engineer as well as a T-4. Initially the *Columbia,* flagship of Squadron B's five ships, had been sent to examine four M-type planets that had been used, and abused, by the Hivers: one – named Marengo – being on the verge of total ecological disaster. The massive effort initiated to save the world was well under way and some encouraging succession of hardy grassoids had already been triumphantly broadcast. Ruins of Hiver occupations were evident on two of the other planets, Waterloo and

11

Talavera, while the fourth, Ciudad Rodrigo, seemed to have an active Hiver colony.

'I should be aboard the *Columbia*. NOW. Not still stuck here.'

'Don't fret so, Roj,' Thian said, broadcasting soothing thoughts to his pacing brother. 'Our orders were approved by both High Councillors, Admiral Mekturian and Glmtml. They'll handle any interference to the rest of our mission.'

'Not to mention Earth Prime Jeff Raven and Callisto Prime Rowan,' Clancy added. 'I see no reason for anxiety, Roj.' Clancy at least forbore to tease his cousin about the real reason for his fretfulness – missing Asia.

'All we have to do on our way home,' Thian said, 'is find ALL the Hiver-occupied planets . . . and *constrain* attempts by any of *them* to despatch another colonial venture.'

'That's all!' Rojer's voice dripped with sarcasm.

'Which will probably take the best part of our lives,' Clancy said, not particularly depressed by the prospect. 'I might even make commander by the time we're done.'

'I doubt we'll devote *our* lives to the project,' Thian said, gesturing to include his brother.

'No, you're Primes,' Clancy agreed without rancour.

There was a pause.

'Think I can talk the admiral into letting me get down on the Hiver world we're heading for?' Thian asked wistfully. He clasped and unclasped his hands in frustration.

'You're a Prime, Thi,' Clancy said, 'too valuable to be risked.'

'And far more capable of defending myself than anyone else on the ship,' Thian said, then bowed quickly to his brother, 'and you, too, Roj. I'm sure I'd find something no-one else could.'

'You're a Lyon, aren't you?' Clancy said, 'as well as a Prime? You will,' he added with a reassuring grin and stretched his legs out, yawning. 'The admiral won't deny you anything.'

'Well, then again, Ashiant may be under orders not to risk you on anything, Thian,' said Rojer in a knowing drawl.

12

'Oh?' Thian's raised eyebrows encouraged Rojer to elaborate on that statement.

'You can't be risked, bro,' Rojer said with a snort. 'They need you to take over from either Grandmother or possibly Grandfather.'

Thian gawked at his brother. 'How do you come to *that* remarkable conclusion?'

'You've been the focus for all our Mind Merges. I'm surprised you didn't guess. It's obvious to me,' and Rojer looked over to Clancy who nodded in agreement, 'that you're the logical successor.'

Thian sat for a moment, mouth aghast, then he 'glanced' into the minds of his younger brother and cousin and realized that both were certain of that. Slapping his forehead dramatically, he flung himself back on the couch, staggered by that prospect.

'Not for a few more decades,' Rojer said consolingly, 'since, praise be, our grandparents seem in excellent health.'

'Spare me!' Thian said groaning, his hand still clapped to his forehead.

*What's the matter, Thian?* asked Alison Ann Greevy, T-5, nursing empath from the sickbay.

Thian let his lover, Gravy, as Alison Ann was known, 'hear' the conversation.

*Oh, I thought something was wrong,* she said with a mental sigh of relief, and her mind touch left his.

'What's wrong with that sort of future, bro?' Rojer asked. 'You're at least getting a chance to travel now and see real life and all that good stuff. Besides, you've got Gravy. And it isn't as if you can't pick a nice inaccessible spot to live in to enjoy your private life when you do get stuck with being Earth Prime.' Rojer rolled his eyes, colouring his thoughts with envious scenes of marital harmony.

*That's enough of that!* Thian said, sternly, abandoning his shocked surprise.

Rojer only grinned, delighted to have annoyed Thian. 'And don't keep me here one moment past getting the last load of supplies on board.'

13

'I'll be well rid of you,' Thian said emphatically.

'I'll never be more than a thought away,' Rojer said and teleported himself out of the room before his brother could take a physical vengeance.

Thian caught Clancy's amused glance and, with a laugh, was restored to his usual good humour.

'Younger brothers,' Clancy murmured sympathetically.

That evening in the privacy of their quarters, Thian and Gravy talked over the prospect of him having to take up either of those tremendous responsibilities – Earth Prime or Callisto Station. Since both his parents and grandparents had expressed their approval of Alison Ann, the couple no longer needed to conduct their liaison as discreetly as possible. Indeed, once Thian knew his attachment to Gravy was approved, he teleported her belongings into his quarters.

'Frees space up for someone else,' she'd muttered as she saw her things neatly being fitted into his closets and drawers. 'Though it was kinda fun being zapped about by you, Thi darlin'.'

'You never knew where you were going to wake up, though,' he'd teased, hugging her tightly against him.

'Well, I'm here where I belong to be,' was her contented reply.

She was, however, surprised when Admiral Ashiant adroitly started including Lieutenant Greevy when he invited the FT&T personnel to his mess table, a tacit recognition of their current status as well as public approval. Once Alison Ann got over the shock, she rather enjoyed the perks that now came her way more frequently.

' 'Sides which, no-one dares complain about 'em, either,' Gravy added, tweaking Thian's nose. 'They're jealous and can't do a thing about it.'

The next morning Earth Prime Jeff Raven contacted Thian.

*Supply drones are ready, Thian,* said Jeff. *Let's see how many we can forward at a time, shall we?*

*As you like,* Thian replied, accepting the challenge, and

14

allowed his grandfather to hear him summoning the merge on his end of the exchange. He smiled to himself, remembering Rojer's prediction, though he kept that very much in the back of his mind. He didn't intend to be styled a 'cocky boy' by his grandmother, the Rowan. *Incoming cargo,* he 'pathed to the other ships in the Fleet in a broadcast alert.

Thian's team quickly assembled in their 'command' room, with its comfortable couches: Rojer teleported in, Clancy and Commander Semirame Kloo used their own feet and so did CPO Lea Day since she had been nearby when she received Thian's summons. The Fleet electrician was a new addition to the team but was improving steadily with each new opportunity to use her previously unexpected parapsychic Talent. She liked being what she called 'a power weasel'.

They had only just arranged themselves on the couches when Jeff warned them of the first shipment – nine drones.

*And we thought the big daddies from Iota Aurigae were heavy,* Rojer said and warned the boat bays to stand by to receive the drones about to be imported.

*On their way,* Jeff said and the team caught the first shipment at the halfway mark and deftly brought them into the readied space.

*That's for the* Washington. *Are the other boat bays alerted?* asked Jeff.

*They have been,* Thian replied and, checking briefly, knew the other ships' Talents were standing by to receive.

Then Jeff called out which drones went to which ship and they spent the next half an hour completing the reprovisioning.

*Now can I go to the* Columbia, *Grandfather?* Rojer asked.

*Are you packed?* And there was a malicious laugh tagging along with that question.

*Half a mo,* Rojer replied, frowning in concentration.

'We'll send on anything you left behind,' Thian said at his most helpful. 'And say hi to all when you get there.'

Rojer disappeared from his couch, his 'Dinis, Gil and Kat, with him.

*We're set. Takes longer to get into the carrier than . . .*

15

Thian didn't really need his team's help to push Rojer's personal capsule to the *Columbia* for he felt his grandfather's touch assisting him, then Flavia's when Rojer arrived at the Constellation Class *Columbia* flagship.

*Thanks, Jeff, Thian. We've been expecting him.*

*Keep him out of trouble,* Thian said and sent a fleeting kiss to Flavia and his younger sister, Zara, who was present in the *Columbia*'s reception team.

*You couldn't,* was Zara's pert reminder and Thian kinetically tweaked her nose to remind her of his seniority. She sent a laugh back over the incredible distance between them.

*How soon will you arrive at the first suspect system, Thian?* asked his grandfather, all business after the sibling exchange.

*Admiral . . .* and Thian paused to emphasize the new rank and felt his grandfather's satisfaction . . . *Ashiant advised us last night that we should make the heliopause by tomorrow evening. We're slowing now. The first exploratory probe indicates that the M-4 is occupied and has an old Hiver ship in orbit.*

*Strange the Hiver didn't notice the proximity of such a close match for their home world.*

*There's quite a distance between the two star systems, sir. And besides, if the ship's as old as it looks to be, the colony queens probably didn't know it existed when they stopped at this one.*

*Same sphere ship design?* asked Jeff.

*Hive design never changes . . . except to get bigger. Anyway, analysis of the pitting and metal fatigue on this Sphere suggests it has been hanging in orbit a long time.*

*Garbage?* Jeff asked succinctly since Hiver planets invariably used space as a refuse dump.

*Not as much as you'd think from the age of the Sphere.*

*Hmm. Check it out thoroughly.*

*Why? Does another 'Dini planet want its own display?*

There had been four vacant Spheres captured in orbit around other Hiver-occupied planets. These had been brought back to the 'Dini home worlds, much honour accruing to the colours of the prize crews.

*No. We're more curious about length of settlement as well as*

16

*its current population. There doesn't seem to be a hard and fast rule of when queens send out new expeditions.*

*Or when their planet begins to get overcrowded?*

*That's it.*

*Why is that important, Grandfather?* Thian asked.

*If we knew precisely what factors precipitate a need for migration, we might know how to inhibit them and contain the queens on the planets they now inhabit.*

*Trouble with the conservatives? Or the bleeding hearts?*

Thian caught the amusement in his grandfather's response. *A bit of both.*

*From which source? Human or 'Dini?*

A laugh echoed between minds. *A bit of both.*

*All right. I'll refrain from asking questions you have no intention of answering.*

*Your grandmother sends her regards, so do your mother and father.* And the presence that was Jeff Raven left Thian's mind.

When he took notice again of his immediate surroundings, Gravy was there with a glass of his favourite restorative. Even though that had not been a particularly taxing use of his Talent, Alison Ann in her capacity as Talent nurturer insisted that they all replenish their bodies after every teleportational session. She had half finished her own drink. Clancy, Semirame and Lea Day were dutifully sipping theirs. The 'power weasel' didn't look as tired from this day's work as she had been from others. She was shaping up nicely into a good backup kinetic. She raised her glass in a toast to him. As he returned it, his eyes fell on the couch that Rojer had so recently occupied. He blinked.

*Didn't you think you'd miss him, Thi?* Gravy asked, cocking her head at him.

*Actually, no, but I do.* And that surprised Thian. *And if you say he's only a thought away, I'll . . . I'll . . .*

'Quickly now, Prime, think of something,' she teased and ruffled his hair.

He patiently smoothed it back with his free hand just as the com unit bleated.

'Yes, sir,' Thian said promptly for the call originated from the admiral's ready room. Ashiant's rugged face filled the screen.

'Will you and your team please join me for dinner tonight, Prime Lyon?' Ashiant asked.

'We'd be delighted, sir,' Thian replied. 'Did your steward get all he ordered?'

'He's still checking but I understand the manifests included all his requirements and he wishes to make full use of the freshest.'

'Very thoughtful of you, sir,' Thian replied.

'My choice, Prime,' Ashiant said and disconnected.

'No more than he should,' said Gravy staunchly. 'You should get pick of the crop.'

'He doesn't mean me, does he?' asked Lea Day, surprised. CPOs did not normally dine at the captain's table.

'You're part of the team, Lea,' Thian said. 'What's the matter? Don't you like slumming in officers' territory?'

'Not really . . . if it's only us, the team, I mean. I try not to disappear from my station, you know. Might cause bad feeling.'

'We'll avoid that whenever possible,' Thian said though he doubted the problem was immediate since the whole Squadron was still elated by their destruction of the final Hive Sphere. As Lea Day had been part of the Talent team to help effect that destruction, she was a *persona* very *grata*. But envy was common among the non-Talented for those who had a measurable quantity of psychic ability. Maybe he should discuss her position with the admiral and see if Lea could be bumped up to ensign. He suspected she'd rather stay a CPO, top of her own pile, than become an ensign and bottom of another. Not that, in the final analysis, a Talent was ever bottom of anything.

She was an attractive woman, her dark hair crew-cut like a velvet skullcap in the acceptable fashion that did not, in her case, disguise her essential femininity. In her early forties, she was nearly as tall as he, lean and trim in her shipsuit; a career petty officer, having come up from the ranks: a native of Earth

18

from the old American continental mass who'd joined as soon as she was old enough to enlist. Her electrical skills – especially her uncanny ability to avoid 'live wires', unnecessary shocks and dowse exactly the trouble spot in the mass of circuit conduits needed by spaceships – should have alerted someone long ago to her latent Talent. Commander Kloo had spotted it when CPO Day had been assigned to the crews examining the captured Sphere that Rojer and his father had 'teleported' back to Phobos Mars Base. Admiral Ashiant had had her transferred to the *Washington* on Kloo's recommendation.

'Now that Rojer's gone,' Thian went on to put Lea at ease, 'we'll be needing you more, rather than less. We'll add another of the crew Talent to keep you company. By the time we're through with you, Chief, you'll definitely be able to integrate into any Talent team.'

'Gee, Talent captain, sir, that's real nice of you.'

Thian wanted to grin at her ambiguous reception of that threat. Instead he took her rejoinder at face value and gave her a bow.

'If that's all, Talent captain sir?' she said, coming to attention, 'I'd best return to the profession of my choice.'

'Can we send you on your way?' Thian asked, his lips twitching to keep his grin under control.

'Thanks, but no thanks, sir,' she said as she strode on quick long legs to the door. 'I can do just fine the ordinary way.' She closed the door firmly behind her.

They all had a good laugh then at her hasty retreat.

'Any truth in what she said about envy, Rame?' Thian asked the commander.

Kloo made a face and tilted her head from one side to the other. 'I haven't *heard* of any disgruntlement. I'll keep an ear open. Mind you, that power weasel can take care of herself. She's been in the Navy long enough to know how. But you're wise to shift around with the other lower Talents. Give all of them a break as well as practical lessons.'

'Some are much better than others,' Clancy said. 'See you at dinner?' he added as he and Kloo also took their leave.

*     *     *

19

*Well?* asked the Rowan, Callisto Prime, pointedly of her husband, Jeff Raven, Earth Prime.

*Well what?* was the innocent response.

*I don't want to have to drag it out of you.*

*I'm waiting for Damia . . . ah, there you are,* Jeff said, ignoring the exasperated snort from his wife. *All your kids are fine and healthy in tone and we shipped every single one of those heavy supply drones with nary a variation on either gestalt support. Rojer and his 'Dinis are now on board the* Columbia *and that should prove interesting.*

*Are you sure about Thian?* Damia asked.

*Can't you feel the truth in my mind?* Jeff asked.

*Don't be difficult, Father,* Damia said. *You keep taking my children and depositing them where YOU want them and wonder why I worry.*

*It isn't as if they haven't improved,* her mother said in a slightly censorious tone.

*Just remember the pressures they are NOT subjected to right now,* Jeff said with no humour at all in his mental touch.

*Is it getting worse, Dad?* Damia asked contritely.

*Anything we can do to help?* added Afra. The two Primes had sensed his presence but Afra waited for the appropriate moment to join conversations between his wife and her parents.

*Just keep our good friends on Iota Aurigae happy and ship off as much of that fine ore as possible.*

*More ships?* asked Afra.

*The Navy wants six* Washington *class so it can reduce the number of support vessels needed. They plan to use the Con-stellations and Galaxies to stand guard on Hiver worlds that might be about to send off a new colony ship.* Jeff's tone was droll. *That Genessee ploy the kids invented has given both Navies tremendous confidence.*

*Too much?* Afra asked.

*We'll see.*

*Even if there's been such criticism about Talents abandoning our 'traditional' non-combative role?* Damia asked, her tone wry. She'd been very proud of Thian and Rojer for coming up with a strategy that had ended the need of suicide missions to

20

destroy Hiver Spheres. It had gone against Afra's methody pacifism that events had caused his sons to think of such a tactic, even if it had saved lives and, in another application, destroyed Hiver Spheres.

*Defence has always been permissible,* Jeff replied. *The Council now has other more pressing worries.*

*Then the estimated ratio of Hiver-occupied planets has gone up?* Afra asked.

*Unconfirmed. Probably down, since some of those probed show dead installations, but that doesn't reduce the threat the species poses. The results of Kincaid's report while on search with Squadron D have to be revised if four of the twenty probed are either ecologically non-viable or prove to be failed colonies.*

*Those were all further out from the original home world,* said Afra pensively.

*True, so we've just begun to search.* The humorous note in Jeff's voice as he paraphrased an old adage showed his incredible resilience in the face of constant attacks and criticisms from the various factions of the two allies, Human and Mrdini. *I'm only the messenger,* he added, as if he had perceived Afra's thought. The two knew each other to their fundamental conscious levels.

*For which we are all eternally grateful,* said the Rowan crisply.

*What's being reported from the other side of the galaxy?* Afra asked.

*I'm waiting to hear. Perry's the Prime with the Fourth Fleet. I should have told Thian that Admiral Ashiant's Squadron is to be called First Fleet from now on.*

*My, we are getting fancy,* the Rowan said.

*I'm so glad you got Perry and Morgelle away from old David,* Damia said at the same time.

*Yes, their Talent was being wasted,* Jeff replied, *especially since David is now willing to train up Xahra and that youngling Prime he just discovered in his own backyard. I'll have to reassign Morgelle from Second Fleet shortly but she's learned enough, Flavia said, to run a Tower. You provoked him, you know, Damia, with all your brood . . .*

*Not ALL my brood, Dad, and you leave the babies alone. I don't want them to have to grow up fast like Thian and Rojer did.*

*That's a low blow, Damia,* said her mother and her husband almost in the same thought.

*No-one can regret the attack on Thian or Prtglm's outrageous wasting of Gil and Kat and its effect on Rojer more than I,* and there was such deep remorse in her father's voice that Damia was immediately contrite, laving him with affection and apology.

*They DID mature from those experiences, Damia,* said the Rowan in a neutral tone . . . and Damia was further rueful when she knew her mother obliquely referred to her brother, Larak, dead these many years, lost in the necessity of countering the mental entity Sodan. She had been the designated focus but Larak had gone in first and Sodan's mental strike, aimed at her, had killed her T-2 brother. *And we are all exceedingly proud of them.*

*Which David would like a little of, please, for his children,* Jeff continued, getting over that sad reminder quickly. *You'll be happy to know that Gollee Gren's found a half-dozen new potential high Talents. One who had a near-death accident which brought out latent kinetic Talent. He's testing well at the 2 Level.*

*Is he? That's very good news,* and Damia meant that sincerely. *So I get to keep my younglings a while longer?*

*We'll see how they develop,* her father said in a teasing tone, as if he didn't expect much from the four younger Lyons.

*Dad!*

Jeff chuckled. *You do leave yourself wide open for a tease, you know, dear heart. To business – when's the next ore shipment?*

*Miner Mexalgo has four big daddies but wants to wait till he has the full half-dozen. To make our effort worthwhile. Another hull from the mines of Iota Aurigae?* Damia's tone held pride for her world's ability to supply the raw materials that would become elements of the expanding Allied Fleet. *I'll let you know. It shouldn't be too long at the rate they're working: humans and Mrdini.* She chuckled and heard her father echo that.

Iota Aurigae had as many Mrdini settlers now as it had Human. The 'Dinis missed their hot fierce primaries but in a mine, who sees the sun? They had space, their own settlements including fine hibernatories, better than those on their home planets, Clarf and Sef, although there was considerably more prestige in going to a Clarf facility.

As a Prime Talent, Damia was far more aware than most people that the Mrdini worlds were overpopulated and the pressure on them needed relief: much of her awareness derived from her oldest daughter, Laria, who was Clarf's Prime. The High Council had discussed the disposition of colonial expansion in private and public debates. Since the seven Human colony worlds had been free from the Hiver assaults until the Hivers' abortive attempt on Deneb – known as the Deneb Penetration – Human worlds were by no means as critical in population densities as the five Mrdini planets were. With the Alliance, fewer 'Dini were dying in combat against Spheres although their birth rate remained as high as it had been when more spacers were needed. The Allied Council had voted, almost unanimously, that the first nine suitable planets would be given to the Mrdini and the tenth made available for Humans. That decision had immediately met with resistance from a new faction, calling themselves 'Planets for People', adding to the many disparate 'voices' on the twelve Alliance worlds. However, the High Council was not moved to award an equal distribution of suitable worlds since the intent of that opposition was specious.

In the first place, an 'ideal' Mrdini planet would be hotter than those comfortable for Human habitation. In the second place, few Humans realized how desperately crowded the five Mrdini worlds were: in conditions no Human would tolerate. The Humans had only begun to spread out across the earth-type planets in the Capella, Deneb and Iota Aurigae systems. Their need was not as urgent – unless it was prompted by obvious tit-for-tat mentalities. On Clarf and Sef, the two most overpopulated Mrdini worlds, a corresponding faction immediately erupted, demanding that the first twenty suitable worlds should be Mrdini, since their race had struggled alone for two hundred years against the Hivers.

In the third place, the disposition of any new colonial worlds depended on many factors, the most important being that the relevant planet was not already occupied by an emerging sentient species. To which the obvious argument was that, if the Hivers had already rid the planet of any large, possibly predatory, life-forms, that wouldn't be a problem, would it? Since Talavera, a world that had been 'prepared' for Hiver occupation, was ecologically ill, how many other prospective planets would be in a similar state?

There would probably be as many theories – and opponents of those theories – as there were M-type planets in the galaxy. And who knew what other intelligent spacefaring species might exist in the quadrants not yet explored by Mrdini, Human and Hiver ships?

While most Humans met Mrdini on equal terms, not all Humans and not all Mrdini were in favour of continued close association now that the enemy – the Hivers – had received a major setback. Matters closer to home and divisive individual concerns often received more attention and publicity than the problem that still faced the Allies: finding Hiver-occupied worlds and somehow restricting the alien creatures to them.

Masses of details needed to be gathered by elements of both Navies: discovering which worlds the Hivers occupied, how full they were, which M-type planets ignored by the Spheres trying to find a new home world would be suitable for Mrdini or Human occupation.

One loud group didn't want any further Human expansion. A more virulent sect wanted to control FT&T because FT&T were 'weasel-lovers' and should not be trusted to conduct the Towers in strict accordance with its original Charter. This ominously growing group took note of the most minute variation, discrepancy, or minor modification undertaken by Towers or emanating from the Blundell Building, the main FT&T headquarters on Earth. Some of the dissidents were medium to low Talents, dissatisfied by their assignments or claiming professional partisanship.

'Everyone knows that the Towers are dominated by a few families,' was the accusation most frequently lodged and, unfortunately, accurate. The fact that Primes were rare enough did not apparently enter into the complaints. In the matter of Tower Primes, nepotism was far more benign than malignant or inefficient. In reality, the responsibilities and duties of a Prime far outweighed any reward: remuneration was strictly controlled although a Prime could, by virtue of his or her ability, live anywhere they chose. Genetics played a critical part in providing more high Talents, though some emerged from unexpected sources as had the Rowan, Callisto Prime, reared on Altair, and Jeff Raven, Earth Prime, who had come – rather reluctantly – from Deneb to assume the responsibilities which had been Peter Reidinger's until his death. Children on every human world were now routinely tested at puberty for any vestige of trainable Talent. Every scrap of latent Talent was carefully nurtured, developed and trained to make the best possible use of it. If some had delusions of strength, they were soon ineluctably placed in the category appropriate to their real abilities. Oftentimes a minor Talent increased with usage and FT&T was only too pleased to reassess and upgrade that person.

It had been a matter of necessity that four of the five children born to the Rowan and Jeff had been encouraged to produce large families. Jeran, Cera and Damia were T-1s, Ezro was a T-3 physician, while the deceased Larak had been a T-2. Even his one child, Grayhan, was a T-2. All of the offspring in the Raven-Lyon marriage were T-1s, though for some time it was thought that Zara, the second daughter, might be a dysfunctional T-1. She was now fully trained in a medically oriented Talent so it was unlikely that she'd be asked to assume the responsibilities of a Tower.

David of Betelgeuse had three T-1 children: Perry, Morgelle and Xahra. Jeran, now Denebian Prime, had four, Barry being of an age with Rojer, while Cera had three, also potential high Talents. The Bastianmajani couple from Altair had produced a T-1 in Flavia though her brothers and sisters were lesser Talents. They were completely unrelated to the Gwyn-Raven-

Lyon group. Rather more Denebians had latent Talents than other first-generation colonial worlds. They were lazy about using them, though the Eagleses, Ravens, Sparrows and other clans supplied many of the high 4, 3 and 2 Talents – when they chose to move off-planet. No-one could be forced, against personal inclination, to make use of Talent. The Denebians, as a group, were far more interested in developing their world. Unfortunately, Talents were still an élite and limited group and their abilities more and more in demand now that Humans and Mrdinis were spreading ever outward from their home worlds. The plain facts, of course, rarely figured in the complaints of nepotism that were lodged.

*Any good news?* the Rowan asked, so pointedly her daughter winced.

*If you mean great-grandchildren, no,* Damia said with a sigh. She had so hoped that Laria would be able to win Vanteer's constant affection. The T-6 engineer at Clarf Tower had one failing: he couldn't settle to just one woman and already had several offspring from different women, Humans living on Clarf. That two of the infants seemed to have Talented minds augured well for any children he might give Laria.

*What's the problem?* the Rowan asked.

*I think,* and the reply came from Afra, *that Laria intimidates him.* A T-6 would have no defence against a mental invasion by a determined Prime. Damia was glad that Laria had not resorted to that in her wish to become pleasing to Vanteer.

*What?* The Rowan found that hard to believe. *She's not aggressive.*

*Like some you could name,* Damia put in, referring to her teenage experiments in finding a partner.

*But you sorted yourself out,* her mother said.

*Laria is a different personality entirely . . .*

*For which we are grateful,* said Jeff, teasing again, but his touch was fond.

*So don't you two meddle,* Damia said sharply.

*We have our ethics,* Jeff said, *though there are some who do not believe it.*

26

*Father, of course you do. I'm sorry I said that,* and Damia was once again contrite.

*We might shift some more willing prospects to Clarf now that we have some breathing-space,* Jeff suggested.

*I can't think who would be suitable,* Damia said with another sigh.

*Well, this latent T-2 kinetic, the one Gollee Gren's been training, is an attractive person,* the Rowan said. *I think he's also related to Yoshuk at Sef Tower, a younger brother.*

*Yoshuk's a good man,* Damia said with a lift of hope in her voice. There was a hint in her mind that she found Vanteer's reluctance to ally *her* daughter an insult to the entire Family.

*She's twenty-six and a bit,* Afra reminded them. *Give her time to settle on someone who is compatible. And no need to remind us, Damia m'love, that you'd had four children at Laria's age.*

*I was lucky* and the deep love and affection she had for Afra were a vibrant note in her voice.

*You were!* the Rowan said softly.

*I was the lucky one,* Afra said firmly. *Worth waiting for and let us give Laria that option, too.*

*Agreed,* said Jeff and on that comment he and the Rowan left the merge.

'How can Vanteer say that Laria intimidates him?' Damia asked, sliding upright and swinging her legs to the side of her couch. 'Zara might but not Laria. She's very careful with relationships. Look how well she and Kincaid get along . . .' She made a face. 'I so wish he was interested in women.' She gave a gusty sigh. 'As a T-2, he'd be an ideal match.'

Afra sat up, too, his expression thoughtful. 'Kincaid is so good with our younger ones when he visits.' Damia gave him a sharp look. But he shrugged. 'Just an observation. She and Kincaid have a very good rapport.'

'Not that good . . . At least as far as it goes.' Then she continued more briskly, 'If Gollee has someone to send to Clarf for training, it might even make Vanteer jealous. After all, there'll be a lot of activity from that planet once colonization starts. Another Talent might be needed.'

27

'Kincaid's certain that Clarf has already started provisioning colony ships, choosing specialists and colour groups, ready to go the moment First Fleet – I rather like that new designation . . .'

'So do I,' Damia agreed, standing up and arching her back in a stretch.

'. . . The Tower will be overworked, sending off personnel carriers, message tubes and cargo drones. Up, up and away.' He grinned at her over such eagerness.

'Well, the 'Dinis need the room to spread out in, that's certainly true. I just hope the Hivers haven't ruined other perfectly good worlds as they did Talavera.' She frowned, having heard from Zara in detail about the ecological damage wreaked on that planet. She put on her coat and prepared to leave.

Putting an affectionate arm about his wife's shoulders, Afra guided her to the Tower steps. They met Keylarion on her way up.

'Oh, you haven't gone,' their T-6 station manager said, surprised.

'Oh yes we have, and you haven't seen us,' Damia said.

'Unless it's urgent,' Afra appended, giving his wife a reproving look. She made a face at him.

'Xexo and me are set to do some recalibrations, that's all,' she said and, as if on cue, the T-8 engineer arrived from his section of the Tower, diagnostic equipment hanging from both arms and down his back.

'Ah, you're finished. Good,' Xexo said as he went past them on the stairs, grunting at the weight he was carrying.

'Anything serious?' Damia asked, since Afra's reproof had recalled her sense of duty.

'No, just to be sure,' Xexo said and Keylarion winked as she followed him.

Damia grinned back at her, knowing how particular the engineer was about his beloved generators.

Outside in the brisk late winter air of Iota Aurigae, Damia folded her coat about her and huddled against Afra's long frame, to shield herself from the worst of the wind.

Their 'Dinis came rushing out of the house, chattering as if their friends had been gone for weeks instead of a few hours. Tri caught Afra's free hand while Fok took Damia's and escorted them the rest of the way.

# CHAPTER TWO

Rojer joined the *Columbia* in the middle of ship night, just before the dogwatch came on.

*Sorry, Flavia. Should have checked to be sure it was convenient,* he said. *We'd just finished hauling the drones and there was Grandfather ready to ship me out so it seemed silly to waste the ride.*

'I'm here, I'm here,' said Flavia, appearing in the boat bay and nearly colliding with the duty officer, Lt Sadler Ismail, who was on his way to the personnel carrier. 'Zara went back to bed.'

'Oops, sorry about that, Prime.' He took Flavia's arm to steady her precipitous arrival. 'Good to see you, sir,' Ismail said, belatedly saluting as he remembered that Prime Talents had the honorary rank of captains while on Fleet manoeuvres. 'Need some help there, Gil, Kat?' he added as the 'Dinis emerged.

*I'd've had Asia greet you but she stayed below on some minor emergency . . . If I'd known . . .*

*That's all right. So we're orbiting Talavera.*

*Sure*, and Flavia looked surprised. *Didn't you know?*

*No, I didn't know. Grandfather just whisked me away from the* Washington.

Just then various items dropped into the personnel carrier: one soft-soled boot, a cascade of disks, and two worn, obviously dirty shipsuits.

'I left the suits behind for a reason,' Rojer said, making a face in the general direction of his previous ship. He pointed to a shoulder patch that displayed a clearly printed 'ASS *Washington.*'

Flavia grabbed the offending suits and they disappeared: a disposal hatch hissed receptance. She gave him an affectionate hug, touching his mind with warm greetings.

'You needn't have come down yourself, Flavia.' And he returned her embrace. 'But I'm glad you did.' Despite the hour, she felt as vibrant and self-assured as ever. He could wish, feeling her very womanly body against his, that she wasn't already attached to Jesper Ornigo, T-6 from Betelgeuse.

*I know. It's sad we can't replicate ourselves and share the wealth,* she said, half-teasing. 'C'mon, I'll take you to your quarters. Thanks, Sadler. He's my problem now.'

'Yes, ma'am,' and Ismail signalled for one of the yeomen on duty to take Rojer's luggage.

'No need to disturb your watch,' Flavia said airily and with a gesture the duffels disappeared, including the shipshoe and the disks.

'We'll go the easy way,' she said, turning to say good night to officer and watch. She took his hand and 'ported him to the passageway outside his assigned quarters.

'You go on back to bed, now, Flavia. I'll settle myself in,' and he gave her a mental push.

'I'm just two doors down,' she said and walked away. 'G'night!' ''Night,' he responded with an airy kiss for her cheek. He put his hand on the door-plate and it slid open, showing him a room that contained both bed alcove and a lounge. Not as luxurious as the specially designed quarters for the Talents on the *Washington* but larger than his original accommodations on the *Genessee* and Phobos Moon Base. *You wanted the change of assignment,* he muttered to himself.

He had indeed half-hoped that Asia would have been there

31

to welcome him. That was the trouble with Primes. Always launching people when it was convenient for *them*. He glanced at his duffels, wincing because of the speed with which he had stuffed them. Ah, well, he could sort them out tomorrow. Right now he'd follow Flavia's example and get some sleep. He took off his shipshoes, loosened the top cover of his bunk and slid under it. With a mild suggestion to his diurnal self, he was asleep in moments.

*Is that all, Van?* Laria asked as Clarf Tower's generators hit an even pitch after the latest drone launch.

*Yup!* was the relieved response. *I told you we were going to get busier.*

*It's to-ing and fro-ing freight,* Laria said, somewhat disgusted.

*Throwing freight, you mean,* Lionasha, Tower's T-7 expediter, corrected. *It's much more fun fro-ing 'Dinis about.*

*Ah, ah, ah!* Kincaid Dano said, with a mental image of a wagging finger. He grinned across the way at Laria as they both sat up on their Tower couches and stretched against the long session.

'I don't feel like a mule,' Laria said, rotating her shoulder-blades and rubbing her neck. 'I feel like I've been kicked by one.'

Kincaid swung his long legs over the edge of his couch and, with equally long arms, reached across the narrow space and began to massage her neck, his strong fingers sensitively touching just the right spot. Laria let her head hang and murmured appreciatively.

*Van's a damned fool,* Kincaid said on a tight link with her.

*Leave it, Dano,* Laria said.

*Why should I?* the T-2 asked. *For all he's one of the best Tower engineers, he's an aggravation.*

*Do I sound aggravated?* Laria asked.

*Patient is what you sound and you're too good for him.* He gave her a final hard rub, nearly sliding her off the smooth surface of her couch. He caught her body with a mental block and she couldn't help but giggle. *That's better.*

32

*He's handy,* she said with a shrug.

*You should tell him that and depress his ego.*

*It's the thought of a T-1 in his bed that depresses him,* Laria said and sighed.

*I don't think you're in love with him anyway, Laria. Not the way you* should *be. He has been, as you say, handy. And in an attractive enough package.*

Very, very deeply, Laria thought that Kincaid was in an even more attractive package but his preference lay with his own sex. Meanwhile that didn't interfere with them understanding each other as perfectly as she could have wished Van and she did.

'Which idiot was it that said once we've got the last Sphere, work'll slack off?' Lionasha said as Laria and Kincaid descended the short flight of steps from the cupola above the station building that acted as a 'tower'.

'Wasn't me,' Kincaid said, making for the cold-drinks cabinet. 'What'll you have, Laria, with your electrolytes?' he asked.

'Do we still have any of that real old-fashioned lemonade flavour?'

'We do,' and Kincaid 'ported her a nice cold flask, grinning as she deftly caught it in her open hand. 'Not a drop spilled, either.'

Vanteer joined them from the lower level that housed the great generators needed for Talent gestalt. He was wiping his hands on a greasy cloth.

'I need a beer,' he said and 'ported one without quite the same deftness as the others used. He shot them a look as he peeled off the cap. 'Number three needs servicing. I had to rev it manually during the last three 'ports.'

'Will it be down long?' Laria asked.

Lionasha also looked apprehensive. 'We've the same schedule for tomorrow, you know.'

'So you told me. I'll have it up and running sweetly by tomorrow when it's needed,' he said, turning to retrace his steps, 'even if I have to work all night.'

Lionasha looked from Laria to Kincaid and rolled her tawny eyes.

*Keep a lid on it, Lio,* Laria said, aiming the thought at the Tower expediter whose eyes matched her hair, set off by a skin that took Clarf's sun well.

Kincaid gave a low snort. *Likes to rub it in, doesn't he!*

*You, too, Dano.* And Laria glared at the T-2.

Lionasha returned to her desk, shaking her head, and began checking the next day's schedule on her screen.

*We're a good team. Let's never forget that,* Laria said. 'I'm going swimming.'

'You'll fry,' both Lionasha and Kincaid told her.

She held up sun-browned arms, as dark as acorn hulls, and laughed. 'I've sunblock. I need the exercise.'

WE COME, TOO cried her 'Dinis, just entering the Tower from the landing-field.

Kincaid stretched, yawned. 'I'm for a nap, frankly,' and his 'Dinis, who arrived in on the heels of Laria's, vehemently agreed: all three sauntered down the cool hall to their quarters.

She went to her room and changed into her swim togs, struggled into the long caftan that would also be a protection against Clarf's late-afternoon sun. Tip and Huf rummaged to find pads to lie on, and the umbrella that Laria wisely carried to shield herself from the sun at the swimplace.

'Have fun,' Lionasha said as she watched the three of them file out the door.

Halfway there in her ground car, her caftan clinging to her sweating body, Laria wondered why under any sun she was doing this now. She could have waited until sunset, when the air was less humid and Clarf's primary was not shining directly in her eyes as it was now she was heading west. If Vanteer was going to work on the generator, she couldn't remain on the Tower premises, especially after Kincaid's remarks.

She knew Van had acquired another girlfriend: a chemical analyst just in from Betelgeuse on a three-month assignment. That was a long enough stay for most Humans who came from colder Human planets. They might exude joy over a world that rarely had any rain. When they had to endure the constant heat and humidity night and day, the novelty soon wore off. An unlucky minority would prove to be allergic to the harsh

34

rays and have to be transferred, to the annoyance of their contractors, Human or 'Dini. Meanwhile, there was no point in trying to get Van's attention: this Marjolee Hess-Tukin monopolized him. Laria had seen her at the very party where Van first met her: a pretty little woman, Laria admitted impartially, with long eyelashes, which she used to good effect on any male. Ironically, it was because Vanteer was Talented and part of the Clarf Tower staff that he was such a conquest for Marjolee. Doubtless one of the other, less tactful females who had also been wooed by Vanteer would warn the girl of his fickle nature. Laria had come to the reluctant conclusion that Van couldn't resist the challenge of a new female to be courted and won. He required diversity. And how he kept up with the demands made on him by his other women – he had once sworn to Laria that he loved her to the exclusion of any other woman he'd ever known – astounded his colleagues in the Tower.

'How *does* he do it?' Lionasha often remarked when Van had lured yet another girl into his bed.

'I know plenty of men who'd like to know,' Kincaid had replied, grinning. 'Of both inclinations,' he'd added with a droll smile.

Whatever, Laria needed to get out of the Tower. She thought wistfully of cool, dark-sun Iota Aurigae and home: with the wild wind and the mountains, and riding Saki to hunt scurriers and avians. But now was not the time to ask for home-leave.

One of the four planets that Kincaid had discovered, of those he had probed on his unhappy stint in Squadron D on the Galaxy Class *Valparaiso*, had been named Talavera, following the nineteenth-century naming of his other three M-type finds: Marengo, Waterloo and Ciudad Rodrigo. Its primary was not quite as fierce as Clarf's but would certainly suit 'Dinis better than Humans. With so few dying in combat against the Hivers, all five worlds were bursting with candidates willing to undertake the immense task of colonizing, even if it meant heavy ecological work. No birth-control methods existed for the 'Dini species. Indeed their prolificacy had been an advantage during their two hundred years of fighting the Spheres. They could 'lose' suicide crews, knowing that others of the same genetic pattern would be born in the hibernatories at some later date. Such a 'reincarnation' allowed the 'Dinis, if it became necessary, to sacrifice themselves willingly. This was, of course, a fundamental difference between them and Humans, who did not waste their space personnel. Fortunately, Mrdini High Command and all its Councillors were aware of this major psychological difference between the two species or the mindset might have brought about an insuperable schism. The difference occasionally caused trouble on mixed-species crew ships despite continued lectures on the subject.

Ironically, the Mrdini race had originally been attracted to the Humans because they had witnessed the seemingly effortless destruction of the first Hiver Sphere to approach Human space at Deneb: the Mind Merge of the Rowan and all female Talents had paralysed the Hiver queens and the Male Mind Merge of Jeff had sent their Sphere into Deneb's sun.

The 'Dinis had come to the point where, with dwindling resources, they were hard-pressed to continue their defence against the Spheres. So they had used 'dreams' to make contact with Humans – with Laria's mother and father, Damia and Afra, recuperating on Deneb from Larak's tragic death and their exhaustion in battling the mental entity Sodan. An Alliance had been promulgated between Human and Mrdini. Now, if suitable worlds could reduce the population density on the five 'Dini home worlds, much of the growing dissatisfaction on the 'Dini half of the Alliance would be eased.

Laria reached the river swimming facility before the place became crowded. 'Dinis liked water sports. Though sun-warmed, the water was noticeably cooler – since the current was swift – and Laria sank gratefully into it up to her neck. Tip handed her one of the rope harnesses that the wise swimmer looped around the arms. She let her body be carried flat out to the length of the rope by the current. The river flowed over her in a rippling massage. Tip and Huf joined her, their furry bodies silkily touching hers now and then in the current. Letting herself relax with her head back, Laria closed her eyes. She was facing east so that the sun was no longer in her face. Tip and Huf gurgled happily and there they remained until the Clarf sun with its customary abruptness sank below the distant hills, and darkness spread across the deep plain with its thousands of 'Dini dwellings and the occasional lump of a hibernatory.

As soon as Laria heard the revving of other ground cars and the put-put of individual fliers approaching the river bank, the chatter of 'Dini tongues, she flipped over and began to pull herself, hand over hand, to the bank. Shucking off the harness, she swam vigorously to the slanted permacrete lip that assisted entry and exit. Almost before she reached her car, Tip and Huf dancing beside her, totally refreshed by the swim, her skin and her suit were dry. But the water had been therapeutic. She made a private wager, that Vanteer would have finished the servicing and be gone when she returned to the Tower.

She won.

Lionasha had left a note saying she was dining with friends in the Human Compound, lavishly air-conditioned. Lio had a new male interest. Kincaid was probably still asleep but he was always a restful and undemanding companion.

Laria woke in the night, gasping with panic, her heart pounding against her ribs, her 'Dinis twitching in their sleep and mumbling. She had been caught in their dream and it had been . . . What had it been? Terrifying? No. But charged . . . heavy with emotion and an odd 'dead' smell.

'Laria?' Kincaid 'ported into her room, striding to her bedside and gathering her up in an anxious embrace. 'What is it? What's the trouble?'

She clung to his bare arms, her head against his chest, struggling with the aftermath of such intense sensations, gasping for breath.

'Easy now, easy now,' he said as he stroked tangled hair back from her face, his hands gentle. ' 'Dini dream?'

She nodded.

'Are they due for hibernation?' he asked.

37

Tip and Huf were still flapping at her side in whatever dream held them.

'Possibly,' she said and knew that had to be part of the problem. Humans might not know how 'Dinis mated – the hibernatories were off limits and even 'Dinis did not mention what went on – but sometimes, when her pair were close to that part of their life cycle, their dreams could be extremely erotic. Her own frustration had magnified the intensity of their dreams and she had been frightened by her own response. That was what had wakened her. 'They usually know and tell me.'

Kincaid pulled her closer, holding her against him, soothing her with soft touches and a wave of mental consolation. It felt so good to be held – a thought she kept very, very tight. Good to be held by Kincaid. That rider startled her and, her panicky breathing under control, she started to push away from him. His hands resisted.

'I offer myself, Laria,' he said softly in her ear. 'You *need* someone right now and I am here.' He gave a self-deprecating laugh.

She gripped his arm, unable to answer yet desperately wanting to agree.

'You offered me friendship, dear Laria, when I needed it so badly. Why may I not assuage your need now?'

She could feel his mind touching hers, lightly at first, then stressing his remarkable offer, as his arms folded her more closely to him. She could not deny the honesty of his gesture. She most certainly could not deny her need of relief.

'Admittedly I'd be a virgin sacrifice,' and the laughter in his voice found an amused response in her, 'but I like you better than any other woman I have ever met. And I am not the least bit intimidated by you being a Prime.' He kissed her forehead and then held her away from him, seeking her eyes in the darkness as his mind sought hers on a deeper level. She did not resist. 'After all, it's much the same with either partner,' and his mouth curled in an ironic smile. 'Shall we see if we can make it together?'

She opened her mind completely and felt within him the

desire to console, the respect and admiration he had for her, and a suddenly fierce yearning for sexual release.

*I am honoured*, she said.

*I am horny.*

*That's my problem, too.*

*Let's solve that mutual problem. Just don't . . .* he added, *shield for or from me.*

Gently he pushed her backward onto the rumpled bed, stretching his long self beside her, and then pulled her tightly against him, one arm about her shoulders, the other fondling her bare body. She let down all mental and physical barriers, felt him do the same, saw all that had troubled him before he came to Clarf Tower, and was shaken by an incredibly powerful desire to erase such devastating memories with a selfless abandon to the growing passion that Kincaid's deft lovemaking roused in her.

Laria hadn't had many lovers and the fulfilment they had given her had been satisfactory enough. But nothing was like the climax she achieved with Kincaid and she felt the surprise in him, the exaltation, when he collapsed against her, shuddering in release. They lay together for a long time in the sweet aftermath, his mind wondering at his response to Laria, hers savouring the fullness of rapport with the personality that had taken refuge in irony and detachment.

*That was rather more than I expected*, he said wryly.

*And exactly what I needed, dear friend.*

*I am more than your friend, now, Laria.*

*Are you?*

*You can see that easily enough, Prime.*

*Yes, but is it right for you?*

She could feel his mental shrug, vividly accompanied by the lingering astonishment of completion with a woman.

*You would consider that aspect, dear heart,* he said. *I feel we should explore the possibilities without prejudice. Certainly I have never felt such rapport with anyone since Josh died.*

Because he still had all his shields dropped, she knew who Josh had been, how deeply they had loved each other, and how Josh had died in a sporting accident that happened so quickly

39

Kincaid had 'seen' only when it was too late to save his lover. Struggling to find equilibrium after such a terrible loss, Kincaid had welcomed the assignment to the *Valparaiso* in an effort to distance himself from increasingly painful memories, only to find himself torn in two directions by the officers who vied for his company.

*One thing is sure,* Laria said sternly, *I cannot hurt you as those two did.*

*Of that I'm sure,* he responded with one of his droll chuckles and he gave her a hug. 'Now get some sleep. Tomorrow will be busy.' And made a move to sit up.

She made a sound, closing her mind quickly lest he see how reluctant she was to have him leave her.

'On second thoughts,' he said, settling back down, wedging the pillow under his head and replacing his arm around her shoulders, 'that would require more effort than I care to make right now.'

*Thank you.*

*Don't mention it. Now sleep, Prime.*

*Yes, sir,* she said in a meek tone and wove her fingers into his hand.

Beyond them, on the wide bed, the 'Dinis also sank into a deeper, more restful slumber.

'That swim did you good,' Lionasha remarked as Laria started up the steps to her Tower the next morning.

'Yes, I think it did,' Laria replied as casually as she could because Kincaid let out a burst of laughter in his room, and let her hear it.

'I'm glad,' Lionasha said with obvious relief. 'We've a very busy day. Oh, the generator wasn't as much of a problem as Vanteer thought.'

'I know. He wasn't here when I got back,' Laria said over her shoulder, unperturbed.

*No, Lio can't read us, my dear,* Kincaid said and, then as he swung into the Tower hall from the private quarters, added: ' 'Morning, Lio. Good evening?'

'Yes, indeed,' and the other two Talents caught the unmistakable smugness of her satisfaction with her evening's pleasure.

'Good for you,' Kincaid said affably, trotting up the stairs. 'At least you didn't get a burn yesterday at the river,' he added, grinning at Laria as he reached the Tower. The mischief in his smile made Laria quickly stifle her amusement lest Lionasha catch it. He shook his head, indicating that he was not projecting his ebullient mood.

' 'Morning all,' said Vanteer, striding into the Tower. He leaned into the stairwell, calling up to them. 'Fixed the generator, Laria. Did you have a good swim?'

'Yes, thanks,' she called back cheerfully. 'Start 'em up, Van, we've a busy day ahead. Got two hours before that sun starts scorching again. Let's get to it.'

Kincaid touched her with approval as he settled back on his couch and got into position for the work ahead.

They had had a very full day by noon and took time off for a siesta. Even their 'Dinis grumbled about the heat on the plascrete of the landing-field. There were not as many loads for the late afternoon but enough to tire them. Laria made a salad for supper with fresh fruit that Yoshuk had sent them from Sef. They all ate together, while Lionasha sorted out the orders for the next day's teleportations. Soon after Van had wandered off by himself, Plrgtgl arrived, its poll eye draped in vivid magenta lace, with endless questions for Laria and Kincaid about the progress of the explorations.

Over and over, Laria repeated that as soon as she heard something she would most certainly inform Plrgtgl. Kincaid brought up the files on their lounge screen, showing Plus, as Laria called her 'Dini contact, what was so far known about the four planets that he had found, paraphrasing Laria's reassurances with his own. Their 'Dinis, of course, served Plrgtgl the juice drink it preferred and got whatever their human partners asked for, as well as some of the bits and nibbles which Plus had come to like.

SEF IS MUCH LIKE THAT, Plus said in 'Dini, pointing its flipper at the surface of Talavera.

41

THE PLANET COULD EASILY BE SEF RENEWED, Kincaid agreed. IT SUFFERED DAMAGE BY HIVERS WHICH MUST BE REPAIRED AND WILL NEED LIFE-FORMS FROM THE SMALLEST . . .

NO, said Plus firmly, THERE ARE SOME THAT WE CAN DO WITHOUT THIS TIME. LIKE THE LICE, AS YOU CALL THEM, AND THE STINGERS. NO HARM TO THE ECOLOGY BY LEAVING THEM OUT.

HOW CAN YOU BE SURE? Laria asked, amused at Plus's vehemence as well as its wish to leave behind such bugs. She saw that Tip and Huf as well as Nil and his Plus were keenly interested in both queries and answers though they did not voice their own opinions: not in the presence of such a senior 'Dini.

WE HAVE STUDIED CAREFULLY, Plus said, shaking the lace on its poll eye until Laria was afraid it would come loose. WE USE THIS AS PROBLEMS IN TEACHING THE YOUNG. WHAT MAKES A GOOD PLANET BETTER. WHAT IS NEEDED TO SPREAD POLLENS AND SEEDINGS. WE WOULD BE UP AND RUNNING, AS YOU SAY, and Plus's large frame shook with its delight in using Basic slang, BEFORE YOU CAN SAY BOO? IS THAT WHAT YOU SAY . . . BOO?

'Boo' came out in Basic. Laria and Kincaid agreed that it had used the slang properly and then listened as Plus enumerated the various plans for the revitalization of the planet.

Full night had settled on Clarf before the two Talents tactfully managed to get Plus to leave.

'I thought it'd never go,' Laria said, exhaling with exaggeration.

'They've been doing a lot of research on reviving Talavera's ecology,' Kincaid said thoughtfully.

'From the way Plus was going on, that must be their latest game to play at night.'

'As useful an occupation as many, certainly,' he agreed.

'I'm for a shower and bed,' she said, waving over her shoulder at him as she left the lounge for her own room, Tip and Huf following on her heels.

'I won't be far behind.'

*   *   *

She was tired and, when she had soaped and rinsed herself, turned the shower to cool to reduce her body temperature. Wrapping a towel about herself, sarong fashion, she left the bathroom. Her 'Dinis were already curled up.

'Let's have nice dreams tonight, shall we?' she said but they did not answer.

She had no trouble falling asleep. But, once again, early in the new day, she woke with the same panic syndrome, gasping for breath, unable to remember what had roused her so thoroughly.

*Again?*

*Again, and worse this time,* she said, tears dripping down her cheeks.

Kincaid seemed to step into the room at the bedside and was enfolding her in his arms, mentally soothing her alarm and helping her control the ragged breaths and agitated respiration.

'What are they doing to you?'

'I don't know. They've . . . never been like . . . this before. And I'm in much better shape . . . after you . . . last night,' she said, leaning her head against his shoulder, gripping his arm with both hands and trying to still the shudders that ran up and down her spine.

'You were fully asleep, weren't you? I wasn't,' and he said the last ruefully. 'I couldn't seem to get comfortable. Odd smell in my room the circulator isn't removing.' His hands smoothed down her back, as if he were trying to push the shudders from her.

Gradually they ceased and she lay limply against him, her hands still on his arm, keeping her by him. When he felt her totally relax, he shifted slightly and she grabbed reflexively to keep him close, as if he were the talisman to ward off the frightening dream.

'Don't worry. I'll stay. Perhaps you can help me get to sleep?' His voice was oddly wistful and she giggled.

'Why not? We both got to sleep last night.'

'This could get to be a habit,' he said, chuckling, as he put one hand on her chest and pushed her back into the pillows.

'Not if it has to start with me scaring myself to death,' she said as she reached out with her hands to collect him to her.

The third night was worse as Laria and Kincaid woke at the same instant, both feeling the shafts of intense emotion. Sobbing, Laria was struggling out of the twisted sheets of her bed when Kincaid arrived, tripping over the sheet he had 'ported with him in his haste. Laria shot up, reaching to steady him and then they clung together until the spasms gradually eased.

*I think both sets of 'Dini pals,* and his tone was sharper than she had ever heard from him, *need to go to the hibernatory. That smell ought to have alerted us. I remember it from 'Dinis in our Squadron. They've been having fun and games with us.*

*They have?* Laria was astonished. She didn't want their new intimacy to be anyone's fun and games, even her devoted 'Dinis.

*Can you explain this any other way?*

*Are you angry with them?*

*Ah!* And his arms tightened about her, his lips turning up in a soft smile as he gazed down at her. *I can't say that I am, dear heart, but I'll be damned if I'll let them manipulate us like this. I can do without the panic triggers and I know you can.*

She glanced over her shoulder, half-expecting to see two bright poll eyes watching them. *They're fast asleep,* she said, seeing only the two lumps to one side of her wide bed.

*And so were Plus and Nil when I staggered out of bed, but that doesn't keep them from conniving dreams. You'd have had more experience with 'Dini dreaming than I.*

*Not I. My parents were the first to have 'Dini dreams. Tip and Huf have always given me nice dreams.*

*My pair kept me from going crazy on the* Valparaiso, Kincaid allowed, his tone puzzled now. *Tomorrow we'll take all four to the hibernatory and see what their condition is. D'you want to bet they've used their sex drive to stimulate ours?*

Laria tried very hard not to giggle at the outrage in Kincaid's tone. Of course, he could feel the rising laughter in her under his hands and he held her off to look into her face.

44

*And it worked,* she said meekly just before a chuckle broke from her lips.

*All right, all right,* he said, rocking her from side to side in his arms. *I'll give in. Will you?*

She hesitated, not quite sure how to handle this because she had no intention of forcing herself on Kincaid, despite how deep her feelings for him had become. She felt him begin to withdraw and tightened her arms about his neck.

*I just want to be sure you want to, too.*

*I do,* and she couldn't doubt he meant it.

The next morning, just as false dawn lit the skies, they hauled all four 'Dinis into the ground car and drove them to the nearest hibernatory. The large keeper, unusually gaunt for a Mrdini of its age, took one look at the quartet and started scolding them.

HOW DARE COLOURS GET INTO SUCH CONDITION, MAKING SUCH DEAD SMELLS! NPL, PLS ARE YOUNGER BUT TLP AND HGF KNOW WHEN SMELL TOO BAD. WHY DELAY? THIS SPECIAL TIME AND SPECIAL PLACE THIS TIME. DELAY CAUSE PROBLEMS. COULD BE ALL WRONG. TIMING IS ESSENTIAL NOW OF ALL TIMES. Railing at them angrily, the keeper pushed them ahead of it, swatting first Kincaid's Plus and then Tip, Nil and Huf because they weren't moving fast enough to suit it, through the door which was emphatically slammed shut.

As much amused by the scolding their friends had received as relieved by the knowledge they had acted properly, Kincaid and Laria locked arms and made their way back to their ground vehicle.

*Such dead smells?* Kincaid said rhetorically, grinning. *Could cause great problems?*

*They did smell and they were trying to put something over on us.*

*And succeeded very well, didn't they, dear heart?*

*I concur, dear man. I concur.*

He stopped and in the peculiarly pellucid light of Clarf, looked deeply into her eyes and touched her mind.

*If they were the problem, Laria . . .*

She caught his hands. *I haven't asked for any promises, Kincaid. I am first and always your friend.*

*Yes, that you are, dear heart. That you always are.* Then he gave her a gentle push towards the ground car and he drove them back to the Tower.

# CHAPTER THREE

The *Washington* hung behind the largest of the three moons that circled the subject planet, while probes began their exploratory flights. Thian had control of those investigating the planet while Clancy and Semirame Kloo had sent theirs to the Sphere, set in a geo-synchronous orbit above what appeared to be the same sort of flat field used for Hiver scout ships on the Xh-33 Hiver world.

'That ship is ancient,' Clancy reported to Admiral Ashiant who was seated behind the Talents' couches.

'It is?'

'The hull's pitted,' Rame Kloo added. 'And that odd covering they use on their Spheres has all worn away. Never seen that before. We should ask the 'Dinis about such erosion.'

'I'll send a message to Captain Spktm on the *KSTS*,' Clancy said and gestured for Rame to continue searching without him for a moment.

'Can you get inside the Sphere, Commander?' the admiral asked Kloo, leaning forward, elbows on his knees as he peered at the screen which did indeed show the deterioration of the surface of the Hiver vessel.

'Indeed we can, sir,' Rame said. 'They left a door open for us,' she added in a droll voice.

The admiral recoiled slightly in reflex as the probe dived for a jagged hole in the exterior. For a moment the screen was black. Then the probe's lights came on and displayed the now familiar drive area, did a sweep and then focused on the hull fragments from the hole littering the deck.

'Just what we need,' Clancy said and activated the probe's sweeper to collect the debris. 'I'll just 'port them to the lab, sir, and we should get an estimate of its age from forensic examination.'

'I'll tell them to expect it,' the admiral said, raising his wrist com to his lips.

'If you wouldn't mind, sir,' Clancy said, grinning to himself. Sometimes he had the notion that Admiral Ashiant felt somewhat at a disadvantage in the presence of the Talents. 'Spktm is querying its experts on the deterioration of the Sphere's skin. It'll come back if it has any information.'

'Ah, here we are, sir,' Thian said, gesturing to the screens he had just activated, showing pictures of the surface taken by the probes he was controlling. 'Odd.'

'What's odd?' the admiral asked, lowering the com now he had contacted the lab technicians.

'I'd've expected a much larger facility if this planet has been settled as long as the age of the ship seems to indicate.'

'Yes, you're right in that. The Xh-33 had a much larger installation near its field. Can you see the entrances to the underground scout storage?'

Thian shook his head. One probe swooped lower to the ground and then quartered the field area. Thian halted it a few centimetres above the ground.

'I can just make out a long seam, sir . . .'

'Yes, yes, and covered with sand or dust or whatever.'

'Hangars don't look to have been opened in a long while,' Thian said.

'No, they don't.'

'And if you'll look to the other screen, sir, there doesn't seem to be as much under cultivation.'

48

'Is this colony then dying?'

'Doesn't look to be, not with those flourishing crops which seem to be well tended. In fact, it's a rather nice world, Admiral. There's a good balance between cultivated and fallow fields. See that stretch just coming up . . . and forestry. And that lake . . . lovely. Almost Arcadia,' Thian remarked.

'Arcadia?' the admiral echoed. 'What's its designation on the Mrdini Star Maps?'

'Huh? Oh. Let me see.' Thian tapped a few keys before he said, 'Cj-70.'

Ashiant gave a disapproving grunt deep in his throat. 'Shame to stick to alpha numerics on it, pretty as it is. Let's refer to it as Arcadia. Agreed?'

'Willingly, sir,' Thian said obligingly and keyed in a substitution. 'However, it's certainly not as active as Xh-33 was.'

With this the admiral agreed, seeing the neatly weeded rows of greenery, the adjacent field sporting some dark purply-green foliage.

'Go on, will you, Thian?'

And Thian sent his two probes, in opposite directions, skimming over the surface at a height of twenty metres. In each screen they saw several of the collection squares, none as big as those on Xh-33 but substantial enough. Finally the right-hand screen showed movement and homed in on it. Workers were trundling along in their ordered phalanx down to yet another collection point. The creatures were head to tail, moving on six limbs at a brisk trot. Two more limbs were cocked at each 'head' and the watchers could see the specialised arrangement of trowel and fork.

'Those creatures aren't as large as the ones Rojer recorded on Xh-33, are they?' Ashiant said, puzzled.

'No, they don't seem to be,' Thian concurred and activated another screen with the relevant disk of Rojer's exploration of that planet. 'Much smaller.'

'But carrying the same sort of tools, so they're similar to the Xh-33 workers. Why would they be smaller?'

'I haven't a clue, sir. Shall I get one of the xenbios in here?'

'Aren't you projecting all this on their lab screens?'

49

'I am, but there's no reason you can't have a running report on their assessment.'

'Ask Lieutenant Weiman and 'Dini Grm to join me at the Talent post, will you?' Admiral Ashiant said into his wrist com, his eyes not leaving the screen.

While they were waiting for the specialists to arrive, Ashiant gave Thian a curious look. 'Would you mind my asking you,' and his glance included the other Talents, 'a little *more* about Talent? I mean, I know that Primes do both telepathy and teleport over enormous distances but Clancy here's a T-2 and I know he 'paths as well as 'ports and . . .' Ashiant shrugged, his rugged face indicating a sincere desire for a full briefing on the distinctions.

Thian grinned, saw Clancy reddening and Kloo trying hard not to grin.

'It's basically a difference in strength and length, and combinations of inherent skills, sir. I can 'path or 'port with or without generator gestalt. Clancy's got more kinetic ability than telepathic and, while he's strong in kinetics, he can't really 'path or receive far, even in gestalt, but his abilities multiply mine. And Kloo. Now she didn't know she was a latent Talent until the Phobos examination. At first she could only "send",' and Thian smiled again at Kloo rolling her eyes over her discovery of latent abilities. 'Now she can receive, and come in to add strength to *our* . . .' and he pointed to Clancy, 'merge. Alison Ann was a T-5 empath but she's advanced in skill, learning to 'port as well as 'path, but her initial ability made her a superb nurse.'

'It's association with us lot that have improved her at least a full grade up,' Clancy said, slyly grinning at Thian.

'It does help to be continually in use, as it were, sir. Our father, Afra Lyon, was originally a T-3 but constant association with our grandmother increased his skills to T-2. He may even be as close to Prime as he wants to get.'

Clancy made a grimace of surprise.

'Not that he'd admit it,' Thian went on. 'However, two T-2s, one with more telepathic strength, the other with kinetic, like Yoshuk and Nesrun on Sef, or the Bastianmajanis,

50

Flavia's parents, on Altair, mesh Talent so well they are all but equal to Prime. My sister, Zara, as another example, has both kinetic and telepathic ability but her empathic level is too high for her ever to be a Tower Prime. Like Elizara, she's best fitted for the medical and healing profession. So not all T-1s can automatically be Tower Primes . . . which, as you know, sir, FT&T badly needs.'

Ashiant nodded and gestured for Thian to continue.

'Below the 2s, you get variations of the abilities to 'port or 'path, sometimes just one and not the other at all. Or some can receive but not send. Or send a fair distance on a gestalt but not receive. T-3s are useful as aids to T-2s or Primes. There are far more T-4s and downward available as backup but they don't have the inherent stamina, even in connection with a gestalt, to work on their own, or for very long. However, engineers from T-4 down are apt to work solo anywhere and we've a lot of choice among them.'

'I thought that your cousin, Asia,' Ashiant turned to Clancy, 'trained with Rojer as engineer.'

'Yes, she did, sir, and is on the *Columbia* as T-4 and will probably get a post on a Tower.'

'That's just the Federated Teleport and Telepath side of Talent,' Thian went on. 'Sometimes we get T-2 rank for clairvoyants, finders, and empaths. FT&T tries to contact anyone with latent Talent, assess and train them. Some are better off going into private firms where their particular level of other aspects of Talent, like dowsing or affinities to water and fire, makes them invaluable to their employers.' Thian made a face and scratched the back of his head. 'I know my grandfather's trying to lure some of the higher ranks away from commerce and industry because FT&T never expected to expand so heavily into this sort of assignment . . .' and Thian gestured to indicate the *Washington* and naval duty.

'Damned glad FT&T permits it,' Ashiant said, nodding his head and then giving Thian a wry smile, 'though I wouldn't have thought I'd admit that when you first came aboard.'

Thian laughed out loud, remembering how many naval regulations and traditions he had set on their ears in his first

51

few hours aboard the old *Vadim*. Ashiant grinned back and nodded his head.

'We've both learned a thing or two since then, haven't we, Isthian?' Ashiant said, using his Prime's full first name.

'I know I have, sir,' Thian said. He turned towards the entrance to the Talent quarters. 'The xenbees're here.' And a discreet knock on the door panel followed his words.

However, when Ashiant explained the reason for their summons, neither Sam nor Grm could give him any answer to the puzzle.

'The queens activate whatever sort of worker they need for the task,' Sam said, rubbing his chin, while Grm, a dusty brown 'Dini, rocked gently on its flat feet. 'I have been noticing, Admiral, that this planet doesn't seem to be as densely farmed as Xh-33.'

'I have decreed,' and the Admiral glanced about in a pseudo-pompous manner, 'that this planet is to be referred to in all documentation as "Arcadia".'

'That gives it more personality than Cj-70,' Sam said with a big grin.

Grm pondered this, fingering its chin. AGREE. ARCAD-EE-A.

At that point, the admiral's wrist com bleeped quietly with an incoming message.

'Yes? Now that's very interesting. Thank you, Commander,' Ashiant said. 'They've dated the Sphere by the deterioration of the metal fragments at five hundred and eighty years old.'

'That's old!' Sam added a soft whistle. 'What is the oldest Sphere you ever encountered, Grm?'

'This one older than any seen,' Grm replied in good Basic, still rocking on its feet. 'We have only two hundred years fighting. That is much older.' Now it shook its head up and down and clicked softly in its throat. 'Far, far from home world, too.'

'Rather daunting, actually,' Ashiant murmured. 'Just how deeply have they penetrated our galaxy?'

The probes had entered the night side of the planet.

'Shall we continue, sir?'

'Yes, since I believe those probes are equipped for dark-vision. I want to know just how many and where collection points and the queen installations are.'

'Queens live deep under the ground,' Grm said, pointing to the deck and jabbing its digit to indicate considerable depth.

'Have we got any probes sensitive enough to pick up queen life-form readings?' Ashiant asked Thian.

'Rojer managed to do some probing in the collection facilities on Xh-33,' Thian said, 'but he didn't actually find a tunnel that opened into a queen's living quarters. It was a maze . . . with low-ceilinged waiting places for the various types of workers.' Thian shook his head at the immensity of such an undertaking.

'Much smaller workers,' Sam said, still rubbing his jaw. 'Don't understand what that could mean. Prime, can you get us some soil samples from . . .' he grinned, '. . . Arcadia's surface? Dr Tru Blairik, the bio on the *Columbia,* suggests that the soil on Marengo and Talavera was deficient in a variety of minerals and earths. We also have the components of the Xh-33 for comparison.'

'I'll direct the probes to start collecting soil samples. Random selection, Lieutenant?' Thian asked.

'Yes, please.'

'We can help you now,' Clancy said. 'There's nothing left in that Sphere that we haven't seen in the others, though it doesn't have escape pods. Maybe that was a brand-new innovation for the Hivers when they met Mrdinis, Grm.' He grinned at the 'Dini who swivelled its poll eye around to Clancy.

'Int'rusting,' and Admiral Ashiant began to rub his chin thoughtfully.

'Indeed,' Grm agreed, continuing to rock as if that was as much an aid to thought as jaw-rubbing.

'Prime, have we any updates from Squadron . . . excuse me, Fleet B?' the admiral asked.

Thian leaned across to Clancy and indicated the T-2 was to take over the manoeuvring of the probes. Clancy nodded as he and Rame took firm control of the two while Thian leaned into one of the *Washington*'s generators for the gestalt needed for a far sending. While he could have done it without aid, he had learned to save unassisted contact for emergencies.

*Rojer? You available?*

*Always,* was the cheerful reply and a mental sketch of a deep bow.

*Is it daytime wherever you are?* Thian couldn't be sure since it was his brother's touch that he had contacted, not the ship or a planetary surface.

*It is – and I'm on Talavera where we've started investigations.*

*And?*

*This is the one with a failed Hiver colony and we've about concluded that the soil lacked some element vital to the queens. There's one queen corpse left and a few workers but they've been here a long time.*

*Five hundred and eighty years or so?*

*What? No. At least I don't think so. Why?*

Thian informed his brother of their discoveries on Arcadia, emphasizing the size of the workers.

*That's int'rusting,* Rojer said. *Yakamasura and Blairik noticed that with the worker shells here. Much smaller than those at Xh-33. You can see the difference with the naked eye. Are you telling me that the planet you're investigating is that old and not overcrowded?*

*That's what I'm telling you.*

*What's the soil analysis?*

*Just getting in samples now.*

*Tsck, tsck, you're slow.*

*Not at all,* Thian replied, refusing to rise to his brother's jibe. *Just being cautious. THIS planet is occupied.*

*Hmmm, yes, that would advise some caution, I suppose. Five hundred and eighty years? That's grabbed the xenos' attention.* And there was laughter in Rojer's mental tone. *Yes, that's what Thian said. How'd you arrive at that estimate, they want to know?*

*Forensic analysis of fragments of their Sphere.*

*Pass that along, would you?*

Thian flipped the file in a 'port to his brother's position.

*Hey, close shave, bro. So your planet's off the colony list? It's occupied.*

*Well, this one isn't. The 'Dinis can have it. All except this compound until we've scraped all the data we can from it. Those Hivers obviously didn't do enough homework. But then, they had queens to waste, didn't they?*

*Looks like.*

*'Deed it does. Send me your soil analyses when they're ready, will you, bro? Blairik is doing comparisons. We're moving to a more felicitous site . . . to erect the Tower.*

*I'll send on the samples.* And, with an image of himself giving Rojer a brotherly pat on the back, Thian disengaged.

He did not however resume his control of the probes.

'I would like to get down to Arcadia's surface, Admiral Ashiant,' he said after a long thoughtful pause.

'WHAT?' Ashiant was astounded. 'I don't think I can allow that, Thian. You're far too valuable to us . . .'

Thian held up his hand. 'I'd run no risk, I assure you.' Then he turned to Grm and Weiman. 'The queen kept at the Heinlein Centre . . . is she still ignoring the presence of Humans or 'Dini?'

'It has made no response at all,' Grm said, shaking its head.

Sam Weiman sighed. 'I had the opportunity to transfer to the . . . ah . . . facility,' he said. 'Stood as close to her as I am to you right now, sir. I have never been so completely ignored in my life.' His moon face creased into a droll grin. 'No-one has ever had a reaction from her. There have been so many attempts at some form of communication. Every method has been tried: sound, colour, every radio waveband and electromagnetic frequency modulation. We don't even know if she's been aware of them.' He sighed again. 'It is so terribly frustrating,' he added with considerable vehemence.

Thian turned to the admiral. 'I would be in no danger because the Hivers do not recognize us as enemies or friends, or anything. They don't *recognize* . . . any . . . other . . . living species.'

'Not even those who have recently blasted all their Spheres to bits?' asked the admiral, cocking one eyebrow at Thian.

55

'I won't be IN the ship, sir. I do need to be in their ambience,' Thian said in a slow, measured way. 'I will bring a full squad of marines, if you feel that is necessary. I don't. And Clancy would be here to snatch me right back if I were threatened.'

Sam Weiman jerked his index finger up and down, the eagerness on his broad pink face suggesting that he'd be very willing to accompany any such expedition. Grm gave Thian a long, searching, hopeful look.

'You go, Prime. I go and Sam,' it said with more than usual firmness.

All three regarded the admiral, who looked from one to another as if he doubted their good sense.

'Such a mission, seeing the queens in their natural habitat, would be most instructive, sir,' Sam said, his body taut with anticipation. 'I'd like to take as many readings as possible, of soil, air . . . anything that might be useful for our study of the Hivers as a species. And perhaps leave remotes to view while we're still in orbit?'

Ashiant gave a snort, then exhaled with a combination of impatience and irritation.

'Very well,' he said, flicking his fingers to show that he was not happy with the request but permitting it. 'If there is *any* reaction groundside, you'll be hauled out instantly.' He fixed a basilisk stare at Clancy who nodded vigorously in agreement.

Sam's face was beatific, Grm did a little dance on its feet and Thian grinned.

'And that squad will be right there beside you . . .' Ashiant pointed at each in turn. Then he twisted around, finger pointing at Clancy who was trying to maintain an imperturbable expression, though his eyes danced. 'And you don't lose sight of them for one moment.'

'No, sir, of course, sir,' Clancy replied, sitting up as if at attention. One of the probes zigzagged and he instantly rectified its course.

'Sir, if I may be allowed to lead the surface party,' Lt Commander Semirame Kloo said, 'I'd be able to assist Lt Clancy with a speedy evacuation.'

Ashiant widened his eyes, threw both hands in the air and rose to his feet.

'You're all mad. Very well, Commander. Assemble a squad. Hand-picked martial-arts experts. I've seen the clips of how fast that queen can move the few times she has. Side arms, missile-loaded. I want to see where you intend to land! And YOU,' Ashiant pointed again to Thian, his finger shaking a bit, 'wear body armour.'

'Yes, sir.'

Ashiant glared about the room once more and then with an exasperated 'whoosh', went through to the bridge.

'Admiral on the bridge,' was plainly heard just as the door slid shut.

Thian brought his hands together with a loud clap. 'Let's get with it, team,' he said enthusiastically. 'Sam, you get into body armour, too. Grm, do you have anything similar?'

Grm drew itself up to its full metre and a half. 'I am 'Dini. I need no armour against queens.'

*I could throw Grm back by myself, if I had to,* Semirame said with a sniff. Then she held up her wrist com and started snapping out her orders.

'Shall I keep on with the probes?' Clancy asked.

'Please, Clancy. We ought to have a full surface scan so we can map all the Hive installations. Get Lea Day up here to help and who's that other good telekinetic on board?'

'Vlad Ivanov in the machine shop,' Thian said. 'He'll do fine if he's available.'

'He is,' Semirame said, interrupting herself. 'Thought he'd be needed. And have you picked out our landing spot?'

'Yes.' Thian pointed to one of the unused screens in the bank ranged across the bulkhead. A scene came up from some of the initial footage of their day's scanning of Arcadia.

'By a collection facility?' Semirame asked in surprise.

'Why not? That space right there,' and Thian put the cursor on the spot. 'Nice open space for the shuttle, good visibility. Computer, print screen 5.' The hard copy rapidly extruded from the unit and he handed it to Semirame who frowned as she scanned it. 'Copy to Admiral's screen. I'll leave it up for you, Clancy.'

'Thanks,' his cousin said drolly.

Then Thian flicked his fingers at Sam Weiman and Grm. 'C'mon. Get ready. I don't want to hang around . . . in case the admiral has second thoughts about this.' He grinned, once more, mischievously before he turned. With a skip and hop more suited to a much younger person, Thian made his way to his room to suit himself in the gear specified by the admiral.

*Any sign we've been noticed, Clancy?* Thian asked when he felt the slight bump as the shuttle landed on Arcadia's surface. *Nice 'port. You're improving.*

*Thank you,* and Clancy's tone was droll. *Nary a flicker on the telltales!*

Thian turned. 'Let's have a reading on the air, Mocmurra,' he said and the woman promptly held up the peculiar device she carried. A long thin spiral tube contained a worm of intricate, flexible coils coated with a polyamide material that turned them brown: a compact and efficient gas chromatograph.

Mocmurra grinned. 'Air's fresher than the *Washington*'s.'

'Let's move out, men,' Commander Semirame said, touching the shuttle's hatch control as her squad instantly got to their feet. She nodded to Thian, allowing him to be first, but Grm slipped in ahead of him and jumped deftly to the ground, the tools on the belt it wore clanking together.

'Soft,' it said as it flipped its feet through the greeny-brown ground cover that stretched beyond and over the collection facility. Tendrils from the vegetation had spilled over the wide entrance but were trimmed short of covering it.

'Keep the place tidy, don't they,' Semirame said, right at Thian's elbow as he stepped onto the surface. She gestured for her squad to spread out and around the shuttle, checking on all sides.

'All clear, sir,' her sergeant reported.

'Now what, Thian?' she asked.

'I don't quite know,' he said, looking around at the plain that extended in all directions, at the cultivated land with an

58

occasional access alley for the workers. He took deep breaths of the air, tasting it, feeling it on his skin. 'Faint odour?'

'There is,' and Semirame took another deep breath. 'Sort of . . . crisp.'

'Yes, exactly,' Thian said, having been unable to find the right descriptive word for the lingering smell in the air.

It was extraordinary to be standing here, on a Hiver world, and he didn't bother to hide the slight smile of wonderment and incredulity this moment provoked. He snapped mental fingers at Rojer's jibe that he'd never be 'risked' on a personal tour.

Semirame pointed. 'Look at it move!'

Thian saw the 'Dini, cavorting over the ground cover, headed right for the collection facility entrance, down the slope.

Semirame whistled for her squad leader's attention but the sergeant had already allocated two men to follow the 'Dini.

*Any activity, Clancy?*

*Not so much as a pip out of place. Admiral's in here, on your couch, eyes glued to the screen. His expression – well, I'd call it avid, I think. Certainly nothing's going to surprise him. What's it like?*

*Like any other M-type planet we've been on. Air has a nice crispness to it. We've taken GC readings and Weiman's taking samples of the ground cover. Grm's on its way down the embankment to the entrance and we're following. Keep track of me.*

*Just don't expect me to move ALL of you out of danger if you run into it.* Clancy's tone was slightly sour.

*You can come on the next excursion, Clancy.*

*Do I have a choice?*

Thian only laughed as he started down the steep slope that led into the subsurface collection centre. He was elated in a way he had never before experienced, not even when he and Kiely-Austin had penetrated the nova-seared Great Sphere and found the egg repositories intact. Even the familiar sting-pzzt that was now noticeable couldn't dampen his mood. Anyway the body armour somewhat deadened the sensation.

He hoped that it would continue to do so when they were in closer proximity to the Hivers.

Semirame had sent men trotting on ahead of the adventurous Grm whose short legs could not match the jogtrot of the marines. She gave a brisk nod of her head and then tilted it to mentally inform Thian that her advance scouts had seen nothing inside to alarm them. Thian stepped onto the approach ramp, excitement rising inside him. With his special senses, he couldn't hear, see or feel anything. No, that wasn't quite right. There *was* something . . . a presence . . . not something truly sentient, but something alive. Some things, he corrected himself.

The ground beneath his feet had been trampled down for so long that it was now below its original level by several centimetres. In fact, if he looked closely he could see the slight ruts worn by workers that had tramped up and down it for centuries. In the depths beyond the overhang, he could see light – Semirame's scouts checking it out.

'Scouts say it's all clear. Stinks a lot, like rotted vegetation,' she said with a snort.

She raised her arm to call the rest of her team forward. Sam Weiman had knelt down to scoop up more soil samples, grunting as he forced his tool to loosen the closely packed dirt. Semirame pulled down the dark-vision visor from her helmet and Thian followed her example as they moved into the facility.

The prevalent smell *was* indeed of slightly rotting vegetation. The odour deepened as they penetrated further in. The flooring was clean and their boots scraped on a different surface. Thian leaned down to touch it.

'Some sort of plascrete,' he said.

Another of Semirame's noncommittal grunts.

'Lots of low tunnels now, sir, leading deeper in and down to other levels,' said the tinny voice issuing from Semirame's wrist com. She looked at Thian for orders.

'Can you navigate them?' he asked into his own wrist unit.

'Can do,' was the answer after a slight pause.

'Hands and knees job?' Thian asked.

'Can do,' was repeated.

'Found where the stuff must get dumped, sir,' another voice reported. 'Straight ahead of you. 'Bout ten metres.'

Semirame and Thian rapidly covered the distance, their quick steps echoing in the underground space since stealth did not seem to be required.

The smell was heavier as they reached the dumping point. Peering down the slide that was at a forty-five-degree angle, they could see a parallel chute and conveyor belt. Despite the smell, their handlights showed no refuse at all: the plascrete was clean.

'Down and down they go,' Semirame remarked at her driest. 'Hemmer, Vale, Singh, take a look below.' To Thian she added, *Mark 'em as they pass you, Thian, so's you know 'em to bring 'em back up, like you did the crews in the Phobos Sphere.*

He could see her wide grin, her teeth showing brightly in his visor. He nodded, getting a touch of each of them as they imperturbably slid down the ramp and started examining the direction of the belt.

'Found a whole bay or holding level full of . . . workers? Sir? Sir?' another trooper reported. 'Smells bad but no garbage.'

'Got enough light to send me back a scan, Wixell?'

'Do my best. Place's as dark as . . .' Wixell paused, cleared her throat, and went on, 'dark, sir.'

Thian watched his wrist unit and the scan came up, lumps of darkness then illuminated by a slowly moving beam of light.

'The workers,' Thian said when he saw the tool extension crossed lifelessly on the front of the creature. 'Standing by for orders from the queen?'

'Can't move any further in, sir,' Wixell went on. 'Place is stuffed with them and the ceiling's just high enough for them to lie down, or whatever it is they're doing. More vegetable stink, too.'

'Any other exit from the . . .' Semirame paused, grimacing as she tried to find an appropriate word.

'Stable?' Thian suggested.

61

'Stable's are for living things. That's a garage,' she said, sounding disgusted.

'No, sir, blank walls.'

'C'mon back then, Wixell.'

'Sir?' and another scout reported in. 'Found a bigger tunnel, leads down and straight ahead for several hundred metres.' Her voice had an edge of excitement. 'Big enough for a queen, I think, sir. I'm getting static from the GC so I'll take readings.'

'Do that, Mocmurra,' and Thian could see the commander grinning. 'Go on, Thian. I'll call them,' and she jerked her thumb towards the slide and then her finger in the direction Thian should go. 'Captain Lyon's on his way, Mocmurra. Wait for him, will ya? Bessy, Trainor, scout ahead for the captain.'

Thian trotted across to the light held by the figure at the opening to the tunnel's slit. It wasn't very wide, but then the queens weren't either; they were tall.

'This way, sir,' Mocmurra said: the sturdy marine was grinning over her discovery. 'Only one the size for Humans.'

'Anyone know where Grm is?' Thian asked, realizing he hadn't caught sight of the 'Dini since it had entered.

'It was with me, sir. It's up ahead.'

'Let's move it, then,' Thian said. It wouldn't do for a 'Dini specialist to get hurt or captured by the Hivers. He picked up his feet and ran down the straight tunnel, blessing the visibility of the visor.

*It's OK, Thian,* came Clancy's reassuring thought.

*Can you track Grm?*

*It's got a locator on its tool belt.*

Thian kept running, trying to keep the nail-studded boot heels from hitting the tunnel floor too loudly, just in case the queen could feel vibrations. He nearly ran Grm down when the 'Dini appeared in front of him, at the T-junction. Actually, it was more than a T, for additional tunnels, all queen height, opened up like a delta. Nine more.

THIS WAY, Grm said, pointing to the first one on the left-hand side, its poll eye gleaming with excitement and the fur at

62

an almost perpendicular angle to its body. When Thian would have moved forward, it held up a flipper, bringing it around to its mouth to indicate a necessity for stealth. Then Semirame yanked at Thian's sleeve and slipped in front of him. Well, she was right, of course, to guard him. They cautiously moved forward, placing their feet noiselessly.

A snatch of an old song, *'with catlike tread, upon our way we steal,'* sprang to his mind.

*No sound at all, we never speak a word,* Alison Ann's voice continued.

*Tracking me again?* Thian said, amused that Gravy was in touch.

*A fly's footfall would be distinctly heard,* was Semirame's addition, surprising a gasp out of Thian. *Just happened to remember it* she added with a touch of bashful humour in her voice. Thian grinned. The commander's mental tone was quite different from her vocal one, and far more revealing of her personality than her spoken words.

Another smell impinged on their senses.

*Queen stink?* Semirame asked Thian.

*Heavy sting-pzzt, that's for sure.* And Thian tried to ignore the concentration of that phenomenon, though the body armour did help. *Tell Mocmurra to get more readings.* He heard her give the order. *My sister Zara's the only one of us who's been close to a queen. Sam didn't mention smell as a factor in his confrontation with her. And nothing recorded about the ambience in her . . . quarters . . . suggests a poisonous emanation. Of course, we had spacesuits when we were on the Great Sphere but the vacuum of space would have erased any residual odours.*

*Wasn't much reek on the refugee Sphere by the time it got to Phobos Base but this smells a bit like it. Ooops!*

Semirame had caught up with Grm and her halt was so abrupt that Thian walked into her. She pointed to her right and Thian saw the opening and what was beyond it, as plain in his visor as if they'd been in full light – a queen, standing, with its groomers, its upper limbs extended for the attentions of its minions.

63

*She isn't that big,* was Thian's first thought.

*She isn't? Where are you?* Clancy demanded brusquely. *That's the admiral's question, not mine.*

*We seem to be at the entrance to a queen's quarters. I don't think she's as big as the one at Heinlein Station.*

*Estimate!*

*A metre thirty centimetres, give or take a centimetre,* Thian said, looking at Semirame who nodded, though she kept her visor focused on the queen.

Grm tugged at Thian's arm and Thian leaned down to let it speak softly in his ear.

SHE IS NOT BIG. SHE IS OLD.

Thian passed on that information though how Grm could tell the creature's age was beyond him.

*I'll go in,* he told Semirame at the same time as he announced that intention to Clancy.

*NO!!!* came at him from two directions and he shook his head against the blast.

Semirame looked at him, her eyes hidden by the visor, but there was no mistaking the negative posture of her body or her raised hand, ready to clout him if he moved.

*All right, then. You go first, Rame,* he said, trying to sound pleasant when he wanted to lift her up and shake her for being so damned cautious about his Talented self: he could react faster in his own defence than anyone else could because he'd instantly sense injurious intent.

Semirame must have caught some of that because she lowered her hand and shrugged. Carefully she entered the queen's quarters, Thian with equal stealth right behind her, so they were almost moving in tandem.

*This is much bigger than I expected,* Thian said and Semirame gave a barely perceptible nod of agreement.

*Palatial, considering where she stashes the guys that do all the work.*

*Describe!* Clancy demanded. *Admiral talking,* he added a second later in an explanatory fashion.

Thian could just see the scene, with Ashiant stiff with apprehension.

*The main room is say thirty metres by thirty metres and half that to the ceiling. It's crammed with bodies, her attendants, and there's a ledge against one wall, and, against the wall perpendicular to it, another sort of seat – it may be where she extrudes her eggs . . .*

*Yeah, it does look like a birthing stool with the big hole in the back AND a sort of tube opening in the wall,* Semirame said, then added in a tone of disgust, *I don't know why I'm 'pathing. We could be roaring and this lot wouldn't hear us. We're right in front of them . . . they've got to know there are three individuals staring at them. And something just scurried over my feet . . . it didn't even notice it was canted to one side doing so. Hey, wait a minute, Grm.*

*It doesn't hear you, Rame,* Thian said, quickly following the 'Dini as it went further into the room. Grm did have the good sense to move slowly but the 'Dini was determined to see all it could of the habitat of its lifelong enemy. He caught up with Grm and planted one hand firmly on its shoulder, tightening his grip when the 'Dini tried to evade. He squeezed his fingers to make certain Grm knew it wasn't supposed to go on unattended.

*Look at the walls, Thian,* Semirame said urgently and Thian glanced upward, having been far more aware of the queen and her bustling attendants. He really hadn't noticed more than the size of the room. Now he saw that on three walls, just above the height of his head, there were glowing screens or monitors.

*Their communications boards?*

*Why not? The queen's reading the one in front of her. Look at her head. She's tracking something,* Semirame said. *But I don't see as much change in the panels on the side walls.*

Thian watched long enough to be aware of changes, rippling top to bottom of the panel, as if scrolling.

*CAN YOU SEND SAMPLE?*

*Only if you and the admiral stop roaring at me suddenly. I damned near jumped onto something,* Thian said testily. *Rame, tape a recording of the side panels. I can focus on the one she's watching from where I am now.* He lifted his wrist com, activating the record touch button, and grabbing Grm's arm before it took advantage of his need of both hands and got loose. Grm did pull its feet out of the way of several rapidly moving attendants who passed where it had been standing and went out through a hole in the wall. *Get Mocmurra in here, too, to record the smells.*

*I think Sam would call them 'pheromones',* Clancy said.

Then something rammed into Thian's heel and he lifted his foot as another variety of attendant charged out, only momentarily thwarted by him being in its way.

*Place is crawling with bugs and beetles,* Thian said, dipping his hand so the watchers could see the rammer skittering into the heap that surrounded the queen. With two of her nether limbs she was tilted slightly backward, her egg-bulb just clearing the floor. Thian could see that it was being coated, or cleaned, he wasn't sure which, by those surrounding that section of her.

*Admiral and Lt Commander Britt, the science officer, say that she is not, I repeat NOT, as large as the Heinlein queen. Commander, please focus for one minute on the left-hand panel. Then for a minute on the right-hand one. We seem to get some sort of variation but very erratic. Thian, go back to the wall she's watching. This may be a significant breakthrough.*

Making sure he wasn't going to walk on anything scuttling about, Thian backed up so that his recorder would catch the full screen of the front wall the queen was watching. She opened her mouth. Thian and Rame both froze. A creature, slightly larger than most of her attendants, held up a lump. She lowered her head slightly, and the lump was inserted into her maw. She seemed to inhale the material because it certainly didn't go down her throat as a lump.

*Did you see that? A male? Feeding her?*

Before Semirame could answer, Thian was distracted when something connected hard against his shin. He danced off that foot. Then replaced it to lift the other and avoid what was scurrying about.

*Keep the camera still,* Clancy said.

*I will if they'll stop kicking me in the shins. There! That better?*

*Frankly, I couldn't tell,* Clancy said, *but the experts sure are excited.*

*Why?* Semirame asked in her droll fashion. *We'd need a Hiver to decipher it . . . maybe even read it, and none of 'em are talking to US.*

*If it keeps the experts happy,* Clancy said, his mental tone amused, *let 'em try it.*

*Wonder what would happen if we could replicate this for the Heinlein queen?* Thian said mischievously. He heard Clancy's mental chortle and Semirame's snort.

*Ah, that would be sheer mental cruelty, Thian,* Semirame said, *after 'porting her into a functional Sphere so she could start it up for us and then whisking her back to prison.*

Thian grinned in the green darkness around him at the memory of that incident. Well, the ploy had worked and the queen had shown them the sequence of start-up controls that the Human engineers had been unable to fathom. They'd 'ported the queen without the knowledge of the Phobos Base commander but the tactic had worked.

*That wouldn't work this time, Rame. She won't talk to us and how what they might be saying to each other would help us, I don't know.*

*You're right,* Semirame said wistfully.

*Admiral asks could you set up a surveillance unit in her quarters?* Clancy asked.

*Sure. But I'll need a night-vision unit and some heavy-duty stick'em,* Semirame said. She added quickly, *and it has to be an odour-free adhesive!*

*Can do,* Clancy said. *Just hang in there a few minutes, if you can.*

*We can,* Semirame blithely assured him.

*On their way,* Clancy said.

*To get it really stuck proper in position, I'm going to have to stand on your shoulders, I think. You're good for something now and then, you know.* Semirame gave him a picture of her, patting his head. Only she was on stilts and he was much, much shorter.

Suddenly Thian heard a mechanical whirring and air was blowing against him.

*That's odd,* Semirame said.

Thian felt Grm tug at his sleeve and he leaned down.

THEY SMELL US, the 'Dini murmured in his ear.

*Grm seems to think we smell,* Thian said.

*I don't doubt that in the least,* Semirame said. *They gotta have clean air.*

*If they smell us, why don't they SEE us?* Thian asked.

*I dunno and I'm happy they can't. Hurry up with that spy-eye, will ya? If they're cleansing the air, they might look for . . . thanks.* A package landed against Rame's chest and she clutched it firmly to her.

*Good catch,* Clancy said.

Now Semirame pushed Thian to the back wall, gestured for him to make his hands into a footrest. He shook his head, grinning, spread his legs slightly and 'ported her to his shoulders. Wincing, he also lightened her not insubstantial weight before her heavy boots could dig welts into his shoulders. Instinctively, he put his hands up on her muscular calves to steady her. He could feel her smear on the adhesive with quick movements, then the pressure as she stuck the surveillance unit into the goo.

*Can you see, Clancy?* she asked.

*Ah . . . yes, coming through . . . as clear as it'll get, I guess.*

*Now's the time to know, Clancy,* she said in her best have-you-done-as-I-told-you commander manner.

*We'll fiddle with resolution up here. Admiral says get out of there before you do stink up the place enough for them to start looking for you.*

*Right.*

Thian 'ported her back to the floor, and she gave a curt flick of her fingers to indicate they should leave. Grm tried to resist Thian pulling it along but, with the air circulation blowing across his face, Thian really did think it was high time to leave.

*We got lots of pictures, Thian. Landing party's recording all over the facility. Clancy sent each of the teams night-vision remotes,* Semirame said and the group at the entrance now stepped back to allow them to leave the queen's quarters. As soon as she was some way down the passage, Semirame gave low-voiced orders to reassemble in the main chamber.

There was a substantial breeze flowing across the chamber when they got there.

'All units here?' she asked, scanning the figures in front of her.

'All present and accounted for,' said the squad sergeant.

'Let's get outa here before they try to find who's making their house smell,' Semirame said and, raising her arm in a forward sweep, trotted up out of the collection point. Pushing up her visor, she ran backwards as she checked again that all who had entered were coming out. Then she turned forward again and kept up the trot the short distance to the shuttle. She stood by the door, with the sergeant, checking once more. In minutes everyone was seated, ready for the 'port back to the *Washington*.

*We're ready,* Thian told Clancy.

*Steady as you go,* Clancy answered.

'Sir,' and, having got the commander's attention, Wixell pointed out the window.

They just had time to see low-slung creatures flowing up out of the collection facility, waving antennae about.

'Trying to find out where the smell comes from,' Semirame said, chuckling. 'Have to remember to neutralize us stinking types the next time we do a reconnaissance.'

Thian grinned. 'I wasn't sweating. Were you?'

'Naw,' Semirame replied. 'Might be our boots.' She looked down at her dirt-stained footwear. 'Or our uniforms. Always did say the dye's got a vicious pong to it.'

*All set?*

*All set.*

A moment later Thian nodded approval as the shuttle landed so smoothly only he and Semirame were aware that they had been transported the thirty-six thousand kilometres to the geo-synchronous orbit above the surface of the planet. Though there was a startled look on Wixell's face as she'd been facing one of the two portholes.

*Should we run a GC on us to see if we do stink enough to*

69

*register with those ultra-sensitive queens?* Semirame asked, cocking her head at Thian. *And what we smell like?*

*Wouldn't that upset our ultra-sensitive and efficient troops?*

Whatever she might have replied was lost in the next second. Someone pounded on the door, to indicate that they should undo the hatch. Instantly the entire squad had weapons at the ready, aimed at the hatch.

*Nothing wrong with their reflexes.* 'Re-lax, troops. We're back.'

A gusty sigh of relief came from all sides, and with it a whiff of garlic.

'*Garlic!*' Thian said to Semirame.

'*Yeah, just noticed. Wonder if that's relevant, but we'll use a stink 'graph just to be on the safe side.*

*Garlic used to be a specific against witches, ghosties, ghoulies and things that go bump in the night,* Clancy said.

*Whose side are you on?* Thian asked while Semirame muttered orders through her wrist com. Then she smiled up at him, giving her head one sharp nod to show that the pong-test would be accomplished.

'Sir,' said the boat-deck watch officer, 'Admiral's compliments and can you report to him immediately.'

*I'll just hold 'em up a moment and then they can file past Exit 5 and get odorized,* Semirame told Thian.

*Should make an interesting appendix to the mission report.*

He waved his hand at her as he exited the ship and strode to the nearest lift, busy formulating his report to the admiral. *He's going to love the garlic.*

# CHAPTER FOUR

Laria and Kincaid got the announcement of the release of Talavera to the Mrdini from Earth Prime who was nearly as jubilant as all of Clarf would shortly be.

*That's marvellous, Grandad. You don't know how happy that'll make everyone here.*

*I've a very good idea, Laria, but doubtless you'll fill us in. Please inform Plrgtgl immediately as a courtesy and – here's the written notification – in Basic as well as Mrdini.*

Both Tower Talents heard the message tube rattle into the basket.

*Good shot, Earth Prime.*

*The hand hath not missed in decades.*

*How soon can they set off?* Laria asked, grinning in triumph at Kincaid who was smiling, too.

*How soon can colony ships be loaded?* Jeff Raven responded. *Who's catching?*

*Rojer, Flavia and the* Columbia *team. No problem on the receiving end.*

*No, there won't be. May I leave the Tower to take the message to Plrgtgl?*

*You are Tower Prime, Laria Raven-Lyon, YOU can leave the*

71

*Tower any time you wish. I'm sure there's nothing coming in that Kincaid can't handle by himself. Right?*

*Right,* was Kincaid's instant reassurance. He jerked his head at Laria to urge her to leave.

The note of the generators slid deeper without Laria using them. She remembered to use a glove to pick up the message tube still freezing from its 'portation through the vacuum of space and ran down the steps.

'We got it, we got it!'

'Got what?' Lionasha asked.

'HEY, what's wrong with the Tower? Generators are off . . .' Vanteer called from his level.

'IT'S OFFICIAL,' Laria yelled back. 'The 'Dinis get Talavera!'

Vanteer was up the short flight in one leap. 'They do?'

She waved the cylinder. 'I'm off to make a personal delivery of the go-ahead,' she said, leaving the cool of the station and, stopping dead in her tracks, gasping at the hot air outside. But she persevered on to her ground vehicle. YOU'VE GOT THE PLANET, she shouted in 'Dini to Fig, Sil, Dig and Nim who were on yard duty.

'Dinis did exultant cartwheels all across the plascrete. She laughed at such antics as she got into the ground car. Someone had already turned on the air-conditioning full blast – Kincaid, no doubt, getting rid of the trapped heat inside. She took off fast enough to raise a dirt cloud and pebbles that pattered against the undercarriage. She turned out of the Tower Compound, heading for the Clarf Administration Building. She drove at daring speed through the afternoon traffic and into the compound where Plrgtgl had its office. Braking in front of the main entrance, she didn't wait for the air cushion to settle before she flung herself out of the car, through the roasting air and was in the relatively cool building in four long strides.

'What's the rush, Prime?' one of Plrgtgl's Human assistants asked, surprised at her appearance.

'You'll hear, you'll hear,' Laria said, brandishing the message tube. 'Is Plus here? Oh, do tell me it is?'

'Far's I know,' was the reply. 'Naciana's at her desk.'

As Plrgtgl was responsible for managing all the Humans currently employed on Clarf, it employed Human staff assistants, too. So Laria courteously knocked on the door before sliding it back.

Naciana looked up. 'Laria?'

'Is Plus in?'

'Yes,' Naciana said, waving her to the inner door, but half-rising from her seat as she sensed Laria's excitement. And also saw a tube that must contain important documents if Clarf Prime was hand-carrying it.

Plrgtgl looked up at her entry, rose to its full height.

EARTH PRIME HAS REQUIRED ME TO GIVE THIS DIRECTLY TO YOU, HONOURABLE PLRGTGL, she said in 'Dini and, with a flourish, handed it the tube.

Plus lowered its poll to eye her for a long moment.

IT IS THE NEWS WE WISH FOR, IS IT NOT, Plus said, holding the tube tightly to its chest for a moment. Then, with a flick of its flippers, it opened the container and disks fell onto the desk along with a sheaf of hard copy. NACIANA?

YES, SIR? Naciana had followed Laria to the threshold.

PUT THIS ON MY SCREEN, Plus said, tossing Naciana one of the disks which her eager fingers fumbled into the appropriate slot on its desk while Plus was unrolling the hard copy. AHHHHHHHHHH, and Plus's ecstatic warble echoed out of the office, through the door Laria had left open, to startle Humans and 'Dinis alike in the halls. WE HAVE IT! WE HAVE IT! WE HAVE IT!

Laria, knowing what the 'Dini meant, leaned back against the desk to avoid a collision as it charged past her, waving what looked like a Mercator projection of Talavera. Plus danced up the hall, knocking bodies aside in its exultation. Then, almost ricocheting off across the hall at the end of the main corridor, it returned, giving everyone in its path a glimpse at the map, babbling in a combination of Basic and 'Dini that made no sense to anyone. Except Laria, who knew enough to understand its garbled comments.

73

The moment Plus re-entered its office, it altered completely, becoming dignified and organized. After her first surprise at Plus's reaction, Naciana, well accustomed to her superior's volatility, had put the full report up on the screen.

COPIES, MAKE COPIES, LOTS OF COPIES, Plus said, flipping its free arm at her to show great urgency. Once behind the desk, it smoothed the Mercator projection out, holding the map down with objects on its desk, and then unrolled the rest of the hard copy. CALL THEM ALL. WE MEET AS SOON AS THEY GET HERE. OH, THIS IS MARVELLOUS. OUR WORLDS WILL ALL REJOICE, Plus said to Laria. Then it scrutinized the documentation with a poll eye that was shining with its inner joy.

Communications units buzzed from Naciana's desk. Plus waved her to answer while it picked up its own unit and began what Laria was certain would be a string of calls to Clarf's administrative personages.

'Good luck,' she said to Naciana who was listening to the caller whose audible tone was as excited as Plus.

Naciana waved her free hand and gave Laria a thumbs-up sign, her eyes wide with excitement as she tried to get a word in edgeways to the caller. In the hallway, Laria was stopped time and again by Humans and 'Dinis for an explanation.

'The High Council has awarded 'Dinis the planet Talavera,' she said, again and again and again as she ploughed her way to the entrance.

There she was almost knocked down by excited 'Dinis, large and small, who were trying to get into the building she was trying to exit. She 'ported herself out of the way and got into the car, sweat in rivulets down her face and body. When she started the vehicle, she realized that there were so many other cars parked every which way, she had no clear exit left, even on air cushion.

*I'll help,* Kincaid said, laughter in his tone.

*You'll have to. There's no other way I'll get out of here.* She linked her mind with his and together they 'ported her car all the way back to the Clarf Tower compound. *Just as well,* she added, *because the traffic's backed up on all the roads and the air's thick with incoming 'Dinis on belts. How come?*

74

*We do have 'Dinis here, you know, and I think they broadcast the news even before you got to Plus.*

*You should have seen the old grey dear!* Laria said, grinning, and gave Kincaid a replay of the 'Dinis' ecstatic hall dance. Then she 'ported herself out of the car and into the cool Tower. 'Phew! Only something as important as this news could get me out in that heat.'

'I take it there is great rejoicing on all Clarf's streets?' Lionasha asked in a wry tone.

Laria gave the T-7 a repeat of what she'd 'pathed to Kincaid.

*Is there any hard copy for us here on Sef?* And Laria was astonished to hear Yoshuk's voice.

*How did you hear?*

*Earth Prime was kind enough to repeat the good news to us. He figured it would take you a little time to get it to Plrgtgl and we'd need to be forewarned. Care to wager on how long it takes the 'Dinis to start the immigration?*

*NO,* Laria said firmly. *But I suspect both Towers'll be overworked.*

*In fact,* Lionasha said, holding her com unit slightly away from her ear, *Clarf Tower is being asked to facilitate the despatch of the* KLTL . . .

*. . . They* can't *have organized a ship and crew in . . . what is it, half an hour?* Laria objected.

*You were wise not to bet, Laria,* Yoshuk said laughing. *Nesrun has just received a request from the* KLLM *to be lifted as soon as possible.*

*Have they had ships just standing by? In case?* Laria demanded of no-one in particular as she 'ported herself onto her couch in the Tower. *Let it never be said that we dallied in transporting them to their desired location.*

*Here's where the* KLTL *is right now, Laria,* Lionasha said. The co-ordinates came up on the Tower screen. *Good thing you know that ship so well.*

*Is it all ready?* Laria demanded. *I'm not about to send a ship that far with its hatches still open.*

*I checked,* said Kincaid. *It's ready. Let's shift it to Talavera.*

*ROJER, are you ready to receive?*

*READY?* Rojer was as astonished as she was but caught the excitement in her 'pathed words. *Let no moss grow on 'Dini flippers. Yes,* now *I'm ready.*

Laria felt his mind firmly contacting hers: she felt Kincaid's strong support and, reaching out for the *KLTL,* 'ported it off its field and towards the distant system.

*Got it! Nice throw!* Rojer said.

*The first of many, I'm sure,* Laria said.

*I'll get the rest of 'em up then.*

*You did that alone, brother?* Laria turned from sister to Clarf Tower Prime in an instant.

*Me and the* Columbia's *generators! We're able.*

*Don't try it again, Prime Rojer.*

*Yes, Prime Laria.* And Rojer's tone was anything but penitent.

*He'll burn himself out if he doesn't take care,* Laria said privately to Kincaid, scowling.

*A Lyon burning out?* Kincaid made a scoffing noise deep in his throat. *Highly unlikely.*

*Not even Lyons are infallible.*

*I heard you say it,* and Kincaid, grinning mischievously from his couch, waggled his finger at her.

She couldn't stay angry with Rojer when Kincaid was in such a good mood.

A half-hour later, in the midst of congratulating themselves on the 'portation of the *KLTL,* Lionasha received official notification that two more ships, one a large freighter (and its tonnage was included in the information) and the other a passenger vessel, awaited teleportation.

'Have they been LIVING on board just in case a planet was released?' Laria demanded, lying back down on her couch.

'Wouldn't surprise me. Shouldn't surprise you, considering how overcrowded Clarf is right now,' Kincaid said.

No sooner were those big ones shifted than three smaller units requested assistance from Clarf Tower. After them, two more of the big naval K class ships reported readiness to be 'ported.

76

'Never even remotely suggest that our 'Dini allies are unprepared for any contingency that might rear its head,' Lionasha said as Laria and Kincaid came down for a restorative drink after such heavy duties.

When a request to transport three more loaded freighters and two passenger ships came in, Vanteer had already left the Tower and the others were eating a late supper.

'Get me Plrgtgl, Lio,' Laria said, trying to keep her exasperation under control, since Lionasha was nearer the Tower office.

'It's unavailable,' Lio replied.

'Is Naciana still at the office?'

'It's her I'm talking to.'

Laria 'ported the com unit out of Lionasha's hand. 'Naciana, tell your boss no more tonight after this lot. And only one an hour tomorrow. Talavera's a long way to toss anything and there really is a limit to what this Tower can process in one day.'

'I'll tell him,' and Naciana didn't sound too happy about it. 'I've never seen them in such a frenzy. You'd think the planet would disappear . . .'

'It's more likely to get as crowded as Clarf with this rate of traffic. And have they brought enough food? There's nothing there, you know.'

'Oh, they know. That's what's on the three freighters. They do have to be sent as fast as possible, Laria . . .' and Naciana let her voice trail off with a silent plea.

'No more after these five until full daylight tomorrow. We have got to get some rest. I absolutely will not 'port when I've reached my limit. And Rojer will be AS tired at his end.'

'I'll tell Plus,' Naciana murmured in a deflated response to Laria's ultimatum.

'Mules we're not,' she muttered darkly to Kincaid and Lionasha.

'Yes, we are. You just kicked!' Kincaid said and at the sight of his roguish grin, some of her exasperation drained.

*   *   *

77

Rojer seemed in better spirits than Laria was when they touched minds again, but he had Primes and high Talents to assist.

*That is absolutely the last delivery tonight, Rojer.*

*I should hope so, but they make quite a display orbiting Talavera. I am reliably informed that that's what it will now be called. Or Tlvr, if you prefer.*

*I prefer my bed right now, thanks, brother.*

*Until tomorrow then.*

Laria made the barest formal acknowledgement, and rose wearily from her couch. Kincaid put a helpful arm around her waist as she gracelessly thumped down the steps and turned towards her quarters.

'I did wonder if the 'Dini tongues would be up to Talavera,' she murmured.

'Tlvr is very 'Dini-ish.'

'Yes, it is.'

It was Kincaid who pulled off her station boots, pushed her into the bed and drew the light cover over her.

*Sleep well, my friend.*

Laria yawned, turned on her side and was asleep.

The next day both Clarf and Sef Towers operated on all the power the generators could give them. Sef, with T-2s Yoshuk and Nesrun, handled the lighter shipping and much of the drone traffic. Clarf Prime 'ported one major ship an hour for the next twelve, interspersed with message tubes and 'urgently required' cartons of equipment which had not been ready to leave when the mass migration began. Almost as many messages came back in from Talavera within that hour-frame as went out. 'Dinis were busy collecting and delivering tubes and cartons in response to the shower of messages.

The experts on the *Columbia* had recommended a wide valley, near one of Talavera's large inland lakes, as the primary site. The land around it supported some vegetation and was pronounced arable and without the lethal trace elements that had been found near the queens' original installation. The water would have to be treated before it was

78

potable by Humans or 'Dinis but it wouldn't harm the millions of plants being sent to begin the resurrection of the planet. The initial 'Dini swarm from Clarf and Sef managed miracles in their first forty hours on Talavera, assembling prefabricated headquarters buildings, living quarters, storage barns, ground vehicles, heavy earth-moving machinery, making landing cradles for all sizes of incoming drone deliveries as well as personnel carriers. A second swarm were planting and seeding large areas around the lake. A Tower was erected to one side of the landing-field, with living accommodations for the Humans who would staff it.

Rojer, Roddie, Asia, Jesper Ornigo and Flavia's brother Mallen transferred down from the *Columbia*, leaving Flavia as Prime with Zara, assisting until the Tower was fully operational. Rojer, Flavia and Zara had agreed to take turns as Prime. Morgelle had been returned to Earth to await reassignment. The ecological team, Dr Tru Blairik, Mialla Evshenk, Rosenery Mordmann and Yakamasura, set up their camp to one side of the Tower. Without being asked, the 'Dini work teams arrived with additional housing units, offices and a field laboratory, and staffed the facility with trained 'Dini assistants by the same evening.

'They must have gone hyper to have all this ready to teleport so quickly,' Roddie said, eyes wide with amazement, when they arrived on what had so recently been empty land. 'They even have shade trees for us.'

'All the comforts of home,' Rojer said, grinning. 'Even the sun,' he added, shielding his eyes from the glare of Talavera's primary.

'Not quite as bright as Clarf's,' Roddie said, with a quick glance in the direction of the sunset. 'Thank all the gods!'

'I envy Laria's tan,' Asia said at Rojer's side.

'You be careful of the sun down here, Asia,' Rojer said, as usual assuming she needed his guidance.

'I have sunblock on, dear,' she replied, unruffled. 'See!' and she made him examine the slight sheen the cream gave her clear complexion.

Rojer grumphed. 'Just don't forget to put it on.'

Jesper and Mall rolled their eyes and Roddie regarded Rojer as if he were slightly bereft of common sense.

'As long as you do, too, Rojer,' Asia said in a sweet voice without a tinge of sarcasm.

Their effects neatly dropped into a pile just beyond them. *Thanks, Flavia.*

*You're welcome, Roj, but please stop treating Asia as if she was an imbecile. She's extremely competent,* Flavia added with a bit of asperity in her tone.

'I know, I know. Let's get settled in, team,' he said and found his duffel. He would have taken Asia's as well, but she forestalled him and was already trudging up to the Tower quarters, Rojer's 'Dinis supporting the end of her sack.

Dr Blairik, whom Rojer found a pain in the neck, intercepted him before he could catch up with Asia.

'I really do feel, Prime Rojer, that we should have been informed that the 'Dinis were going to take over *every*thing,' he said, clearly disgruntled.

'Why? Because they're so highly organized?'

'Well, I would have expected to be consulted about my requirements . . .' Tru Blairik began sententiously.

'Is there anything wrong with the facility provided?' Rojer asked.

'I haven't had time to really investigate . . .'

'Why don't you do so, and *then* we can rectify any problems,' Rojer said and quickly moved away from the astounded biologist. An indignant 'well, I never . . .' followed Rojer into the Tower.

'Good on you, Rojer,' Rosenery Mordmann said, grinning. 'Saw him corner you.' She had a message tube. 'When you've had a chance to settle in, I was asked to provide ecological reports to various groups on Earth.'

Rojer gestured towards the worktop that would serve Jes Ornigo as Tower expediter. 'It's first in line.'

'Thank you,' and, putting the tube down, she left with a cheerful farewell wave.

Rojer continued on his way to the personnel quarters and nearly knocked into Jes coming back to the Tower proper.

'Yours is obviously the one at the end of the hall, Roj,' Jes said, his arms laden with disk files. 'They've done us proud even with the speed they put all this up.'

'We've already got our first message to 'port from Talavera,' Rojer said over his shoulder.

'We'll be ready when you are, Rojer,' Jes assured him.

Rojer peered into the next open door and the room was empty. So was the one on the left-hand side of the corridor. So he walked on to the end and opened the door into a large lounge room, subtly decorated with 'Dini artefacts and Human-type furnishings: a thick plain green carpet on the floor – restful. Windows gave onto the space that was already lined with trees and the beginnings of a patio. The inner wall had worktops and several screens mounted on the wall. A proper office. On the short wall to his left were two doors. One was a closet and the other was locked. He crossed the room to the door beyond the office space and entered a spacious bedroom, complete with the extra wide bed that also featured a 'Dini trundle. Another door gave into a well-equipped bathroom, attractive restful 'Dini designs on the tiles. Laria's accommodations on Clarf were not as fine as this. He grinned with satisfaction as he swung his duffel onto the bed.

'Mine is nice, too,' Asia said, startling him, and Gil and Kat came racing into the room behind, taking a running jump to land on the bed.

'Where are you?' he asked her. To his 'Dinis he said, 'Act your age, you two. You'll make holes in the mattress before I ever sleep on it.'

'I'm around the corner,' she said, grinning as the two 'Dinis flowed down onto the trundle and began rolling around on it, testing its surface. 'Jes said there's already a message tube to be sent. Or did you want to unpack first?'

He gave his duffel a diffident look. Then, smiling at the thought of opening a brand-new Tower on a now Dini-occupied world, Rojer threw a proprietary arm about her shoulders and guided her back through the lounge. Then he could hear the generators chugging quietly.

'Who started them?' he said surprised.

'I did,' Asia said. 'After all I'm the engineer,' she reminded him almost pertly, and continued on her way to the three steps down to where the generators had been housed.

*Do you mind working with me as back-up?* Mallen asked, an odd smile on his face.

*No, no, of course not . . .*

*It's just that Asia's prettier than I am,* Mallen said.

Rojer adjusted his thinking quickly, for he'd assumed that this was his chance to work with Asia and he'd really looked forward to such rapport.

*I have to admit to that,* Rojer said, colouring his tone with amused chagrin. *But I'll need your strength as T-3, Mallen. No insult intended.*

'Let's get to work, team!' he said, reaching the lounge and clapping his hands. He heard the generators kick over. 'Jes, you're expediter?'

Jes Ornigo pulled out the chair at that workstation. 'That's me.' He peered down at the message tube, rubbing his hands together as if eager to start the day. 'I'll send the co-ordinates up to your screen.'

'Thanks.' Then Rojer made a flourish at Mallen towards the Tower. 'Shall we ascend?'

'By all means, Captain,' Mal replied with a flourish of his own.

Mallen Bastianmajani took the left-hand couch with a sigh of satisfaction.

*Didn't you think you'd make a Tower?* asked Rojer, amused but entirely understanding Mallen's reaction as he settled in the right-hand one, a perfect fit for him.

*Frankly, no.*

*You may wish you hadn't,* Rojer said drolly. *Asia, generators up to speed?*

*Yes, Prime,* was her quick response.

Jes screened the co-ordinates in the High Council Buildings in Old Europe and Rojer, checking to see that Mal had them, nodded once. He felt Mal's mind joining his as easily as a foot slips in an old shoe.

*Here we go!* And the message tube disappeared.

82

*You didn't hang about, did you?* Earth Prime said to his grandson.

*Can't set a bad example, Grandfather. Not the way the 'Dinis are swarming in here.*

*Welcome to Tower life, Rojer, Mallen, Asia,* said the Rowan graciously.

*Thank you, ma'am.*

*Enjoy it while you can, Rojer,* his grandfather said. *Don't know how long I can spare you from the Operation Search.*

*OH?*

*Later, lad, later. Morgelle's in line for the next Tower. Good sending.* And, as abruptly as Jeff Raven had touched his grandson's mind, he was gone.

*That was nice of them,* Mallen said. *I've never been in contact with either of their minds before. Awesome.*

*Hmmm, well, yes, I guess it was. Only how'd he know we'd started sending? The Blundell building was not the destination.*

*They always know,* said Jes sardonically. *And our next service will be four messages for Clarf. How'd they know we were up and ready?*

*Because they are,* Jes said.

*Stop the chatter. Four to Clarf?*

The generators lifted briefly as Rojer made the 'port. *Coming in, Clarf Prime,* he said formally.

*Rojer? You're on the Talavera Tower?* Laria asked him. *They set that up fast enough.*

'Talavera Tower'? That sounded very good to Rojer. *That they did. So you can lob anything to me now, on the surface. Flavia and Zara are still on the* Columbia. *We'll bring down what's being held in orbit.*

*But you're on the business end. Good. I've a lot more to send you.*

*Tired, sis?*

*Well, it's been hectic here. I put my foot down and we only do one big one an hour . . . every hour . . . and they are weight, but . . .*

*I won't let them overwork her,* Kincaid said, joining the conversation.

*She can make sure of that herself, thank you both,* Laria added with some asperity. *Here's the latest one: freighter, cargo all inanimate. Got a big enough cradle?*

*I've enough delicacy of touch not to warp our brand-new cradles,* Rojer replied. *Thank you, sis. Nice 'port.*

*There're two more scheduled for today and that's it for Clarf Tower. What time of day is it there for you? I'll mark it up for a 'Talavera Tower' rotation.*

Rojer glanced up at the multiple-time displays, each identifying a different main Tower time, nicely placed for easy reading for the couch occupants. *It is 14.30 of a 26.50-hour day.*

*I have that information. Thank you, Talavera Tower.*

*Incoming from Earth,* Mallen said.

*Five drones. Inanimate,* was his grandfather's terse message.

Rojer linked and brought the drones in the rest of the way, slotting them neatly into the waiting cradles. 'Jes, ask my 'Dinis to come up here, will you? We're going to need more drone-size cradles if they keep sending us job lots like that.'

Kat and Gil came tumbling up the steps, front limbs forward to prevent slipping back down in their haste.

KAT, GIL, PLEASE SEE WHO IS CONSTRUCTING CRADLES. WE'RE GOING TO NEED MORE OF THE SAME SIZE AS THE ONES . . . Rojer broke off because the yard manager was already organizing crews to empty the drones and load the grav sleds. Then a crew of ten 'Dinis manually lifted the light drone shells off their landing web. IF THE YARD CREW CAN DO IT THAT FAST MAYBE WE DON'T NEED TO.

MORE COMING, Kat said. WE ASK FOR MORE. BETTER MORE THAN FEW.

'That's fer sure,' Rojer said. 'Off you go, then, and please ask who is the yard manager. I haven't met him yet.'

*That's Seelbat Buffer, a Capellan and a T-5 kinetic,* Asia informed them from her station by the generators. *He has 'Dinis.*

'How many?' Rojer asked, since the yard seemed to be swarming with all the colours Mrdini bodies came in.

84

*He's a friend of Flavia and she pried him loose from Capella Tower Yard. She's very good at that sort of thing, you know.*

Rojer cleared his throat, remembering that Flavia had got her brother and her mate included on the crew of the *Columbia*. But if Seelbat worked as well as Mallen and Jes Ornigo, he'd have no complaints.

'Isn't it unusual for a Capellan to have 'Dinis?'

*Yes, he was the first* . . . and some edge to her voice suggested to Rojer that likely Seelbat had taken a lot of criticism and dislike from the methody folk of his home planet for being partnered with 'heathen aliens'.

'He's here now and that's good,' Rojer said.

*Incoming from Sef,* warned Jes.

*Congratulations, Rojer,* chorused Yoshuk and Nesrun from Sef's Tower.

*Or do we commiserate?* asked Nesrun in her droll way.

*I'll let you know in a day or so,* Rojer replied. *Speaking of which, our day is 26.50 hours long and you are slinging me at* . . . he caught their send, a medium-sized passenger yacht, *precisely 14.45.*

*We'll mark it down. You'll be keeping standard Tower hours?*

*I'll have to or be worn down to a nubbin. Is Laria all right?*

*Overworked but I think things'll ease off once the impatient get to Talavera. Oh, and we added a little welcome gift. The 'Dini bean-counter, Fsslm, has it for you.*

*Bean-counter?* Beside Rojer, Mallen chuckled.

'Accountant,' he said. 'We've a full complement of governing officials down here already, you know, from the passenger ships we caught on the *Columbia*.'

*Let's hope that Fsslm doesn't complain about the luxury they've provided us,* Jes said.

*Here it comes,* warned Sef Tower, and Rojer met the Mind Merge which Yoshuk and Nesrun used and placed the yacht carefully into its cradle.

*Seelbat, full honours to the passengers,* Rojer said. *Fsslm is to be especially treated. It's got something for us from Yoshuk and Nesrun.*

*I've the steps in place and Put and Car acting guard, Rojer.*

85

*Thanks, Seelbat. Sorry I didn't get to greet you formally.*
*Who has time for formality right now?*

Rojer grinned. Seelbat's tone had rippled with amusement. Since the Tower was glassed all round, Rojer could observe the arrivals: all but the first one carrying heavy sacks. Fsslm was a mature blue-grey, large enough have earned its five-letter name. Ground transport wheeled into the yard, ready to accommodate Fsslm's party and their accoutrements. Not all the disembarking passengers were admitted to that vehicle, so Put let out one of the shrill whistles a 'Dini could emit and a second air cushion appeared to transport the remainder of the newcomers.

As soon as the vehicle was cleared of its animate cargo, the yard tractor tackled the yacht and moved it to the storage area.

Rojer leaned back on the couch, pleased with such efficiency.

*Fsslm's directed its car here, Rojer. You'd better get down.* KAT, GIL, COME WITH ME. HONOURABLE FSSLM ARRIVING. *Come on up, Asia.*

*Should I?*

*Yes, you should,* Rojer said firmly as he rose from his couch, gesturing for Mallen to join him below. *It isn't that you don't know 'Dinis, m'love.* He paused at the foot of the steps until she joined him, tucked her hand under his arm and, ignoring her pull to free herself, proceeded to the Tower entrance.

Their timing was perfect for the car arrived just as the four Talents emerged, Kat and Gil slipping around them to flank the vehicle.

WELCOME TO TALAVERA, HONOURABLE FSSLM, and Rojer calculated his bow, his arm pulling Asia's upper body down to the appropriate level for a five-letter name 'Dini.

AH, IT IS A PLEASURE FOR FSSLM TO MEET RJR AT LONG LAST, Fsslm said, bowing just a tad lower to emphasize its pleasure, and handed over the large box it carried. Rojer had to drop Asia's arm to accept the package that had a suspiciously cold bottom. THIS IS SMALL TOKEN OF ESTEEM FROM SEF TOWER AND FROM SEF PLANET FOR THE RELEASE OF THIS MARVELLOUS

NEW WORLD TO MRDINI OCCUPATION. SOON THIS WILL BE AS BEAUTIFUL AS CLRF, SF, TPLU, KF AND PTU.

OF THAT I AM CERTAIN, HONOURABLE FSSLM, NOW THAT YOU ARE HERE TO HELP ORGANIZE AN ORDERLY AND ACCOUNTABLE FINANCIAL STRUCTURE. Rojer and Fsslm bowed simultaneously.

*Rojer, incoming,* Jes warned.

WITH GREAT REGRET I MUST SHORTEN OUR FIRST MEETING AS THE TOWER IS EXTREMELY BUSY AT THIS HOUR. WE WILL MEET AGAIN IN THE VERY NEAR FUTURE, FSSLM. OUR GRATITUDE AGAIN FOR THIS GIFT.

Rojer was stepping backward, the package beginning to freeze his hand. Asia kept pace with him, with several more bows.

BE COMFORTABLE, HONOURABLE FSSLM, she said in well-accented 'Dini which surprised Rojer.

*I only know a few of the polite phrases, Roj, but Flavia said I must have some.*

*Indeed you must, m'love.*

Fsslm bowed once more and then mounted the steps into the car that it imperiously waved to proceed.

The door slid open and Rojer and Mallen made for the steps to the Tower, Rojer pausing long enough to deposit the package at Jes's station.

'What's in it?' Mallen asked as they clambered two steps at a time.

'Don't know but it's cold. See to it will you, Jes, when you've a chance.'

'Probably Sef fruit. It's the right season,' Asia called up from the generator level.

'What's incoming?' Rojer called over his shoulder as he and Mallen made it to their couches.

*Drones, of course. Another five.*

*We really will need more cradles if we're getting this much traffic in,* Rojer said.

*It should level off. How much more stuff do they need to get a planet started?* was Mallen's complaint.

His sentiment was echoed when Talavera Tower signed off

87

for the day at 22.00 of its 26.50 hours. The traffic had been steady the entire day, and the Talents had had to snatch meals – and some of the excellent ripe fruit that Sef Tower had sent – in between the almost continuous bombardment of large, medium and message tubes, many from Earth or the other 'Dini planets. Seelbat was possibly the weariest when they finally called a halt. He had worked non-stop even with all the 'Dinis helping him to empty cradles and stack the drones, or park the vehicles.

'Who have we got up on the *Columbia?*' Rojer asked, slouched on one of the recliners in the main lounge. Asia, with a smear of generator oil on one cheek, lay curled up on another couch.

*Flavia, Zara, fifteen T's of various abilities,* she answered him, too weary to speak aloud.

*Well, we're going to need Zara. I'm not burning Mallen out with such loads.*

*I'll be all right, Rojer, really I will,* Mallen assured him. *Didn't I keep up with you all day?*

*You did and you're a pleasure to merge with, Mal, but if we get several weeks of this sort of heavy traffic, we need to spell everyone. Tower experience is useful for any Talent,* Rojer said firmly. *But we don't have the extras that Callisto, or Iota Aurigae or Earth have. Look at Seelbat. He's a shadow of his morning's self,* and Rojer tried for a little levity since he could sense Asia's apprehension. *I don't* need *another engineer if I have you, but we do need someone to share the load with Jes, if only to keep the data in order.* He turned to Jes and pointed a finger at him. *And you're to go to bed when we all do, not stay up till dawn to file today's receipts. We'll get a yeoman down to help with* that. *If we should, the gods forbid, lose a drone or a freighter, we've got to know what it was and what was on it or our bean-counter will not be pleased with us. And Seelbat cannot work at such a clip without relief. Did you get anything to eat at all?*

*Wasn't hungry.* Seelbat didn't even open his eyes though his right hand idly stroked Put's back. His 'Dinis were sound asleep, heads pillowed on his thighs.

*Who've you worked with on the* Columbia *who can assist you in the yard, Seel?* Rojer asked.

*Yeoman Dorot Bay or CPO Esther Stapleton. Kinetic T-6s who can receive but are not much good at sending.*

*As we're on the receiving end, that'll do us. Where did you get all those 'Dinis?*

Seel chuckled without opening his eyes. *Their bosses send them to make sure they get the packages they're expecting. Some of 'em stay because they prefer the prestige of working in the yard to whatever manual work they've been stuck with right now.*

*A never-ending supply?* Rojer asked, grinning at 'Dini tactics.

*Just about.* Seel gave a weary smile.

Rojer rose to his feet with a sigh and walked out to Mallen's workstation. Flopping down into the chair, he activated the com unit to the *Columbia.* Despite the hour, someone would be manning communications round the clock – whichever time the ship operated on.

'Yes, sir?'

'Rojer Lyon here at Talavera Tower.'

'Good evening, Captain Lyon, how can I help you?'

'Is that Lentard?'

'Why, yes, Captain, it is,' replied the CPO, obviously pleased to be recognized.

'Don't wake anyone at this ungodly hour, but would you please ask Captain Soligen if we can borrow my sister Zara, CPO Esther Stapleton and Yeoman Dorot Bay for auxiliary Tower duty? We're swamped here, and probably will be for the next week or ten days while everything gets 'ported in.'

'Yes, sir, Captain. I've recorded the message. Is it a priority?'

'Not before tomorrow at breakfast, Lentard.'

'Yes, sir, Captain. I understand. Thank you. Over.'

'There. That should do the trick,' Rojer said. 'And I'm for my bed.'

The other four managed to get to their feet and slowly made their way down the hall to their quarters, 'Dinis following those who had them.

\*    \*    \*

89

*Talavera Tower holding up OK?* Jeff Raven asked as he contacted Rojer with the warning of a passenger ship full of experts, coming from Earth, to help establish the 'Dini colony.

*A good night's sleep helps a lot, sir, and I drafted Zara off the Columbia . . . to keep her out of mischief . . .*

*I wasn't IN mischief, Grandfather,* Zara said with a dire look at her elder brother. She had arrived just after breakfast Talavera time and, after one look at Mallen, announced that they'd work shifts. She was taking the first one. Mallen could go back to bed.

*I had brothers, too, Zara,* and Jeff chuckled. *Never any respect for siblings. Handle this bunch carefully. Some of 'em are fragile.*

*Do they have quarters, Grandfather?* Zara asked. *'Dinis don't mind sleeping rough. Humans do.*

*They'll use the ship. If you can set it down near the 'Dini headquarters, that will suffice quite nicely.*

*Good idea,* Rojer said as Jes sent up the size of the liner. *I don't happen to have a cradle that big anyhow. Come to think of it, the Tower Yard isn't that long either.*

*Ready?* Jeff asked.

Roger shot a look at Zara who instantly merged her mind with his, all that practice in the Tower at Iota Aurigae making a smooth meld. *Ready.*

*Oooof,* said Zara. *What are they carrying beside themselves?*

*Equipment for three major laboratory facilities as well as botanical and biological specimens that the zoologists think will do well on Talavera,* Jeff said. *I trust you didn't crack so much as a beaker.*

*Nary a one, sir,* Rojer said, grinning at Zara. *There's a Talent aboard who hasn't realized they've landed here.*

*That'll be Dr Seyes Real Esperitos,* Jeff said and there was an edge in the tone of his mind to indicate to his grandchildren that T-5 Dr Esperitos was not high on Earth Prime's 'will-see' list. *Man has no control when he's excited. He is often very funny without being aware of either his humour or that he's broadcasting it. He's tolerated for his very excellent knowledge of xenobiology.*

*Good heavens, you mean we've left Earth and are on Talavera already? How could that be? I felt no motion whatever.* Esperitos blinked in surprise.

*Sir, this is Tower Prime Lyon and I assure you that your ship is on Talavera, as you will see if you would care to look at the nearest screen or porthole. May we take this opportunity . . .*

*Jes, are they on our screen?* Rojer asked privately.

One of the smaller screens instantly displayed the substantial liner landed just beyond the four-storey headquarters block.

*. . . To welcome you and your associates. We shall be meeting at some later date, sir, but you must excuse me as more cargo is 'porting into the Tower.* And Rojer cut off the beginning of an effusive paean of gratitude. 'Remind me not to go to any parties he's at, Zara,' he said, grinning at his sister.

*I should imagine you'd hear him coming and 'port out of his vicinity,* she said.

# CHAPTER FIVE

'They HAVE to have occupied the whole continent by now,' Laria said, trying to keep desperation out of her voice. It was the end of another long day of 'porting loaded vehicles, drones and importing message tubes that resulted in additional drones or tubes sent back to Talavera. Attuned as he now was to her moods, Kincaid heard her aggravation and sent soothings at her. She glared at him. 'I'm not *that* badly off.'

'You're not?' he asked mildly.

'It seems to me,' Lionasha said, 'that we haven't sent anything to anywhere BUT Talavera for the past three weeks. WHAT are they doing with all that raw material?'

'Where are they storing it, for that matter?' Vanteer put in.

'According to my brother,' Laria replied in a somewhat caustic tone, 'the heavy freight we've been struggling to 'port is loads of prefabricated partitions which the 'Dinis seem to be able to make up into whatever shelter is needed. HE says that they've a first-class Tower with every amenity possible.'

'Well, at least the 'Dinis got *that* priority right,' Lionasha remarked. 'Not that we can complain. They do right by us here on Clarf.'

Laria grimaced and finished the last of her lemonade. Lio was right: Plrgtgl was forever enquiring if there was anything the Clarf Talents required to ensure their comfort. And their quarters were luxurious. What was wrong with Clarf was the heat. Talavera would enjoy a winter season of some six months: it had a longer rotation around its primary and three degrees more of axial tilt than Clarf had. Clarf was just constantly hot! Nights did get cool . . . well, relatively cooler . . . but the daytime heat was enervating in full Clarfian 'summer'. Once again she thought longingly of home, the darker sun of Iota Aurigae and the cool breezes that came down from the mountains . . .

*As soon as this migration is over,* you're *taking a holiday,* Kincaid said sternly.

*How?* Laria demanded and this time there was a wail of desperation in the tight tone she 'pathed at him. *Every T-1 Grandfather can find is working full time somewhere.* She got to her feet; somehow managing to keep her expression from revealing her inner despair. 'I'm for bed. See you all in the morning, fellow mules.'

'It's a light day tomorrow, Laria, if that's any consolation,' Lionasha said encouragingly.

'Oh, they're sure to find a half dozen emergency drones to be sent,' Vanteer said.

Lionasha rolled her eyes. 'You would!' She pushed herself up out of her chair and, with a disgusted look in Van's direction, left the lounge.

'What'd I say wrong?' Vanteer demanded of Kincaid.

'If you can't figure it out, Van, I can't help you,' the T-2 said and left the Tower engineer alone.

Van shrugged, finished his drink and left the Tower. He had a date. It suddenly occurred to him that Kincaid had stopped visiting whatever friend he had in the Human compound. But then, they were all tired these days. Not that he was *ever* too tired for his favourite off-duty occupation. He grinned as he left, bracing himself for the sultry air outside the cooled Tower.

\* \* \*

'You do need a break, Laria,' Kincaid said, entering her room. She was eagle-spread on the bed, as if she had merely fallen backward onto its surface.

'I don't know what's wrong with me, Kincaid,' she said, raising her head briefly to acknowledge his presence. 'It's all I can do not to snap at folks and no-one deserves that. Not with the loads we're 'porting. All I want to do is sleep.' She let out a long sigh.

He stretched out on one side, propping his head up on one hand, and looking down at her, letting his mind reach hers with gentling thoughts.

'I think we're both missing our 'Dinis. I know mine have kept me balanced in times of stress,' he said softly. 'Only three more weeks.'

'Well, let's hope they don't try any more tricks on us,' she said glumly. Then immediately turned remorseful and reached out to touch his free hand. 'I didn't mean that the way it sounded, Kincaid.' She could feel her face flushing with embarrassment. 'Whyever they did it, I really, truly enjoyed . . . I mean . . . I'm just sorry it wasn't . . .' She rolled her eyes as her attempt to explain the pleasure she had had came out all wrong. *We were together, Kincaid, and it was wonderful. I just would rather it had been not forced on you . . .*

*Nothing could have forced me, Laria.* He gave her hand an affectionate squeeze and then began to smooth her hair back from her face. *Oh, our 'Dinis heightened the atmosphere a great deal, that's for sure.* And he chuckled softly, wrapping a strand of her hair about his index finger. Then, turning his body and propping himself on both elbows, he dropped a light kiss on her cheek. *However, we aren't being manipulated by sex-driven 'Dinis right now and plain ol' sex between consenting adults usually relaxes the sort of tension we're both under. If you're not too tired . . .*

Kincaid cocked his head at her, a one-sided grin curving his lips, as if he was amused to be making such a suggestion.

'I think I'd like that very much, Kincaid,' she said softly, reaching up with both hands to run her fingers through his hair and then bring his face down to hers.

94

They were gentle with each other, as much from weariness as from a genuine and leisurely interest in making sure each would be satisfied. While not as passionate as their encounters had been when the 'Dinis were involved, release was unexpectedly and delightfully prolonged so that they drifted into sleep in each other's arms.

They woke together, one mind's consciousness awakening the other, and they were still entwined. Kincaid lifted himself on one elbow and gently outlined her mouth with one finger, smiling a little.

'I might even get accustomed to this, my dear. You're very restful.'

He had no barrier set and she perceived how much his mind and emotions had healed. He had been a desperately weary, disillusioned and battered man when he'd arrived at Clarf Tower.

'That's as you wish, Kincaid,' she said lightly but oh, so very pleased to know the healing was now complete. 'And thank you.' She raised her head high enough to reach his lips and gave him a soft kiss. Then immediately rolled to the side of the wide bed to rise. 'Let's hope that Van wasn't right and today's load doesn't include sudden emergencies. And we *are* all going to take a holiday when we finally get Talavera completely supplied.'

'Good idea,' was his amiable reply. 'I'd best shower . . . in my own room.' And he 'ported himself away.

*It would be more fun to shower together,* she thought very quietly and to herself alone. But she did feel much better today. In fact, she was aware of some very important change in herself as she bathed and dressed.

'All I needed was a good night's sleep,' she told Lionasha as they met for breakfast.

'Does wonders . . . that is if you spend your night sleeping,' Lio said, and for one startled moment, Laria wondered if Lionasha could possibly know how she really had spent the first part of the night. But Lio was looking significantly in the direction of the engineering section and obviously meant Vanteer. Laria felt his weary but satisfied presence doing the usual dawn check on the generators.

95

Kincaid was whistling when he emerged into the lounge and started building himself a breakfast.

'Let us devoutly hope, Lionasha, my dear, that you were not enjoying any adverse prescience for today's workload,' he said as he filled his tray.

'There's not an ounce of clairvoyance in my Talent, Kincaid,' Lio said. 'Besides which I can't imagine what can have been left out of what we've sent streaming out to that planet.'

'Officials to make sure the work's being done well and on time,' Laria had occasion to remark drolly later that morning when a small passenger craft begged 'portation to Talavera. 'And Plrgtgl's on it so let's set it down as lightly as possible by Headquarters.'

'At least that's the only one,' Kincaid said, stretching until his joints audibly popped when they had despatched it. 'Was that Zara aiding Rojer this morning?'

'No, actually, it was Flavia. But they're both T-1s and strong.'

'I thought Zara was more of a healer than a Tower Prime,' he said, slewing sideways and resting his elbows on his knees, his big hands clasped lightly.

'That's her personal preference but Rojer's been rotating the T-1's. We're not the only ones sending him 'portages.'

*You know, I'd like to see what they've done with all the stuff we've sent to Talavera,* Lionasha said, busy sorting the day's files into their respective piles.

*Want to rotate with someone there?* Laria asked.

*Well, not exactly rotate, but just have a good look round,* Lionasha said in a careful tone.

Kincaid and Laria chuckled at her qualification.

*I think I would, too,* Kincaid said, winking at Laria. *Sort of busman's holiday.*

*Busman?* Lionasha repeated, confused.

Laria grinned at Kincaid since she did understand the archaic reference.

*Like a spaceman taking a cruise on a liner for the fun of it,* she explained.

*Oh! Wouldn't he have had enough space travel?* Lionasha asked.

*That's the point,* Kincaid said.

*Not much of a point, or a holiday,* Lionasha said with a little snort of contempt.

Laria and Kincaid exchanged glances, his eyes twinkling with an amusement he kept well covered from Lionasha. She had a pedantic tendency and misunderstood the subtler whimsy of Laria and Kincaid.

*Laria, a special cargo – quite animate – and just for you,* said Jeff Raven with such a smug tone to his voice that Laria was very much surprised, and curious. *I know both 'Dini Towers have been hard-pressed with outgoing. Gollee suggested this T-2 so kindly don't bang him up.*

*As if I would,* Laria replied tartly.

She heard her grandfather's chuckle and then felt the incoming personnel carrier that she deftly caught and landed gently in an appropriate cradle. 'Dinis swarmed to greet the newcomer.

*Messages, Laria,* said Rojer at the same instant. *Priority.*

When she realized from his mind that there was a drove arriving, she immediately linked with Kincaid to prevent any of the incoming tubes from getting lost. The mass of them took up every available rack, with several rolling onto the ground. The 'Dinis who had opened the personnel capsule were now chasing the fugitives.

*Well, at least it's all inan . . . ahhhhh,* and Lionasha's exclamation of total surprise and her sudden surge of immense sexual attraction caused Laria and Kincaid to exchange astonished looks.

As one, they made for the stairs. Kincaid halted but Laria continued, curious to see who could have such a startling effect on Lionasha. The tall man was holding both Lionasha's hands in his – a surprisingly tactile contact from one T for another. She was gawking like a teenager at the very handsome and somehow familiar man bending towards her. Vanteer was standing stock-still on the top step of the stairs down to engineering, his face expressionless.

The new arrival, still holding Lionasha's fingers in his hands, turned slowly towards Laria, smiling with such charisma that Laria had no trouble at all understanding Lionasha's reaction. What she didn't understand was the immediate and intense antipathy that his expression generated in her.

'Vagrian Beliakin, T-2, reporting from Blundell Tower to assist Clarf Tower and Prime Laria Lyon,' he said, showing very white and even teeth in a wide grin that was meant . . . Laria knew instantly . . . to have the same effect on her that it had had on Lionasha. 'Kincaid,' and, his smile altering subtly, he gave Dano a glancing look, 'I look forward to merging with the man who developed the probe techniques on the *Strongbow* . . .'

Laria caught the spurt of absolute rejection from Kincaid: a violent abhorrence at the thought of even the lightest merge with the mind of this man. Fast as it was, Kincaid's reaction also had something to do with his long tour on the *Strongbow*.

'It's required reading now, you know,' Vagrian went on, totally unaware of anything save his making a very strong impression on everyone in Clarf Tower. Laria shot a quick probe at Vanteer and caught envy, distrust, and, unusually enough, a touch of fear from her engineer. Lionasha was still smitten, the undercurrent of her thought wondering if she had a single chance of getting him into bed along with a sense of puzzlement because Vagrian looked familiar to her, too.

Familiar to whom? Laria wondered, although the impact of his forceful greetings on her staff had diverted her briefly from that thought. Now he advanced on Laria, hand extended sideways in the prescribed position for Talent-touching.

Inadvertently she took a backward step, banging her heel into the first riser. She felt Kincaid descend to stand directly behind her and never had she needed his support more.

'You're Yoshuk's younger brother,' Laria said, looking down at the extended hand and wondering how she could avoid touching him.

*Do it and know,* Kincaid said on a very tight tone.

She couldn't smile but she did manage to make the touch –

98

red/acerbic/pepper – as briefly as she could, and being very careful not to let him see past a tightly shielded mind.

A wry smile pulled Vagrian's sensuous mouth to one side. 'Yes, my elder brother by a scant year. I am late come to my Talent.' His smile became winsome but slightly embarrassed, and he smoothed back his wavy dark hair. 'A freak accident stimulated it and I was lucky enough to save others from sure death.'

'Yes, such stimuli do activate miracles of self-preservation,' she replied, trying to fathom why she was having such a negative response to the man.

She had never felt the least bit threatened by Yoshuk whom she had always considered the handsomest man she had ever met. Vagrian was the taller by at least eight centimetres and, tall as she herself was, she felt dominated by his almost offensive nearness. But she couldn't step back with heels already pressed against the first riser.

'Dinis, rushing in with the addresses of the piles of message tubes, broke the tableau.

'Ah, I seem to have arrived at a propitious moment to start work,' he said, his smile promising eager co-operation as he glanced up to the Tower.

'In point of fact, Vagrian,' Laria began, 'it's not so much Clarf that needs bulwarking as Sef. A third T-2 – and I know how easy it is to merge with a brother or sister – would ease the burden which Yoshuk and Nesrun have been struggling with. So, if you'll just get back in your personnel carrier, Kincaid and I will 'port you over.'

Vagrian's expression was stunned, his jaw dropped and all the good nature and camaraderie of his first minutes in Clarf Tower dissipated in a sudden blast of angry rejection of such a transfer. He recovered so adroitly that Laria wondered if she had accurately read that split second of fury. His disappointment she could well understand but not that flash.

'Alternatively, I'm sure Earth Prime can find you another posting, where your charismatic personality will work in your favour.'

As Laria stepped to one side before turning to mount the

99

stairs, she heard Lionasha's gasp, was aware of Vanteer gawking in surprise. She caught Kincaid by the arm and urged him up to the Tower.

'Prime, I was posted *here*,' Vagrian said, the wave of his hand taking in all of Clarf Tower, his voice edged with a barely concealed and increasing anger. 'By Earth Prime himself. Your grandfather.'

Laria turned on the top step, staring down at him, her body rigid with her rejection of him, and his effect on her Tower personnel. She started to tremble and felt Kincaid's sudden support as she drew herself up.

'I am Prime. I was not informed of this posting and I do not need an additional T-2. Kincaid is more than adequate for any merging I need. You have a choice, Vagrian Beliakin: Sef Tower that does need a third T-2, or back to Blundell Tower.'

'But I was *chosen* for *you*,' he said, allowing disappointment to show in his face as he lifted one hand in appeal. His emphasis informed her all too succinctly of why he had been posted here. Her fury at such tactics now included her grandfather.

'For me?' Laria said softly. *Never!* She turned back, sliding into her couch and leaning into the generators. *If you do not walk straight out of this Tower and into the personnel carrier, I will 'port you there myself, Vagrian Beliakin. You have exactly five seconds. And I have decided that you will cause just as much trouble with the excellent team at Sef as you would here, so you are going back to Blundell. MOVE!*

*He is moving,* Vanteer said and there was deep satisfaction in the engineer's voice. *Wise decision, Laria.*

*I don't understand you, Laria,* Lionasha said, baffled.

*He's in the carrier,* Van reported.

*Earth Prime! This is Clarf Prime. I am returning that man undamaged but only because I wouldn't waste the time or soil my hands with him.* She acted with such alacrity that the carrier was back in the cradle on Earth before she finished speaking.

*Laria! You can't have given Beliakin time to present his credentials.* Nor did Laria have any doubts that her grandfather was considerably annoyed by her rejection.

100

*What did you tell him about me? Or was he Grandmother's idea? Because he is the most repellent personality I have ever encountered: self-centred, aggressive, domineering, worse than a 'Dini days late for hibernation! He had Lionasha drooling like a teenager. It was all Van could do to keep from punching him and he had the effrontery to decide he could displace Kincaid in the first merge we made. Nor will I permit Kincaid to be exposed to such bigotry! I would sooner mind merge with twelve Hiver queens than that odious man.*

There was silence from her grandfather. A silence that meant he was digesting her polemic. *You have stated your case, Prime. I was attempting to arrange for a relief team to allow your entire Tower some well-earned rest. Vagrian was the first candidate Gollee felt capable.*

Laria gave a bark of laughter. *Not him. Send him to a Squadron where his . . . peculiar personality will be controlled by naval discipline. We may be tired but we haven't shirked a single responsibility yet.*

*No, you have not,* and Jeff Raven's tone commended their efforts.

*If you will forgive me, Earth Prime, we have two score message tubes to 'port to their recipients.*

*Do so, then.* This time the silence was his absence.

Battered by the encounters with her grandfather and Beliakin, she covered her face and started to weep from reaction. Kincaid gathered her into his arms, stroking her hair and laving her troubled mind with reassurances.

'Try this,' said Lionasha. The expediter had a cup of steaming coffee in her hand, eyes and face anxious. Vanteer stood beside Lio, looking both concerned and amazed.

'We heard,' Vanteer said. 'Couldn't help it, Laria.' He blinked and gave her a little rueful grin. 'Never heard you speak to anyone like that before. Especially not to your grandfather.' Vanteer was awed. Just beyond him, on the step below the Tower level, his Dig and Nim, and Lionasha's Fig and Sil were ranged, poll eyes startled and wide.

Laria took several quick sips of coffee, then the tissue Lionasha offered and dried her eyes and cheeks.

101

'Kincaid, you knew that man, didn't you?'

Kincaid nodded slowly, his eyes reflecting the sadness that had carved lines in his face in the space of a few minutes. 'Once,' and then with a noticeable effort, Kincaid forced his taut body to relax. 'Slightly longer than just now. And that was before his Talent asserted itself. But I was just as happy to see him leave *without* making the kind of trouble he's often caused.'

'He *was* trouble, all right, and all too ready to do what *he* intended here,' Van said. 'I'm only a T-6 but he was coming over loud and clear.' His hands were still clenched into fists.

'I've never met anyone like him before,' Lionasha said, shaking herself as if to dispel an unwanted burden. 'He was . . . overwhelming.' And she let out a self-conscious little laugh, then shook her head again more vigorously.

'Too fecking sure of himself,' Vanteer said.

GLAD YOU KNOW THAT, Dig said and the other three 'Dinis nodded vigorously. BAD DREAMING WITH THAT HUMAN. BAD DREAMING.

Laria regarded the 'Dinis with surprise, and a certain gratification that they concurred with her own instinctive and almost unreasonable rejection of a person in such a short space of time. She gulped down most of the coffee, handed the cup back to Lionasha.

'We do have work to do, team. Let's get to it. Day's heating up.'

The tubes were duly 'ported to various locations on Clarf.

'Most of 'em are from that bunch we just sent out,' Lionasha said. 'How could they report back so quickly?'

'Whaddya wanna bet they forgot half the stuff they now find they urgently need?' was Van's suggestion.

He was proved correct, for small and large drones made up the rest of the morning's imports to Clarf Tower and exports to Talavera. By lunchtime, Lionasha announced with some surprise that the Tower had cleared all cradles and nothing else had come in for the afternoon.

'May I respectfully suggest that we enjoy a siesta until

102

something does turn up?' Kincaid said as he made his way to the kitchen. 'What can I get you, Laria?'

'Salad, sandwich,' she answered from the Tower. Vanteer had left the generators idling but she didn't need assistance for the quick call she felt she should make.

*Yoshuk?*

*Laria?* There was pleased surprise in the man's voice. Sometimes there was little resemblance between siblings of the same parents.

*Your brother Vagrian was here.*

*Oh no!* Yoshuk didn't sound pleased. *Ah! You used the past tense? My congratulations on your perception and immediate dismissal of Trouble on Two Feet.*

*Yes. I sent him back to Blundell. I nearly sent him to you two to help with your workload.*

*Merciful heaven, I thank you from the bottom of my heart for that show of common sense.*

*Is he as . . . difficult as I read him, Yoshuk? You're not.*

*Most emphatically I am not my brother Vagrian. Whyever was he sent to YOU of all people?*

*I think my grandfather had dynastic notions.*

*Ha! Earth Prime's slipping or his initial screening has developed serious flaws. Not that Grian couldn't – without half trying, I might add – give the right answers. Unless someone thought to deep-probe him. Did you? So that you found out how poisonous he is? Accept my profound apology for being related to him. That might have had something to do with your grandfather's momentary lapse of good sense. Or he was taken in by circumstances of Grian's sudden emergence as a Talent.* Chagrin coloured Yoshuk's tone.

*You've relieved my mind, Yoshuk. I didn't think my judgement had failed me. Especially when Kincaid's reaction was total rejection and abhorrence.*

*Kincaid was right on line and the first thing my dear brother would have done is to displace Kincaid.*

*That isn't possible.*

*Oh, yes, it would be if Vagrian desired to . . .* Yoshuk paused. There was a smile in his tone as he continued. *Kincaid deserves*

103

*your loyalty, Laria, and I'm glad it's in such deep measure for him. You will never regret it.*

*Are you peeking, Yoshuk?* Laria was surprised and clamped her thoughts down.

*Me? You're the Prime! I do suggest that you stop broadcasting quite so loudly or both Vanteer and Lionasha'll hear.*

*Thanks, Yoshuk.*

*On the contrary, thank YOU, Laria, for sending that bad package right back where it can be dealt with.*

'Laria?' Kincaid called at the base of the Tower steps.

'Coming,' and she ran down the flight, taking the plate of sandwiches from Kincaid's hand, smiling as she did so. 'Yoshuk is not enthralled with his younger brother either,' she said, joining the others at the table. 'Good thing I didn't send him there. We could probably have heard the roar of rejection all the way from Sef.'

'A bit of a shame, though,' Lionasha said, casting a sideways glance at Vanteer. 'He'd've cut a fascinating swathe through the Compound here.'

'Not if he intended to make a handfast arrangement with Laria, he wouldn't,' Van said in a low growl of dislike. 'I wouldn't've liked that for *you,* Laria. Or for you, Kincaid,' he added. 'What I'd like to know is how he passed Gollee's screening?' He directed that query to Laria.

'Oh, that one could pass any screening he'd a mind to,' Lionasha replied. When the others regarded her with surprise, remembering her reaction to Vagrian's charm, she grimaced. 'I may have been susceptible to all that masculinity, and the smarmy way he came on to you, Laria, but I came to my senses pretty quick. Especially after I caught that shaft he aimed at you, Kincaid.'

'I appreciate that, Lio,' Kincaid said with a wry grin as he regained his equilibrium. 'I thank you, too, Van.'

'We haven't worked this Tower so long that I'd let you down when someone like that piece of ego threatened you,' Van said staunchly. 'You're a helluva lot more man than that one can ever be.'

Kincaid looked slightly bemused and surprised.

'Well, it takes all kinds to make this universe, you know,' Van went on, a little abashed.

'The devil you know?' Laria said teasingly.

'Better than that one, that's for sure,' Van said, one hand unconsciously closing into a fist again. Then he rose. 'Dig, Nim, would you clear this away for us so we can get that siesta while it's quiet?'

SURE, SURE, SURE, and the chorus came from all four 'Dinis.

'When are yours due back?' Lionasha asked. 'I've missed them.'

'We all have.'

YES, YES, YES, was the unison reply as the four 'Dinis began to pile dishes and take them to the recycling unit.

The Humans were all smiling as they dispersed to their quarters. When Laria heard the last door close, she 'ported into Kincaid's room. He had his back to her, pulling down the top sheet of his bed.

*Yes?*

*Kincaid,* she began, not knowing exactly how to break her news to him.

He turned, eyebrows rising up in surprise at her obvious hesitation.

She walked up to him, took his hand and laid it on her stomach. *We started a child last night.*

*How can you be so sure?* he demanded, astonished.

*It's one thing a Prime knows almost instantly: that a new life has started. I wasn't positive . . . because this hasn't happened to me before . . .* and she reached up to stroke his hair with an affectionate hand. *I knew when Vagrian threatened you . . . because he threatened me as well. If you do not object, I shall nurture the embryo. If you do object, I can remove . . .*

He pulled her into his arms, embracing her as tightly as he could, as if warding off any possible harm to her or his seed in her womb. *No, no, no. Please. To father your child? More luck than I ever dreamed would happen. As much as I can, and in spite of my orientation, I love you, Laria, and as much as it is possible for me to love a woman.* As tightly as he already held her, the pressure of his arms increased. *Did you know how terrified I*

105

*was when Vagrian appeared? Terrified to lose the gift of friendship you gave me when I arrived here sick and desperate and wanting far more to die than live?*

*I knew you were in very bad shape . . .* And she let him see that she had not known how close to suicide he had been.

He held her away from him and she saw the tears in his eyes. *You healed me then with such a simple acceptance of what I was. What I am now is all your doing.*

She put her fingers on his mouth. 'No more regrets, my friend. No more looking back. I don't require any promises from you, Kincaid Dano. I do however require a father for the child.'

He folded her tightly against him again, and said with a shaky laugh that was almost a sob, 'That would give me the greatest possible joy.'

'Even if I should require more children from you?' she said, her lips against his ear. 'We Lyons tend to be prolific, you know.'

'Let's see how we do with this one first, shall we?' he asked, but his voice rippled with amusement. Then he picked her up in his arms and, carrying her to the bed, laid her down, settling beside her and 'porting the cover over them both. 'It's more important than ever that you take a siesta,' he said in a stern voice, turning his head to frown at her. 'And if your grandfather will talk to you again in the next few weeks, d'you think we can get a more congenial T-2? Or even a couple of 3's?'

She put her fingers on his lips. 'Ssssh. Morag's just about old enough for some Tower training. I'll ask Mother first.'

'Good idea. Now close your eyes and sleep.'

*I don't think I can, I'm so wired . . .*

*I'll help . . .* Gently he put his hand over her heart.

*As if you could overcome a . . . T . . .*

'I've a few tricks you don't know about, dear heart,' he said softly as her face relaxed and her breathing slowed to the rhythm of a natural sleep.

'How could we possibly have missed Beliakin's overweening self-importance, Gollee?' Jeff Raven asked, rattling his fingers on his desk with aggravation.

106

'Because he's an exceedingly clever young man,' Gollee said, and tossed over a folder of hard copy. 'With good shields that only you, the Rowan and perhaps Damia could have penetrated. I certainly caught nothing more than an intense pleasure at activating a Talent he was sure he had, since his only brother is a T-2, and the hope that he would get a "good assignment". No harm in such thoughts and aspirations. However, if you run down the names of those who passed him through the testing process, there's only one male. To be quite candid,' Gollee sighed briefly, 'with the workload in my department, I was delighted to find a T-2 proving out. I reviewed the assessments and had no reason to doubt them since he most certainly possessed a strong kinetic T-2 when I put him through his paces. With a sibling as capable as Yoshuk already working as Talent, I made the mistake of assuming a more familial integrity and rectitude than he appears to have.' Gollee thrust the file into the reader, scrolling down to nearly the end. 'I just looked over these comments from acquaintances again. I should have paid more attention to them. While he doesn't appear to have made close personal friends, that is not uncommon for the Talented. I originally dismissed the references as malice or understandable envy. On a closer perusal, all of them were men and women of sound judgement and personal integrity. They were attempting to warn us.'

'And I, like a damned fool, was so delighted to find a splendid young fellow for Laria, I didn't question those careful comments either.' Jeff flipped the folder shut. He sighed. 'Well, no-one's perfect.'

Gollee chuckled. 'So you figured he'd suit Laria?'

'If he hadn't this serious personality flaw, as a T-2, he'd've been ideal. I think we'll give him to the Navy as Laria suggested. God knows we're hard-pressed to provide kinetic T's to keep the distant elements of Hive Search supplied.'

'Good idea. He can hardly take over a ship as he evidently planned to take over Clarf Tower. Send him out on the *Strongbow*,' and Gollee's grin was definitely malicious. 'That should pay them back for the gauntlet they ran Kincaid through.'

'You're not the vindictive sort, Gollee,' Jeff remarked, raising his eyebrows in surprise.

'Only in particular cases,' Gollee said with a droll grimace. 'I just don't like manipulative Talents when they're as strong as Beliakin and can so easily inhibit lesser Talents. We can at least employ his unquestionable abilities where they will do the least damage.'

'I believe I concur with that. Which brings us back to the original problem: who do we have to assist Laria's team? They're overloaded right now and the traffic is not likely to ease off for several more months.'

'Morag's how old now?'

Jeff regarded Gollee with surprise and chuckled. 'With all those complaints about nepotism colouring the political scene? Do we dare augment Clarf with yet another Lyon?'

'She won't be in charge. And why shouldn't she visit her sister and get some on-the-job training?'

'I'll ask Damia. Morag is close to seventeen now and has been merging with her parents on a regular basis. She'd know the procedures, so that would be a decided advantage. Afra says the four local Talents they've discovered after that mine collapse are fitting in very well as support staff. Xexo's snagged one as an engineering prospect . . . a T-5. Nothing like a brush with calamity to stimulate resources.'

'Which,' Gollee said, rising to his feet, 'is exactly what brought Vagrian Beliakin to our notice.'

'We shall be more careful, shan't we?'

'Indeed we shall. And make sure we have an even distribution of the sexes in the initial interviews.'

'And for anything above a T-3, a Prime does the final check probe,' Jeff said.

'When, that is, you can fit it in,' Gollee remarked and 'ported himself out of the office.

*Did you hear all of that, my love?* Jeff asked, leaning back in his comfortable chair and propping his feet on his desk.

*Can I never eavesdrop but you know I'm doing it?* the Rowan asked with some asperity.

108

*We are of the same mind and heart, lady of the Tower. How can I not know when our minds are linked?*

*Hmmm. Beliakin seemed almost too good to be true. But then I've no clairvoyance even if I should have been more suspicious just because it was such a perfect solution.*

Jeff heard his wife's mental sigh of remorse.

*Send Kaltia with Morag, Jeff,* the Rowan said after a moment's pause. *They are accustomed to working together and will be company for each other in what is definitely an older grouping.*

*What? And deprive Damia of more of her childer?*

*I've an even better idea . . .*

*Send Beliakin to Iota Aurigae?* Jeff snatched the notion from his wife's mind with the ease of their long association and closeness. *What a splendid solution! Damia and Afra will handle him and he's unlikely to realize he's being tutored and having his thinking adjusted. When he's suitably reformed,* and Jeff chuckled, *THEN we can responsibly send him to a Search ship.*

*He can't do any damage at Damia's at all. Not even to the two youngest. He may be a strong kinetic but, looking over his file, I think that's all he has. He's not strong on telepathy, only on short sends and receives. Also, we must do all we can to redress the embarrassment he received at Laria's hands . . .*

*Embarrassment?*

*All right, humiliation,* the Rowan corrected herself, *but I suspect he came on too strong, so cockily sure of his ability to enchant any female that he succeeded in alienating her. Isn't that what the therapist said?*

*You hadn't read the report?*

*No, you didn't give it to me. But I know Laria and she doesn't respond well to such masculine assertiveness. You know that she's been puzzled, and hurt, by Vanteer's vacillations because she genuinely likes him and trusts him as engineer. Not as a male companion.*

*We could transfer him . . .*

*No, because Damia thinks she might yet overlook Van's . . . ah . . . failings. Let's give her the assistance of Morag and Kaltia while the pressure's on the Tower. Then we'll have more time to find a reliable male.*

*Reliable male!* Jeff pretended to be affronted.

*I could wish,* and Rowan ignored that reaction, *that more Denebians could bring themselves to explore their latent Talents. You are unique, dear heart, but there must be some male for my granddaughter. And you* know *your home world keeps ignoring their most exportable assets.*

*If Gollee senses no definite bias from Beliakin when he proposes a Tower posting at Iota Aurigae, his being available might ease Damia's reluctance to part with the girls. Afra and Damia really do need a good kinetic to keep on shoving those big daddy ore-drones.*

*Morag and Kaltia like Kincaid, too. Then we could send them on to Rojer at Talavera . . . Oh, you're reassigning him, too?*

*I have to, love, with Operation Search expanding in all directions.* However, and he forestalled the objection she didn't even have to think at him, *I'm formulating a valid reason for Asia to accompany Rojer, if that partnership is coming along as well as Flavia thinks it is.*

*IF,* and the Rowan's thought was tinged with criticism, *he'll stop acting like her protector and more like a lover.*

*She's developing a good self-image, according to Zara.*

*About Zara, Jeff . . . can we now use her more efficiently?*

*Doing what?*

Then the Rowan went so quiet he wondered at the silence.

*Making contact with the queens. Somehow we must achieve communications with them.*

*Why?* Jeff asked. *Even when Thian was in the queen's quarters he and his team were totally ignored . . .*

*They were smelled.*

*I'm not so sure we can manage a communication level based on smell, m'dear.* Jeff guffawed. *Unless we found a stink that drives them out of their lairs or exterminates them.* Then he turned serious. *But I have been wondering how we could capitalize on the fact that only Zara, of all the specialists who have tried to establish communications with the Hive species, has been able to sense* something *. . . even if it was only that the Heinlein queen was suffering from hypothermia.*

*I do so wish we could make some sort of a breakthrough. If*

110

*only to silence those who want us to eliminate the species entirely, wherever Hivers are found. I can't believe, when we have become so sophisticated in so many areas, that that sort of barbaric thinking can still exist.*

Jeff sent reassurances to her, sensing her distress over a large, very vocal faction, which was growing stronger and stronger, especially since estimates of the number of planets occupied by Hivers were also increasing as the Fourth Fleet went further on their segment of the Search, in the opposite direction of the First Fleet. Three species were vying for the same sort of new M-type worlds to ease population densities. Fortunately for Humans, their Mrdini allies preferred the hot-sun worlds that could scorch the hide off Human beings. The marginal, semi-tropical worlds might cause contention that could become a serious issue. And each new settlement insisted on having the benefit of FT&T, causing Jeff Raven, as Earth Prime, more and more headaches as he tried to accommodate the growing pressure of requests. There were only so many Talented minds available and he was sensible of the risks overburdening could cause. Overburdening and the same sort of problem which the emergence of a flawed T-2 like Vagrian Beliakin could cause. Federal Teleport and Telepath had enough to cope with, without internal dissension.

*We'll find a solution,* the Rowan said, in her turn reassuring her beloved husband.

*We usually do* was his equable response.

They both turned back to their separate responsibilities, each gaining strength and courage from their momentary rapport.

*Incidentally, have you considered introducing Beliakin to Tarmina d'Estres?*

Jeff allowed his chuckle a lascivious edge.

*I believe she introduced herself to him the first hour he was back here in Blundell.*

The Rowan sent an image of a saccharine smile on her face. *No better woman to pour salve on a wounded male. On the other hand, I hope Damia doesn't know that Laria rejected Beliakin.*

*I'll know when I suggest Beliakin to her.*

111

# CHAPTER SIX

'My father's up to tricks again,' Damia told Afra.

Afra turned amused yellow eyes at his wife of twenty-seven years, patiently awaiting further explanation.

They had completed the day's stint at Iota Aurigae Tower and were walking back to their house that sat well above the bustling, growing capital, its noise muted by the distance.

'Because he's offered us a strong kinetic T-2 in return for sending our daughters to their sister?' A slight smile tilted one corner of the Capellan's narrow, attractive face. He had the kind of features that improve with maturity. He reached for Damia's hand, as much to reinforce their intimacy as to fathom her remark.

'I'll bet you anything this Vagrian Beliakin, for all he's Yoshuk's younger brother, poses a problem we're supposed to solve for Earth Prime.'

'What's wrong with that?'

Damia didn't need to shoot him an annoyed glance: he could easily feel her agitation.

'Haven't you solved enough Gwyn-Raven problems, Afra?'

His answer was to throw his arm about her shoulders and

drag her close against his lean body. Being so much shorter than him, she fitted in under his arm quite easily.

'I admit to things being a little dull lately . . .'

'Oh, you . . . you . . . methody Capellan . . .' she said in exasperation, making a brief attempt to slip from under his arm, but he was far stronger than her and she couldn't escape. Not that she really wanted to. 'We're enjoying such a nice respite, with even Petra able to manage without constant supervision . . . and isn't training our own Aurigeans enough of a challenge? If we *needed* yet *another* one?'

'Then you don't object to Morag and Kaltia getting some experience at Clarf?'

'Not at all. Summers on Deneb are well enough, and Isthia is superb with them, but they haven't really left home, as it were, for something completely alien.'

'Clarf's that, even if they've been raised with 'Dinis,' Afra admitted in a droll tone. He frowned briefly. 'Will Kaltia's very fair skin be at risk?'

'Sunblock helps and she already knows she has to be careful after that awful case of sunburn she had on Deneb. And that primary's not at all as harsh as Clarf's . . .' Damia's voice trailed off, and she too frowned slightly. 'Well, she's old enough to know to keep out of the sun.'

'That's right, my dear, and she could always make parasols fashionable on Clarf.'

'They are . . . but to get back to this Beliakin T-2 . . .'

'Let's worry about him when he gets here. Didn't Jeff say that Gollee's giving him some extra training?'

'Gollee doesn't train, dear, he tests.'

'Hmmm. For what?' Afra asked, at his blandest.

That casually dropped remark from her father was what really alerted Damia to a possible contretemps.

'If the fellow's already been passed through the assessment process, why is Gollee handling him and not one of the regular trainers?' Damia asked, lengthening her stride to match her husband's long-legged pace.

'We'll know soon enough . . .' They both heard the staccato rhythm of hoofbeats on the path winding up the hill behind

113

their home. 'There they go . . .' and they caught sight of their four younger children, galloping out to hunt. 'Oh, well, dinner's soon enough to give them the good news.'

Afra tightened his grasp on her, pulling her closer yet, looking down at her.

'It'll be good to have the house all to ourselves for a while,' he said.

Damia caught the gleam in his eye and put her arm about his lean waist. 'Yes, it will. How convenient that Tri and Fok are hibernating. We really will be alone again.' She sighed in gratitude.

'Except for the tribes of Darbuls, slithers and Coonies that infest our house,' Afra teased her.

'This time of day they'll all be asleep. Let's hurry.'

Laughing, they 'ported into their spacious room at the top of the house.

They were grateful for that respite by dinnertime when they informed their ecstatic daughters, Morag and Kaltia, that they were to go to Clarf and assist their sister's Tower team with the vast loads still being poured onto the planet Talavera.

'So we're going to do something more than push big daddies,' Kaltia said, her unusual yellow eyes, legacy of her Capellan father, glistening like miniature suns.

'Huh. We'll be pushing just as much around, and Laria'll be bossing us,' Morag replied sourly.

'Laria has never been bossy,' her mother said firmly. 'And if you need bossing, you'll take it, young miss, if it comes from a Tower Prime.'

'I'm going to be a Tower Prime when I'm old enough,' Kaltia informed them with the complacency of her youth.

'That remains to be seen,' Afra said, for he was methody enough not to condone bragging. Kaltia gulped, subsided and concentrated on eating.

'Kincaid never bosses,' Morag said, affecting a pose, 'even when he's hunt leader.' She got on well with her sister's T-2. She'd been impressed with how well he rode and what a good shot he was. She considered him a very comfortable person to

114

be with. 'Is Vanteer still engineer?' Her sly attempt to wheedle information from her mother was duly noted.

'Yes, and we'll have no gossip, Morag,' Damia said firmly. 'Lionasha's Tower expediter.'

'Have they 'Dinis?'

THEY DO, THEY DO, chorused Kev, Su, Sim and Dar at once. WE'LL GO TO CLARF. The four of them started to do cartwheels and other acrobatic antics around the dining-table.

WE'LL HIBERNATE IN CLARF ITSELF, said Dar, bouncing higher than one would expect from a 'Dini.

WE'LL SEE TIP AND HUF, AND NIL AND PLUS.

'You'll have to help in the Yard,' Morag said sternly. 'No running off to your colour houses whenever you want to.'

NO, NO, WORK IS FIRST. ALWAYS, Dar assured her and then began to twirl Sim round and round until Morag was dizzy watching them.

'So, who's this T-2 you'll have to do *our* work?' Kaltia asked in a proprietary tone.

'Yoshuk's younger brother,' Damia said.

'Isn't Yoshuk the T-2 with Nesrun at Sef Tower?' Kaltia asked. 'Thought so,' she added when Damia nodded. She was silent a moment. 'There won't be ponies, will there?'

'No, not on Clarf, silly. No room. 'Dinis there use flying belts,' said Morag.

'And you will not,' Afra said, pointing an admonitory finger at Morag who was more athletically inclined, and reckless, than Kaltia. 'You already drive a ground car and they've the same models there. Or you can 'port.'

'That's not bad manners on Clarf?' asked Kaltia, surprised. On Deneb it was but then, on Deneb, they had had ponies.

'You will first inform anyone in the immediate vicinity what you intend to do,' Damia said firmly. 'Otherwise it's just as ill-mannered as it would be here or on Deneb.' When Kaltia made a long-suffering grimace, her mother added, 'Not that I want you out in the Clarf sun any longer than is absolutely necessary.'

'I know, I know. I must use enough sunblock. Why,' and her tone turned petulant, 'did I have to get the fair skin and the freckles in the family? No-one else has them.'

'Grandmother says you're a throwback,' Ewain said, as helpful as teenage brothers generally are.

'And you're a . . .'

'That's enough,' Afra said firmly and the three subsided and resumed eating.

'I think it's great,' Petra said suddenly. 'There'll just be you and me, E, and no-one to tell us which pony we can't ride.'

'Yeah, but we'll have to do all the hunting.'

Petra grinned. 'But we won't have to hunt so much with just four of us here . . .'

'Possibly five,' Afra said, 'unless Vagrian Beliakin chooses to live down in the city instead of here.'

'Forgot about him,' Petra said, turning glum. 'Do we have to have him here? It's E's and my turn to have you,' she added, looking sternly from one parent to the other. 'We've waited long enough.'

'When were *you* ever neglected?' demanded Morag tartly.

'I said, that's enough,' Afra repeated, adding a mental quietus. 'Good hunt, today. Where'd you go?'

'Laria's valley. It hasn't been hunted in just ages,' Morag said. '*It* has been neglected . . .' and she cast a daring glance at her father, 'so the hunting was good.'

Afra regarded his daughter with such a long thoughtful look for her impudence that she turned her whole attention to her dinner plate.

*She* needs *more work and responsibility,* Damia said though her tone was amused by her daughter's clever wordplay.

The rest of the evening passed without incident, Damia and her daughters making certain the guest quarters, private from the main living area, were in order for the new arrival. Both Afra and Damia felt that a man of thirty would want to live nearer the city with all its possibilities of entertainment, though he would need to stay at Tower House until he'd found accommodations.

'You're Vagrian Beliakin, aren't you?'

Since the words were spoken close in a tone that was almost a challenge, Beliakin looked up at the woman who had

116

stopped at his table. He felt her shields resist his initial touch. She was only marginally attractive and he was far too involved with Tarmina d'Estres to need to seek additional female companionship.

'I'm T-2 and a far sender,' she said with a twist of her lips that bordered on mocking.

Beliakin rose and gestured for her to be seated opposite him. He had chosen a table well away from the other Talents enjoying meals in the spacious and restfully decorated Blundell dining-room. He had had an exhausting morning with Gollee Gren, and really did not want any company. Since she had in effect challenged him, he had to respond, however briefly.

'Clarissia Negeva,' she said, sliding awkwardly into a chair.

Nerves, Vagrian thought and gave her one of his reassuring smiles. Her reaction was a deep flush of blood to her face and she averted her gaze to some point over his left shoulder. She'd be easy, he thought.

'I lasted longer at Clarf Tower than you did,' she said, composing herself and her tell-tale colour, clasping thin hands in front of her on the table and leaning towards him. Now she regarded the pulse in his throat rather than his face.

'Did you?' He fought to stifle the burst of anger her comment roused in him. He had been given to understand by Gollee Gren that the abortive incident had been expunged from the record. His common sense took over. Tarmina certainly hadn't known, nor had any other of those he had been in contact with. All the testers had assumed he was being reassessed. He was certain that if that abortive mission were known he'd've been aware of either ridicule or prurient interest. He managed to keep his expression pleasantly puzzled as a third consideration occurred to him. If somehow this Negeva woman had information that was not normally available to others in Blundell Tower, she might be worth cultivating. He intended to pay back Clarf Tower's Prime no matter how long it took. 'May I ask how you knew that I had been to Clarf?'

Her lips moved slightly, and although she did not give him a direct look, he felt positive that she, too, had a bone to pick with Laria Lyon.

'I have a friend, a good friend, in the Yard,' she said. 'He had been on duty when you were 'ported and saw your precipitous return. He thought I should be informed.'

'Why?'

Even though Vagrian had come late to his Talent, he knew from his brother's conversations at home that Talents did not generally avoid direct eye contact – since they could shield their true thoughts from all but the most determined invasion. In the point of courtesy on a first encounter, Negeva had neglected to offer him her hand . . . almost an insult between Talents. While he was not a strong 'path, this close he could read her deep enough to find some reason for her approaching him. He ignored the fact that she'd been rattled by his smile: few women failed to respond – generally in positive ways. He resolved to ensure they made a tactile contact before she left his company.

She leaned even closer, and now her eyes met his, anger and a sort of implacable hatred easy to note.

'That family dominates FT&T and they have no right to do so. They make arbitrary decisions and enforce them on us in an unjust and humiliating manner. They are weasel-lovers, every single one of them!'

'You're referring to the Gwyn-Raven-Lyon clan?' he asked, lounging back in his seat because her breath was sour. Probably from the curdled enmity that festered in her skinny frame.

'Who else? They have all the best Towers, all the best accommodations. They sit in judgement on every single Talent and they don't . . . have . . . that . . . right!' Her eyes had narrowed and she had had to lower her voice as she stressed that opinion.

'Who's to oppose them?' Beliakin asked.

'They haven't enslaved all the T-1's in our worlds.'

'Really?' And this was news to him.

'By no means. Nor all the T-2's. Furthermore,' and she gestured for him to close the gap between them, 'they ignore the clairvoyant as if they were dirt.'

118

'And there has been a prediction that the mighty will fall?' he asked, feigning a hopeful anticipation.

'Of course. The higher they are the harder they will fall. And fall they will. Then *we* will assume our rightful positions in the Towers, and annul the infamous Alliance. We have no more need of those . . . creatures!' She gave a shudder of repugnance.

'Disgusting,' Beliakin said ambiguously.

'And giving worlds *we Humans* discovered with our advanced technology to . . . *them* . . . when *we* are to be given what's left over is intolerable. No more promising colony sites can be so summarily just *given away*! Our future generations will be denied their rights of expansion on worlds that have been just *handed over* to . . . *them.*'

Beliakin tightened his shields against this woman's intrusion, though it occurred to him simultaneously that she was so wrapped up in her angry spiel that she was taking no notice of his reactions. Personally, he had no objections to the Mrdini. She was patently xenophobic. That species had taken the brunt of centuries of war against the Hivers. Their long struggle should have some rewards. As far as he knew, the one world released to the Mrdini would have been too hot to be comfortable for Human residence. On the one hand, he didn't like the Hivers at all, having taken an opportunity to see the queen imprisoned at Heinlein Moon Base. That creature revolted him more than 'Dinis did . . . it and the scurrying forms that it had hatched from its mound of eggs. So the Mrdinis were welcome to Talavera. The sun would fry an egg on a rock by midday. However, he was definitely curious about her group and wondered just how many Talents might be involved in any effort to overthrow the Primes. Though how that could be achieved was beyond him. On the other hand, reporting on their dissidence might be one way to nullify the Clarf disaster with FT&T.

'Are there many who feel as you . . . and I?' he asked in a low conspiratorial tone, as if he agreed with her opinions.

'More than you'd believe,' she murmured. Then abruptly she rose. 'I shall contact you. I shall use the word "expunge" so that you will know it is I contacting you and you will open your mind to me.'

Not if I can help it, Beliakin said very privately to himself. He rose, too, and, tightly shielding his thoughts as he'd been taught, extended his hand. She regarded it suspiciously and he could certainly sense her hesitation without any benefit of Talent. Her fingers gave his a glancing touch. He gleaned very little from it, but enough to know that this Talent could be dangerous in her hatred of the Gwyn-Raven-Lyon family. As he watched her stalk . . . yes, that was the right word . . . out of the dining facility, he wondered if he could effect a revenge on Laria Lyon without being tainted by whatever devious plans Negeva and her group had in mind. That is, if these had not already been 'seen' by other, more sensitive Talents. She was, however, a T-2, and a sender was apt to have better shielding from any but a T-1. What a very odd creature she was. And viciously xenophobic! Talents were supposed, by the very nature of their abilities, to practise tolerance. Of most things . . .

He finished his meal, discarded the dishes and made it to his appointment with Gollee Gren to see what his new assignment was going to be. He wondered to which boondock he'd now be sent after his utter failure at Clarf. Hopefully where that wretched female couldn't reach him, no matter how strong a sender she claimed she was. He did wonder, however, just how many agreed with her sentiments. Generally speaking – and this had been why he was so jealous of Yoshuk – Talents enjoyed many more privileges and more prestige than any other profession in the Galaxy. Few made full use of all such advantages. He intended to if, that is, he was any place where he *could* use the perks. What he found hard to understand in Negeva was why any disaffected person would wish to destroy . . . no, she didn't wish destruction, she wished a larger role. Beliakin knew there were factions dissatisfied with the Alliance and with the distribution of colonizable worlds (once Hivers had been dispossessed), to the Mrdini in particular. Since 'weasel-haters' generally had little if any contact with the 'Dinis, he couldn't see what upset them so much. In any event,

120

he still had a score to even with Laria Lyon by whatever agency that came his way, even as unattractive and virulent a one as Negeva. And he'd get Kincaid Dano at the same time. Whistling happily at such a prospect, he took the lift to the administrative level.

'Iota Aurigae?' Vagrian stared with disbelief at Gren.

'You'd be working with two of the top Talents in FT&T, you know,' Gren said, 'and I can assure you that the con-tretemps at Clarf will not be repeated. In fact, your kinetic ability is very much why you're being posted there.'

'I thought the family handled all traffic,' Vagrian said, temporizing as he assimilated the fact. Such a posting had been so far out of possibility that he couldn't believe it. Was this a tacit apology for Laria's treatment? Damia and Afra Raven-Lyon offering him such a post to make amends for the vagary of their daughter? Considering its distance from the other main solar systems, Iota Aurigae could be considered a boondock, being a very recently developed mining world, but it was gaining prominence and expanding as the need for its ore resources increased. Topmost in his mind was the realization that he'd be able to hunt there – an activity frowned on by the more sophisticated worlds as archaic, or non-existent as on Clarf, and one that he thoroughly enjoyed and excelled at. Afra was almost legendary as the Rowan's T-2 partner until he married her daughter, Damia Gwyn-Raven, and they took over Iota Aurigae Tower, producing . . . what was it . . . eight T-1 offspring? Or were all the kids gone now? Not that it mattered. If he proved his capabilities as a strong kinetic at their Tower, he'd achieve an enviable reputation at FT&T. And he might also just happen to find out how to get back at Laria. Nothing like the home ground to discover the precise way to wound her the most. He had absolutely no reservations about working with the Capellan T-2 but Damia was known to have inherited the volatile temper of her mother, the Rowan. Well, most of the Primes he knew anything about had tempers. Came with the awesome responsibility, he supposed. Were they aware of his calamity at Clarf? Could there be an ulterior motive to that posting? Apart from rectifying their daughter's unexpected rejection of him?

'The family has, until recently, handled the Tower,' Gren was saying and Beliakin paid attention, trying to catch any shielded thought. Gren did have unusually tight barriers but his public mind was quite open as he went on. 'As you probably know, all the Raven-Lyon children are T-1s so they are assigned off-planet to broaden their experience. They're down to the two youngest who are not old enough to assist as fully. You would be working with several indigenous Aurigaeans who had break-through stimulation similar to your own – a mining accident in their case.' Gren's expression was rueful. 'It's easier if one comes less abruptly to the emergence of Talent but we can use every one we can classify. Both Damia and Afra have had experience with bringing on latent Talents.'

'Yes, of course,' Beliakin said, realizing some comment on his part would be courteous.

'That also was a factor in assigning you to Iota Aurigae. A T-2 of your kinetic strength is such a find for FT&T at this particular moment in time,' and Gren smiled in a manner that bordered on apology, 'that perhaps we might have pushed you a tad too quickly where your abilities were most needed with the mass of material Clarf Tower's had to process lately. The Lyons – and rightly – are treated with great caution and respect. It wasn't easy to find suitable Talents for Clarf.'

Gren sounded sincere, Beliakin thought. Perhaps Clarissia Negeva had simply not been up to the work on Clarf and transferred before she could mess things up. Or the Prime hadn't liked her. That was more understandable. Negeva was not an attractive person . . . and xenophobic, too. Not a good mindset for working on Clarf. Perhaps he should avoid any further contact with her. Their cases were not at all similar.

'There's also good hunting on Iota Aurigae which is, I realize from your transcript, one of your avocations. Tower House has an excellent stable and the hills are full of game, large and small and not so easy to bring down, I might add.' Gren's lips twitched as if remembering unsuccessful experiences. 'Damia has issued an invitation for you to stay with the family if you wish – though there are new and well-appointed apartments in the city and transport would be no problem for you.' He consulted his notepad, checking off another item. 'Living accommodation is in addition to your salary, and you have the usual privileges of importing whenever drone space is available. It usually is. Drones may be full enough leaving Iota Aurigae but they're mainly empty on the return trip. Personal effects above and beyond what will fit in a personnel carrier will be forwarded . . .' Beliakin waved aside that consideration since he had little in the way of impedimenta, and no wish to import anything from a home world that had little to recommend it except that he had escaped its bucolic lifestyle. 'Would you be agreeable to leaving here at 22.00?'

'Today?'

'Yes, if that's convenient. You'd arrive late afternoon at Aurigae and be able to settle in before dinner.' Gren regarded him and then added, 'I believe there're six big daddies – as they call the ore transports – to be heaved to Betelgeuse tomorrow so you'd have a chance to demonstrate your kinetic abilities. Which, may I say, are the strongest we've ever measured in a late-comer.'

While Vagrian Beliakin knew this to be very true, he modestly accepted that assessment. Gren flipped down the cover of his notepad to indicate the formal interview was over and stood.

'I am certain that Iota Aurigae Tower will appreciate your presence and your willingness to accept the posting on so little advance notice.'

As Beliakin reached the door, considerably relieved, Gren had a final comment.

'You also have the best wishes of Earth Prime and his regrets that he could not be present at this hour to wish you well.'

If that was an additional apology for the humiliation Beliakin had suffered at the whimsy of Earth Prime's grand-daughter, Vagrian accepted it in a gracious manner. He might come out of that initial disaster well ahead in FT&T. He would certainly bend every effort to do so.

\*     \*     \*

'You're just getting us out of the way before Beliakin arrives,' Morag said fiercely, although she wanted to get to Clarf as fast as her parents seemingly wished her there.

'How old are you?' her mother asked with a slight strain showing in her patience.

'Well, he's supposed to be absolutely gorgeous . . .' Morag said wistfully.

Afra laughed. 'A good fourteen years your senior, love, and far too practised a . . .'

'Lover,' Damia said bluntly, 'for my young and relatively inexperienced daughter.' She cocked an eyebrow at Morag, making it plain that she was aware of Morag's experiments with young miners in the capital city.

Morag made nervous adjustments of her personal belongings under the couch of the carrier rather than meet her mother's shrewd and knowing eyes.

'You've been well instructed on how to handle . . . such matters,' Damia went on, 'and do not fail to protect both yourself and the object of your affections.'

'No, Mother,' Morag said solemnly for she vividly recalled the pain in Damia's eyes when, in the course of handling her daughters' sex education, she had confessed the terrible damage she had inadvertently done her first young lover.

'No, Mother,' Kaltia agreed as quietly.

'There is quite a large Human Compound on Clarf now so I suspect that there will be opportunities for a social life while you're there.' Damia hugged first Morag and then Kaltia, keeping an exceedingly tight hold on how much she would miss them, despite their sibling bickering. There had been a certain justice in Petra's remark that she and Ewain would have more of their parents' time now. Both she and Afra intended to spend more time with the two youngest of their brood. Indeed, Damia was not too old . . .

*You may not be, lover, but I most certainly am,* Afra inserted into her mind with such intensity that she had to keep from laughing at his vehemence.

Then it was Afra's turn to bid his daughters farewell and he held each for a long moment in his arms before he released

124

them to enter the double personnel carrier. Their 'Dinis were chattering excitedly about actually getting to Clarf, the Mrdini Homeworld.

Xexo and Keylarion smiled and grinned as the cover locked into place. There was no need for the practised Talents of Iota Aurigae to return to their Tower couches to speed the light carrier on its way. But all could hear the generators change tone as first Damia alerted Laria at Clarf Tower that her sisters were on their way, and then father and mother sent the carrier on its almost instantaneous long-distance journey. Xexo muttered something about an odd squeal from Generator B and Keylarion said she'd best check that the big daddies would be ready to ship once they had this strong Kinetic Talent in the Tower.

'Kaltia did put on sunblock, didn't she, Afra?' Damia asked belatedly.

'Half a tube. You have some on your cheek if you'll check,' Afra said.

'Oh, so I do.'

'Have we time for lunch before they send Beliakin on?'

'Gollee said he wouldn't arrive until the girls were away,' Damia said. '22.00 Earth time.'

'Late afternoon here, then. We've time for lunch and a swim.'

'We've enough from the last hunt?'

Afra sighed with amusement. 'I'm not sure there'll be any left for this Beliakin. Gollee says he likes to hunt.'

'Well, we certainly won't stand in the way of that, now will we?' and she started back to the house.

'How long did he and Clarissia talk?' Jeff Raven asked Gren.

'Not long, but perhaps long enough.'

'What was his reaction to his posting?'

Gollee chuckled, crossing his legs at the ankles and relaxing. 'He was startled because he certainly didn't expect to be at a major Tower, especially at the one managed by the father and mother of the woman who humiliated him so. From the first I've maintained that Laria's rejection is known only to you, me and Clarf Tower which has not even mentioned it. If he thinks we've told Damia and Afra, and they're in some way expiating their daughter's rejection, all to the good . . . Unless of course Damia reads it in him.'

'She's got the capability,' Jeff said, 'but she's got to have a strong Kinetic and both Afra and Damia know the pressures Laria's under. Considering how Beliakin comes on to women, my hindsight is now clear enough to realize that his brand of charisma would put Laria's hackles up.'

'True,' Gollee said, grinning. 'He certainly cut a swathe through the feminine complement of Blundell Tower. Tarmina allowed as . . .' and Gollee paused, 'how he's most unusual.'

Jeff chuckled. 'She'd know.'

'She's offered to take on any others like him any time you choose.'

'She would.' Jeff caught Gollee's tilted eyebrow. 'None of that, Gren. I know she tried to get you in bed, too. If I wasn't well married to Rowan, I should have been sorely tempted.'

'At least Tarmina takes refusal in good part,' Gollee said, clearing his throat. 'If we could be sure Beliakin might forgive and forget, I'd rest easier.'

'I count on Damia's expertise as well as her immunity to the sort of charisma Beliakin dispenses. You handled this well, Gollee, and I appreciate it. However, did you perceive how susceptible he might be to what Clarissia's group is peddling?'

Gren snorted. 'Depending on his success at Iota Aurigae, plus the fact that Clarissia was exactly the wrong female personality to make contact with him, I doubt he'd jeopardize what could be a very useful career with FT&T. She's her own worst enemy, that one, even if she thought she could capitalize on Beliakin's abrupt dismissal from Clarf. Though how she knew of *that* needs to be discovered.'

'Damn,' and Jeff swung his gimballed chair from side to side in an agitated manner, running his hand through his thick dark hair. 'It's so *much* more to our advantage to catch Talents young enough so that the basic conditioning is completed. A wild card like Beliakin could prove very dangerous, especially in today's volatile political and economic situations.'

'Well, he's in the best place for some fine tuning, Jeff. And if he does well there, there's any number of postings where he'd be invaluable. I think that's the ploy to use . . . support that ego of his . . . nurturing it until what the dissidents offer wouldn't tempt him.'

'It's that ego of his I worry about.' He slapped one fist on the desktop. 'Stupid of me to assume the man would have sense enough to be tactful. At least until he'd settled into Clarf Tower. He was so deferential to Rowan.'

'Who isn't?' Gollee said with a laugh. 'And, if he managed to fool her . . .' Gren let his sentence trail off. 'Your children tend to find their own mates, Jeff. And so far, they've done exceedingly well. Give your grandkids the same leeway.'

Jeff made a face. 'My dynastic leanings *are* obvious, aren't they?'

'The Gwyn-Raven line is not the only one to produce T-1s.' He paused. 'Just the most reliable.'

All four of the senior Tower staff at Iota Aurigae were in the yard when Vagrian Beliakin's personnel carrier was gently cradled. His ear caught the contented purr of generators that had had little to do with his transport. The lid was cracked and crisp cool air with a mountainy tang to it flooded in.

That was enough right there to please him after the blast of hot air that had greeted him on Clarf.

'Welcome to Iota Aurigae, Vagrian Beliakin,' said one of the most stunning women Beliakin had ever seen. And not just beautiful in a classic way, but so vital that she seemed to have an almost visible aura around her. To his surprise, she extended her hand and he found himself responding, while all his initial impressions were reinforced by rich/green/spice in that deft, but far too short, contact. 'I'm Damia Lyon. This is my husband, Afra.'

The lean man, much, much older than Damia, smiled in warm greeting as he extended his hand. Vagrian was still so shaken by touching the Prime that he almost missed the strength of Afra's equally electric contact.

What a pair, Beliakin thought as deeply as he could keep such a startled assessment. The mother was so dramatically different from Laria that he couldn't believe they were related, save for the distinctive white lock all Gwyn-Raven-Lyon offspring seemed to have. He took a second, longer look at Afra. Then he saw where Laria had inherited her looks.

'Let me introduce you to Keylarion, our station expediter,' and though the woman – probably the same age as Damia – touched hands with him, he got very little more than deep blue and pine.

'Xexo here is our engineer,' and Damia now presented the gnarled older man who stepped forward.

'Pleased,' was Xexo's comment and his touch was oily, black, pungent. Exactly what one would expect of an engineer.

'We've four trainees but you can meet them later, Vagrian,' Damia said. 'You didn't bring much with you,' she added as Xexo casually slung the heaviest of the duffels out of the personnel carrier.

'Always travel light,' Vagrian said, keeping his smile pleasant and his manner quiet, struggling to restore his composure and a public show of confident ease. He hauled out the other two.

'I'll just 'port them to your room,' Damia said and all three disappeared.

'I should have done that,' Vagrian said.

'I know where the room is,' she said with an engaging grin. Then she gestured towards the well-worn path to the house he could see sitting on its height. 'Bit of a walk.'

'Not in this marvellous air,' he said, breathing deeply and catching himself before he had expanded his chest ostentatiously. 'It's like a fine wine.'

'One of the fringe benefits,' Afra remarked as they set out.

Aware that neither Xexo nor Keylarion was following, Beliakin looked around.

'Xexo isn't happy with the B generator,' Damia said, grinning at the vagaries of her engineer, 'and Keylarion's

128

checking the co-ordinates for tomorrow's cargo. Did anyone warn you that you'll be put to work tomorrow and that we lift them straight from the mine yards?'

'Gollee Gren did mention big daddies,' Vagrian said, 'not that we lifted them from sites.'

Into his mind with alarming ease he caught a picture of the immense drone that he was to help shift the next day.

'Well, there'd be few cradles that size,' and, while he responded as surprised as he was supposed to be by the size and tonnage of a drone full of ore, he felt no qualms at all about managing such weights. That had been his speciality ever since he'd diverted that mudslide on Altair. 'Did I understand Gren correctly that your children have been helping you shift those things?'

Damia chuckled. 'Only when they are old enough. In a merge with Afra and myself, we could add their strength without stressing them. I've seen your testings, Vagrian, and I must say that I'm impressed by your solo shifts.'

'I'm not good at much else, though, in any other Talent range,' he said with what he thought was exactly the right note of modesty.

'You wouldn't need to be,' Afra said with a chuckle.

By then they had reached the steps up to the house and Beliakin emitted a startled cry when Darbuls, slithers and Coonies charged out of wherever they had hidden themselves.

'Forgot to warn you, Vagrian,' Damia said as she 'ordered' the mass of striped, mottled, tabbied, plain-coloured creatures to clear away. 'Don't tell me Gollee didn't mention the menagerie.'

'He mentioned horses,' Beliakin was looking all around him, not wanting to step on someone's favourite beast . . . unless one of Laria's was identified to him.

Suddenly all of the beasts were sitting, quietly, watching him; even the slithers had coiled their supple bodies into compact circles.

'Each of our children and their 'Dinis have favourites which, of course, are prohibited from going with them so we inherited the whole zoo,' Afra said, picking up one of the

129

Coons and stroking its creamy-orange fur. 'You don't have an allergy to any of these, do you?' and he gestured to the herd.

'Oh, no, no. In fact, the only ones I recognize are the felines. I thought they didn't like snakes,' and Vagrian had been able to stifle the brief panic he'd felt surrounded by so many strange beasts.

'Slithers are not precisely reptilian,' Damia said, allowing one to twine itself about her forearm, 'but they are the favoured pets of our 'Dinis. If you don't care for them, just gently disengage any that try to cling to you. They take hints quickly.'

'Yes, that's good to know.'

'They also stay outside,' Afra said, 'unless their 'Dinis are here.'

'I see.'

'This way, Vagrian,' Damia said, gesturing up the broad stone steps to the wide sheltering porch of the house. Three Coons and two Darbuls followed her, none of the slithers did. 'Our 'Dinis are currently in their hibernatory though you'll meet the pairs my two remaining youngsters have. They're out hunting. I gather you enjoy the sport?'

'Yes, I do,' Vagrian said.

'And you ride?' Damia gave him a measuring look. 'I suspect we can mount you adequately.'

'Yes, I originate from Altair . . .'

'Yes, you'd ride all right,' Afra remarked approvingly.

'Your room is just up these stairs,' Damia said. 'If you'll do the honours, Afra, I'll get us something to snack on.'

The room was certainly an improvement on his quarters in Blundell Tower, Vagrian thought, and Damia had neatly 'ported the two smaller sacks to the wide bed and the large duffle to a luggage stand. The door to the right was ajar and showed the usual bathroom fixtures. It was however the view from the double windows of the room which got his full attention, showing a breathtaking panorama of the distant city and the shore that it bordered.

'Never seen anything like it,' Vagrian said quite truthfully, going to the nearest window and opening it. He took another deep breath of the exhilarating air. 'Blundell never smelled this good.'

Afra smiled. 'I'll leave you to get settled in.'

*Well?* Damia asked pointedly when Afra joined her in the kitchen.

*Interesting personality.*

*Dangerous personality with all that masculine charm.* Damia gave a shudder. *I had this awful sensation that he was Sodan come back to haunt me.*

*Did you?* Afra looked surprised.

Damia flushed. *Well, he has a similar dynamic charisma and you can't deny he's decidedly attractive.*

*Not at all my type.*

*It's not a laughing matter, Afra. Young Naja's just the age to be bowled over and ready for an infatuation.*

*He'll be an equal shock to our three Aurigaean lads,* Afra said with a teasing glance. *He's not a threat we can warn them about.*

*He's so* much *on his best behaviour,* Damia said thoughtfully. *Maybe it'll last. I can't imagine why Father thought he'd do for us. When Laria . . .* Damia paused and turned wide eyes on Afra who grinned knowingly back at her. *He did? And she sent him packing? My father sometimes exhibits very poor judgement for a Prime. Did Mother know?*

*If she did, she was perhaps too hopeful and not as astute in her reading of Vagrian's character as I would have thought.*

Damia regarded her husband with a measure of dismay. *He is absolutely the wrong sort for Laria, especially after all she's been through with the wayward Vanteer. How could Father have been so stupid?*

*Don't think he was stupid, m'dear. I think he was so glad he'd found a strong T-2 Kinetic to ease the load at Clarf, he sent the man ahead without preparing Laria at all.* Afra poured cold Aurigaean wine for them both. Damia absently accepted the glass and took a slow sip of the dry vintage. *I'd venture to say Vagrian blew it. Probably took the trouble to charm Lionasha, ignored Vanteer and then made a fool of himself trying to impress Laria. He's only just discovered his Talent and you know how witless that can make someone.*

131

*It hasn't made Numto, Clunen or Deferson witless.*

*They're younger by a few years whereas I'd be very surprised if Yoshuk's big younger brother hasn't been having his way with any girl he chose on Altair. IF – and we can always confirm this with Gollee,* Afra went on, holding up one hand, *Vagrian made a balls of meeting Laria, and they've sent him to us to . . . ah . . . adjust . . .*

*. . . Of course they have,* and Damia scowled into her wineglass.

*Then let's see how well he performs and what we can do. Neither your father nor Gollee would have sent him here unless he has real ability that they wish to channel and save.*

Damia was too accustomed to Afra's sense of justice and common sense to ignore his comments.

*Small wonder he wanted Morag and Kaltia away before Vagrian arrived,* she murmured. *Can you imagine the impact he'd've had on Morag?*

*With no trouble at all,* Afra said with a chuckle. *He's descending.* 'I thought we still had some of that Brie-type cheese left, or did Morag eat the last of it?'

'I've pâté and the local soft cheese,' Damia was saying, having swiftly 'ported crackers and spreads from the larder and cold store, while Afra opened a second bottle of white wine to the one they had nearly finished, as well as other liquors.

'What's your preference, Vagrian?' Afra asked. 'There are two local lagers that are quite palatable and something the miners drink that they call "bitters".'

'Isn't that an Altairian white?' Vagrian asked, pointing to the wine.

'Indeed it is,' Damia said, smiling approval. 'One of our perks as Tower staff. You can order anything in when we've empty drones returning. And we have them in fleets,' she added in a weary tone.

'Let's go into the lounge. Sunset's rather unusual here on Iota,' Afra said, the indulgent host, and carried the drinks tray while Damia and Vagrian followed.

They were still on broad conversational topics when Petra

132

and Ewain arrived in, their Darbuls and Coons at their heels. Vit, Buf, Jan and Tiv followed, each with just one slither.

*Thank you, dears,* Damia said, nodding and smiling before she introduced her youngest aloud to their house guest. *He'll need time to become accustomed to the slithers, I think. Reptiles on Altair are too dangerous to be considered pets.*

When they wished to, Petra and Ewain could be the epitome of well-behaved children. Attuned to parental attitudes, they assumed that pose and passed snacks, then politely urged Vagrian to try some that they preferred. His enquiry about what they hunted on Iota met with such explanations and eagerness for him to join them, that Damia was able to go out to the kitchen with the 'Dinis to finish dinner preparations.

The hunting topic was pursued during dinner because Vagrian – with every appearance of good nature – was quite happy to compare his forays as a young hunter on Altair with the experiences of Petra and Ewain. Listening with an acute ear for any false tone, Damia had to concede that Vagrian was not exaggerating his prowess. Both she and Afra knew that some of the game he had pursued on Altair was a good deal larger and more dangerous than anything on the coasts or mountains of Iota Aurigae.

'We've nothing like ballbites and beartards here on Iota,' she said at one point.

'Frankly, it's never been the size of permissible prey that's attracted me, Damia,' Vagrian replied with perfect sincerity, 'but the skill the hunting requires. If you do hunt here for the table, I'd be very happy to take part, if you'll tell me what is and is not permitted.'

'What's your weapon of choice?' Petra demanded, her eyes keen, mouth half open awaiting his answer. Damia was relieved that Petra was still a trifle too young to be seriously affected by Vagrian's good looks. After all, her older brothers were just as attractive.

*But . . .* Afra put in wryly, *merely brothers.*

'What's available?' asked Vagrian with a shrug.

'Just about anything,' Afra said, 'from slingshot . . .'

133

'Slingshot? You can bring down prey with that?' Vagrian's surprise was not feigned.

'Sure,' Ewain said nonchalantly. 'Get most of the avians that way. Head shots that don't bruise the edible parts.'

'Bow and arrow?' Vagrian asked now.

'Yup, and spear now and then against the bigger scurriers,' Petra said and then grimaced, 'though that's kinda overkill. I mostly stick to my .22.'

'Head shots?' Vagrian asked.

'If I don't have a clear view of the eye.'

'Will I be safe out hunting with this pair?' Vagrian asked their parents.

'We haven't eaten a guest yet,' Ewain answered, giggling.

After dinner, Petra, who was in charge of evening stables, asked if Vagrian wanted to come along.

'We've turned most of the ponies out,' Petra explained.

'And you've a favourite mount?' Vagrian asked.

'Yes, I'm allowed to ride Saki now. She was Laria's special mount but she's such a brilliant ride, we've all used her until our legs get too long.' She spared a glance at Vagrian's legs. 'You're much too tall already.'

'Which is Saki?' Vagrian asked as they entered the stable.

'Here she is,' Petra said and turned to the first box on the right. 'Isn't she beautiful?' She held her hand out flat and Vagrian had a brief glimpse of a tidbit that quickly disappeared into the mare's eager mouth. When Vagrian stepped closer, the mare backed up, ears flat.

Once more startled, Vagrian wondered if the animals in this unusual household were also telepathic. The diverse herd that had taken him by surprise in front of the house had immediately withdrawn and sat in patient order until released. And now this mare seemed to sense his keen, and inimical, interest in her.

'She'll behave better when she sees you more often,' Petra said airily. Then she tugged at Vagrian's sleeve. 'The horses are further down and I'd say China will be up to your weight. She's very sure-footed which you need in our hills and quite onward bound.'

134

Seeing a bucket of horse pellets, Vagrian took a handful, determined to make a positive impression on this mare. The dappled grey accepted his offering quite willingly and allowed him to stroke her neck and scratch her ears. When Petra clicked twice, China stepped back and he got a good look at her.

'Good bone, and strong hindquarters,' Vagrian said appreciatively and when Petra gave him an approving glance, left his assessment at that. He was going to have to be very careful in this household, even in its stables. He must certainly remember that every one of the Lyons were T-1s. He wondered if such ratings extended to the animals. He would try to make friends with at least one of the Coon cats. They were an expensive import on Altair so he had little direct experience with the breed. Canines were another matter since he'd used dogs in hunts. He wondered how close to canines the Darbuls were.

'So what are our duties now?' he asked Petra.

'Oh, we just check to be sure their water bowls haven't clogged, and clear out droppings. We already checked for prods or scratches. We have to be careful about them here on Iota. Lots of odd stuff even the horses born here can't handle. There's the medical kit.' She pointed to the green box on the wall. 'Everything's marked in case you need to use something and no-one's here to help. Though we always hunt in pairs at least.'

'Wise,' he said. 'So let's clean the boxes.'

Petra went to an elongated object, held by brackets to the wall at the entrance, and she pointed to a similar affair on the other side. 'Xexo did 'em and these vacuum brooms save so much trouble. Try to lift only the droppings. Too many shavings mean you gotta empty more often.'

Vagrian had not seen such a handy device before, since Altair tended to use old-fashioned methods on its farms. However, following Petra's advice, they had cleaned up the droppings in a fraction of the time such a task usually took. Then she showed him where to empty the now filled containers: a large tank.

'It processes the manure for use in agriculture,' she said, deftly handling the transfer. Having watched closely, Vagrian repeated the process. 'Hey, you're good,' she declared approvingly. 'Do it wrong and it's all over you.'

'I'm doing my best to make a good first impression,' Vagrian said.

'Oh, you're doing all right,' she said so airily that Vagrian once more tightened his guard. 'Oh, don't be so silly. Nobody here imposes even if we are T-1s. It's such bad manners. Just keep on my mother's good side,' she added in a whisper. 'That should be easy for you.' And with that cryptic remark, she motioned for him to replace the gadget on the wall.

Although the minor job he had just completed with Petra had required very little effort, he felt tired as he climbed the steps back up to the house.

'You look all in,' the girl said, cocking her head up to him as he held the door open for her. She frowned. 'If you got here late afternoon, it'd've been 22.00 hours at Blundell. You'd better get to bed. Tomorrow you'll be initiated into transporting big daddies and they're something else again.'

Damia appeared in the hall. 'I apologize for forgetting the time difference, Vagrian. And all of us handle the big daddies first thing when we're well rested. Sleep well.'

Though the dismissal was kindly meant and Vagrian could not deny that he was tired, he wasn't too pleased to be sent to bed like an adolescent who wouldn't admit to fatigue.

The next morning, after an excellent breakfast, he joined Damia and Afra in Iota Aurigae's Tower. If the views from the house had been splendid, the positioning of the Tower in a gap of the mountains gave breathtaking panoramas of the foothills that culminated in an immense range of snow-capped crests and endless ridges.

As they entered the facility, Keylarion, at her workstation, gave them a good morning and turned back to the screens showing the big daddies they would shortly send on their way. The throb of generators pulsed through the floor of the building as Vagrian followed Damia and Afra up the stairs to where three couches were centred, wall-mounted screens mirroring those at Keylarion's desk. Several smaller couches had been pushed back against the outer wall. The one on the left that Damia pointed out to him was brand-new, while the ones onto which the Prime and Afra settled showed years of use and frequent repairs.

Vagrian was not the least nervous once he settled onto the couch that fitted him as if it had been custom-made for his tall, wide frame.

'What's first, Keylarion?' Damia asked. One of the screens brightened. 'Maltese Cross, huh?' She turned to her left, to Vagrian. 'You have been trained in Merge techniques, haven't you?'

'Of course,' he said, and tightened his inner shields.

'Let Afra take you in. And relax!'

He felt the gentle push of Afra's mind against his and did manage not to resist. He was still unsure of Merging despite the practice sessions at Blundell. But this was almost effortless and he could relax. And did. Then felt the incredible strength of Damia joining and picking up the existing Merge. Afra increased and drew him to a higher level. An unexpected excitement began deep inside him to respond to the 'draw' on his Talent.

*Easy, Vagrian,* Damia said, *now follow my lead to our target. We'll need your heft . . . DAVID, coming your way . . . at top speed! NOW!*

As if he were part of the drone they were manipulating, Vagrian felt its dead weight, felt the Merge lifting it with incredible ease and then shift it until he, within the Merge, felt the contact of another Merge, taking the drone the rest of the way to Betelgeuse.

He was aware then of the generators, dropping from the height at which they had assisted the gestalt of mind and direction.

*Well done, Vagrian,* Damia said, grinning at him. *Keep in mind we've five more of these brutes to shove. Allow me to draw the heft as I need it. Don't anticipate. It'll take even you a little time to feel the needs of a Merge.*

137

The second screen brightened with the second target. 'Trefoil Mine, this time, and then back to Maltese Cross.'

Afra was still in Merge with him and Vagrian had to appreciate the experienced delicacy of the other T-2's touch. But then, the man had decades of practice, first with the Rowan at Callisto Station and the twenty-six or more years with his wife. No matter, the Capellan's deftness was remarkable and most certainly did not give Vagrian any sense of violation or intrusion. He had thought that most Merges occurred with the focus mind initiating the process, then including the others involved.

*Damia's strong even for a Prime,* was Afra's discreet remark. *Especially working with our children, I could lead them into Merge.*

*Ready?* Damia asked.

*Ready.*

*When you are,* said another male voice that must be David of Betelgeuse. *Who've you got throwing today? Certainly not Petra and Ewain.*

*Vagrian Beliakin,* Damia said. *ARE you ready, David?*

*Quite!*

This time Vagrian was ready for the sensation and the weight and, remembering not to anticipate, this thrust was, indeed, easier.

By the sixth and final 'portation, Vagrian knew he had worked hard. There was sweat on his forehead from the mental and physical effort. He was reassured to notice Afra mopping his forehead and that there was a glow of perspiration on Damia's composed and beautiful face.

Keylarion came up the steps with a tray of tall drinks, handing each of them one. She grinned at Vagrian.

'I see you survived to tell the tale,' she said. 'Didn't even have the generators at max, either. Xexo's going to love having you here.'

He was debating a retort when Keylarion turned to Damia. 'Some incoming scheduled in half an hour. OK?'

'You bet,' Damia said, tipping her glass at Vagrian. 'We could damn well push to the Magellanic Cloud with this one assisting.'

'All in a day's work,' he said, taking refuge in a trite reply because he hadn't expected such approval. After all, she had had to tell him to exercise restraint. And she was Laria's *mother?* Would he have made such a balls of it at Clarf if Damia had been the Tower Prime?

'Work's not over yet,' she said teasingly and took a long drink.

He did, too, knowing that the stimulant would restore the energy those heists had taken, even if he didn't feel them . . . yet.

He concluded his first day's work at Iota Aurigae Tower well pleased with himself and this assignment. This was a real challenge for any Talent and, for the first time, he felt he had used his mental muscles since he discovered he had Talent. It was also the first time he had not had a nightmarish flash of that mudslide. He was glad that little reminder was receding. He'd been one of the senior Wardens of a large game preserve on Altair, accompanying a big group of hunters, and he had managed to include in their number his current female companion. Alcibaca had claimed an enthusiastic interest in hunting: feigned, he suspected, in an effort to capture his attention. For once, his suspicions were false. She'd kept up with him and the others whom he had escorted on a regular basis. Without a murmur of complaint, she'd done her share of camping chores and had bagged three of the largest beartards, skinned and dressed down the meat properly.

They were on the fourth day of the week, and its third rainy one, when he led them, carefully, up a steep slope to a narrow valley he knew was the home of a large enough 'bear' clan which should be culled. He had his charges spread out across the slope since he was well aware of the dangers of mudslides in these hills. Between keeping an appreciative eye on the rear view Alcibaca presented and the other on the weakest of his group, he did not see three of them closing up, ahead of him. Nor did he see the avian that one of the hunters, who ought to have known better, fired at. The sharp crack was all that was needed to set the treacherous ground moving.

139

The three men had time to leap to the far side, clinging to the nearest saplings and bushes, but the slide, once it started, picked up momentum in an awesome inexorable cataract of moving mud, heading right at the rest of the hunting party. Horrified, Vagrian had kept his wits, seeing that there was one chance to protect himself and his group. The slide was heading towards a granite outcropping. If there was only a way to *push* the slide to the opposite side of that, instead of over it, the mud would head harmlessly into the valley below. With every ounce of body language, he valiantly pushed the bulging rippling head of the slide and, when it actually did pass on the far side of the rock, he fell to his knees, gripping his head against the most appalling blinding headache he'd ever experienced.

Alcibaca and one of the executives had the good sense to call in their position and airlift the hunting party out – all of them. The one who had fired without checking with him was served with a lifetime ban at that preserve. He had been interviewed by a T-4 and the outcome was sufficient to alter the course of his life. His one regret for the precipitous way in which he was 'ported to Blundell for further assessment was that he hadn't been able to persuade Alcibaca to accompany him. She had expressed gratitude for saving her life in a time-honoured fashion and he would miss her.

# CHAPTER SEVEN

Laria's delight in having her sisters coming was sufficient for her to be the one to open their personnel carrier in the dawn cool of Clarf. She hugged them both, introduced them and their 'Dinis to those doing the Yard duty.

All of a sudden, Morag pulled out of her sister's embrace and, her jaw working in astonishment, pointed skyward. 'What's sparkling up there? Or is it my imagination?' She squinted towards the distant, but visible, shining point. 'Or do you have a morning star I didn't know about?'

'Oh, that,' Laria said dismissively, without bothering to look up. 'That's a Hiver Sphere!'

Kaltia's eyes widened with some apprehension as she, too, peered at the sparkling spot.

'It's empty, though occasionally Mrdinis go up to prowl around for the fun of it,' Laria said. 'That's the one Captain Klml brought back as a trophy for its colour. Then every other 'Dini world had to hijack one to maintain the honour of their colours.'

Morag, eyes still on the Sphere, hanging like a malignant metal moon in the morning sky, shook her head. 'Thing still looks dangerous.' Then she wiped the beads of perspiration that, despite the relative cool of very early morning, oozed out of her pores.

'Wouldn't think that would have bothered you, Morag,' Laria said, somewhat concerned.

'It's not the Sphere that made me break out in sweat. It's what you call climate here.'

'Why, it's cool right now,' Laria replied.

'You call this COOL?' Morag demanded.

'All is relative,' Laria said, grinning. 'You'll gradually get acclimated and I don't expect you'll want to go out much at first but the Tower's set to Iota temperatures. Don't worry about the duffels. The 'Dinis'll bring them in.'

Laria paused only long enough to 'port the personnel carrier into the storage shed where its interior wouldn't heat up when the full sun appeared. Then she turned both girls, who were still staring up at the Sphere, firmly towards the Tower as eight 'Dinis argued over who was to carry which duffel.

EACH OF YOU GRAB ONE END. THEN CART THEM TO ROOMS 3 AND 4, WILL YOU PLEASE? Laria told them so she could introduce her sisters to her Tower crew.

'You know Kincaid, of course,' she said, 'Lionasha here is our expediter and Vanteer our engineer. And that's all of us, bar the 'Dinis. We've got four off in hibernation – mine and Kincaid's – but they're about due to come home.'

Lionasha hugged both girls, Van treated them to a bow and a kiss on their hands, grinning mischievously when Morag gave him a mock scowl and Kaltia pretended to swoon at such courtesy. Standing slightly to one side of the others, Kincaid appeared uncertain as to what form his greeting should take but Morag dragged him down by the shoulder and kissed his cheek, laughing at his startled expression.

'Missed you hunting with us, Kincaid,' she said, winking at him.

Kaltia, less the hoyden, extended her hand and when he took it, folded her other hand over for a closer contact. She grinned up at him.

'My sister hasn't worked you to death then . . .'

142

'Not yet . . .' Kincaid added with a mock grimace. 'But your presence will make my demise much less likely. I couldn't believe it when Laria said your mother had relented.'

'I thought it was Grandfather's idea?' Morag said, looking from Kincaid to Laria.

'His idea, but Mother had to agree to parting with you,' Laria said, linking an arm about both shoulders and hugging them into her. 'Oh, but it's good to have family here. You may, once you've got accustomed to Clarf, wish to take an apartment together in the Human Compound because there's a lot more going on there than here. I've asked for another ground car since I know,' and she cocked a finger at Morag, 'that Dad passed you for driving years before he let me solo.'

'Had to,' Morag said with a grin.

'We can settle in later. We came here to work,' Kaltia said, rubbing her hands together with a roll of her eyes.

'You will,' Lionasha said, gesturing to the load of disks. 'We've some heavy drone freighters to go . . .'

'Ah, piffle,' said Morag, with a toss of her heavy dark hair, the silvered lock that was the family's trademark falling neatly down the centre of her tresses. 'We've done big daddy ore-drones until it's second nature.'

'Why else do you think you're here?' Vanteer remarked dryly but he was grinning at the ebullience of the sisters which had lightened the semi-gloom emanating from Laria since she'd 'ported the unwanted T-2 back to Blundell. Surprised as he had been at Laria's precipitous removal of Yoshuk's brother, he had been intensely grateful. Vanteer had just a touch of prescience in his Talent and warning ripples had gone down his spine the moment the man had entered the Tower. Morag and Kaltia, by their very presence, eagerness to work and delight in being able to help their sister, had dispelled the last of that unpleasantness. He knew that Kincaid had visited the Lyon home on Iota Aurigae and both girls were obviously glad to renew the acquaintance. The nebulous worries that he recently sensed in the Tower dissipated in the giggles of two more Lyons. 'Is there anyone left at home?' he added.

143

'Sure, Ewain and Petra,' Kaltia said and dismissed them with a wave, 'but they're still too young so Grandfather sent in a strong kinetic T-2 to help Mother and Dad.'

'Really?' Kincaid said to break a stunned silence, since all the adults in the Tower had a good idea just who that T-2 could be.

'We had to leave but he's supposed to have more than enough heft for the big daddies. And Mom and Dad will break him in properly.'

'Yes,' Laria said, an odd look on her face, 'I'm sure that they will.'

Lionasha suddenly started sorting disks, Vanteer retreated to the generators and, if Morag caught some undercurrent, Laria distracted them by urging her sisters to follow her to their quarters.

'We won't really have much time before the Tower's busy, but as near as I can remember, you'd've left home at about nine thirty?'

'On the nose, sis, or do we have to call you Prime?' Kaltia said.

'Have you ever called Mother Prime?' Laria retorted, chuckling.

'Only Grandmother,' Morag said pertly.

'Oh, but I AM glad to have you here!' Laria repeated.

'And we're glad to be allowed out,' Morag said, 'but that sun is incredible!'

'You brought sunblock, Kaltia?' Laria asked anxiously.

'Half of what I brought IS sunblock,' Kaltia replied sourly. 'I shall just have to be the night bird.'

They all heard the unmistakable sound of generators turning over and speeding up.

'I don't think there's time now for more than a quick look into your rooms,' Laria said, sliding open a door on one side of the hall and pointing to the one just opposite it. 'See which one your duffels are in, wash your faces or whatever but come on back to the Tower. Today'll be so *easy*.'

And it was, despite six hefty drones loaded with machinery and spare parts, two large passenger vehicles, and the usual

144

incoming shower of message tubes. That caused Morag the most astonishment.

'It's raining tubes out there,' she cried, watching the canisters falling into and all around the cradle.

'We could use something else,' Kaltia said. 'Like a big round bin. They're too short to land in a cradle and too many to stack neatly.'

*Bins are a great idea,* Lionasha said. *Why couldn't we think of that?*

*Because we've been too busy catching,* Laria said with a note of exasperation.

*New brooms sweep clean,* Kincaid said, grinning at the girls.

*Or a ramp to slide them into a big enough enclosure so it doesn't matter how many come in at once,* Morag suggested, projecting the image of such a device.

*Roll 'em in like bowls in an alley,* Vanteer said. *Good notion. Let's get the 'Dinis on it. They'll know where to get the stuff we'd need.*

*And we thought the mining companies got lots of messages!* Morag exclaimed, remaining in the Mind Merge but at the same time 'porting loose message tubes into an orderly pile. *How long's this been going on?*

*Since Talavera,* Laria said. *We've one more crate . . . easy does it! It's fragile.*

The crate, the machinery inside it visible through the slates of its carrier, landed without so much as a bump.

*What's the waybill on that, Lio?* Kincaid asked.

*A return to the FCR Works at Fl. Malfunction. Needs recalibration.*

*Well, let's put it in the shed, out of the way, then, until FCR tells us it's ready to receive it,* Laria said. *They'll have to reschedule to take on repair work.*

'That's the lot for the morning,' Lionasha said. 'Be right up.'

Morag stretched, arms above her head, toes pointing out, and Kaltia turned on her side and assumed a brief foetal position – each relaxing in a different fashion. Kincaid looked casually over at Laria. As deftly as he could as the next in line to Laria in the Mind Merge, he'd drawn more heavily on the vibrant young strength of the girls, knowing they'd have enough experience to ease some of the burden that fell to the Prime.

She turned her head slowly towards him and cocked her finger at him, letting him know that she was well aware of what he'd been doing. She was not, apparently, going to reprimand him.

'That was good work, kids,' she said as she heard Lionasha coming up the steps with the restorative beverage.

Kaltia took a long swallow, her eyes widening with pleasure at the taste. 'Hey, where does this come from?'

'The ever-tropical planet of Clarf,' Laria said. 'There are some advantages to it and this is one of the nicest ways to drink replacement electrolytes. Of course, the 'Dinis prefer lemonade but they're not shifting tons about.'

'Do they grow citrus fruits on Clarf now?' Morag asked, licking her lips to be sure she'd got all the liquid.

'A varietal grows here but it's Earth lemonade they adore,' Laria said. 'Now, we all take a siesta at this time of day, especially newcomers.'

'Why? We haven't been outside or anything?' Morag said.

'I'm conserving your energies for the afternoon session which can be heavier,' Laria said, swinging her legs to the side of her couch before she finished her drink. 'Besides, you should get settled into your rooms.'

Sliding from their couches, the girls went down the steps where Morag halted, eyes widening at the stacks on Lionasha's desk.

'Hey, I can help with that. I used to do it on Iota and you've far too many. May I?' she said, already finding a chair to draw up to the littered desk.

'I really would appreciate the help. It's all those tubes!' And the word came out with an emphasis short of resignation.

'Vanteer? Do you think we could rig some sort of a ramp to channel the tubes into stacks?' Kaltia said, stepping down into engineering as he began to drop generator power to idle.

He handed her a stylus and a pad. 'Go to it, gal.'

'That's what this Tower has needed,' Kincaid remarked, offering a hand to Laria. 'Young eager blood! A transfusion for us weary weight-lifters.'

'I've these sorted, Lio,' Morag was saying. 'Now how do I contact the recipients?'

'That,' and Lionasha took the pile from Morag, 'is where our 'Dinis assist. Here's another set. Fraggit, but I'm glad you read 'Dini that fast. I still have to puzzle. Fig, Sil, Nim and Dig,' and she beckoned the 'Dinis over, 'as soon as you've got these done, you can show Kev, Su, Dar and Sim how we arrange them for collection. THEN you may take the girls' 'Dinis out for a look round.'

GOOD, GOOD. WE DO FAST, and Fig, who was organizing things in the absence of Tip and Nil, handed out the sorted files. The experienced 'Dinis picked up com units from the rack and, as they dialled the appropriate numbers, explained to the newcomers how distribution was handled. Fig was as good as its boast and within half the time it usually took, thanks to Morag's deft help with Lionasha, the 'Dinis went out of the Tower to rack the message tubes where they could be collected.

WE'RE DONE, WE'RE DONE. WE GO. BACK LATER, Sil announced, opening the door just wide enough to lean its head inside and deliver the message.

'Wow,' exclaimed Lionasha, looking with deep relief at the clear workspace. 'No wonder Lyons are the Primes of choice,' she added, grinning at Morag.

'Well, we're still learning, you know,' Morag said with such modesty that Laria, overhearing, laughed. 'Honest, sis. There's a lot more in such a busy Tower as Clarf than there ever was at home, for all the big daddies we had to heave.'

'What do you think about a set-up like this, Laria?' Vanteer asked, showing both the Prime and Kincaid the sketchpad. 'This'd be easier to construct . . .' and then the stylus tapped the third drawing, 'but this might be more efficient. And dead easy to put up. Could have one done by morning, I think. I know Lvlr can get us the materials and have them here by dark. Might even get it to give us the benefit of its expertise. Lev's done some bits and pieces for us before now.'

'Then you'll keep us?' Morag asked, eyes round and mocking.

'You just bet we will!' Laria and Lionasha chorused and they all burst out laughing.

*Your report and the materials collected on the surface are still being analysed,* Jeff told Thian on the *Washington.* His mental chuckle echoed in his grandson's mind. *I am reliably led to believe by no less a personage than High Councillor Gktmglnt that the planet you've so adroitly investigated is completely a-typical of the Hiver colonies and has confounded all the Mrdini experts. Ours, as well, despite the fact that we may not have had as much experience with the species as the 'Dinis.*

*What's the gist, Grandfather? The enbees here will want details.*

*When such are formulated, a copious report will be sent. Right now confusion reigns. 1) Your Hivers do not appear to have sent out any Spheres, since you say there has been little use of the available ore deposits and the Sphere they used to arrive there is deteriorating. 2) The queens are a third smaller than our specimen at Heinlein Base. 3) Eighty installations on a planet that size are unusually few since Xh-33 had ten times that many and, to judge by the age of their oldest Sphere . . . fragments have been analysed . . . Xh-33 is a much younger settlement. 4) The inactive workers you found in the stable, holding place, whatever, are also much smaller than usual. 5) According to Mrdinis, Hivers* always *send off excess queens.*

*If there are no excess queens?*

*Aye, there's the rub, Thian. There should be and there aren't. Yet that colony is by far the oldest – judging by the analysis of the Sphere fragments – it should have sent off colonies in keeping with the currently understood Hive patterns.*

*So, what do you wish us to do now?*

*Check your findings by infiltrating at least ten of the other queen hives and more GC readings. The pheromones you got from the one queen's quarters are not at all what emanates from the Heinlein queen. Get us more soil samples from as many cultivated fields as possible near existing hives for cross-check-*

148

*ing. And as a treat, snag us samples of the various worker types. If, as you've discovered, they're dormant or resting or whatever it is that keeps them immobile until needed, that shouldn't be difficult or expose a team to queenly retribution. It would, however, be very interesting if the queens did respond in some fashion to . . . ah . . . losing some of their working types.*

Thian couldn't help but chuckle at his grandfather's droll tone.

'Let us in on the joke, will you, Thian?' Admiral Ashiant asked dryly.

When Thian had recited exactly what his grandfather had reported, Ashiant guffawed.

'Well, frankly, I don't see that we'd have any trouble absconding with a few specimens.'

*The experts want several of each from different installations,* Jeff Raven said, having been able to hear the admiral's response through the link with his grandson.

'Don't want much, do they?' Ashiant said with a sniff. 'I suppose the experts'll want some of the queens' attendants, too, for comparison's sake.'

*Yes, indeed. But not if it puts teams at risk.*

'I shouldn't indulge myself with whimsical remarks in your presence,' Ashiant said.

*Who's to know what risk is involved until we try it, Grandfather?* Thian also vocalized that query. *We will neutralize the smell of us, though, since odour does seem to get through their chitinous skulls.*

*Inform the admiral that's a splendid idea, to get queens' attendants, too* was Earth Prime's response. *And might prove a salient factor in figuring out this a-typical situation.* Thian obeyed.

'Humph,' said Ashiant, looking pleased. 'It is an oddity, to be sure, but how that can help us reduce the threat of Hivers in general is beyond me. We'll still need to identify any, and every, planet they occupy and somehow render them unable to colonize.'

*Inform the admiral that I could wish his view was more widely held.* Again Thian relayed the message.

'Are the militant still asking for species annihilation?'

149

Ashiant asked, his bushy eyebrows raised in dismay.

*With growing fervour. The High Council remains unanimously in favour of some solution that does not include genocide. The militant annihilationists refuse to be pacified by planetary containment and insist that the queens would only find some other way to 'terrorize occupied space'. Odd that you, Admiral, are more of a pacifist.*

'As Admiral of the first Star League[1] Fleet that managed to destroy an enemy without sustaining casualties of our own,' Ashiant replied when Thian conveyed that information, 'I would prefer to keep that record. Going up against a *planet* of belligerent Hiver armies might ruin such a worthy aspiration.'

'If you'll pardon my intrusion, Admiral,' Thian said, speaking for himself. 'They didn't even know we were in the queen's inner hive. How would they recognize a punitive force if they refuse to "see" us when we were patently present? The only objects they appear to recognize as a threat are other spaceships. Even one of their own Spheres, as Xh-33 proved to us.'

'Ah, but an attack launched on their installations would surely result in some reaction,' Ashiant said. 'You identified a great quantity as well as variety of creatures in the underground Hives.'

'None of them armed with anything but farm tools and a lot of limbs,' Thian said.

*History is full of examples of very poorly armed insurgents managing incredible victories over much stronger better-armed foes,* Jeff said. *However, we do have the advantage of being able to 'port specimens into a secure container, especially if you can replicate the environments of their Hive accommodations to prevent their being aware they've been moved.*

*It's the sting-pzzt we'd have to endure that bothers me, Grandfather,* Thian said and gave a shudder at the thought of proximity to such a concentration of that uncomfortable Hiver emanation despite the muffling the body armour provided. Eighteen Hives to visit? That first one had been enough.

1 The Nine Star League of the original yarns had increased its membership and is now referred to as Star League.

150

*Only need to handle them long enough to get them in a personnel carrier to 'port 'em back.*

*Where?*

*Offhand I'd say Heinlein Base. There are other facilities within that Base, well separated from where the queen is. Of course, if you can acquire enough, I'm certain there are enough eager xenbees elsewhere in the Star League desperate to check their theories about the creatures.*

*Thank you, Grandfather, for this interesting and challenging assignment.*

*Cheeky boy,* was the retort but Thian sensed only Jeff Raven's amusement in his use of the Rowan's favourite epithet.


As Thian suspected, far too many scientists back on Star League Worlds and Mrdini home planets were eager to examine live specimens of the different hive workers.

*Will I be expected to fill that order list, Grandfather? It'd practically depopulate the planet.*

*Certainly not,* Jeff replied. *Both Gktmglnt and Admiral Mekturian reaffirmed the original orders. There may be other Hive planets where more specimens can be gleaned . . . that is, if the militants calm down. Heinlein Base is out and another, less obvious destination is being considered. I'd limit those who know about this operation.*

*Even on the* Washington? Thian was surprised.

*Especially on the* Washington. *We have reason to believe that the militants managed to get a few aboard despite our precautions.*

When Thian discussed his order with Clancy, Gravy and Commander Kloo, Semirame immediately confirmed Earth Prime's suspicions.

'How did that happen? I thought security checked everyone on board.'

'There's been some scuttlebutt,' Rame said with a shrug. 'Sleepers or those who were halfway in agreement anyhow.'

'After all we DID?' Thian found himself appalled at such

151

intransigence. He'd achieved far more than his original brief by removing eight Spheres with no Fleet casualties.

Semirame gave him a sympathetic smile. 'You remember the reaction we had at Phobos Base when we wanted to import the queen to show us how to start up a Sphere? Well, Commander Baldwin may be an asshole, but he's heading a long line of 'em. Then, too, Day heard some scuttlebutt she wasn't too happy with. Couldn't identify the speakers 'cos she was in the messhall. About why didn't we just use one of the little bombs in every installation and end the problem for ever, and wasn't that why the *Washington* was out here?'

'I think I check everyone we do decide to use on this mission,' Thian said.

Clancy gave him a hard stare. Probing without the permission of the individual was one of the most stringent Talent prohibitions.

'Not when it's for security purposes, Clancy. Even the admiral would agree on those grounds,' Kloo said, siding with Thian. 'Especially if the High Council finds this planet a-typical. Looks pretty typical to me,' she added with a grin.

So, disliking the necessity, Thian did a quick probe of those on the list of possible team members that Kloo submitted. He deleted nine names, two of which Gravy had already had doubts about. One that he was happy to discover unbiased was a T-7 petty officer who had been along on the reconnaissance of the other installations. Hazur Adi had automatically taken soil readings that he said would be no trouble to duplicate, especially if they managed to grab some from each holding cavern to replicate the dominant odour.

'Mostly the right temperature is what keeps them dormant until the queen activates them,' Hazur said when he sat in on the second briefing session. 'Love to know how she does that.'

'There has to be some communication between her and her workers,' Lea Day said as she often did. 'Even if it's on no frequency we can hear/identify. One thing, Prime, I thought I'd better ask . . . if you'd planned to stash them on board until you know where they're to be 'ported?'

Thian looked at her for a moment, snapped his fingers, and

152

dramatically slapped his hand against his forehead. 'That damned sting-pzzt'll be obvious to anyone as low as T-9.' Then he groaned.

'There's one place we could use wouldn't reach anyone,' Lea said with a broad grin on her face.

'You got me, Chief. Where?' Thian asked.

'Gee, sir, you surprise me,' the CPO said, savouring the moment for a beat. 'On board that old Sphere, a'course. As I remember the report, it wouldn't be hard to repair one of the boat bays the Hivers use for their scout-ships. Send over enough oxygen, park the carriers inside and no sting-pzzt to clue even a lamebrain T-9 to what we're about. The critters'd be safe. More ways than one.'

Because it was Lea's idea, Thian ordered her and Gravy, who was immediately brought into the project as well as Hazur who would do the environmental adaptations, to accompany him in spacesuits to the long-inoperative Sphere that circled the a-typical planet. Clancy and Semirame 'ported ahead the supplies. In the weightlessness of the aged Sphere, it was relatively easy, if tedious, to seal the least damaged of the boat bays and pump in the necessary oxygen. Once the area was airtight and no loss of oxygen visible in space from the *Washington,* the medium-sized drones which would accommodate the captive Hivers were 'ported in for Hazur to 'doctor' to approximate the underground accommodations from which they'd be shanghaied. Three nights later, when Thian, Lea Day and Hazur Adi had recovered from that expedition and their other preparations were complete, Thian initiated the raids.

He kept each infiltration to the most effective minimum team so that Human odours would not alert the queens. They'd been careful to eliminate any new-plastic stink from the body armour. They'd also smeared their gear with dirt from the worn tracks that led underground. On two occasions they were able to make off with workers returning at twilight from cultivation duties. Though they did 'remove' some of the varieties tending the queens, this set off an unexpected agitation in the queen so deprived. Since they had installed

153

monitors in each of the queens' quarters, they watched anxiously to see what would happen, ready to replace any or all of the variants rather than incite the queens to action. After a period in which Kloo said she was sure one queen counted up her attendants one by one, the queen had extracted an egg from one of the tubes of embryos and evidently prepared the egg to replicate the missing attendant.

It took five nights to complete the project which Thian code-named 'Shanghai', complete with soil and a replication of the food pellets found in the various underground caverns.

'They'll never even know they're not at home,' Hazur Adi said with an understandable pride in having completed his part of 'Shanghai'. Monitors within the drones indicated that all the captives remained in a passive state.

Somehow word of the importation of 'hordes of Hive creatures' for scientific purposes set off a reaction that proved just how strong the militant annhilationists were. The very notion that Hive creatures would become laboratory specimens on 'civilized' planets turned many of those as yet undecided into fierce opponents to the prospect. Human militants took full advantage of the panic and fear, agitating in every capital city of the Human-occupied worlds against such an 'invasion'.

Heinlein Base was ringed by private yachts, orbiting just beyond the legal limit and obviously determined to prevent the landing of any of the 'deadly' specimens. Another useless display of protest, since anyone who thought twice would have realized that Talent could 'port the objectionable creatures anywhere without alerting the sentinel craft.

Commander Baldwin had his revenge on the Talents on the Phobos Base Project who had started up the intact Sphere. He reminded them that the biggest danger came from Talents who were 'minions' of the High Council and determined to subvert the will of the Majority. Blundell's answer was a calm restatement that they were a-political and that it was impossible to subvert Talent to purposes other than those described in their Charter. That this happened to include the transportation of approved carriers of all types and telepathing of any messages, overt or covert, was not open for discussion or for intervention. Any attempt to interfere with the operation of FT&T would result in the closure of every Tower and the facilities on which all interstellar trade depended. Further, any attempt to interfere with Talents of any grade could result in stoppages in the locality of the interference.

There were, of course, renewals of the frequent accusations of the monopoly of FT&T. The response did remind the public in general and dissidents in particular that there were, indeed, other ways of transporting goods and messages, even if these methods required considerably more time and considerably more Human effort. Hence FT&T was not a monopoly, merely the best and most effective method currently available.

The Mrdinis, showing amusement at these demonstrations of Human intransigence, contacted Gktmglnt who quietly informed Earth Prime that the best possible place to install the specimens would be in the various captured and intact Spheres, in geo-synchronous orbits about the main 'Dini planets. Quarters and laboratories could be arranged to accommodate those Human scientists who wished to join the Mrdini specialists in the evaluation of the species.

*So when can we 'port these dangerous, vicious, creatures to an 'unknown' destination?* Thian asked his grandfather.

'I'll handle the security, Thian,' Admiral Ashiant said. 'Major Gefferny has uncovered a ring of sympathizers – some of those we'd already suspected of militant tendencies. You'd best get on with "Shanghai" as unobtrusively as possible.'

'We've already "shanghaied", sir,' Thian said. He ignored his grandfather's delighted guffaw.

'You have?' Ashiant blinked in astonishment. Thian also did not mention that Earth Prime was bellowing with laughter at his grandson's efficiency.

'In fact, sir, if I may be bold enough to suggest it,' Thian went on, 'it might put a stop to the unrest on board as well as those demonstrations if you leave this orbit and get on with the Search.'

Ashiant grumphed, jutted out his chin belligerently before

155

replying. 'What? And give those militants the satisfaction of thinking they won this round?'

'Since they haven't, sir,' Thian replied with understandable amusement, 'why not let them deceive themselves? It'd make it that much easier for the scientific work to proceed without interference.'

'They can't be on board. Can they? Where that sting-pzzt you tell me about could be detected?'

'No, sir,' Thian said, shaking his head, noticing that Gravy, Clancy and Semirame were having trouble stifling their amusement at having confounded the admiral.

'Are you going to tell me, young Thian?'

'I'd've thought you'd've figured that out, sir,' and Thian turned his head slightly in the direction of the planet they were orbiting. The abandoned Sphere was just in sight.

Ashiant began to nod his head. 'In plain sight, so to speak. Well done, Prime Lyon. Well done all,' he included Clancy, Gravy and Commander Kloo. Then he pounced. 'How'd you manage transfers without it showing up on generator use?'

'Didn't need to use gestalt, Admiral,' Thian said, 'not with these three and the others we tagged for the job. We were very cautious, too. By the way, if you could see your way clear to a commendation, Petty Officer Hazur Adi was of inestimable assistance and deserves one.'

'I'll speak to my flag captain . . . without specifics.'

'Well, *she's* safe,' Thian said, since he knew Captain Ailsah Vandermeer from his time aboard Ashiant's first ship.

'She'd better be,' was Ashiant's unequivocal reply. 'Well done, people. Well done. Only . . . when are they leaving . . . where they are?'

Jeff Raven then confided the co-ordinates of the ultimate destinations to Thian.

'Grandfather has informed me, sir, so we'll just wait until we're underway again when the fluctuations of the generators will be less noticeable and the 'port can be effected with the least possibility of anyone noticing it.'

Ashiant chuckled all the way out of the Talents' lounge until the door slid shut.

Then Gravy and Semirame could indulge in the howls of laughter they had been holding back. Clancy was grinning from ear to ear at their notable success.

'And Baldwin can go . . .' Semirame began and then clamped her mouth shut, long habit interfering with her yearning to castigate a senior officer. Even one who richly deserved it.

'You know, after seeing that ring of yachts around Heinlein Base and some of the nastier militant demos, is there any chance some idiot might try to breach Blundell?' Clancy asked soberly.

'Sure, if they want to stop all interstellar transport.'

'I meant, more personally, against Jeff Raven?'

Thian seemed to consider this and then, so abruptly that he was a blur of motion, he launched himself at Clancy who instantly 'ported himself aside. Thian spread both hands at the success of his demonstration and walked back to his seat.

'Unlikely. And Clancy's just a T-2. With good instincts, I might add,' Thian said. 'Grandfather's guarded. So's Callisto Base and every single Tower FT&T operating. Even if all the lower Ts became disaffected, some of it would leak to a higher rank and they'd be . . .'

'What do Talents do to those who transgress?' Gravy asked when Thian didn't go on.

'I haven't heard of any . . . reprimands,' Thian said, 'but, in the early days of Talent, those who didn't obey the tenets of Henry Darrow or subsequent Talent leaders got . . . mind-locked.'

'They got their minds burned,' Clancy corrected coldly.

Gravy shuddered, hugging her arms. Semirame nodded, her agreement with such a dire punishment apparent.

'That's why it's so imperative to find Talents young and train them up so they can't be subverted,' Thian added with a sigh, looking out the porthole. 'Well, we're not the only ones who haven't wasted time,' he said, pointing. The Sphere was no longer visible and the view of the starscape was altering slowly.

Being nearer, Semirame flipped on the panel that showed the helm's manoeuvres.

'We are definitely leaving orbit,' she said with satisfaction. 'How soon can we 'port the Hivers?'

'Show the engineering board, will you, Rame?' Thian asked, rising and going to his couch. 'I'll just warn Grandfather to tell the Spheres to be ready for their new inmates.'

'Nine carriers are going to make some generator noise,' Clancy said, sliding onto his couch just as Semirame got to hers. Gravy stretched out in her lounge chair.

'Do 'em one at a time. Two a couple of times, Grandfather is telling me. Just merge with me. Three, two, one . . .'

The Merge was completed with the ease of long practice. Semirame raised one hand, eyes on the engineering board.

*We won't need much push,* Thian told the others in his mind. *Here's the first pair . . . any variation, Rame?*

*None that isn't consistent with our breaking orbit.*

*A pair to the next Sphere at Sef. Rame?*

*No problem.*

It took only ten minutes to despatch the carriers, the last one the longest since the *Washington* was picking up speed with every passing moment.

'She's one sweet ship,' Semirame remarked with a sigh of understandable pride.

Thian lay still on his couch much longer than the others and only seemed to rouse himself when Gravy brought him the restorative drink. She sat down beside him on space he instantly made for her slim self.

*What troubles you, Thi?*

*That's only the first occupied planet, Gravy. Are we going to have trouble with every one we find?*

*Probably,* being candid since she had no reason to hide her thoughts from him.

*What if they want specimens from every other Hiver planet?* Thian let the others in on his quandary.

*It's likely they will,* Semirame said, not at all concerned. *We did it successfully this time. We can probably manage again.*

*Not if the local Sphere is occupied.*

*Let's worry about that when, as or if it happens, Thian,* Semirame said.

158

*We've given the experts enough to chew on . . .* Clancy hastily added, *metaphorically speaking, of course.*

Thian swung his legs over the couch, keeping as close to Gravy as his altered position allowed. *I want us to check every Talent, major and minor, on this ship and see who's affected by the militants. I want to be able to trust ALL of them, not just a few.*

Semirame regarded him, her expression almost sad. *We can't check every Talent in the entire Fleet, Thian.*

*I'm more concerned with the morale of those on this one, since it's the flagship.*

*And what do we do to the ones we already know are suspect?* Gravy asked, her expression blank.

*There's a way . . . a safe one . . . of suppressing the Talent of anyone under a 5. A sort of lid on their Talent. It can be removed but it would keep them from tumbling to any stray 'paths and it would keep them from feeling any sting-pzzt. We might need to do that at some point. I'd ask Grandfather for permission first, and inform Admiral Ashiant if Grandfather says I should.*

*I'd rather you did,* Semirame said bluntly, *even if Grandfather says you shouldn't.*

*Raven would insist you told the admiral, Thian,* Clancy said, glaring at Semirame.

'OK, OK, so I'm new at this,' she said, holding up both hands in surrender.

*Ever regret we took advantage of your Talent, Rame?* Clancy asked, quirking one eyebrow at her.

*It sure gave me a chance to get off Phobos Base with my records still clean,* and she reached over and tousled Clancy's neatly combed hair. *Oh, hey, one last thought . . . to still the voice of the militant. We all know,* and she swung her finger in a circle to include them all, *that the Sphere down there ain't going nowhere, not with the metal fatigue in its hull, much less all the holes. But, if we were to ostentatiously plant one of your little packages, Thian, to blow it to kingdom come if any queen tried to bring the engines up . . .*

*Those engines,* and Clancy snorted derisively, *wouldn't go . . . Oh, I see what you mean. Smart idea!*

159

*I do get them. Part of being around you guys so long.*

*By all means mention that to the admiral, Commander, and I'd rather it came from you since I would be exceeding my orders to do so. That ought to earn you a commendation, too,* said Thian, grinning. *There'd be no way it could be detonated without* knowing *the detonator code.*

*I sort of hate that we have to placate* them, Gravy said, looking rebellious.

*Not when it anticipates a possible demand they might think of,* Clancy said with a malicious grin.

'I don't know about anyone else,' Thian went on aloud, sliding off the couch and hauling Gravy after him, 'but I'm starving of the hunger.'

'Considering how little you've had to do lately,' Gravy said, 'I can't imagine what's been developing an appetite in you.'

'Whatever it is, it's catching,' Clancy said, taking a comb from his hip pocket and giving a few swift, accurate passes over his messed hair. 'Coming, Commander?'

'Now that you mention it, it is past my lunch-break.'

# CHAPTER EIGHT

The announcement that the *Washington* and its Fleet were moving onward in its Search for other Hiver-occupied systems was at first met with some jubilation as the militants did, indeed, believe that their agitation had had an effect on the 'weasel-lovers'. Admiral Ashiant's advice to the High Council that an explosive device had been left on board the decrepit Sphere – as a deterrent – brought a loud demand for its immediate detonation.

The admiral had Commander Yngocelen announce that detonation was automatic should the Sphere be boarded and the militants would have to be happy with that.

Thian sent Earth Prime a message tube full of the recordings taken of the Hivers, complete with the interesting altering 'panels' which the queens had been watching. He copied all the boards in the various queens' quarters. Maybe some expert could find the Rosetta Stone that would translate those weird patterns. He also recommended that they see what reaction they got from the Heinlein queen by playing them in her presence.

The euphoria over forcing the *Washington* to remove itself from the 'dangerous, Hiver-occupied planet' did not last long.

161

Militant leaders must have engaged in considerable discourse and they decided that the High Council had deliberately ordered the *Washington* onward in an attempt to cool the volatile situation. They were certain that an even more egregious plan was being formulated by 'weasel-lovers' to subvert what was, to them, so obviously the 'will of the people'. The *Washington* was still searching and who could know what might be the next attempt to 'pollute Earth or one of the other civilized Star League Worlds'. The only sure answer to the threat posed by the Spheres was the complete annihilation of the Hiver worlds. Renewed agitations stressed the formidable weaponry of the *Washington* and the other ships in that Fleet: the availability of weapons that could scorch the surface of any planet, wiping out all life-forms, including the hated Hivers. The rebuttal that this would only put Humanity on the same level as the Hivers was scorned and ignored.

Two larger yachts attempted to bomb the Heinlein Base where the captured queen was being 'coddled'. The missiles were repulsed by the automatic shields that guarded the facility against stray meteors. The resultant explosions midspace caused damage to ships that had not been warned of the action. There were forty fatalities on nine of the small craft ringing the moon, some of which did not have escape pods so that all aboard perished when the hulls of their ships were penetrated by debris. The crews of both large yachts were arrested on charges of manslaughter, endangering the lives and property of twelve other ships, and malicious damage to a government facility.

A more devious mission by dedicated militants came closer to success when a heavily armed and well-drilled group, using moon vehicles, made an assault on the installation. Their advance was seen in time by the Observation Post and marine units were 'ported in – again arousing intense criticism of FT&T – to deal with the invaders.

More splinter groups evolved from those abortive attempts, disgusted with the inefficiency with which these had been conducted. In general, the two attacks on the Heinlein Base had an adverse reaction on the militants. Such unnecessary deaths roused to action those who felt that it was immoral to wish to destroy an entire species. Broadcasts replayed ancient examples of genocides, hoping to remind Humans that such vengeance produced longer-lasting problems than it eliminated. Surely Humankind had grown beyond such heinous solutions, whether the target of such annihilation was Human or alien.

The issue began to involve many Mrdinis since they were well known to side with the militants on the issue of destroying any planet occupied by Hivers. However, there was dissension within the largest militant group about including aliens to achieve their God-given objective. Fortunately, the oldest of the Mrdini colours held the power to control the official Mrdini political position and they were of one mind on the immorality of annihilation. Since the adulation of and obedience to their elders was a fundamental concept of Mrdini social behaviour, no Mrdini would disobey their leaders. The example of Prtglm, who had murdered Rojer's Gil and Kat on board the *KTTS*, was a constant reminder that no unauthorized or independent action could be taken against their ancient adversary without the most stringent redress.

The hope of the High Council rested on the abilities of their Human counterparts and the combined scientific research into finding a way to restrict Hivers to the planets they now occupied. Such a constraint would placate the most vengeful of the younger Mrdinis, such as Captain Klml and others in positions to vent their belligerence. A formidable task but one in which both Human and Mrdini scientists were determined to succeed.

Another dedicated faction still dreamed of finding a way to communicate with the queens: by odour since that had provoked some reaction from the queen during the *Washington*'s infiltration of their quarters. Though ridiculed by some xenologists, the idea was not without merit. The odours of Human perspiration and/or the smells of the uniform material and gear they had carried had provoked the only reaction from a queen yet recorded.

*     *     *

163

With the Talavera settlement expanding so rapidly, the High Council decreed the opening of Marengo as well. Exhaustive investigations of Marengo's environment showed that it was suitable for either Mrdini or Human occupation. Since the planet had a decided axial tilt, similar to Earth's, with large continental masses making almost a complete circuit at the equator, as well as four medium continents in the temperate zones, the planet would be opened to dual colonization: the Mrdini concentrated in the tropics while Humans could settle the higher, more temperate areas.

Of course, the militants were joined by other factions in an outcry that this was so obviously an attempt to placate everyone, and please no-one. There were enough Humans and Mrdini – especially Humans paired with Mrdinis – volunteering for the mixed colony that the Marengo Expedition was enthusiastically acclaimed by the moderate and the conservative elements. At least FT&T was able to place Morgelle of Betelgeuse, who was no relation to the Gwyn-Raven-Lyon Primes, as Tower Prime so that much publicity was attached to her appointment. That accord was brief but a return to the insistence of the militants was deflated by the Second Fleet's discovery of a second Talavera-type world, bearing traces of a failed Hiver colony. The disquieting element of that news was that no Sphere remained in orbit. The optimists said that meant that the Hivers were unlikely to return to that solar system again and the pessimists wanted to know *where,* in that case, had the Sphere gone. This planet was named Clariflor, since its surface had elements that resembled Clarf's terrain as well as climate, and a vast primeval swamp area reminiscent of the old American state of Florida. There were highlands and cooler areas suitable for Human occupation but Clariflor would be mainly a Mrdini world.

After the disasters befalling both Thian and Rojer and the overuse of T-2 Kincaid Dano, FT&T had initiated the practice of never sending a single high T out on an assignment without a support Talent. Unfortunately that left insufficient T-2s and T-3s to establish a Tower, until a suitable Prime could be released from other duties. Naturally this allowed the militants the chance to complain that FT&T was not doing its duty by supplying Primes when needed. No amount of argument could explain that Prime Talents were thin on the worlds comprising the Human part of the Alliance. All who could be useful were in full employment. Meanwhile, the Clariflor expedition was being serviced to the best of FT&T's ability by Talents on shipboard.

'And that's that!' Jeff Raven remarked to the meeting that he had called to explain the current FT&T situation to the two High Councillors. 'We can't supply what we do not have. The militants may cry "nepotism",' he went on, making quote marks with his long fingers, and seeing the answering grins at the conference table, 'and ignore the exhortations of FT&T to test every child at an early age to cultivate and develop even the slightest bit of Talent. The best way to GET more Talents is to breed them FROM Talents.'

'And *we,*' said the Rowan firmly for she was present in one of her rare in-system trips to attend this conference, 'have certainly done our part. Now if a certain other planet . . .' and, leaning both elbows on the table and propping her chin on her clasped hands, she gave her mate a penetratingly meaningful stare.

'All right, all right, Rowan, Deneb is well endowed with latent Talents – but damned few Primes – old enough, that is,' he hastily corrected himself since his son, Jeran, had fathered several likely ones, 'to take on the responsibilities of a Tower. Young Barry's not quite old enough. He needs more training. We'll have to put Xahra in for a while at the beginning, and let her break him in. He could just do for Clariflor. But you have to admit that more Denebians are voluntarily coming forward . . .'

'Even if their willingness smacks more of nepotism than the critics would like,' Gollee Gren added, since he referred to those of the Sparrow, Eagles and Hawk clans who were loosely related to Ravens.

'Do we have to use Primes for Towers everywhere?' asked Elizara Reidinger whose T-1 gifts were used medically rather than in communications.

'Not always,' Jeff said, 'but finding matching pairs of T-2s, or triplets of T-3s with sufficient versatility to manage the Tower duties is almost as hard as finding a Prime. THEY at least need little training . . .'

'Especially if they are Tower born,' the Rowan said with a hint of pride for her grandchildren's recent achievements.

'Right now, all the T-2s we can spare are on the main Search expeditions. And if you consider how far we will have to range to identify all the Hiver-occupied planets . . .' and Jeff gestured to the 3-D tank which replicated the scope of the Alliance's exploration, marking those systems which had at least one Hiver-occupied world. There were a depressing number of them.

'Hivers have been in space far longer than we have,' Admiral Mekturian remarked with a weary sigh.

MUCH TOO LONG, said High Councillor Gktmglnt, large enough to tower over everyone else at the conference table, even the tall Jeff Raven. ARE WE ASKING TOO MUCH OF OUR NAVIES AND OUR PEOPLES TO CONDUCT SUCH AN ENDLESS SEARCH?

NOT IF IT ALSO DISCOVERS NEW PLANETS FOR BOTH OUR SPECIES, Jeff replied in faultless Mrdini.

THERE EXISTS A SECONDARY PROBLEM TO FINDING SUFFICIENT PLANETS TO HOUSE OUR EXCESS POPULATION NOW THAT SO MANY DO NOT NEED TO GO ON THE LINE, said Gktmglnt, and it closed its poll eye long enough to indicate that it had a sensitive subject to discuss. WE MRDINI, IN ONE ASPECT, RIVAL THE ENEMY IN REPRODUCING. It turned to Elizara. YOU ARE THE MOST RESPECTED OF THE MEDICAL PEOPLE WITH WHOM WE HAVE HAD CONTACT. AFTER MUCH DISCUSSION WITH OUR PEOPLE, WE REQUEST THAT YOU ASSIST US IN DISCOVERING SOME MEANS TO . . . REGULATE AND REDUCE THE MRDINI BIRTH RATE. Then Gktmglnt closed its poll eye and lowered its head.

BUT YOU HAVE MANY TRAINED HEALERS, HONOURED GKTMGLNT, Elizara said, surprised. She remembered how Thian's Mur had been treated by the *KLTL* 'Dini medic.

SUCH MEDICS TREAT SICK AND WOUNDED MRDINI. Gktmglnt

166

shook its head slowly from side to side. HIBERNATION AND CREATION ARE THE RESPONSIBILITY OF THE KEEPERS. A DIFFERENT MATTER ENTIRELY.

*Specialists, huh?* Jeff murmured.

*Oh, this can be very difficult then. I understand the keepers are a law unto themselves and share nothing of their work.* Then she inclined her head with great respect to the High Councillor. ONE UNDERSTANDS THE DIFFICULTY. HUMANS RESPECT THE HIBERNATORY. HOWEVER TO DO AS YOU REQUEST, Elizara began slowly, HUMANS WOULD NEED TO KNOW MUCH MORE ABOUT THE PROCESS WHICH, WE DO COMPLETELY APPRECIATE, IS THE MOST SACRED ASPECT OF MRDINI CULTURE.

IT IS, Gktmglnt said, bowing even further in either embarrassment or humility so that Gollee cast a frantic look at Jeff, fearful that the huge Mrdini might overbalance.

Jeff held up a reassuring finger and Gollee, who was sitting beside the Mrdini, relaxed back into his chair. As discreetly as possible, Gollee did tighten the shield on his right side . . . just in case. Being smothered in a Mrdini mass was not high on his list of priorities even if the personage was one of the most prestigious of that race.

IT IS KNOWN THAT HUMANS ARE ABLE TO . . . REGULATE THE NUMBER OF OFFSPRING. IT IS BECOMING MORE IMPERATIVE THAT MRDINI DO SO. ATTEMPTS TO EFFECT A REDUCTION IN THE HIBERNATORIES OF OUR MAJOR PLANETS HAVE NOT BEEN SUCCESSFUL. Having delivered the burden of its message, Gktmglnt straightened, though its colour remained less vibrantly grey than usual. THIS MUST BE CAREFULLY DONE . . . WHATEVER MUST BE DONE . . . NOT TO OFFEND . . . NOR TO ALLOW SUCH TO BECOME PUBLIC KNOWLEDGE ON OUR PLANETS FOR THE NECESSITY IS NOT PERFECTLY UNDERSTOOD AND MIGHT BE CONSIDERED A RESTRICTION OF LIFE. BUT IF THE ALLIANCE IS COMMITTED TO RESTRICTING THE POPULATION OF HIVERS, IT IS IMPERATIVE THAT MRDINI SHOULD NOT INDULGE IN UNRESTRICTED BREEDING, TOO.

DISCRETION CAN BE MAINTAINED, Elizara said, emanating reassurance, understanding, approval and praise for the Mrdini decision even though she knew Gktmglnt was not empathic.

IF IT IS POSSIBLE TO BE ABLE TO EXAMINE SUFFICIENT MRDINI IN A HIBERNATORY TO. . . UNDERSTAND THE PROCESS OF CREATION . . . OUR BEST BIOLOGISTS AND GENETICISTS WILL BE PREPARED TO THUS DISCOVER A METHOD BY WHICH REPRODUCTION CAN BE REDUCED WITHOUT LOSS OF REFRESHMENT TO MRDINIS. *Although who,* and Elizara's mental comment to the telepaths around the table was fraught with her astonishment at such a monumental task and how best to proceed when so many of the most important practitioners of their specialities were up to their eyeballs trying to make some headway with the Hiver problem, *can I find to deal with Mrdini reproductive procedures . . .*

*Zara,* said the Rowan in a tone of voice which indicated *that* problem had just been settled. *She's been raised with 'Dinis and, more than once on Iota Aurigae, helped when there were injuries in the mines.*

Elizara blinked and then grinned. 'She'd need laboratory facilities and other xenbees specialists but it need only be a small team.'

'I doubt you'll have trouble finding one,' Gollee Gren said with a grin of pure relief. Zara was, indeed, the exactly perfect selection. 'I could give you a long list of trained personnel dying for a chance to know about the hibernatories and 'Dini reproduction.'

THAT MIGHT POSE SOMEWHAT OF A PROBLEM OF CONFLICTING LOYALTIES FOR ZARA AND PLG AND DZL, Gktmglnt said.

NOT IF THE MATTER IS HANDLED AS ADROITLY AS I SUGGEST YOUR ZARA RAVEN-LYON IS CAPABLE OF DOING. 'DINIS DO TRUST HER IMPLICITLY, Elizara said, AND YOUR INVOLVEMENT IN THE MATTER, HONOURABLE GKTMGLNT, WOULD APPEASE ANY POSSIBLE DOUBTS THEY MIGHT HAVE.

I WILL SO INSTRUCT THEM. IN PERSON. IF IT IS POSSIBLE FOR THE ESTIMABLE PRIME ZARA AND HER COMPANIONS TO ATTEND GKTMGLNT IN THE NEAR FUTURE. THIS PROBLEM MUST BE SOLVED BEFORE MORE MRDINIS ARE AFFECTED.

Elizara looked concerned. AND HOW, COUNCILLOR GKTMGLNT, ARE MRDINI CURRENTLY BEING AFFECTED?

Once more, Gktmglnt bowed its poll eye, covering it

with several of the protective lids, expressing chagrin and embarrassment. BY LOWERING THE TEMPERATURE OF HIBERNATORIES IT WAS HOPED THAT CREATION WOULD BE ADVERSELY AFFECTED.

*Odd that they would seize on temperature to control reproduction,* the Rowan said, her eyes glinting with irony, *since we damned near killed that queen by keeping her quarters too cold.*

ESTIMABLE GKTMGLNT, WHAT DID RESULT? Elizara asked at her gentlest.

Gktmglnt's head lowered further and Gollee could not help but lean slightly away from the huge 'Dini whose bulk seemed to widen in remorse. Erect, the great grey 'Dini did not take up quite as much horizontal space.

MANY VERY UNHAPPY MRDINI. UNFULFILLED WHERE FULFILMENT WAS NEEDED. UNCREATIVE WHERE CREATIVITY IS JOY AND REFRESHMENT.

THAT'S CERTAINLY NOT WHAT YOU HOPED TO ACHIEVE, IS IT, Jeff said wryly. *I wonder just what the repercussions will be, especially on those Mrdinis who are vital to the workings of the Alliance.*

*If we do it correctly, few will be aware,* Elizara said, *and that is exactly what Gktmglnt is anxious to ensure.*

Elizara reached across the corner to lay a reassuring hand on Gktmglnt's flipper, lying so lax in an attitude of resignation and despair. ONCE WE KNOW MORE ABOUT MRDINI BIOLOGICAL FUNCTIONS, WE SHOULD BE ABLE TO RESTORE JOY AND FULFILMENT. FOR WE HUMANS ARE ABLE TO SO DO EVEN AS WE RESTRICT CREATION.

Reassured, Gktmglnt straightened itself. BEGIN AT ONCE, ESTIMABLE PRIME ELIZARA REIDINGER. THE SITUATION HAS BECOME CRITICAL ON ALL OUR PLANETS . . . Then he bowed towards Jeff Raven and the Rowan sitting side by side. WITH THE NOTABLE EXCEPTION OF IOTA AURIGAE.

IN THAT CASE, the Rowan said, PERHAPS THAT WOULD BE THE BEST PLACE TO START SUCH INVESTIGATIONS. WITH MRDINIS WHO TRUST AND WORK SO CLOSELY WITH HUMANS.

ADMIRABLE SOLUTION, and Gktmglnt's colour acquired an instantly brighter sheen. THOSE OF US WHO UNDERSTAND THIS

169

ALLIANCE BEST WERE CERTAIN OF HUMAN SUPPORT AND ASSIS-
TANCE IN THIS VERY DELICATE AND FUNDAMENTAL MATTER.

Gollee Gren was looking down the agenda for the next item
to be discussed at this conference when, of a sudden, alarms
warbled shrilly. Despite all the security measures on this level
of the Blundell Building, three humans and one large blue
Mrdini appeared in the conference room, spraying the occupants of the table with dart-like missiles which were spat out in
a deadly almost inaudible burst.

The intended victims had faster reflexes than their attackers:
Jeff and the Rowan 'ported themselves high up, out of range;
increasing his shields, Gollee Gren covered Gktmglnt's body
with his own, while Elizara 'ported herself and Admiral Tohl
Mekturian to the far corner. The four attackers were themselves mind-stunned by Talents and collapsed, paralysed. The
door to the conference room burst open and the security
guards rushed in, immediately taking charge of the intruders.

*May I ask,* Jeff said in a tone not even his lifelong partner
had ever heard him use, *how Clarissia Negeva got in here?* And
he indicated the paralysed forms.

*Sir, the location of this conference room is protected,* said an
exceedingly red-faced and furious T-3 security officer. *We do not
know how the security system could have been so compromised.*

'*Clarissia Negeva?* Why so it is,' said the security captain as
he turned over the first of the two women sprawled on the
carpet.

'She's the xenophobic T-2 Laria bounced out of Clarf,' Jeff
went on . . . Elizara was 'porting restorative drinks to the
Rowan, who was ashen-faced, and to the stunned admiral,
while Gollee apologized profusely to Gktmglnt for both the
intrusion and his rough handling of the Mrdini's person.

'The others – both T-2s and strong kinetics – are Duvona
Tselligan and Nyol Greb, both Capellans,' Jeff said, having
touched their stunned minds.

THE MRDINI IS A DISGRUNTLED MEMBER OF MY OWN STAFF,
said Gktmglnt in a tone dripping with distaste and disillusion.
IT IS TO BE SENT BACK IN A PERSONNEL CARRIER IMMEDIATELY
AND . . .

PLEASE, NOT TO CLARF THIS TIME, the Rowan said, raising one hand in appeal.

IT IS FROM KIF AND WILL BE SENT TO THE MOST PUBLIC PLACE POSSIBLE.

WOULD IT NOT BE WISER TO DISCOVER WHO ELSE AMONG YOUR STAFF MIGHT BE INVOLVED? asked T-3 Security Officer Harry Sargent with a formal bow to the High Councillor.

THE MANNER OF ITS PUNISHMENT WILL BE SUFFICIENT DETERRENT FOR ANY OTHERS WHO CONSIDER ELIMINATING A HIGH COUNCILLOR WILL REDRESS WHATEVER GRIEVANCES EXIST.

*FATHER! GRANDFATHER? GRANDMOTHER? FATHER? GRANDFATHER? SIR? UNCLE? SON?*

*Commendable reactions, all of you,* Jeff said with a wry smile as his mind was flooded by the queries from various alarmed offspring and other relatives. *All is well. A discreet and very private message will be forthcoming. Allow us to deal with the matter in our own time. Thank you.*

*They'd've been too late,* the Rowan remarked very quietly to her mate. *I had no idea I'd broadcast this . . . recent untoward event.*

*I suspect all of us did,* Jeff said, managing a grin at Elizara and Gollee.

Harry Sargent, his hand carefully gloved, picked up one of the many darts scattered about the room by the deflection the Talents used in self-protection. He examined it, sniffed cautiously and his expression became even more implacable.

'Poisoned. A particularly virulent type. Even Elizara couldn't have saved all of you. Especially these,' and he indicated a scatter on the table in front of Gktmglnt, 'would have been impossible to neutralize.' He bowed his abject apologies to the High Councillor which had resumed its seat, its figure regally erect.

TAKE THAT AWAY IMMEDIATELY, and Gktmglnt nodded at the immobilized 'Dini.

CERTAINLY, HIGH COUNCILLOR, said Sargent.

ALLOW ME TO ASSIST, Gollee said and he 'ported the body to one of the many personnel carriers available at the Blundell

171

Building's Yard, an action the others followed with their minds.

WOULD YOU KNOW THE CO-ORDINATES OF ITS . . . FINAL PLACEMENT, GKTMGLNT? Jeff asked.

THE BIG SQUARE ON KF WOULD BE THE MOST PUBLIC PLACE.

WE KNOW THOSE CO-ORDINATES, Jeff said.

YOU DON'T GET TO DO IT BY YOURSELF, the Rowan said, rising up from her chair until she was nearly as tall as the High Councillor, I INSIST ON . . .

NOT UNLESS I AM IN ON THE THROW, TOO, Gollee said in an equally arbitrary tone.

IN THE TIME IT'S TAKING US TO ARGUE WHO DOES IT, IT COULD HAVE BEEN DONE, Jeff replied.

WE'LL ALL DO IT, Elizara said at her most reasonable. ONE, TWO, THREE.

*WHAT'S GOING ON UP THERE? MY GENERATORS DAMNED NEAR OVERLOADED!* was the outraged roar from T-2 Viling Iredit, the Blundell Tower engineer.

*Operation Overkill* was Jeff's unapologetic reply. *It's not likely to happen again.*

THE TRANSFER IS COMPLETED? asked Gktmglnt.

MOST DECIDEDLY, Admiral Mekturian said, leaning across and lightly touching the Mrdini's arm, a big grin on his face.

Jeff held up his hand, looking first to the Rowan who gave a slow nod of her head, then to Gollee who was also in accord. Elizara hesitated.

'You'll need to know who else is involved. I shall attend to that when the meeting is concluded,' she said.

'That's my job,' Gollee said.

Elizara, her usually sympathetic expression neutral, turned to him. 'In this instance, I disagree, Gollee. You are an excellent T-2, but I am the Medical Prime and these three had . . . sick minds.'

The Rowan leaned across the table, her eyes bleak. 'Their minds are not to be healed, Elizara.'

'That is a given, Angharad Raven, since they have abrogated any consideration by such an unwarranted attack.' She turned to Harry Sargent. 'Secure them in the Infirmary and

172

request my assistant to administer the necessary suppressant. They are to be placed in separate rooms and are not to be allowed to move or communicate with anyone, even my assistant.'

Harry gestured to his team who bowed respectfully. The team, Harry and the three remaining limp bodies 'ported out of the room.

'I should review security features,' Gollee said with a grim expression.

'Three kinetic-strong T-2s could, and did, manage it,' Jeff said, rubbing his jaw.

'Who'd've expected we'd be bearded in Blundell after all,' Rowan said, grinding the words out, obviously still coping with her anger over the attack.

'I'll see it never happens again, no matter how many dissident Ts they can assemble,' Gollee said in a tight, implacable tone.

'I shall discover *why,* which I believe to be even more important,' Elizara said, 'there are dissident T-2s at all.'

'Consider me available, Elizara, if necessary,' the Rowan said.

Elizara nodded in compliance.

'Now that that's all settled,' and Jeff gave himself a shake, indicating he had been more upset about the incident than he was willing to admit, 'how far had we progressed on the agenda, Admiral Tohl?'

'Item nine,' Mekturian said, blinking slightly in reorienting his attention as he touched his notepad. When he looked up, his expression suggested that Jeff knew exactly what the next topic should be. 'Having a surface team investigating the occupied Hive planet named Ciudad Rodrigo.'

'Yes, we could do with more comparative samples of pheromones and soil,' Elizara said. 'As has been remarked, the Hivers might test the air and remove any life-form large enough to be considered a predator, but they don't seem to test soil for its components. They just dig in, as it were.' She gave her mouth a quirk at her phrasing.

'We'll be taking Zara from the *Columbia* and Talavera Tower,' Gollee Gren said, scrolling down on his notepad.

173

'Flavia can do the surface inspection of Ciudad Rodrigo?' the Rowan asked.

'Hmmm, I'd thought to send Rojer . . .' Jeff began.

'Not without Asia,' Elizara interrupted him, waggling a finger.

'I know, I know,' he said, nodding his head to the caution and holding up one hand. 'I want him to have some surface experience as well, with Asia,' as he turned to Gollee. 'Is that mixed team you've been training ready to tend Talavera Tower? If they work out, that'll free Rojer . . . and Asia . . .' He held up his hand before anyone could remind him.

'Five to replace that cheeky boy?' the Rowan asked.

'Well, if three T-3s can't handle 'porting and two good T-2 'pathers can't manage in the Tower, we'll have to see just how much support they'd need in a larger Merge,' Gollee replied. 'Denebians, too.'

'Really?' Elizara said with a sly grin at Jeff.

*That's quite enough of that, if you don't mind.* Out of deference to the two High Councillors, Jeff added, 'How soon does the *Washington* make its next destination?'

'Two more weeks, I believe,' Gollee said.

'Mmmm,' Jeff murmured ambiguously.


'I can't reach any of them. Neither can Mother,' Laria told everyone in the Tower who had rushed up the stairs at her scream. Kincaid, who had been in Merge with her, was clutching his temples in pain. Morag and Kaltia quivered with reaction to the fright they had heard all too clearly. Vanteer and Lionasha had rushed into the Tower. Now Lionasha passed restorative beverages to everyone with the firm advice to drink first, talk later.

Laria was still too full of the panic she had sensed, despite the distance between Clarf and Earth, to do more than take quick sips between phrases.

'Somehow . . . they were all . . . Grandfather, Grandmother, Gollee, Elizara . . . and I'm sure I felt the presence of the two High Councillors as well . . . had all been in danger. I do apologize for broadcasting to all of you, too.' She

174

swallowed the rest of the drink, rose and started to reduce the headache she had given Kincaid.

'We all felt surprise, distress, not so much panic,' Kincaid said, gratefully allowing Laria to heal the splitting headache. He felt that his eyes were crossed and kept them closed.

'You shielded us,' Morag said to him almost accusingly. 'Nice of you but *we* should have been shielding you,' she added.

'Habit,' he said, his eyes still closed, and his shoulders slumped.

'When will we get any details?' Kaltia asked softly, more distressed than any of the others, as she kept wringing her hands. 'It's awful not knowing.'

Morag and Lionasha both reached out to comfort her physically, nearly bumping heads in their effort. That bit of nonsense in itself relieved some of the tension.

*Where IS everybody?* Yoshuk demanded. *I gave the co-ordinates but I can't . . . Oh, something's gone very wrong?*

So they had to explain to the Sef Tower Talents what little they knew.

*I'll just get the co-ordinates, Yoshuk,* and Lionasha hurried down the stairs.

'Morag, Kaltia, you 'port with me,' Laria said, glad to have something to DO. 'Kincaid's mind's in no condition to merge.'

'I . . .' Kincaid got that far before he was flattened by three T-1s gently but firmly to his couch. 'I yield.'

*So what happened at Blundell, sis?* Rojer asked. *Grandmother AND Mother shut me up.*

*When I know I'll tell you. I suspect we'll all be told at the same time but if we aren't . . . here comes your shipment, Yoshuk . . .* Laria said, taking her two sisters into Merge as gently as she could.

*Hey, save your strength, Lar . . . Oh, you have Morag and Kaltia? What happened to Kincaid . . . ah, yes, well if he was in Merge, it's to be expected. I'll keep 'em pacified here,* Rojer went on.

Despite the nagging worry about how, under all the Star

League suns, hostiles had invaded the conference room at Blundell Tower, the other Primes continued with their duties.

No-one felt much like eating any lunch but they were all present when Jeff reported the whole incident.

'Clarissia Negeva?' Laria was so surprised that she spoke aloud, although all the other Talents were listening to Earth Prime's explanation. 'She said she'd get even with us "weasel-lovers" the day she left here.'

*Don't blame yourself for her bigotry,* Jeff said sternly. *You warned us that she was xenophobic and that was vital information. We simply didn't realize how vital. That she was able to enlist other Capellans is not surprising. To have got to a member of the High Councillor's staff is more unusual.*

*So, what's happened to them all?* Laria demanded without a shred of pity.

*Elizara . . .*

*Elizara? But she'll . . .*

*Don't ever get on the wrong side of Elizara, my dear,* her grandfather said in a droll warning. *There are limits to even her famous compassion and understanding. The 'invaders' have been unable to keep any of their sordid little machinations from her searching mind. They also have been deprived of whatever Talent they once enjoyed and are being sent back to Capella for their penal servitude as menial labourers in frontier garrisons.*

*And the 'Dini?*

*It is performing the same salutary function as did the un-lamented Prtglm, on Kif, its planet of origin,* Jeff replied dryly. *Gktmglnt pronounced sentence. Gollee is full of plans for more advanced security on this level, too.*

*But how did someone like Clarissia get as far as she did?*

*With two other strong T-2 kinetics, she could get very far once she knew where to look. Now this has been a very tiring day and, while there are other messages for all of you, these will come by tube and are to be divulged on a need-to-know basis. Thank you for your immediate support. Can't imagine how I let out my surprise! I suppose one does react with an instinctive mayday when unexpectedly attacked in what is supposed to be an invulnerable chamber.*

176

For the first time in her life, Laria heard a puzzled, almost uncertain note in her grandfather's voice. HER grandfather insecure?

Kincaid reached over and clasped his hand tightly about hers, broadcasting reassurance, shaking his head.

*Yes, you would appreciate that better than anyone else, Dano,* said Jeff with a chuckle not too far off his usual irrepressible humour. *We ALL had a bit of a shock that we're making very certain cannot be repeated. All right?*

Then the presence of Jeff Raven was gone from their minds.

'Perhaps that was needed, Laria dear,' Kincaid said, leaning towards her and capturing the other hand as well. 'Nothing happened beyond a nasty shock . . .'

'And the punishment of those who dared violate Blundell!' said Morag, her eyes sparkling with anger. Kaltia still looked uncertain.

'We Talents get so we feel we can lick anyone with hands and feet tied down, Kaltia,' Kincaid said gently. 'It isn't true. We all have limits. Even Jeff Raven, the Rowan and the very efficient Gollee Gren.'

'But can you imagine what chaos would result if the Blundell Building had been . . .' Lionasha began . . .

'It couldn't be,' Vanteer said so stoutly and angrily that Lionasha recoiled. 'It's far too well protected from the outside . . .'

'That's what I mean. They were *inside*!' Morag said.

'And they were Talents,' Kaltia said, outraged and appalled.

'T-2s and only kinetics,' Morag went on. 'You heard Grandfather. Three could about get anywhere in Blundell except his office. The meeting was in one of the conference rooms.'

'Clarissia would have known where all the conference rooms are,' Laria said but her voice did not have its usual firmness. 'And she had left here threatening . . .'

'Did I or did I not hear your grandfather say that you are not to blame yourself, Laria?' Kincaid said, making her look at him when he deliberately pinched the hands he still held. 'Then listen to him.'

'Yes, do, Laria,' Lionasha said, her eyes angry. 'Van and I couldn't believe how tolerant you were of that methody Capellan and her prissy ways,' and Lionasha did such a good imitation of Clarissia's long-suffering expression that Laria managed a weak smile. She turned to Kincaid. 'And we thought that idiot Stierlman had been ineffectual!' She rolled her eyes at her understatement. 'YOU,' and she cocked her finger at Kincaid, 'know what you're doing and you do it. How's the headache?' she added.

'Gone, thanks,' and Kincaid used that reply to release Laria's hands and lean back. 'If I may be so bold as to suggest a siesta today, I think we'd all benefit.'

'I know I would,' Laria said and, rising, left the room.

Morag and Kaltia exchanged anxious looks.

'She'll be all right,' Kincaid said, 'but a rest is a good idea for all of us.'

'Indeed it is,' Lionasha said briskly. 'We've more cargoes, and I don't know how many message tubes to be sent all the way to that new planet, Clariflor.'

'Who's receiving?' Kincaid asked, frowning because he couldn't remember.

'Right now, Xahra, one of David of Betelgeuse's kids.' And Morag grinned. 'He must be seething to have had to let another of his precious children leave his control. She's a Prime and has T-2 and T-3 support.'

'Then it'll be all right,' he said with some relief as he, too, walked down the hall to his quarters.

Once out of sight, however, he 'ported into Laria's room. She was curled in a little ball, weeping.

'Oh, dear, I was trying not to broadcast,' she said, lifting her head to show her distressed contorted face. Instantly, he picked her up, sat back down on the bed and arranged her comfortably across his legs, tucking her head under his chin and exuding quantities of sympathy.

*I know misery rather well,* he said gently.

*It's just that it hit me so unexpectedly.* She lifted his free hand to her cheek. *I can't imagine a world without Grandfather and Grandmother* there *and available to us . . . to all of us.*

178

*My very dear Laria, there will come a time when we must let them go. Talents do enjoy long lives, long healthy ones but for even the strongest of us, there comes the day, the hour, the moment when . . . it just becomes . . . too much.*

*They could retire . . .*

*Ha!* Kincaid dismissed that with a laugh that bounced her on his chest. *One day, dear heart, they simply won't wake up. They will however never suffer the debilities that used to depress and made our ancestors demand the mercy of euthanasia.*

*But no-one gets that sick nowadays,* protested Laria, still fighting inwardly against the demise of her beloved grand-parents. And her parents. Afra was much older than Damia . . .

*And he is Capellan who are known to be indestructible.*

*But not invulnerable . . .*

*If you're going to continue to torture yourself with such thoughts, I'm leaving.* And he made as if to move. She held him there with both hand and Talent, immobile.

*Remind me not to try to depart without your full permission,* he said with mild reproof. Then, as she immediately lifted the restraint, he put one hand on her belly. *Here, love, is the real immortality . . . the continuance of the genes which made both your grandparents and parents. THIS is your hope and their eternal renewal. I think such news would be good for them to hear right now.*

*What if they don't. . .*

*Approve of me?*

*I didn't mean you hear that.*

*Then don't think so loudly so close to me.* He hugged her affectionately, to indicate absolution. *The child will be yours, and mine, and Talented. That is the salient fact that will render any minor details superfluous.*

*Are there any other Talents in your family?*

He gave a snort. *No, there weren't.*

Flashing through Laria's mind was a kaleidoscope of pun-ishment scenes, an angry, contorted face of a woman, and echoes of voices from Kincaid's past that gave her a shocking insight into the childhood of a Talent, reared by a family

179

which did not approve of nonconformity. She was equally aware that he didn't know what he had just projected: their minds were more deeply linked than she realized. She wondered if he did, but decided not to mention it.

*I do know,* he went on and those childhood flashes faded, *that your parents welcomed me without reservation to your home and family. I care more for their good opinions than anyone else's.*

*But what if Grand . . .*

*Your grandparents are older and wiser than even Afra and certainly you, dear heart. I'd far rather everyone knew and settled that little detail. Now rest. We both need it after the morning's that's . . . thankfully gone, and this afternoon's traffic is mercifully light.*

They rearranged themselves more comfortably in restful positions, though Laria clung to his arm and nestled as close as she could get to his long body.

*It doesn't matter what earth-shattering things happen, does it?* she said almost bitterly. *Primes have to man the Towers.*

*Responsibility, and routine, give you balance, too, Laria. I'd rather have them both, than be without either. Rest, Laria. You need it after that shock.*

And, much to her surprise, reassured by his presence, she did.

Flavia equably received the news directly from Earth Prime that Zara was required immediately by Prime Elizara. Jeff Raven said that orders were coming for Captain Soligen and her attendant ships to leave orbit around Talavera and proceed to the system that contained Ciudad Rodrigo.

'Earth Prime would like myself,' and Flavia placed a hand on her chest, 'with Rojer . . .' she paused to grin at Captain Vestapia Soligen, 'and Asia, with whatever other team members and security personnel we need to do a survey of that 'Dini-occupied planet. We must gather the usual samples for comparative examination.'

Captain Soligen frowned, obviously rapidly running through who else should go with the Talents.

'Earth Prime is sending Thian's report on his surface ventures . . .' Flavia paused. 'I believe the confirmatory message tube has just come in. Let us do without that dreadful Dr Esperito, if we can. Wayla Gregorian should accompany us as science officer and Yakamasura and possibly Rosenery Mordmann plus whatever team Kwan Keiser-Tau feels is necessary to protect us.'

'I think I'd like to come along, too,' Vestapia said.

'Me, too,' said Rhodri Eagles, rapping belatedly on the half-open door. He had a message tube in his hand. 'This is, I believe, for you,' and he handed it to Flavia, grinning with his usual insouciance. 'You wouldn't dream of leaving me out of the expedition, now would you?'

Flavia grinned at the captain's bemused expression.

'None of us would, Roddie. After all, you've had more personal experience with queens than any of us,' Flavia said.

When Zara was told of her reassignment she was excited to be asked to work with Elizara again, but there were no specifics for her of what that work entailed among the many contained in the message tube. There were certainly enough recordings and readings from the *Washington* as guidelines for the Ciudad Rodrigo landing team.

'Well, at least I'm not being yanked out of here and dumped where I'm going as Rojer was,' Zara said with a slight grimace of exasperation.

'Then we'll have time for a farewell party on Talavera,' Flavia said, pleased. She loved swimming in the lake – careful, though, not to swallow too much water.

*Yeah, but who's Grandfather got to manage my Tower?* Rojer demanded, incensed.

*Don't fret. Asia's coming with you,* Zara said placatingly.

*She has to come with me. Wherever I go.* He snarled when he heard Zara's mental sigh. *Don't come over all sisterly on me, Zara.*

*Stop treating her like a child.*

*I'll court her my own way, with no help from you.*

*Just so long as she knows she's being courted,* was Zara's tart reply.

181

*Whaddayou mean by that?*

*If you can't figure it out by yourself . . . Oh, never mind. Grandfather's sending three T-3s for the 'porting and a pair for the 'pathing and older experienced T-5s as expediter and engineer. I'd say that needing five to replace you is a compliment, Roj.*

*Well, I have brought all the big heavy stuff in with* my *team.*

*Stop grousing.*

*Stop nagging.*

*CHILDREN* and Flavia's cool soprano interrupted their wrangling.

'I think it's a compliment that so many are needed to replace you, Roj,' Asia said when Rojer came into the lounge, still frowning over that exchange.

'Am I leaving, too?' Jes Ornigo asked.

'Yes, it'll be almost a complete new crew,' Rojer said, looking at Asia, cool and pretty in a particularly nice shade of green one-piece that ended at her knees. She had cute knees. He shook his head impatiently at being diverted from the more important news. 'My grandfather wouldn't dare separate you and Flavia,' he said, grinning at the droll glance Jes gave him. 'There're two experienced T-5s as expediter and engineer and we're to break in our replacements.'

'Does Dr Esperito get to go to Ciudad Rodrigo?' Asia asked, her expression anxious. Her inherent shyness had made her one of the few who didn't just leave the doctor. He endlessly pontificated to anyone he could catch.

Rojer laughed. 'No. He stays!'

'That's a relief,' Jes and Asia said in unison.

'So when do our replacements get here?' Jes asked.

*As soon as you lot stop gossiping and get to your couches,* said the unmistakable voice of their grandfather. *I'm waiting . . .*

'Hold your horses,' Zara murmured under her breath as she and Rojer 'ported themselves into position. Asia had darted to her generators and, when they were needed, they sang sweetly in use.

\*     \*     \*

182

From the large personnel carrier emerged seven people, ranging from a man in his sixth decade who was the expediter and had been drafted from Blundell Building. The engineer, a younger man, had also been at Blundell and was clearly delighted with what he saw of his new Tower.

The T-3 kinetics were twin brothers and a sister from one of the western Denebian clans that even Rhodri had never met. They were just out of their teens and eager to prove their abilities. The 'paths, Andy and Ivy Dumas, were in their early twenties but obviously already partnered and they had 'Dini pairs.

'Sorry to rush you into work right away,' Rojer said, not the least bit apologetic, 'but we've some afternoon deliveries and that'll give you some practice while we're still here.'

'You're leaving soon?' asked one of the twins. Rojer didn't stay long enough to know if it was Scott or Stuart who spoke: they were almost identical. Their sister, Sara, was only a year younger and looked enough like them to have been a triplet. The T-5 expediter was from Capella and was known to Jes Ornigo, Flavia and Mallen. Mal was to stay on at Talavera to help the new group settle in.

'No rest for the wicked, you know,' Zara said, indicating that it was her brother who was wicked. Then grinned when Asia stepped to Rojer's side supportively.

'We've another assignment, but most of the heavy stuff's been brought in,' Rojer said, pointing to the settlements so obviously built of prefabricated sections. 'If you've been trained at Blundell, you'll do just fine. And the *Columbia* – and us . . .' and he indicated Flavia and tapped his chest, 'are only a thought away.'

Ivy Dumas rolled her eyes at that oft-repeated Talent reminder, thus recommending herself to Rojer.

'So let's hit the Tower . . . gang,' Rojer said, rubbing his hands together. 'Oh, Mal, see if we can rustle up more couches. We can use comformables from the lounge right now but a good couch is essential for everyone on duty in a Tower.'

The comformables had appeared on the Tower floor by the time Rojer led the five newcomers up the stairs.

*Thanks, sis,* he said since he suspected she had done the 'porting.

*Happy to oblige.*

The two 'paths hadn't caught that exchange but then, they hadn't been included.

Asia was already explaining the vagaries of the Talavera generators to the engineer when the Tower group took their places.

Rojer let the five follow him on a 'port of some faulty units back to Betelgeuse, introducing the new Tower staff to David, and then let the three kinetics bring in some medium heavy shipments from Procyon, again introducing them to the Tower Prime. By the time Altair had fresh produce and nursery plants to send, Scott, Stuart and Sara were much more at ease and Rojer backed off completely. A shower of the inevitable message tubes startled all of them but Rojer explained that most message tubes could be sent the entire way by the deliverer and that this would happen frequently.

*They'll do,* was Zara's verdict.

*They're too tense.*

*They're brand-new at it,* Flavia said. *And Mallen's there to lend a hand. I'll bring down the caterers and the others from the* Columbia, she added. *I'm in the mood for a good party. As a rule, we don't get much chance to celebrate reassignments.*

*Grandfather's way of making all this shuffling palatable,* Rojer replied but he wasn't opposed to a party. It might even give him the chance he'd been waiting for.

*For Pete's sweet sake, don't wait ANY longer.*

Flavia's advice surprised Rojer. She usually minded her own business. But she'd been aboard the *Columbia* with Asia long enough to know how young and shy Asia was, how easily intimidated. Why, she wouldn't even brush off old Esperito when he was boring her with his latest observations, usually at the top of his voice as well as his mind.

The four new 'Dinis of Ivy and Andy had been made very welcome and were delighted to help in the yard. They were quite young and a sort of greeny-grey. There were no others of their colour on Talavera but the greys said they were close enough to join their house.

184

Someone had brought out lights for the Tower Yard where the *Columbia*'s caterers set up their food dispensers. 'Dinis appeared with chairs and tables gathered from the personnel quarters as well as their own homes. Mal and Jes, with the help of the twins, lighted a path in orange to the lake and along the shore. Vestapia and her senior officers had been invited but no-one said a word to Esperito about the upcoming surface investigation of Ciudad Rodrigo.

'He's lonely, you know,' Asia said when Rojer had for the fourth time that night taken her away from Esperito. The old xeno had immediately seized on the old expediter as a listener who was considerate enough to take on the role.

'Small wonder,' Rojer said. 'Why didn't you just invent an errand you'd forgotten?' he demanded, waving his hand about. 'Or remember a message. Or go to the bathroom.'

'I can't keep using the same excuses all the time, Roj,' Asia said meekly, her head down.

'Now, I don't mean that as criticism, Asia,' Rojer said, realizing that one of her more sterling qualities was her innate kindness and forbearance. He reached for her hand and her fingers curled about it in acknowledgement.

They continued along the orange-lit path in a darkness that was already boasting some night insect sounds.

'Sounds a bit like Deneb,' he said, and daringly put his arm about her shoulders. She was so lightly boned. The perfume she was wearing was floral. Pheromones of a pleasant sort.

'Yes, it does,' and she grinned up at him. 'Makes all that hard 'porting worth it, doesn't it?'

'It does.'

Rojer swung them back to look at the Tower in its illumination.

'You're not going to *miss* it, are you, Roj?' Asia asked, astonished.

'I am. Sort of. I think. We set it all up, from scratch.'

'You've not worried about our assignment on Ciudad Rodrigo?'

'Me? Worried about Hiver queens? Never,' he said with

185

such vehemence that she recoiled. But he caught her back, pulling her into both arms. 'Are you?' He knew she didn't like slithers but queens were definitely not slithers. Although Thian had mentioned something scuttling over his feet . . .

'If I'm with you, I'm never scared.'

He looked down at her face, shadowed so that she looked older, mysterious. He wanted very much to kiss her.

*Then WHY don't you?* Zara said in exasperation.

'What's the matter, Rojer?' Asia asked and anxiety flickered across her face, making her his dear young Asia again.

*Not that young, Rojer,* and this time it was Flavia who was chiding him.

*Both of you, get out of my head and my space and let me do my own courting.*

*Then DO it!* the two Primes said in a chorus of disgust. *You're the one who's shy now.*

'I know that look,' Asia said, her voice no longer soft and yielding. 'You're 'pathing, and just when we're in the most romantic setting we're ever likely to have for the next months. Sometimes, Rojer Lyon, you can be the most exasperating of men.' She gave his shoulders a shake and then, standing on her tiptoes, reached up and pulled his head down to hers, kissing him soundly and far more thoroughly than he thought his Asia should know how to kiss.

*Well, it's about time!*

Rojer ignored the snide telepathed whisper and later couldn't remember who had spoken because he and Asia were responding to each other in the passionate embrace. With their emotions awakened and reinforced by mutual desire, Asia 'pathed to him for the first time . . . a far firmer 'voice' than her audible one.

*Your room or mine?*

'Asia!' He broke off the kiss to stare down at her, not that that wasn't what he had in his mind.

*Believe me, Rojer Lyon, I'm grown-up enough!*

*Where did my shy Asia go?*

*She got tired of waiting, Rojer Lyon. Take me.*

\* \* \*

Thian woke, gasping for breath, stunned by a dream so terrible that he clung to Gravy beside him.

'Whatever's the matter, Thian? O, Lordee, look how Mur and Dip are thrashing about. They'll hurt themselves . . .'

Gravy was as fast to assist the two writhing creatures as Thian.

'I just had the most awful dream, Thian,' she said, holding Mur to her and stroking it, thinking reassurance as hard as she could. 'Freezing. Choking.'

Thian was doing much the same to Dip.

'Let's surround them,' and he rearranged himself and Gravy so the two 'Dinis were on their laps, Human arms making a safe cage about the shuddering, quivering bodies.

'Whatever can have happened?'

*Rame, Clancy, Lea, how many 'Dinis on board are having nightmares?* Thian broadcast to the entire complement of the *Washington.*

His com unit started buzzing and the panel at the workstation in the lounge was announcing urgent in-ship messages. The replies were all the same and came from all parts of the ship where Humans had 'Dini friends. As abruptly as it started, the convulsions ended. Whimpering, the 'Dinis were coaxed back to sleep but only when they were held tightly by their Humans.

Thian thought to check with Captain Spktm of the *KSTS*.

WHATEVER IT WAS, IT WAS WIDESPREAD, THN. BAD DREAMS FOR THOSE ASLEEP. FOR US AWAKE, THE MOST HIDEOUS THOUGHTS OF TERROR, COLD, CHOKING. IT IS OVER. WE ARE ON DUTY. WE WILL TAKE RESTORATIVE DRINK.

That was not good enough for Thian. Not when the 'bad dreams' were reported on every Human ship with 'Dinis in their crews and on all the 'Dini vessels.

*Rojer, you had any trouble there?* Thian 'pathed to his brother on the *Columbia, en route* to Ciudad Rodrigo.

*TROUBLE, he calls it,* was Rojer's sarcastic reply. *Every 'Dini went into convulsions. Never seen the like of it. Humans who were unlucky enough to be asleep had nightmares . . .*

*Of freezing cold, choking and terror . . .*

*Yours got it, too? I thought Asia and I'd never calm Gil and Kat.*

*Whole damned First Fleet had it.*

*Do you call Grandfather or do I?*

*As Earth Prime,* and Jeff's voice interrupted their conversation, *I reluctantly report that there seems to have been a major power failure at Clarf Main Hibernatory. Many are dead and we are trying to estimate the losses. It is hoped that a proportion may be saved by restorative methods that are currently being applied.*

*But, Grandfather, how did our 'Dinis know so far away?* Thian asked.

*Who was it said that bad news travels fast? I'll let you know when we can find some Mrdini who will tell us exactly what happened. And how! A rough estimate is that nearly eight hundred 'Dinis of all colours were affected. Those here at Blundell say that the very young and the oldest would have died. I'll send a full report.*

*On another topic,* Jeff said after a brief pause, *the Heinlein observers rigged a screen in the queen's quarters and played selected passages from the material you sent me a while back.*

*OH?*

Jeff's chuckle was malicious. *She took one glance at the side panels and ignored them. She walked up to the main panel, the one where the patterns alter, watched it. Those who have become familiar with what gestures or movements she makes thought she was 1) startled, 2) disgusted and 3) returned to her couch and didn't pay the screen any further attention. The com experts are of the opinion that the side panels are static, with very few alterations, while the main screen gives some sort of running comment on whatever it is queens on the same planet would be talking about.*

*Interesting.*

*Yes, isn't it? I don't know if it's good news but it's better news. Tell your experts.* And before Thian could thank him for the report, Jeff's presence had left his mind.

'Well,' Sam said with a sigh that Grm repeated when Thian gave them the report, 'we did what we could. I don't understand such a negative reaction from the Heinlein queen,' he added, rubbing his jaw thoughtfully.

ONE QUEEN WARLIKE, THE OTHER PLACID. THEY WOULD NOT LIKE EACH OTHER. ALSO FROM DIFFERENT HIVE WORLDS, Grm remarked.

'Would they all use the same language?' Thian asked.

WHY SHOULDN'T THEY? THEY DO NOT CHANGE ANYTHING ELSE THEY DO. And Grm's narrow shoulders raised in a very human shrug.

'Suppose,' and Thian stopped to orient his thoughts, 'the queens did not develop the technology they're using, but adapted it to their use?' The concept clearly startled his listeners. He leaned forward, developing the theory. 'I believe there was an ethnic group that could perfect any sort of mechanical or electronic technology but could not, for some reason, take the next step upward in that technology. Perhaps that's what the queens are: perfectionists but not originators.'

'Hmmm,' and Sam nodded his head, looking at his colleague, and Grm seemed to be considering the notion, too. 'We still have to find a way to keep them contained.' Then, exchanging a glance with Grm and the two xenbees, Weiman excused himself from the lounge.

*I've got a BIG problem, Elizara,* Medical Prime Zara 'pathed to her mentor and instructor.

*And what would that be?* Elizara's prompt reply returned over the distance between Earth and Iota Aurigae.

*I'm not sure it's ethical or medical, but did you realize that there are NO species on Clarf, or any of the other Mrdini planets, similar to them?*

*That's a well-known fact, m'dear.*

*Then how do I experiment?* There was anguish and alarm in Zara's question and suddenly what she said was painfully and dreadfully clear to Elizara. Surprise, and shock, kept her from forming an answer and Zara went on. *We Humans have pigs and mice and rats and other mammalian creatures whose anatomy, and responses, we can use for experimentation. But we bloody don't have ANY OTHER SPECIES like Mrdinis to*

*use in the laboratory. There simply is no OTHER life-form that
does the same thing they do when they are reproducing.*

*Ah, yes, well,* and Elizara bought more time as her mind
frantically went through the known categories of species, some
of which were definitely alien and also definitely NOT Mrdini.
*That is certainly a problem.*

*I mean, I've got all the facilities I could possibly NEED and
some of the best young Mrdini medics to assist as well as their
equipment – which, by the way, I don't know how to use . . . but
I'm learning. But HOW can I possibly do any substantive
experimentation that will give us any sort of an answer? I've
NOTHING to practise on! AND,* the wail of moral outrage
gave way to a far more human despair, *old Frtplm is hemming,
hawing, turning itself upside down NOT to let us try to analyse
what chemicals they put into the air of the hibernatory. And I've
GOT to have that information.*

*Yes, indeed you do. I shall speak immediately to High
Councillor Gktmglnt.*

*Fine. I'd appreciate it. Very much,* replied Zara, punctuating
her phrases with telepathically transmitted sighs that made
Elizara smile, despite herself.

The other ethical issue facing Zara was not something she
could as easily solve. And one that had certainly not come to
her mind when Councillor Gktmglnt approached her with the
Mrdini contraception request. Unique the species was but she
hadn't quite realized HOW or that there were, indeed, no
other even vaguely similar creatures on the Mrdini planets.
Perhaps, in some prehistoric time on Clarf, primitive Mrdinis
had prevented or interfered with the evolution of biologically
similar life-forms. Whatever! That did not help Zara face, or
solve, the problem.

*In this instance, my dear,* Elizara said compassionately, *I
think we must approach the problem on an empirical basis.
While it would be helpful to* have *laboratory specimens on which
to experiment, such are not available. Have you discussed this
problem with any of the 'Dini medics?*

*Oh yes,* Zara replied quickly in such a tone of voice that
Elizara realized she had not received the answer she needed.

*They reminded me that Mrdini do not hesitate to go on the line when it is necessary for the survival of the species.*

Elizara shuddered and felt that Zara had done the same.

*I can't . . .* and Zara's voice was a wail of distress, *do that, Elizara. I just can't.*

*Then concentrate on the empirical, dear. That's all we can do. I shall stand by your* modus operandi *no matter what.*

*Thanks, Elizara,* and a little of the very young Zara whom Elizara had taken in as her student crept into that response.

*I'm always open to you, m'dear.*

And the contact broke.

*Better get out here, Laria. Four extremely dejected Mrdini just walked in,* Lionasha said.

*Dejected? But they've just been in hibernation.* Laria and Kincaid scrambled out of her bed and 'ported to the Tower foyer.

TIP, HUF, and she was down on her knees, embracing the shrivelled weary creatures who stared with hooded polls at the ground. Kincaid was hugging his pair and calling for restoratives that Lionasha was already preparing. The other 'Dinis clustered in an anxious circle, not the usual hilarious and joyous one with which returning 'Dinis were greeted: 'Dinis who were usually eager to resume their duties. WHAT HAS HAPPENED TO YOU?

She remembered how angry the keeper had been to have them arrive at the hibernatory so late, but surely a Mrdini keeper did not exact punishment for delays.

COLD. TERRIBLE. NO JOY. NO REFRESHMENT. Tip and Huf pushed into her arms as if they couldn't get close enough.

THERMAL COVERS, FIG, SIL, DIG, NIM, Lionasha ordered.

SHIFT IN ALL PILLOWS, TOO, Vanteer called after the 'Dinis scurrying to obey, murmuring in disturbed whispers as they went.

*Should we ask for a healer to come?* Kincaid asked.

*How could they be released in this condition?* Laria said angrily, soothing her pair with kisses and fondlings, all the time holding them as close to her as she could. *Their skin's all*

191

*wrinkled and they feel squishy. They've NEVER been this way before.*

*Nor mine,* said Kincaid in a tone that gave warning that he intended to investigate thoroughly.

*What's wrong? What's happened?* And Morag, Kaltia and their 'Dinis 'ported in, fortunately close to the steps as if both had 'seen' where it was safe to arrive.

'We don't know,' Laria said, struggling to keep her tone even.

'They're very sick,' Morag said, as Sim and Dar clung to her legs. Kev and Su had wrapped flippers about Kaltia, their poll eyes wet with fear.

The 'Dinis burst into the room, arms filled with pillows, trailing thermal covers, and instantly Morag and Kaltia arranged these into a nest, into which Kincaid and Laria put their wasted-looking 'Dinis. Lionasha offered the hot drinks she had prepared with herbs she knew were restorative for Mrdini.

'Shouldn't we get a healer for them?' Morag asked.

'There's *supposed* to be healers at the hibernatory for emergencies,' Laria said, barely able to suppress the anger she felt.

Suddenly the door to the Tower flew open and Plrgtgl, followed by other medium-large grey Mrdinis, charged right up to the invalids.

MOST APOLOGIES, PRIME LARIA. CAN NEVER SUITABLY AMEND APPALLING CONDITION OF YOUR DEVOTED FRIENDS. HERE ARE HEALERS TO ATTEND. CLEVER PRIME TO ALREADY START TO DO THE NECESSARY CARING. WE DID NOT KNOW THAT YOUR FRIENDS WERE THERE.

JUST WHAT THE HELL HAS HAPPENED?

*Easy, Laria. It's as upset as you are or Plus would not just barge in here,* Kincaid said. WE AWAIT AN EXPLANATION, he added in Mrdini, folding his arms in a fashion that was tantamount to an insult to Mrdinis.

Plus kept bowing, apologizing, almost incomprehensible in the speed with which it delivered regrets, remorse and promises of restitution.

192

SLOW DOWN, PLEASE, ESTIMABLE PLUS. WE CANNOT UNDER-
STAND WHAT YOU SAY. Laria had caught a garble about
inhibiting creation without harm and how were they going
to treat so many sick 'Dinis with so few to heal the desperately
deprived.

HEATING OF HIBERNATORY AT FAULT. COULD NOT REACH
ASSISTANCE. MANY SUFFER. WE COME TO YOU FIRST OF ALL
COLOURS.

*I'll bet they did,* Vanteer said, for he had folded his arms as
well to indicate the displeasure of the entire Tower. *They can't
afford to lose our goodwill.*

*You would take that position!* Laria retorted, eyes flashing so
angrily that Vanteer flinched as if she had lashed at him
mentally as well. She would have liked to, considering the
mundanity of his remark. THE TOWER SERVES CLARF'S NEEDS
NO MATTER WHAT OR WHEN, PLRGTGL.

HONOURABLE, HONOURABLE PRIME. Plus kept on bowing.
THESE FOUR UNFORTUNATES HAVE NOT BENEFITED. IS IT POSS-
IBLE THAT THEY COULD BE SENT TO IOTA AURIGAE WHERE
SPECIAL TREATMENT IS CURRENTLY AVAILABLE?

OF COURSE. BUT THEY ARE SCARCELY IN A CONDITION TO
TRAVEL ANYWHERE, Laria pointed out. SURELY HERE IN
CLARF . . .

IOTA AURIGAE, MOST RESPECTED PRIME, and Plus made such
a low obeisance that, for one anxious moment, Laria was
afraid it would tip over onto the supine 'Dinis, AS SOON AS
POSSIBLE. AS VERY SOON AS POSSIBLE.

THERE IS WORK FOR THE TOWER WHICH MUST BE COMPLETED.
I MUST ACCOMPANY TLP AND HGF, and she gestured to Kincaid,
NOR WILL KNCD LEAVE NPL AND PLS TO TRAVEL WITHOUT HIS
PRESENCE.

*LARIA!* Lionasha said aghast. *You can't . . .*

*Oh yes she can,* Morag said, taking a step forward, her jaw
set. *There's nothing here at Clarf that Kaltia and I cannot
handle, with you and Vanteer backing us up. The 'Dinis come
first right now and, for once, the Tower comes second.*

*Although it doesn't really since we're still here,* Kaltia put in,
jaw jutting out in stubbornness which both Lionasha and

Vanteer recognized as a family trait. *We are certainly able to do a few days on our own. I'm sure we won't have to pinch-hit for very long. Will we, Laria?*

*No longer than absolutely necessary. You can't know how Kincaid and I both appreciate your willingness, Morag, Kaltia.* Laria managed a grateful wisp of a smile. The relief in her expression at their volunteering underlined her belief in their abilities. She turned back to the Mrdini. IF OUR FOUR ARE IN SUCH POOR SHAPE, WHAT IS THE CONDITION OF THE OTHERS WHO SHARED HIBERNATION WITH THEM?

Plus turned the oddest shade and the healers glanced up from their ministrations with horror-stricken expressions.

I REQUIRE AN ANSWER, PLRGTGL.

THEY ARE BEING CARED FOR TO THE BEST OF OUR KNOWL-EDGE. MORE HELP MAY COME FROM IOTA AURIGAE. TLP, HGF, NPL AND PLS MUST BE GIVEN FIRST ADVANTAGE. CLRF HONOUR REQUIRES THIS. AH, LOOK NOW AND SEE THAT THEY ARE RESUM-ING A NORMAL COLOUR.

Laria looked as Kincaid, kneeling beside the four 'Dinis, gently touched each wizened chest in turn.

*The colour may be improved but I've never felt* spongy *'Dini flesh before. And they are not appreciably warmer.* Though his face did not mirror his concern, Kincaid expressed his sense of urgency in his 'path.

*Lionasha,* Morag said firmly, checking the afternoon's workload, *I see little more than light drones, message tubes and ordinary piffle.*

*Piffle?* Lionasha blinked at Morag. Kaltia leaned around her sister to look at the pad.

*Piffle's all it is, when you consider what we've done from Iota,* Kaltia said, her manner evincing more youthful disdain than Morag had exhibited.

*But your parents were there!* Lionasha said, alarmed.

Laria 'ported Lionasha's notepad to her. *I'd consider it piffle, too, Lio, after what we practised with on Iota. They can handle it. And probably a lot of what will come in, in the morning. Right now, Kincaid and I are going to Iota Aurigae if that's where we can get our 'Dinis treated properly.*

194

Vanteer took a forward step. *You'll check with Earth Prime first, of course?*

*I act on my own cognizance, Vanteer. You will assist my sisters and Lionasha to the best of your ability. Morag, 'port that multiple carrier to the door. Kaltia, 'port my mattress into it and all the pillows and thermals we have.* Then Laria turned to Plus. WE SHALL WASTE NO MORE OF YOUR VALUABLE TIME. YOUR HEALERS WILL HAVE OTHERS TO ATTEND. THE TOWER WILL CONTINUE ALL OPERATIONS. MORAG AND KALTIA ARE PRIMES AND THEIR ABILITIES ARE SUFFICIENT TO ANY TASK REQUIRED OF THEM.

RETURN YOUR 'DINIS TO CLRF IN FULL HEALTH, HONOURED PRIME. And Plus kept bowing itself as it moved backward towards the automatic door which opened, letting in a blast of the hot afternoon air.

*Carrier's all set,* Morag said. 'C'mon, Kaltia,' and she took the steps two at a time up to the Tower. 'We're operational as of right now. Thank goodness we know Iota Aurigae better than the back of our hands.'

*Sure but* you *tell Mother!*

*Don't slither, Kaltia.*

Vanteer heard his generators picking up and darted back down the steps, muttering imprecations about *children*, but Lionasha sent up the Iota Aurigae co-ordinates because she *had* to do something to steady her nerves.

Laria, Kincaid and the nested 'Dinis disappeared right into the carrier without bothering to open the wide hatch.

*MERGE!* cried Laria.

Vanteer, for one moment fearful for his beloved generators being manipulated by novices, put his fingers on the off-toggle but the pressure from the Tower was as deftly executed as if Laria and Kincaid were doing it.

'You left your SISTERS in charge of Clarf Tower?' Damia demanded when she and Afra were awakened by the arrival of a large personnel carrier in front of the house at dawn on Iota Aurigae.

*Considering the urgency of getting their 'Dinis here,* Afra said

195

with quiet authority, gently moving his outraged wife to one side at the window, *they could do nothing else and I'm sure Morag and Kaltia will have Lionasha, as well as the two at Sef Tower, to guide them. ZARA!*

'I'm down here,' and Zara appeared, in the act of shrugging a warm cover over her bare body. She knelt beside the carrier, opening it only far enough to reach in and touch the nearest of the four 'Dinis. Warmer clothing rained down on her. 'You did right. They're in very bad condition but don't worry. I know exactly what to do. Get out, Kincaid. I'm the only Human who has permission to enter the hibernatory here.'

Kincaid did not argue though, after the heat in the carrier, he and Laria began to shiver in the crisp cold morning air of Iota Aurigae.

'Inside!' Damia said, pointing to the house.

'But I said I'd be with . . .' Laria began and disappeared.

Having 'ported her daughter inside the house, Damia gave Kincaid a merciless stare of tacit permission and he 'ported himself inside, too.

'Into the kitchen with you,' Damia said, deftly 'porting herself into unoccupied space in the entrance hall. Then Afra was beside her, throwing woollen wraps around the shoulders of the new arrivals. They pulled them tightly round their bodies.

'I didn't think Zara would have to put her new expertise to the test quite this soon,' Afra said, his hands gently propelling Kincaid and Laria to follow Damia to the kitchen where she indulged in a remarkable display of domestic telekinetic activities. These produced a hot meal, a choice of beverages and additional early-morning snacks that Damia happened to know were favourites of her daughter and Kincaid Dano. While the new arrivals consumed warm food and beverages, they 'pathed the account of the circumstances that had precipitated their arrival.

'And if ours are this sick, I'd want to know what exactly *are* the conditions of the rest of those in Clarf's biggest and most prestigious hibernatory,' Laria said, holding out her cup to be refilled. She was too shaken to do that herself.

196

'The Mrdini are attempting to curtail their birth rate now that so few die in Hive attacks,' Damia said. 'So, in what has turned out to be a very ill-advised attempt to limit creation, they lowered the temperature in the hibernatories.'

'ALL of them?' Laria exclaimed, nearly spilling the hot liquid in her cup in astonishment.

'Fortunately, no. Unfortunately, the main one in Clarf was evidently a test site,' Afra said. 'This is after the fact, Laria, or I'm sure you'd've been warned not to take yours there.'

Laria flushed. 'They were overdue to hibernate and the keeper rushed them in.' She frowned and turned to Kincaid.

'That explains its cryptic remarks, I guess,' Kincaid said ruefully.

Afra paused a moment and then asked, 'You're sure there's nothing Morag and Kaltia can't handle?'

'Nothing. They've been exceedingly well trained,' Laria said, with a bow to her parents.

'They consider the afternoon's quota of tubes is mere "piffle",' Kincaid said with a droll smile.

'And tomorrow's?' Damia asked, not quite scowling but concerned, knowing the amount of traffic Clarf Tower was handling.

'They can handle whatever we can,' Kincaid said with a shrug. 'We'll return as soon as we're certain our 'Dinis are in good hands.'

'You'll get right back to . . .' Damia began, but Afra, making eye contact with Kincaid, put a restraining hand on his mate's shoulder.

'Their priorities are correct, Damia,' he said, using a tone and firmness he rarely directed at her. 'They have left their Tower well attended so they're scarcely derelict in their duties.' He gave her a quick smile then turned back to Kincaid. 'We will ask Lionasha and Vanteer not to reveal who is actually 'porting at Clarf. I doubt Plrgtgl will even know you're here.'

'Plus saw us leave,' Laria was obliged to admit, seeing now through her mother's reaction how ill-advised their abrupt departure was.

*It wasn't,* and Kincaid's hand gripped her thigh firmly.

197

'From what Plrgtgl said, it will be far too busy treating the other . . . victims . . . to question how Clarf Tower is being handled so long as it is operational. I can, of course, return immediately, and leave my friends with Laria to deputize for me.'

'Only when they are well enough not to require the reassurance your presence can give them,' Afra said.

Damia was blinking in surprise at Afra's domination of the interchanges.

'So some idiot decided that freezing 'Dinis would prevent reproduction?' Laria asked scornfully.

'You'd think the last thing a 'Dini would do is emulate a queen,' Kincaid remarked caustically.

Damia did frown. 'How do you construe that?'

'Well, the Heinlein queen nearly died from cold before she started hatching eggs for attendants,' Kincaid replied. 'Or perhaps you never saw the report I did. When they installed the queen at Heinlein, they provided the same ambient temperature that had been in her escape pod. What they didn't realize was that was not the normal Hive temperature: it was low to reduce her activity level by the cold so she'd have the maximum amount of oxygen to take her where she meant to go.'

'So it was plain logic, rather than communication, that Zara acted on that time?' Damia asked.

'She's always been interested in biology,' Afra said. 'She acted on a logical conclusion she didn't know how to explain at the time. I'm glad to hear *what* prompted her.'

'But that doesn't explain why the Mrdini would use cold to reduce creation.'

Afra gave Kincaid a wry look. 'Mrdini logic sometimes defeats Human mental processes.'

'It damned near killed our 'Dinis,' Laria said in a savage tone and added an unreproduceable sound of disgust. 'So how is it that Zara happens to be here in Iota Aurigae and able to nurse 'Dinis?'

'She has had metamorphic training,' Damia began, 'and Elizara felt that, having grown up with 'Dinis, she was the best

198

available medical personnel. Your grandfather as well as the High Councillors considered her the proper choice . . .' Damia paused, emanating a complex blend of pride, anxiety and surprise. 'A select, high-powered team of medical and xenbees has been assembled and permitted to enter a hibernatory to see exactly what does happen. Whatever activities ordinarily take place are limited to specially chosen and trained keepers.'

Laria and Kincaid exchanged respectful glances. 'Well, good on Zara,' said her proud sister. 'So she . . . or someone else here on Iota . . . really can restore ours?'

'I'd rest easy on that score, my dear,' Afra said. Then he rose suddenly and strode from the room.

'What's . . .' Laria began.

'I believe your father is aware that Vagrian is awake,' Damia said.

'Oh, him! I completely forgot you took him on.'

'It may be early, but perhaps we could do stables. I'd find it soothing work,' Kincaid said, rising.

'I'll help.'

'Now just a moment, Laria,' her mother began.

'With all deference, Damia, we'll do stables,' Kincaid said. He took Laria's hand in his and they 'ported out of the room, the height of bad manners for Talents and especially in front of Damia Raven-Lyon.

*How dare . . .*

*Enough, Damia,* Afra said so bluntly that Damia was silent.

Though they were safely out of the house, Kincaid and Laria winced, waiting for Damia's reaction to such a dictate.

'Better we were rude just to Mother,' Laria murmured as she and Kincaid strode quickly up to the stables. 'I'd've been a lot ruder in Vagrian's presence. I wonder how Zara copes with him.'

'I suspect she's not around often enough right now for that to be a problem,' Kincaid said. 'Imagine that! She's allowed in a hibernatory! That's another first for the formidable Lyon's Pride.'

' "Lyon's Pride?" ' Laria stopped and stared at him.

199

'Well, you are, you know, and it's meant as a compliment by all I've heard use the term,' he said in a placatory tone.

'Lyon's Pride, huh,' and Laria savoured the label and then chuckled. 'Does Dad know?'

'I shouldn't wonder,' Kincaid replied.

'Hope Mother doesn't. She's rather partial to being a Gwyn-Raven.'

'So she should be.' Kincaid slid apart the stable doors and grinned as the inmates whickered joyfully at such an early arrival of those-who-fed. There was additional noise of shod hooves scraping against plascrete floors as resting horses rose to all four legs.

In the first right-hand stable, Saki nickered more urgently, stamping her feet in welcome to a well-known voice, demanding her breakfast nuggets.

'The morning feeds are usually made up night before,' Laria said, pausing to let her favourite horse sniff, then lick, her palm. 'The middle door.'

'I remember . . . and so they are.'

Saki pushed at Laria, obviously urging her to speed her breakfast to her, so Laria trotted down to the feed room and helped Kincaid load the trolley. 'We have to start with Saki or she'll damage her knees, kicking the door if anyone else's fed first.'

'Shamelessly spoiled . . .'

'Knows she's the Alpha mare.'

'Will they mind a Lyon-Dano in the Pride?' Kincaid asked, pulling out the feed dish of the brown gelding opposite Saki who seemed to be inhaling her pellets.

'I told you, I don't want you bound officially,' Laria said, moving down the aisle to the next horse.

'Our child will have two parents and that's not negotiable, Laria Gwyn-Raven-Lyon-Dano,' Kincaid said in almost the same adamant tone Afra had used to Damia.

'Like that, are you?' Laria grinned, rather pleased at his attitude, as she dumped yet another breakfast into a manger.

'Unless your parents kick up a stink . . .'

They happened to be facing each other over the feed-flat.

200

'I doubt that, Kincaid Dano,' and she not only made eye contact with him but opened her mind, letting him see her high regard for the person he had struggled to become despite a miserable childhood, 'since they already respect *you*. As well as,' she added in a blithe tone, 'quite likely admire you for putting up with their eldest daughter. Now, let's finish feeding.'

The activity of feeding, haying and straightening stable sheets had a soothing effect on them both, considering the multiple shocks of the day.

'Therapeutic, even,' Laria said, spending a little extra time with Saki to brush a stable stain from the flank of her favourite horse.

'Isn't this the fellow I rode the last time I was here?' Kincaid asked, stepping back to get a proper look at the animal he was tending.

'Sure is, and he seems to remember you fondly enough not to race you around the box.'

Afra appeared in the wide stable opening. 'Beliakin's presence has been requested at Blundell House for the next few days, in connection with Clarissia Negeva's attempt to recruit him,' he said. 'He had the good sense to tell Gollee immediately before he left Blundell. They knew she had, of course, but him coming forward acquits him.'

'He'd've had significant assets to lose,' Laria said blandly, 'but I'm glad I don't have to dodge him.' She gave her father a quick glance to see if she could 'path the real reason Beliakin was now elsewhere.

Afra chuckled but she could read nothing beyond what he wished her to know. 'That young man could see far too many excellent possibilities in the immediate future to jeopardize them. He told us exactly what he recalled of her remarks immediately after that abortive assassination attempt. He was shocked enough, when we heard, to be wide open to us. He *is* a strong T-2 kinetic and once he has cleared himself with Gollee and Jeff, he's liable to be assigned to either a Search Vessel or with a T-2 'path for one of the new Towers that have to be set up.'

201

Laria eyed her father with scepticism and he grinned back, his yellow eyes twinkling.

'Of course, with you and Kincaid here we could allow him the chance to clear his reputation at Blundell. So this will be no holiday for you, though I could wish it were. You are more tired than you should be, Laria,' Afra said and, in an unusual display of affection, stroked her head. His hand stopped and his brows wrinkled in surprise. 'And . . .' His expression was puzzled.

Kincaid instantly stepped to her side. 'Laria carries my child, Afra Lyon.'

Afra nodded briefly. 'The pregnancy is very recent, then, for I can barely detect the physical changes.' He held out his hand to Kincaid. Kincaid did not shield the relief he felt at the quickly proffered hand, taking the gesture as the approval it was meant to reinforce. 'I will have to admit,' Afra continued with a warm grin, 'that I am relieved that you have sired the child, Dano, rather than Vanteer or Beliakin.'

'Beliakin never got near enough to touch me,' Laria said, affronted by the mere thought.

*And too recent to guess its sex!* came Damia's interjection.

*And what if it isn't Talented, Mother?* Laria asked coyly.

*Don't be ridiculous,* Damia said dismissively. *Dano's genes checked out with a very high potential of passing on psychic abilities.*

*Mother, that's . . .* Laria felt a surge of anger.

*Let be, Laria,* Afra said in quick reprimand. *We've known that much data since Kincaid was assigned to Clarf Tower.*

*Then you know what I . . .* Kincaid began when a quick cutting motion of Afra's hand interrupted him.

*That is between you and Laria!* Afra said so firmly that his answer dismissed further consideration of the topic. *Am I not correct, Damia?*

*You are,* was the immediate agreement.

'It may be morning here, but it was late afternoon on Clarf, as memory serves me,' Afra went on. 'The horses are tended. You both need to rest. You may have just to settle for breakfast instead of whatever meal you have missed in your

202

haste to get your 'Dinis here. But you are both tired and anxious. I'd say you'd benefit from a relaxing swim. And some rest.'

Laria swivelled in the direction of the Tower.

'We can handle what's due in or out. We'll wake you the moment there's any news about your 'Dinis,' Afra said.

*Zara says they're already responding to the medicated bath. They absorb quite a lot of nutrients through the skin pores, you know,* said Damia.

'Where are Ewain and Petra?' Laria asked as they followed Afra back to an oddly silent house.

'School, of course,' Afra said. He bent to kiss his daughter's cheek. 'Damia sent them. They don't know you're here yet and we'll keep them out of your hair until you've had a chance to rest.'

Then, with a hand on each to shove them in the direction of the pool, he left them.

# CHAPTER NINE

*Zara's here,* said Damia gently, waking them. *Your 'Dinis're improving rapidly,* she added when she sensed their immediate alarm. *Come down.*

'What time is it?' Kincaid asked, then yawned widely enough to pop his jaw hinge, stretching his long body.

'Late afternoon, Iota time,' Laria said, struggling to lift herself on one elbow to glance out her window and check the way the shadows fell on the hillside. Odd to be waking in her own bed, with Kincaid beside her. Odd, but nice.

'I feel like I've slept the clock round.' He sat up, rubbing a lean and empty belly.

*You did,* said Zara.

Both shot to their feet, grabbing for clothes they had dumped in a chair after their relaxing swim. Someone must have removed the damp towels which Laria vaguely remembered dropping on the floor on her way to the bed.

*You needed it,* Zara went on.

*Morag and Kaltia? Are they all right?* Laria said, hopping on one foot, trying to get the other foot into the trouser leg.

*Take it easy,* and there was a touch of amusement in Zara's voice. *You can bet your bones you'd've been awakened sooner if*

*there'd been a need. Dad says they're doing just great. Blood will
tell.*

*So what's with Tip and Huf . . .*

*And Nil and Plus . . .* Kincaid put in with such matching
anxiety that Zara's chuckle echoed in both their heads.

*When you get down here.*

*There're drinks and things ready,* Damia added.

Speedily dressing, the two lingered only long enough to visit
the bathroom and wash hands and faces before they went
downstairs. Laria led the way into the room Kincaid remembered from his previous stay, where a circle of comfortable
couches ringed a fireplace. Flames danced on the hearth and
they were glad of the warmth by then, accustomed to Clarf's
heat and not the crisp colder temperature at which this house
was generally kept.

Zara was already ensconced on one couch, nibbling a long
thin cheese stick. She pointed to the drinks set opposite her
and the variety of pre-dinner snacks. 'Don't eat too much.
Mother's planning a good dinner to make up for the meals
you've missed.'

'Tip and Huf?' Laria asked, brooking no further delays.

'And my two?' Kincaid added but they both sat at Zara's
gesture.

'What I have to tell you is highly confidential. Dad's out
hunting with Ewain, and Petra and Mother have promised not
to listen.'

Laria regarded Zara with surprise and a touch of trepida-
tion. She sounded more like her grandmother than her kid
sister.

'As head of a team trying to penetrate the mysteries of
Mrdini reproduction, I must also be as discreet as possible in
my explanations. But, to my way of thinking, you're owed.
Your 'Dinis ought NOT to have been in *that* hibernatory. And
the keeper should have had the sense to tell you to take them
anywhere else.'

'That's where they usually go,' Laria exclaimed.

'So what happened there?' Kincaid asked.

'A damned-fool experiment that any zoo-bio would have

205

quashed instantly had we known it was planned,' Zara said, biting off the last of her cheese stick, as if it was something else. She let out a sigh. Then, resettling herself, she turned to Laria and Kincaid and began.

'We're still not sure *what* happens or why certain pairs choose each other, or are put together by the keeper for the express purpose of . . . creating a new 'Dini life-form . . . but Tip would not necessarily be matched with Huf, nor Plus with Nil in a hibernatory. Colours are always paired. As we've discovered, Human bodies replicate every single cell over a seven-year period. Mrdini . . .' and Zara gave a wry smile, 'do it in two months. From what we've been able to discern, dead cells in a 'Dini give off an unhealthy chemical . . .'

Laria and Kincaid exchanged startled glances, remembering that their 'Dinis had been smelling a little stronger than usual . . .

'Hmm . . . the fools were probably delaying as long as they could then. However, the dead cells give off phero-mones up to a hundred units (let's call the measurement. At a concentration of ninety units, 'Dini start getting irritable and try to get to the hibernatory to relieve their discomfort. Most 'Dinis wait too long to come to the hibernatory. But I have discovered that those who come early, say when the chemical is at seventy-five units, are less likely to reproduce. If the concentration got over the hundred mark, they'd probably die but we haven't confirmed that. You see, what substitutes for hormones or glandular activity or cell renew-al and differentiation in their particular physiology works mainly to rejuvenate them cell by cell. From the extra "material" . . .' and Zara shrugged, spreading her hands to indicate she couldn't find a more appropriate word '. . . generated by this extraordinary osmotic process, a new 'Dini is created – between them – but not IN or FROM them . . . just between them. The new life could be con-sidered a clone, but not as we understand or use that process: but they are created, budded, what-have-you from the brand-new rejuvenated material of the process the 'Dinis called "refreshment" – which is actually quite accurate –

206

and they are a mix of the two Mrdini between whom they are made.

'They gorge themselves with a high-protein, high-mineral, complex carbohydrate substance, the recipe for which is known only to the keepers. We've been trying to analyse it but there are some elements . . . Never mind, I digress,' and Zara flapped her hand in self-reprimand, 'and the air in a hibernatory is not only hot, but humid with a special blend of pheromones. The best analogy is the sort of dream state created by some chemicals . . . again a formula zealously guarded by the keepers. I don't know if the pheromones could be altered to provide contraception. Or if the earlier hibernation will do the trick. Frankly, I think our solution is to find out which of the chemicals used can be left out and not trigger the clone/bud to develop. A sort of abortion, if you will, except that it's not taking anything as yet "live". I wouldn't like to think how many eggs we females produce that never get fertilized,' and she shot a grin at Kincaid, 'but that would be an appropriate analogue. The bad news is that some nineteen different components are used in the hibernatory incense. The really bad news is that there are no 'Dini-type experimental animals on which we could try any solution before using it on real live 'Dinis.' Zara heaved a big sigh but that didn't fool her sister. The ethics of direct experimentation on a life-form they considered their equal would have been anathema to any dedicated medical person. 'Then, too, the recipe is so old that the keepers have forgotten exactly what the basic elements are, only how to mix and burn it at a steady rate of emissions. So, we've set up nineteen different wards, you might call 'em, in Iota's hibernatory, and thank all the gods that be that it's such a new facility and we can separate the wards completely. In each ward a different chemical will be omitted, while the rest of the hibernators get the usual incense. When we've figured *that* out, we can decide what chemical to eliminate. One just can't stop all "creation" without some notice being taken of it in the general 'Dini population.' She grinned. 'It's going to take time. But we will succeed.'

'Reassuring yourself, sis?' Laria asked with an understanding grin. She was still close enough in mental rapport with her sister to catch Zara's frustration, despite the very positive statement of intent.

'Yes, I am,' Zara agreed, much to Laria's surprise. 'It's the time it's going to take to be absolutely sure that what happened to your quartet isn't repeated anywhere else that's so frustrating.'

'Did many die?' Kincaid asked.

Zara nodded slowly. Her expression was grim. 'Not the best way to reduce excess population.'

'Were any very important 'Dinis lost?' Laria asked.

'Yes, and some whose matches were also lost so they can't be replaced as Gil and Kat were. No big 'Dinis were involved in the Clarf fiasco. Their hibernations are strictly for the "refreshment" aspect of the seclusion. The "creative" stage is quite individual but the larger the 'Dini the less it is likely to have enough left of the "creative" material required to produce a juvenile.'

'That's a lot more than we've ever known,' Laria said thoughtfully.

'It took us Humans long enough to learn to control our populations,' Zara said. 'We have had many 'Dinis, every colour, come forward and agree to be used as anatomical subjects . . .'

'WHAT?' Kincaid was no less horrified than Laria but she was able to voice her objection.

'Well, they don't leave a corpse, you know. Oh, you didn't know? Since they evolved on such a hot planet, they have a water-regulating physiology, reacting to osmotic pressure. So they sort of turn to mush when the physiology shuts down at death, the cells rupture and essentially the body disintegrates. Unless they are immediately used . . . ooops . . . well, let's not get into the archaic tradition of "going on the line". They were rendered unconscious but had to be used immediately or immersed in a solution of the right liquids until they are used. None of us like the idea of . . . operating on a live entity . . . and keep hoping we won't be forced to that expedient.' Her face had turned as pale as theirs. She went on more briskly. 'They do have a entirely different attitude towards death. You both know that from the history of suicide raids on the Hiver Spheres. They were convinced that they, as themselves, would be re-created. As Gil and Kat were.'

'But to dissect a LIVE 'Dini . . .' Laria could not continue, shaking her head in repugnance.

'I've learned a lot more about Mrdinis since I started this assignment, Laria,' Zara said in the most solemn and respectful tone Laria had ever heard from her younger sister. 'And since we're seeing it more and more as a pheromone problem, we won't need biological dissections. Ooops, sorry. You're looking very green, Lar.'

'Exactly *what* is happening to our friends?' Kincaid said anxiously.

'We're refreshing them. They're in separate tubs, to get the full benefit of that osmotic therapy, and in the same room. At the rate they're absorbing the substance, they should be physically fit again in about three more weeks. You were smart to get them here as fast as you did. I've made arrangements with the head keeper to allow you to come and see them whenever you wish. They're not really conscious right now, but they'll *know* you're there.'

'Three weeks?' Laria was alarmed. There was no way she could be absent from Clarf that long.

'There's not a thing that prevents us from coming back as often as we're needed,' Kincaid said, a reassuring hand squeezing Laria's knee.

Clarf's Tower Prime rolled her eyes as she realized that he was right.

'You've had a shock, sis,' Zara said. Then she shook a finger at them. 'You're not to wear yourselves out – not with the time distortion between Iota Aurigae and Clarf. You especially, Laria,' and her finger settled warningly. 'Not,' and she smiled, 'that I'm not delighted.'

'You looked?' Laria was perversely annoyed at her sister's knowledge of her pregnancy.

Zara guffawed. 'Honey, the change didn't require me to

209

look any further than the glow in your skin and a certain shine in the eye that many pregnant women develop.'

Laria turned to Kincaid. 'Do I look *that* different?'

'If I say yes, you'll thump me,' Kincaid replied with mock fear, pretending to recoil from her wrath.

'Would not!'

'Then you've mellowed, sis,' was Zara's tart response. 'You're built right for having babies, unlike the Rowan, but take it easy – as easy as possible,' she corrected herself immediately, 'in Tower work. Give Morag more of the Merges. She can handle anything. And it wouldn't hurt Kaltia to take a few either. They're well able for it after their apprenticeship here, even if they are technically too young to be full Primes.' She grinned. 'Just as if I had the say in the matter.' *OK to join us, Mother, Dad.*

Damia and Afra did so, Damia carrying a tray of hot canapés.

'You shouldn't've let us sleep so long,' Laria began.

'After your sister the healer said you obviously both needed it?' Damia replied, raising an eyebrow in reproof. 'We've checked with the girls and they're coping superbly.'

'Though they do feel,' Afra added, 'that not every single relative of the many they have – bar Thian and Rojer who probably are unaware of the circumstances at Clarf Tower – needs to check in on an hourly basis.'

'Lionasha would let us know,' Laria started, sharing what she also considered an affront to the capabilities of the pair, as well as a tacit criticism of herself.

Kincaid gave her a gentle nudge with his elbow. 'Where are all the *other* 'Dinis I know live here?'

Zara chuckled. 'The adults are all taking turns nursing your lot and the young are out with Ewain and Petra, hunting. Eat!' and she pointed imperiously at the tray Damia now presented to them.

'I'd sort of looked forward to hunting,' Kincaid remarked in mild disappointment.

'You can hunt all day tomorrow if you want . . .' Damia began.

'Only after we've seen our friends,' Laria said.

'You can come in with me after dinner,' Zara said. 'They'll be lucid enough to know you're nearby.'

'Lucid?' And every ounce of Laria's anxiety returned.

'Because,' and Afra sat himself down on the other side of his distressed eldest daughter, 'they're swimming in a nutrient fluid and so surfeited with regenerative substances that they're not likely to make much sense.'

Laria wasn't sure she found that description any more reassuring.

*I wouldn't lie to you, Lar,* Zara said, passing her cheese-sticks. 'Don't you like these any more?'

*Well, that's nicer than reminding me I'm eating for two.*

*You haven't even started* that.

'Enough,' Damia said.

'Why, Mom? Can't you read us?' and Zara grinned, reverting to her gamine and younger self.

'There's a level at which you two can communicate that excludes us,' Afra admitted as Damia hesitated. He looked directly at Kincaid then. 'The sort of level that develops between two people who are often in Merge and rapport. Morag and Kaltia, being so close in age, have that facility. So do Ewain and Petra. Thian could go in either direction, to you, Laria, or to Rojer. But clearly,' and he waved the cheese stick he was eating from Zara to Laria, 'the girls can activate the old side-slip at will.'

'Side-slip?' Kincaid asked. 'Is it limited to siblings and couples?'

Damia shrugged. 'I doubt it. It works when it works.'

Afra chuckled, deep down in his chest. 'Jeff has often remarked that he can't say anything that your mother doesn't hear.'

'And you, Afra Lyon?' asked Damia, cocking her head at her mate of twenty-seven years.

Afra merely smiled. 'That's for me to know and you to find out!'

'Why, you ornery yellow-eyed Capellan . . .'

'Kitchen timer's ringing, Mother,' Zara said, pointing.

211

'Oh, lord . . .' and Damia moved so quickly she might as well have 'ported.

'Do you, Dad?' Zara asked in a whisper.

Afra's response was another chuckle.

'Oh, you!' she exclaimed in disgust when he refused to answer.

The clatter of horses' hooves, yells from jubilant hunters, provided an additional distraction.

'I can't believe Ewain and Petra hunt for the family now,' Laria said, rising.

'They're pretty good at it, too,' Afra said, unfolding his long frame. He peered out the window. 'They'll need help.'

Which the young hunters did, their horses laden with avians and scurriers.

'Did you bring me in any fresh greens and tubers?' Zara demanded, her expression somewhat censorious as she watched the unpacking.

'Sure, sis,' and Ewain tossed her a sack that had been tied to the front of his saddle. 'Not much at this time of the year but there's enough for your needs.'

In the absence of any of the family Mrdinis who enjoyed helping in the kitchen, the Humans all pitched in, Kincaid electing to dress down the carcasses outside the back door. Avians particularly were best eaten fresh and the scurriers lightly grilled. Vegetables were prepared and, with so many to help, dinner was ready in a very short space of time: a dinner to which Laria and Kincaid did full justice.

'You three go on now,' Damia said. 'We'll clean up . . .' and she included Ewain and Petra.

'Aw, Ma, we hunted,' complained Petra. 'And I've studies . . .'

'You may 'port to save time,' Damia said, 'but don't you dare show off or break a single dish.'

Zara beckoned for Laria and Kincaid to exit quietly before Ewain could start his protests.

The main hibernatory on Iota Aurigae was in the hills above the city and had been built with considerable care by the first

212

'Dinis who came to the mining world. Damia and Afra had insisted on, and 'ported in, the favourite woods and other materials preferred by the Mrdini. A special 'growing' tank had also been constructed though, until very recently, no Human had known what was grown in it, only that the substance was essential for a good hibernation.

Zara did not park the airsled in front of the entrance but swung around back, landing on a ledge that apparently had been built for discreet and private use. Two other small craft were parked. Zara neatly took the single remaining empty space. Emerging, Laria and Kincaid could see no visible entry.

Zara grinned. 'They've left nothing to chance,' she said and walked right up to the apparently seamless rock. She touched something and instantly a door opened outward. She ducked inside, for the lintel was low, gesturing urgently for Laria and Kincaid to enter quickly. The door shut and Laria felt her ears pop.

Zara turned on a wrist light. 'I know the way but it's narrow and I don't want you falling.'

Laria caught the unusual odour and had to cram a finger under her nose to keep from sneezing. Then she became conscious of the incredibly humid heat.

*We've only a few steps to go. Door's to our left. Slip in as fast as possible. That smell can get to you real fast.*

Her wrist light showed them the door and they followed so closely that they nearly stumbled in their effort to enter. The panel slid shut so fast it just missed Kincaid's heels. They were on the landing of a flight of stairs, lit from a brighter light below, and Zara led the way down to yet another door. This opened into a laboratory of considerable size, filled with smells that made Laria very nauseous – those pheromones Zara'd been talking about? There were busy Humans and 'Dinis, diligently peering into microscopes or other instruments at their workstations. Zara's entry with her companions was noted only briefly by those they passed.

'Your 'Dinis are in the private infirmary,' and Zara pointed to her right, to the side aisle in which closed doors were unevenly spaced. 'Third one on the left,' she said. Again a

213

swift parting and then closing of the door. LR AND KNCD HERE NOW, she said, pointing to a viewing window that gave onto a dimly lit inner room.

Instantly a panel slid aside and her parents' two 'Dinis, Tri and Fok, emerged. Laria was immediately surprised at how much larger they'd become as they embraced her, their heads at her shoulder level.

YOU ARE SO BIG NOW, she exclaimed, leaning only slightly down to hold them tightly against her. THANK YOU FOR HELPING TLP AND HGF.

AND NPL AND PLS, Kincaid adding, spreading his fingers on their shoulders.

THEY DO BETTER NOW, Fok told Kincaid, turning to hold out its flipper and squeeze Dano's hand firmly. SHOULD NEVER HAVE BEEN TAKEN THERE IN FIRST PLACE. WHY WERE YOU NOT TOLD?

WE DON'T KNOW WHY, Laria said. THEY NEEDED TO GO AND DID NOT ASK TO BE TAKEN UNTIL WE REALIZED THEY HAD TO GO.

Tri looked up at Laria, its poll eye unblinking. CAN GUESS.

GUESS WHAT, TRI? Laria insisted.

YOU SEE THEM NOW, Tri said and pulled her with it. YOU TOO KNCD.

*Go with them,* Zara said. *I'll tell you one thing: the four of them got chewed to small pieces and spat out when Tri and Fok first spoke to them. Never heard 'Dinis speak like that. Even older 'Dinis.*

*Tri and Fok have grown so much . . .*

*They're four-letter 'Dinis now, too, by the way. Congratulate them when you can.*

Then they were inside the dim room and could make out the four tanks, smell the astringent odour of the fluid in which their 'Dinis were floating. There were other odours mixed in with astringency as well as traces of the strong smell that had assailed them as they entered the hibernatory.

Despite the immersion of her friends almost to the poll eyes, Laria had no trouble identifying Tip and Huf and knelt between their tanks, reaching out to stroke the sides of their heads, below the poll eye.

WE HAVE MISSED YOU AS MUCH AS WE WOULD MISS OUR HEARTS, Kincaid murmured, one hand on each of his 'Dinis' necks.

BETTER NOW, Nil muttered in a voice just barely above a whisper.

OH TIP, HUF, WE ARE HERE FOR YOU. Laria felt Zara touch her mind with reassurance and great affection.

MUCH BETTER, SINCE NOT SILLY NOW AND DO AS TOLD, Tri said quite firmly, coming around the tank to its head and emptying in a small pail of something whose fumes came close to making Laria gag. She felt Zara instantly depress the reaction.

YOU SLEEP, SLEEP WELL, Huf said before Fok emptied a pail into its tank and a second wave of nausea nearly overwhelmed Laria.

YOU COULD HAVE WAITED, FOK, TRI, Zara said with some impatience.

CANNOT WAIT, Fok said, trotting off, empty pail swinging in its flipper. EXACT ON TIME IS IMPORTANT. YOU BRING THEM BACK BETWEEN PAILS. ENOUGH FOR NOW. SHORT VISIT BEST.

*They have seen you and felt your touch and love,* Zara said, putting a hand under Laria's arm and lifting her up.

Kincaid rose, too, swallowing convulsively. His reaction made Laria feel less weak-stomached.

*It affects all Humans that way,* Zara said drolly as she pushed them towards the door. 'But it's always good to breathe fresh air again,' she added as they were once more in the ante-room. OH, THERE YOU ARE, she said to the four 'Dinis who were sitting on stools. THESE HAVE GROWN, TOO, SO YOU MAY NOT RECOGNIZE EWAIN'S VTL AND BFR AND PETRA'S JN AND THV.

IT IS GOOD TO MEET THE FRIENDS OF MY BROTHER AND SISTER, Laria said, executing an appropriate bow to the young 'Dinis. THIS IS KNCD WHO YOU MAY NOT REMEMBER.

WE KNOW NPL AND PLS AND HELP ALL WE CAN, Vtl replied, bowing more deeply.

WE ARE MORE GRATEFUL THAN WE CAN EVER EXPRESS AT THE CARE AND ATTENTION YOU ALL ARE GIVING OUR SICK FRIENDS,

215

Kincaid said and his bow was deeper than Laria's. Vtl was almost embarrassed and Thv, the youngest of them all, slid quietly behind Jn.

DO NOT BE EMBARRASSED BY GOODWILL OF KNCD, Zara told them. OTHERWISE HE WOULD BE WITHOUT HIS FRIENDS AND YOU KNOW HOW PAINFUL THAT IS.

WE DO, and all four of the young 'Dinis now bowed as deeply as Kincaid had.

Laria was still experiencing nausea and she could see the odd greenish tinge to Kincaid's face.

EXCUSE US, GOOD MRDINI FRIENDS. WE LEAVE, Zara said and 'ported all of them out to the clear crisp cold air of the ledge.

Laria leaned weakly against the airsled while Kincaid stood, inhaling and exhaling in deep draughts.

'That's the best way to clear your lungs,' Zara said. 'I'm so used to the stenches that I don't even smell them any more.'

'You mean,' and Kincaid pointed to the solid cliff, 'you can get *used* to that smell?'

'I've smelled a lot worse lately,' Zara said with a wry smile. 'C'mon, Laria, climb into that sled before you fall in. They've seen you, you've seen them, and Flkm and Trpl have reassured you. Those two could have waited until you'd left before they slopped your 'Dinis again,' she added irritably.

'Are they getting even with us then, for not taking good care of ours?' Laria wanted to know, carefully fastening the seat-belt since she still felt woozy. She heard Kincaid's belt click, too.

'No, just being officious. They're actually enjoying the celebrity they've acquired by being able to effect a rapid improvement.'

'How many did die at Clarf?'

'Too many.' It was obvious to Laria from Zara's tone that she was not going to give statistics. 'The very young and the oldest. The mid-age group seemed to have more resilience and are responding to treatment.'

'The same ours are getting?'

Zara nodded, flying carefully around the back of the hibernatory. Of that Laria was just as pleased, for the route

216

they'd taken on the way in had required some dips and veerings that Laria was not certain her innards could have handled.

'I'll give you something for nausea when we get home,' Zara said kindly. 'The big "if",' she went on in a grim voice, 'is whether or not your friends – and the other survivors – will be able to create again. So essentially we have two diametrically opposite problems to solve: contraception and restoration of the creative function.'

'And?' Kincaid asked gently.

Zara gave a shrug. 'If we succeed in finding which pheromones can be withdrawn to provide contraception, the top Mrdini will be happy. We'll try to concentrate on the majority. We'll do the best we can on the other.'

With that to mull over, no-one spoke on the flight back. Zara parked the sled but before the other two could descend, Zara offered Laria a shot glass with a pale green liquid in it. 'Drink. Then go watch the sunset. That's as much a part of restoring your equilibrium as the potion.' She shooed them off towards the steps leading up to the little garden that had been created especially to view the sinking sun of Iota Aurigae.

Very few on Clarf ever knew that there had been a substitution of Tower Primes. At first, quick-witted Lionasha implied that Laria and Kincaid were exceedingly busy helping the poor unfortunate victims of the Hibernatory Disaster. 'Which actually isn't a lie at all.'

'Fiasco, not disaster. You can prevent fiascoes,' Vanteer grumbled from his engineering station.

The *official* story spread by Mrdini keepers was that power had failed at the hibernatory and all attempts by the keeper to repair the damage had been in vain, causing the death of four hundred and five of the seven hundred and eighty-nine using the facility. Very few knew that this had been an attempt to interrupt conception. On Clarf, of course, everyone knew that one did not interrupt hibernation and the keeper had been overly confident in its ability to cope with the emergency. By the time it admitted failure, the damage was done. Top

217

technicians from other Mrdini planets were called in to restore power and cleanse the building. If a discreet new facility was added on one of the upper ranks, it escaped notice in the general confusion of repair. The head keeper and its staff were permanently reduced to menial rank. Three – the oldest who had also been head keeper and its two immediate subordinates – went into an osmotic failure and turned into mush. Of old age, it was said. Whatever their shortcomings had been, their records had been meticulously kept so that it was known which pairings should be repeated to restore the lost Mrdini. When the next group of 'Dinis arrived for their two months' hibernation, an entirely new, younger management was in charge: the new head keeper had just finished advanced training on Iota Aurigae.

Very few *off* Clarf knew that substitute personnel were in charge of the Tower for nearly three weeks. The assignment of a third hot planet, a mere two light-years away from Clariflor, to relieve the overburdened Mrdini home worlds provided an additional distraction. Other Primes receiving or sending material to Clarf were too busy to query any minor differences they might have discerned in 'porting techniques. Quick to learn and already well versed in Tower protocol, the Lyon sisters got the hang of the workload within four days. Morag and Kaltia were quite as diligent in the performance of their duties as Laria had been. To share the learning experience as well as the loads they were having to 'port, they took turns being the Merge mind. Lionasha was punctilious about serving them the restorative drink and they had youth as well as innate strength to support their heavy duties.

Lionasha took it into her head that Laria would have introduced the girls around, and seen that they enjoyed the social life of the Human Compound. She told Vanteer quite bluntly that he would have to act as their male escort. Mrdinis worked longer hours than most Humans – considering their hibernation as their vacation – but Prime Towers kept to the normal Star League eight-hour working day with two rest days in seven.

'You can do what you like the five other nights, but those girls

218

are NOT going to be immured in the Tower,' she said so firmly that Vanteer did not argue. 'They're going to Sixth-day dances and the vid nights, and if they meet someone whom you and I both consider proper, they have every right to enjoy a night off. They aren't nunnies or whatever hermits were called.'

'Nuns,' Kaltia corrected, having been silently cheering Lionasha on in recruiting Vanteer as escort. While the Human Society on Clarf was conducted in a relaxed attitude, neither girl had reached adult status. As juveniles on a foreign world, they ought to be properly accompanied. Lionasha did not mention Vanteer's reputation but she would be along to ensure the proprieties.

'Actually, I think she meant nannies but they didn't have much fun either,' Morag said, looking forward to meeting new people, dancing and having some fun.

'All work is wrong,' Lionasha told Vanteer. 'We need a break and so do they. So, because Laria and Kincaid are far too occupied with Tower management, *we'll* escort the girls. It'd be damned funny if they weren't allowed out of here now and then, you know.'

To that Vanteer had to agree.

So they escorted their charges to functions in the air-conditioned Human Compound. Lionasha took them shopping – Tower personnel had the advantage of knowing in advance if there was anything worth looking at – and both Lionasha and Vanteer escorted them to the dance evenings. The girls were good dancers and rarely sat out. They had the good sense to make themselves as popular with their own sex in the intervals, especially when they tipped the girls off to special imports. They also dropped little clues to support the fiction that they were on an apprenticeship level: Morag moaned a bit at how hard it was to keep track of all the message tubes. Kaltia fretted about getting chapped hands from the cleanser that removed the grease of Clarf's generators.

'We were sent here to learn Tower management, and we are,' Morag said with such sincerity that it was all Lionasha could do not to laugh at her long-suffering pose. 'Sis may be strict, but I can't fault her for that.'

Although they admitted to Talent, they were careful not to mention their actual rank, intimating that they were destined for less glamorous positions than Primes. If any of the more knowledgeable from Terra had suspicions, they kept silent. Since the girls were Primes, they deftly, and shamelessly, used that advantage in 'pathing just enough from the minds of those they met to take the right attitude that would lead to friendly, rather than envious, relationships.

'Well, we never look below the public mind,' Morag admitted to Lionasha and Vanteer. 'But we can't afford to make mistakes with Humans or 'Dinis. We only read surface stuff. That's usually more than enough when people are out to have fun.' Morag grinned. 'They are under the distinct impression that I am training with you, Lionasha, and Kaltia's getting some hands-on experience with the station generators.'

'Yeah, I heard you talking to Scott Attenboro,' Vanteer said with reluctant admiration. 'You know more than he does about station generators.'

'We both do,' Kaltia said flatly. 'Xexo trained us, you know.'

'He did?' Vanteer's eyebrows raised in surprise. 'I didn't think he'd let anyone touch *his* generators.' The Iota Aurigae engineer was a legend in his speciality.

Several times Morag and Kaltia made courtesy calls at the Clarf homes of their 'Dinis' colours and gained much favour from their impeccable manners to the elder 'Dinis. Sim and Dar who were grey and Kev and Su who were blues consequently enjoyed more prestige in their colour houses.

When the sisters were asked about the absence of Laria, they had ready answers: 'Sis is pretty tired right now with all the traffic. You'd think half the planet was emigrating.' 'She and Dano have to do some Tower adjustments.' 'There's a huge shipment to go tomorrow and we're even going to have to help.'

To the amusement of all three women, Vanteer took a very responsible attitude about which males he'd introduce to the sisters. If he was the victim of some joking about chaperoning, he ignored it.

220

'He's almost worse than Dad,' Morag complained. 'He practically hauled that gorgeous Leonid Perutz away from me and all Leonid wanted was a dance.'

'Ha! That one!' Lionasha said, 'and if he hadn't kept Perutz away from you, I would have, and a thump for being so stupid.'

'But he's so handsome,' Kaltia said with a wistful sigh.

'And about as trustworthy as . . . as . . .' An appropriate comparison failed Lionasha. 'Laria won't acknowledge him whenever he's sent here as a troubleshooter. If she snubs him, you will, too. Don't ask the other girls about him, either. Ignore him.'

'Oh!' Morag and Kaltia exchanged thoughtful glances and sighed in unison. Lionasha went on, 'Now young Vince Studebaker may not have Perutz' looks or charm, but he's a good dancer, as funny as 'Dinis on a mudslide and worth much more of your attention than Perutz.'

'I danced with him, and you're right, Lio, he's quick on his feet and he is very funny. He's got some of the most hilarious jokes. Nice ones, too.'

'Just take it from me, girls, and if Vanteer cuts you out from a partner, he *knows* what he's doing.'

'Even if we're wrecking his game?' Morag said with a wicked glint in her eyes.

'We both promised Laria we'd take care of you. Frankly, I think I like Van the better for being so vigilant. Takes one to know one.' Then Lionasha chuckled, her tawny eyes twinkling. 'Though it's good Laria and Kincaid are due back. The strain on Vanteer's beginning to show.'

Just before false dawn, after three weeks' absence, Laria and Kincaid returned to Clarf but without their 'Dinis.

'They're much better, much better,' Laria said, dropping to her knees to embrace the other Tower 'Dinis, clamouring for news of their friends. 'We've missed you all. We're so glad to be back.'

'Not any gladder than Van will be,' Lionasha said, winking at Laria. *I'll tell you later.*

221

'Are we expected to go right back to Iota, Lar?' Morag asked, her expression anxious. 'I've met this real neat guy . . .' Over Morag's head, Laria caught Lionasha's approving nod. 'Vince Studebaker, and there's a fancy dress ball next Sixth day . . .'

'You'll be stuck here a while longer, girls,' Laria said. 'I might even have to send one of you to help Yoshuk and Nesrun at Sef Tower with all that has to go to that latest planet that's been released. Jeff routed quite a bit of heavy stuff through Iota rather than overload you.'

'Overload us! Why, the nerve of Grandfather,' Morag said, outraged.

Laria laughed, hugging her sister. 'You tell him. I won't. Now, fill us in, will you, girls, Lio, and where's Vanteer?'

'He'll be along at real dawn, Laria. He's been more help than you could possibly imagine,' and Lionasha's straight face was belied by the gleam in her tawny eyes.

'Kept all the no-no's from dancing with us, even Perutz!'

Laria's expression froze and she stared at Lionasha. 'If that man got . . .'

'Not with Van acting chaperone, he didn't,' Lionasha said, grinning.

Laria's eyebrows went up in surprise. 'Turned a new leaf, has our Van?'

'Not likely,' and Lio gave a snort and then smiled, 'but he was damned sure he wasn't going to be blamed for any incidents. As far as the Human Society of Clarf is concerned, your sisters were here to learn the lower grades of Tower management.'

'Well done, kids,' Laria said, hugging her sisters once more.

'Hey, you two look a lot better,' Lionasha said. 'Like you got enough sleep or had a vacation.'

'We had both, actually,' Laria said. 'Mother and Dad wouldn't let us near the Tower . . .'

'Not with Beliakin there, I'll bet,' Lionasha said in an acid tone.

Laria beamed. 'We never saw him once. He had to report to Blundell about that wretched Clarissia. He cleared himself of any suspicion.' She paused, with a little smile on her face. 'I wouldn't be surprised at all if Mom and Dad didn't sort of . . . well . . . adjust his general attitude.'

'That couldn't hurt,' Lionasha said, glancing over at Kincaid who grinned back.

'Somehow I don't think he'll stay long now he's had such good experience at Iota.' Laria smothered another grin. 'But you know how valuable strong T-2s are right now. Grandfather's sure to put him in some crucial position. Not that their replacement will be anywhere near the kinetic Beliakin seems to be. Mother said Gollee's description of him is "very young and so eager to learn he's almost pathetic". Kobold von something or other. Well, if Mom can trim down Beliakin's amazing ego, maybe she can build this little fellow's up.'

'Kobold von Gruy? So he developed, did he? He comes from my city,' Kincaid said with droll smile, 'so he'd have to overcome the odd ideas about Talent prevalent there.'

Laria gave Kincaid a quick look and laid her hand briefly on his arm. Lionasha had trouble repressing the questions those brief, and intimate, gestures provoked. She turned away to go get breakfast started.

'He'll do fine with Mother and Dad to sort of ease him into Tower work,' Laria said.

'Didja hunt much?' Kaltia asked so eagerly that it was obvious she missed that task.

'Indeed we did. In fact, I think that between us Kincaid and I finally hunted out that valley of mine.'

'Can't be done,' Kaltia argued.

'Kincaid here,' and once again Laria touched the T-2's arm, 'gets full honours for bagging the most every time we went out, wherever we went. Ewain was disgusted.'

'He would be,' Kaltia said with a snort. 'But when do you get your 'Dinis back?'

*I'll tell you what I can later,* Laria said.

'Zara's still at Iota?' Morag asked, though she already knew the answer.

Laria nodded. 'And likely to be for some time. She's done

223

great work and pulled our 'Dinis round.' Then her face lost all expression. 'Did we lose many we know?'

Returning with a tray of hot drinks, Lionasha nodded sadly. 'I knew twenty, and Van knew another half-dozen. Some eighty of Huf's main house died and thirty of Tip's.'

'Morag and Kaltia made appropriate visits to the colour houses, since their own 'Dinis wished to express condolence.'

'We will, too, of course,' Laria said. 'It was all so needless.' Abruptly she took a sip of the hot drink and then stepped over to Lionasha's workstation. 'Have we much for the morning? You two,' and she pointed at her sisters, 'have the day off.'

'That's fine by us,' Morag said, 'because there were some real neat fashions shipped in from Earth that should be on display and I need something new to wear. We didn't bring half enough good things with us. You coming, too, Kaltia?'

Laria looked queryingly at Lionasha and was reassured by Lio's dismissive wave.

'That pair know Clarf from hither to thither, Laria. Don't worry about them,' Lionasha said. 'Now I don't want you to lose all the good the holiday did you, so if the girls'll stay long enough to help 'port in the heavy machinery, it'd ease you back into the routine.'

'Shops don't open until late morning,' Morag said.

'Sure, don't want to lose my touch,' was Kaltia's reaction.

'That's most unlikely,' Laria said, 'pathing her pride in her sisters.

*Lyon's Pride*, Kincaid added, mischief twinkling in his eyes.

# CHAPTER TEN

An excited Sam Weiman and Grm begged a moment of Thian's time as the *Washington* and the fleet she led made their way towards the next suspect system.

'I know this may sound absolutely ridiculous,' Sam began with Grm bouncing up and down on its flippers beside him. 'But I've been thinking about pheromones, our odours,' he tapped his chest, 'and theirs.' He pointed astern, meaning Arcadia or system Cj-70 that was now a good week behind them. 'I think smell has a lot more to do with Hivers than we may have adequately investigated. When we had Operation Shanghai under way, I automatically took samples of the air as we went from place to place – sort of a headspace analysis, the sort we'd do with alien insects – in each collection point. I believe that the Hivers have been classified as basically insectoids. I also had Commander Kloo add gas chromatography to the remotes to keep track of any pheromone alterations. At any rate, Grm here and I have discovered that these pheromones are distinct, identifiable chemical compounds, especially when the queen made replacements for the attendants we took from her quarters.'

'Really?' Thian raised his eyebrows in surprise. 'More than

interesting,' he went on, 'since Earth Prime forwarded me, in his latest report of the general situation at Blundell, news that my sister, Zara, is working on the Mrdini hibernatory problem.' He turned to Grm and spoke in Mrdini with a quick but respectful bow. YOU MAY NOT HAVE HEARD THAT THE MRDINI FRIENDS OF CLARF'S PRIME AND T-2 DANO WERE PART OF THE TRAGEDY AT CLARF'S MAIN HIBERNATORY. MRDINI HAD GRACIOUSLY REQUESTED HER AS PRIME MEDICAL HUMAN TO HELP REVIVE AND HEAL THE VICTIMS.

Grm, however, bowed, its poll eye covered slightly by its lids in deference to the sad incident. DID HEAR. AS XENBEE, THIS ONE KNOWS THAT SPECIAL PHEROMONES ARE USED IN HIBERNATORIES. BUT NOT WHICH ONES. DEEPEST, MOST SACRED INFORMATION KNOWN ONLY TO KEEPERS WHO ARE TRAINED TO MANAGE HIBERNATORIES. Grm gave a little shudder.

'The point is,' Sam went on, giving Grm another apologetic bow, 'that, if we knew what pheromones the queen produces under which circumstances, we might find a way of . . . of sort of replacing certain pheromones and thus producing a more pacific attitude. Reducing their size and aggressiveness: making them more like the Arcadians. Has anyone done a "headspace analysis" of the Heinlein queen?'

'I can certainly find out,' Thian said at his most co-operative. 'I wonder what sort of smells we exuded on our first visit to that queen's quarters. She sure aired the place out in a hurry. Wouldn't it be ironic if pheromones *were* the key to the Hiver problem as well as the Mrdini?' We've been too busy, he thought to himself, having to eliminate the Hivers to discover how to contain them. But that difference in size between Arcadia's workers and those at Xh-33 and by the Heinlein queens must be significant.

Once Vagrian Beliakin got back from rather intensive sessions with Gollee Gren and with the team investigating the abortive assassination attempt over his one interview with that dreadful Capellan female, he settled back into Iota Aurigae's routine. He learned that he had missed a visit home by Laria and Kincaid Dano. He couldn't figure out if the call to Blundell had been to keep him out of their way but he was happy that he had been absent. He had even had a final quarter-hour with Earth Prime himself and felt he'd made a good impression on Jeff Raven, though the man had kept to two topics: the horses currently at Iota and the hunting that Vagrian had done with his youngest grandchildren. Though Beliakin felt that Raven's geniality had to mask some other devious purpose, he sensed no mental intrusion during their spoken conversation.

Back at Iota, and genuinely glad to be there, he saw little enough of Zara – she rarely even slept at the Tower House right now, trying to save the victims of the Clarf Hibernatory's breakdown. He hunted with Petra and Ewain, careful to keep up an easy relationship with them and their parents. He had no trouble finding female companionship of the type he preferred in Iota Aurigae City.

Two days later, they had just finished shifting another six big daddies when Earth Prime asked for a few words with Vagrian.

Damia grinned and gestured for Vagrian to answer while she and Afra left the Tower . . . just as if, Vagrian thought very carefully, they couldn't have 'heard' whatever Jeff Raven said if they wished. He doubted they would stoop to listening since both were scrupulous in Talent protocol and traditions, and Afra was methody Capellan.

*How would you feel about managing a new Tower, Beliakin?*

*Beg pardon?* Vagrian gripped the armrests of his couch in surprise.

*The Fourth Fleet's released a new planet and your kinetic strength is certainly needed to 'port the supplies the place'll need. I believe they've called the planet Iwojima. I don't know what it is that has the Star League so keen on naming planets after Human battle victories but the Mrdinis don't complain. It'll end up Wjm for them, I'm sure.*

*I hardly know what to say, sir,* Beliakin replied, swallowing figuratively and literally, *but I'll certainly do my best to prove my abilities.*

*Which is exactly why you've been chosen. You'll have a good support in a T-3 'path, a T-3 expediter, a T-4 engineer and, during the initial surge to supply, a third T-3 kinetic, as support. We'll push a lot of the heavy stuff through Perry, the Fourth Fleet's Prime, so initially, you'll do more catching than throwing. We're trying to find a good T-2 'pather to augment you, similar to arrangements that've worked so well with your brother and Nesrun at Sef Tower. But it'll take time to fine-tune a Tower crew so don't be reticent in telling me if there's a mismatch.*

Vagrian was still so stunned at his unexpected good fortune, he said the first thing that came to mind.

*But . . . but . . . what about Iota and who'll assist on those big daddies?*

*Your anxiety does you credit, Vagrian. Gollee's got a T-2 in training, Kobold von Gruy, and they will augment him with their T-2 and T-3 students. All but one are old enough for full Tower work. I need you at Iwojima. How soon can you be ready?*

*Won't take me long at all, sir.* And he was out of his couch and descending three steps at a time, the clatter causing Keylarion to stare at him. Then he also realized that Xexo hadn't come up out of his engineering pit and the generators hadn't been turned off.

'I'm going to a new planet,' Vagrian cried as he passed the two. 'I've got to pack. I'll have my own Tower.' He caught at the door-frame with both hands to stop his reckless forward momentum since Damia and Afra were in the little lounge, grinning at him.

'Take all the time you need to pack, Vagrian,' Damia said cheerfully. 'And congratulations. We didn't think we'd have you long. Not with your kinetic strength.'

'I won't take long,' he promised and stifled the urge to teleport to his room. He did, however, use his kinetic Talent to start gathering up his belongings in the house onto the bed, and was rolling his disks into shirts and sweaters before he was out of sight of the Lyons. *Then* he 'ported to his room and speeded up the process of packing. Since he'd seen Damia 'port his things into her house, he had no qualms about 'porting them back to Tower Yard by the personnel carrier which was always racked in one of the side cradles.

Damia and Afra were coming down the Tower steps as he

jogged up from the house. He said all that was suitable for a leave-taking, grinned at their repeated congratulations, waved a farewell and thanks to Xexo and Keylarion who came out of the Tower to see him off.

Afra closed the cover with one last smile. Of course, Vagrian didn't feel the transfer, not one being done by the Iota Aurigae Tower. He did hear a male voice accept transfer . . . *Got 'im, Damia. Thanks. Greetings, Beliakin. Perry here on the* Asimov. Then he heard a great deal of exterior noise as his personnel carrier settled into its destination cradle. *We'll meet later, Beliakin. Do get into the Tower as soon as possible. We're quite busy.*

The tenor voice sounded slightly breathless which suggested to Vagrian that this Perry – one of David of Betelgeuse's sons, wasn't he? – was multi-tasking. A tap preceded the opening of his carrier and a rush of fresh air, warmer than Iota's, filled with myriad smells – mostly of building materials, paint, oil, grease, and human sweat.

'Hi, I'm your expediter, T-2 Vagrian Beliakin,' said the dark-haired woman looking in at him. 'My name's Beejay, T-3 'pather.' She stepped back to allow him to exit the carrier, her grin broadening with just the sort of appreciation for his masculinity that Vagrian appreciated.

After the quiet of Iota Aurigae's Tower facility, there was hectic activity here – in a hilltop clearing which had obviously been levelled for the Tower – the noise was an assault on his ears. Glancing round to identify what and where the diverse noises were coming from, he saw Humans and 'Dinis everywhere, putting up sections of buildings, roofing, dashing from one of the many open large drones for supplies, so that the place appeared totally populated instead of the most recent colony world. Beyond the immense clearing, beyond the mounds of dirt that had been pushed out of the way for the Tower, he could see wave after wave of odd-looking tree-types spread out in all directions, and up the foothills of mountains not quite as sharp, or young, as Iota's.

'Takes a bit of getting used to,' Beejay said, grinning. 'All that greenery. Hiver ruins are all overgrown, too.' She held out

229

her hand and Vagrian hastily responded by touching her long, blunt fingers: yellow/citrusy/flowing were what he got from their touch. She had an attractive, rather than pretty, face and a compact but feminine body. Her grin widened and she cocked one narrow eyebrow in mutual appreciation of the information conveyed. ' 'Port your stuff into the L section: the lounge is the first room,' and she pointed. 'Nice one, too. We got our quarters built yesterday and nothing's sorted out. Though the Tower is. That's why we're not all here to meet you. Vaclava, our T-3 expediter, is in direct contact with Perry on the *Asimov* with a long list of things we need yesterday. Janfinde's fussing with his generators because he's got a shimmy he has to fix before we're actually operational. Hope you can reach the *Asimov* in just a Merge because we're stuck for so much right now . . . C'mon.'

Vagrian's T-2 kinetic strength was put to an immediate testing, but the Merge techniques he had acquired when Damia and Afra had him work with their Aurigaean latents and their two youngest children couldn't have been better experience. The metal stairs up to 'Tower' lacked carpeting and it was a cupola like Clarf's. Comformable couches were brand-new – someone had guessed his height and width right, though, so he had no fault to find with that, though he hoped the screens were more securely hooked to the still-unfinished walls than they looked. Beejay must have done a lot of Merging because, as soon as she had settled on her couch, she opened her mind to him. By the time Perry called a lunch-break, Vagrian realized how much he missed the 'oomph' of working with T-1s, even Ewain's stolid mind.

'C'mon,' Beejay said, 'the Navy supplies our grub and it's captain's table quality.' He would have eaten anything but he rather thought he'd miss Damia's inventive menus.

The 'lounge' had no furniture, bar the duffels stacked around its circular form and the trestle-table in the exact centre with rough benches on either side, facing windows with magnificent views. Steaming hot food was waiting on the table and shortly the rest of his Tower staff gathered to eat.

'Told you, didn't I?' Beejay said, grinning when Vagrian

lifted the lid from a covered dish and inhaled spicy aromas. Had Damia somehow managed to send along his food preferences: hot and hotter? 'Of course, there's space here for a proper kitchen and I really do like to cook. We can have non-T staff if we want and I suspect you may want to request help. We'll have a lot to do getting started. Hi, there, Vaclava. Meet Vagrian.'

Vaclava shyly offered her hand to Vagrian and he felt violet/lavender scent/liquid. She slipped in opposite him, a quieter, younger personality than Beejay. He'd have to deal carefully with her. He learned later this was her first post after being trained by the Bastianmajanis on Altair. He sensed a charming determination to do everything right the first time. Janfinde, who was brown/nutmeg/cautious, brought the smells of grease and oil with him though he had changed to fresh clothing before joining them at the table.

'I've a CPO coming down tonight, Tower,' Janfinde said, filling his plate, 'to help me tune the number two. We should be running on our own power by morning.' And that was the last thing he said, concentrating on his food.

Beejay had enough conversation to cover his silence and Vaclava's shyness and pulled out of Vagrian the details of where he'd been, what he'd done, and all about the assassination attempt which had been, she was sure, played down by Perry and Captain Osullivan, commander of the Fourth Fleet. She admitted coming from Procyon's planet, Truro, wrinkling her nose because her home world had as much a reputation for oddball cults and preserves as Capella had for strictly methody ways. Truro also harboured many of the clairvoyant or prescient Talents and some of the more gifted Talent therapists. As a T-3 'pather, she'd decided to enlist when the call came out through Truro's Talents that Blundell was in need of high Ts on well-paid short-term contracts that could be extended.

So she'd come to see what a new world looked like.

'Not that I expected it to be a Hiver world, but hey, well,' and she shrugged, her ready grin wry, 'new Tower, good chow, the Navy's been real helpful and those 'Dinis are a hoot and a half. You don't have any?' She made a pretence of looking around her.

'Only the ones I met at Iota Aurigae,' Vagrian replied with a slight, self-deprecating grin. 'But they're likeable and they *can* work all the hours God gave the day. Which reminds me, how long a day do we have here?'

'Twenty-five hours, fifteen minutes. No-one's bothered to figure out a leap year yet, but at this latitude we have about twelve hours of daylight.' She pointed upwards. 'Perry insists we keep to an eight-hour working day,' and she glanced down at her wrist, 'and we're due to work the second half of it, like right now.'

Dutifully Vagrian rose, gesturing at the dirty plates and dishes remaining from a completely consumed lunch.

'You're the kinetic,' and Beejay gave him a vivid mental glimpse of the galley on the *Asimov*. 'The head cook gives us hell if we break anything. Captain's service, you see, not plastic.'

Vagrian nodded understandingly and, with a dramatic wave of his hand, the dishes disappeared.

Beejay jutted her chin out as if she were looking, grinned and straightened up. 'You're neat! Stroganoff will love you!'

'Stroganoff?' Vagrian exclaimed, remembering that he'd been served what Damia called 'Scurrier Stroganoff'.

Beejay made a cross over her chest. 'Swear by all I hold sacred, that's her real name. Mina Stroganoff. And she hates being teased about it.'

'I never tease someone who can cook like that. Let's assume our Tower positions, shall we?' and he included the shy Vaclava Soolit in his courtly gesture. He did a two-fingered salute to Janfinde who nodded in acknowledgement and went back to his truculent generators.

By the end of the eight-hour day, Vagrian was exceedingly grateful to Perry's insistence on set hours. His last task of the day was to bring down the CPO engineer who was going to help Janfinde.

*Anything that comes into the* Asimov *from now on can wait until morning,* and there was something like droll humour in

232

the Prime's tone. *We're expecting fuel drones but there've been priorities going astray so no night-light work down there until our reserves are sufficient. Get a good night's rest and thanks for your help today, Beliakin. Look forward to meeting you face to face. Captain Osullivan sends his regards, too.*

*Thanks . . . Perry and my compliments to Captain Osullivan.*

Another delicious meal awaited the Talents and made the CPO's eyes gleam greedily.

'You guys got it made,' he said, restlessly waiting until Beejay, acting hostess, told him to seat himself and dig in.

'Great grub,' was the CPO's opinion even though Janfinde set the pace of eating to get quickly back to the ailing number two generator.

After he'd cleared the table of dirty china, Vagrian thought to ask would the CPO need to be transported back to *Asimov*, too.

'Well, sir, Captain Beliakin, if it's all right with you, when we finish, I'll just doss down here until after breakfast?' And the man's wide hopeful grin relieved Vagrian of one last duty. What he really wanted was a shower and a bed.

'Which room's mine?' he asked Beejay.

'Yours is the last door facing the corridor. Not much in it yet but the shower water should still be hot. We haven't got everything set up,' she said, 'what with other priorities, but the bed's good. We're to get proper furniture later and you can choose. Wait! Look at that! Worth a few minutes' watching,' she added, pointing to the west-facing window as Iwo's sun set, turning the evening clouds to gold and oranges that seemed to linger long after the primary was finally out of sight.

'See what you mean,' Vagrian said appreciatively. Then he nodded her a good night as he looked down the corridor for his door. He 'ported his duffels in that direction.

Bare the accommodation was with a desk, a chair, a desk lamp, in his 'lounge'. A door set in the west wall led into a bedroom, golden in the last of the dusky light, furnished with a wide bed that had a double sleeping-bag on it. There was a wide bench. Sliding panels covered the closet space on one side of the door and to his left there were rough shelves. In the

233

south wall another door opened into a well-equipped bath-room.

Someone got priorities right. Towels hung on a rack and a variety of toiletries were lined up on the space by the hand basin. As he stripped, he crossed to the bed and tested it. Yes, someone knew the priorities: the bed had some sort of soft layer and was firm beneath. Just right! He walked naked to his bathroom, 'porting shut the doors he hadn't bothered to close behind him. The shower stall was also a surprise: big enough for two. The water, while only warm, was sufficient for him to get a good scrub.

When he left the bathroom, the air had already cooled in the bedroom. A light on the headboard had come on automatically, so he made his way quickly to the sleeping-bag, which he would doubtless be glad of if the night got much cooler, and lay down. He turned on his stomach and applied relaxing techniques to a mind spinning with work and myriad impressions. His last thought was that he had not had time to do something to Laria's favourite mare before he left Iota. Then he remembered that she was also Petra's mount and he owed the Iota Lyons. Maybe he even owed Laria. His own Tower . . . Vagrian Beliakin slept the sleep of the just.

The report of the onset of war on Hiver-occupied world Xh-33 reached Captain Etienne Osullivan on the *Asimov* while he was on the bridge.

'Emergency code from the Xh-33 Moon Base, sir,' the communications officer said, swinging her chair round to face him.

'Put it up.'

There was the usual time lag due to the distance between the *Asimov* and the Xh-33 system.

'Captain Osullivan, Wisla Makako here,' and the screen showed the oriental features of the facility's commander. 'All hell's breaking loose down there on the Main Continent. Queens leading armies of really big dangerous-looking types,' and the screen now switched to the surface carnage with queens leading some of the biggest creatures that Osullivan

234

recognized as augmented 'worker' types from his captaincy of the *Genessee*.

'Is the situation more serious than your reports of earlier skirmishes over field boundaries?' Osullivan asked, his eyes intent on the scene. During the pause between query and answer, the captain sent quick orders. 'Prime Perry, on the bridge right now!' Osullivan had never given the T-1 such a direct order, in fact didn't even realize he hadn't couched it as tactfully as he usually did. Perry 'ported beside him and Osullivan had only to point to the screen's grim scene to explain the summons as he continued firing off orders. 'Helm, set an immediate course for the Xh-33 system. Top speed. Fortunately we're not spatially that far from it. Send a signal to Iwojima that they're on their own for the next couple of days. We'll be back in orbit as soon as we've assessed the situation. Perry, the Moon Base has only a T-3 kinetic.'

Makako was then replying. 'This seems to involve all the queens on the Main Continent, sir, and I wouldn't call it a "skirmish". I'd call it an all-out war. The carnage is unbelievable!' Her wide-eyed expression reinforced her dismay.

'Has she said what started that?' Perry demanded, eyes glued to the scene. 'Is the Moon Base in any danger?'

Osullivan shook his head as the *Asimov* could be felt surging forward in star-speckled space until the stars blurred.

'There's no way the queens can reach the Moon Base. Remember? We destroyed their Spheres and scouts. Makako has reported that they've reopened their mines but ore must be hard to find. New shafts have been sent down. On all the continents, by the way.'

'There must be far too many queens, sir,' Makako was reporting now. 'I've counted forty separate battlefields and several queens contesting ground in one.'

'Nothing you can do about it, Commander,' Osullivan said by way of reassurance and then turned to Perry. 'Prime, please make contact with Earth Prime whether he's at Blundell or Callisto. He needs to know about this. We really do need a telepath at every installation, even if he or she only receives.' The last was said in a low murmur of regret.

'There's never enough to go round, sir. Lieutenant Balido-vino,' and Perry turned towards the duty engineer, 'I'll need to draw on the generators for this distance.'

'As you need, sir,' Balidovino replied, fingers poised on the pressure plates of his engineer panel.

'Yeoman, my compliments to Commander Voorhees and I'd like him on the bridge as soon as possible,' Osullivan added, rubbing his jaw without moving his eyes from the battle.

'Yes, doubtless they'll want an evaluation from the science officer,' Perry said, crossing his arms on his chest. Then he closed his eyes as he telepathically leaped the long distance to Earth.

Quite imposing in that attitude, Osullivan thought, sur-prised at his own observation. Perry was no more powerfully built than any of the other Primes Osullivan had met but there was an aura about the dark-haired, sharp-featured Betelgeu-sian that made him *appear* much bigger and ineluctably more powerful.

'My apologies, Earth Prime,' Perry spoke aloud as well as telepathically so that Osullivan knew what was said. Replies would come back through his mouth but in Jeff's voice. 'But a situation has developed on Xh-33 that you should see through my eyes,' and Perry opened his. There was a slight pause, and then Perry's voice deepened, closer to Raven's tone. 'So that's what happens when queens do not migrate. An awesome sight. Hmmm, and these creatures are much larger than those that were found by the *Washington* on Arcadia. Yet that is a much older colony and hasn't yet overburdened its planet's re-sources. A puzzle, what? Captain Osullivan?' Perry turned to Osullivan with a slight grin, encouraging response.

Lt Commander Jan Voorhees came striding onto the bridge and stopped dead when he saw what was on the main screen, his eyes widening.

'A puzzle indeed . . .' Osullivan waved a helpless hand at the scene and the hideous, unceasing massacre, with broken limbs and scattered parts oozing internal viscous liquid.

'This is one time,' Raven's voice came through Perry's

mouth, 'when we leave the conflict to proceed. Ask Makako to keep recording. I'm calling up our own xenbees to "see" this through me.'

'Sir,' Voorhees murmured to the captain, 'we should get pheromone readings . . . once they've stopped fighting. That could be vital information.'

'Quite right, Mr Voorhees,' Jeff Raven's voice replied, startling the man. Earth Prime chuckled through his link to Perry. 'However, even if Humans have been able to move among Hivers without being noticed, I recommend hazmat gear and full masks.'

'Of course, sir, since we don't know what effect such violent pheromones, even poisonous gases from all those visceral parts, could have on Humans,' Voorhees said, running a nervous hand through thinning blond hair. 'And if the prevailing winds happen to carry the stink to the other continents . . . well, I hate to speculate what reaction would occur.'

'Good point,' Jeff Raven said. 'I'll mention that to our experts. We have, by the way, discovered a T-10 in the perfumery business who has volunteered to lend us his "nose" in identifying the smells. He's supposed to be good at more than the flowery stuff.' Perry's voice dutifully echoed the amusement in Jeff Raven's tone, and one of Perry's eyebrows raised in surprise. 'My xenbees are rubbing their hands in an excess of delight to know we can get samples of the dominant pheromones. Preferably as soon after the battles end as possible.'

'I'll have a team standing by either from here or from the Moon Base, but I request permission to lead it.' Voorhees looked deferentially at his captain who nodded permission. Then Voorhees turned to Perry. 'Is that possible, Prime?' Perry nodded. 'Respond in your own time, Commander Makako.'

The response lag was shortening as the powerful *Asimov* sped towards the Xh-33's system.

'Sir,' Makako replied, shaking her head, 'I would hate such . . . butchery . . . to extend to the other continents. Right now the weather system is mild with moderate winds blowing east to the sea. My met officer says there are rain clouds over the

237

intervening ocean. According to him, we might have as much as thirty-six hours before those winds reach the next landmass. We'll keep a strict eye on it. Continent Two is nightside and doesn't show any disturbance . . .' Her voice trailed off briefly.

'Have you hazmat gear on the Base?'

Another pause. 'Yes, sir, as well as the crew who placed the remotes in the queens' collectives. I've put them on standby.'

'Very good, Commander. Inform us when . . . the fighting is over.'

'Commander Makako, Blundell wants you to copy whatever is already recorded and tube it,' Perry said with Jeff's voice. 'I'll pick it up myself from your Base in fifteen minutes from my mark . . . Mark! We need to have some idea of how they fight.'

'Yes, sir,' Makako said, looking towards Perry and rather startled to hear another voice issuing from his mouth. 'I'm ordering a copy and it'll be in a message tube at Lock Four Eight Two, sir, in fifteen minutes.'

'Thank you, Commander Makako. Let's hope we can stop the . . .'

'Butchery? Slaughter? Genocide?' Perry supplied synonyms in his own voice without a trace of emotion. Then once more Jeff Raven spoke through the link. 'The queens demonstrate a curious killing rage. Similar to old berserkers. My regards to you, Captain Osullivan.' As soon as those words were out of Perry's mouth, he altered his stance and nodded to the captain to indicate that he was no longer in contact with the Earth Prime. The generators whined down to a lower level.

'Berserkers?' Osullivan said, turning to Perry. 'Yes, an apt term. Organize that landing party, will you, Mr Voorhees? We want to be ready. Pheromones? How interesting.'

Voorhees saluted and immediately left the bridge to organize his team.

Perry stepped slightly closer to the captain's chair and said softly, 'One thing is certain, sir, those records may have a salutary effect on those who criticized Admiral Ashiant's destruction of the Spheres.'

'I should certainly hope some good comes of that,' and

Osullivan waved his hand in the general direction of Xh-33. Then his upper body shivered in a sudden convulsive shake. 'Thank you, Prime, for your assistance.'

'You're welcome, sir,' and Perry exited through the door of the short passage from the bridge to the Talents' lounge.

He went immediately to the alcove that housed the lounge's refreshment facility and poured a hefty glass of the strongest brandy of a very respectable selection of spirits and wines. He drank it in one gulp.

'Perry?' his wife Adela asked sleepily, from the door of their bedroom. 'What was that all about? Etienne's never done that before.'

'A question for Earth Prime that was urgent. Want a drink?' and he held up the bottle.

She frowned prettily. 'No, I can go right back to sleep if you're beside me.' She was a T-3 kinetic, able to 'path when in contact with someone, and then only someone she knew well.

'I'll be right there, dear,' Perry said and poured a second, but smaller drink. With her beside him to neutralize what he had just seen, he, too, could go back to sleep.

At dawn, Captain Osullivan requested Perry to come to the bridge. The *Asimov* was already within the Xh-33 system and, with no need for a discreet approach, was still running at top speed. The com screen was scanning the devastated Main Continent on Xh-33, showing the carnage but also a bottom line that gave feeble blips, identifying survivors. Commander Voorhees was dressed in his hazardous-material suit, complete with independent oxygen system. He had the compact gas chromatograph lying across his left arm. Four other hazmat-suited figures stood slightly behind him, and out of the way of the bridge crew, each carrying similar devices, their attention riveted on the shambles of once green, crop-sown fields.

'It seems to be pretty much over,' Commander Makako was saying of the appalling vista of destruction down on Xh-33. 'We know some of the queens have taken refuge in their quarters and suspect many are injured. Haven't established how many died but, of course, their . . . "workers" or "warriors" or whatever we should call them . . . were without leadership. While we watched some fled. A lot of the leaderless were just killed by whatever actively directed queen's group was nearby. Winds remain moderate. When Commander Voorhees joins us, my surface party's ready to go.'

Holding up his device, Voorhees said, 'It might be a bit clumsy but it'll give the readings needed.' He nodded to the captain who was regarding the instrument with a frown. 'Probably selenaldehydes or selenoketones. I've accessed what data we have on queen pheromones. They can vary a lot. Include thioketones at times if there's enough sulphur around.'

'I also have four portable GCs,' Makako said, with practically no pause between his words and her response. 'We used them when we made our first surveys down there to plant the remotes.'

'I've four xenbees to come along from the *Asimov* to help, if that's all right.'

'No problem,' she replied. 'Main boat bay is cleared except for the shuttle to get us downside.'

The screen switched from the battlefield to Makako in her hazmat gear in the boat bay, her surface team and the shuttle behind her.

'Prime Perry, would you be good enough to 'port the *Asimov* party to the Moon Base?' Osullivan asked.

'I'll even give them a boost,' Perry said with a droll grin. The generators whirred and Voorhees and his team disappeared. 'When you're settled, sing out.' He paused in a listening attitude and then leaned on the generators.

'They're here,' Makako said on the screen, blinking her slightly slanted eyes in acknowledgement of their arrival. 'Commander Voorhees is now transferring his men to my shuttle.'

'Where do you want to be set down, Commander?' Perry asked.

'Sir?' Makako's expression was a query.

'See that relatively empty spot, Perry?' And Osullivan pointed to the area: a vegetable field that had been trampled

240

down but was clear of corpses. It wasn't far from a queen collecting facility.

'Yes, sir. Are you ready, Mr Makako?'

'As ready as we'll ever be!' Makako sounded resigned.

'Get us as many samples in and out of the queens' quarters as possible. I know that the Hivers generally ignore us, but how they'd react now . . . is debatable. Keep alert. Is that clear?' Osullivan asked.

The baritone of Voorhees chorused with Makako's lighter soprano in a unison 'Yes, sir.' The hum from the generators was deeper and Perry reached out and deposited the shuttle. The com officer switched to the planet's surface and the shuttle was already in place.

'Neatly done, Perry.' Osullivan settled back into the bridge chair, rubbing his jaw as he watched. 'Please inform Earth Prime that Operation Nose is under way.'

'I have, sir, and I'll gather my team in the lounge and keep a watch, just in case we have to rescue anyone.'

'Good idea,' Osullivan said.

Balidovino transferred the landing site to the main screen as the figures emerged cautiously from the shuttle and began spreading out. The four under Voorhees's command headed towards the nearby Hiver facility while Makako was gesturing for her group to fan out, making for the first of the many piles of inert worker bodies, a dead queen lying on the ground at the forefront. 'Hope they don't need any rescuing.'

Perry nodded and exited through the door to the Talents' lounge, calling up his team members. He was rather pleased with those unassisted 'ports, especially the shuttle.

*Your father would pin your ears back, Perry,* came Jeff Raven's voice in his head.

Perry shrugged. *Sorry, Prime. My team would have taken time to assemble since this wasn't on today's schedule.*

*First law of the Prime is to conserve energy, Perry.*

*Yes, sir.*

Perry kept his reply neutral but he *was* strong and able for the work he'd just done.

241

*'Path me their reports as soon as they have anything significant to be passed on.*

*Yes, sir.*

*Especially if that weather front alters and the winds pick up. I get the distinct impression that, while pheromones cannot be transmitted in space, they could well affect the entire planet.*

*Not all the queens died in this fight, sir.*

*That's not what interests the xenbees here,* Jeff replied and absented his presence from Perry's mind.

'What's the problem?' Adela spoke from their bedroom door. 'The team wasn't due to meet . . . Oh, yes. I see. Can I get you something?'

'I can get my own,' he said with a grateful smile. 'You get dressed.'

At Osullivan's quiet command, the main bridge screen was split so that both teams could be observed. As they neared the queen's collection building, Voorhees and his men had to step around and over dead forms, kicking aside severed limbs. They carefully skirted the few that were struggling back to their hive, leaving behind yellowish trails of vital fluids. Then Voorhees hunkered down by a dead worker and looked it up and down, lifting one limb and measuring it against his hand span.

'Admiral?' Voorhees spoke into his com unit, turning his head up in a reflex action towards the *Asimov* and the observers he knew were watching.

'What's wrong, Voorhees?'

'Sir, if I remember the dimensions of the workers, mentioned in Prime Thian's report on that planet he surveyed – called it Arcadia, didn't he?'

'Go on,' the admiral encouraged him.

'This fellow's a good twenty centimetres longer in the leg, and its body is at least ten longer. And see . . .' Voorhees poked at an extendible limb, hacked off at the first joint. 'This one's got a mallet, hammer . . .' He prodded it with his finger so that unbroken spikes were visible. 'Now that's a wicked modification, or do I mean mutation?'

242

'It certainly is,' Osullivan said. 'Get it recorded and do a spot check on other worker bodies . . . or should I call them "warriors" if that's what they've put in place of shovels and rakes?' Osullivan turned to his com officer. 'Put me on a wide comline. I want to get *all* surface units to check if all the . . . workers . . .' and he made an ironic grimace, 'are the same.'

The order was duly given and accepted.

Makako's fan was also avoiding the stumbling wounded forms that blindly retreated back towards Voorhees, or dragged themselves in the opposite direction.

'Can't tell the players without any markings,' one of her team remarked.

'According to my GC readings, each queen must stink different,' said another, 'and boy, am I glad I'm in a hazmat suit and can't smell a thing!'

'Button up,' Makako said firmly.

Then Voorhees's voice came on line just as he and his four entered the facility. 'There's a badly wounded queen in here, her egg-bulb is collapsed on one side, lost most of her hind legs to the second joint and has only one front arm with palps. She's making for her quarters and there're little scuttlers coming out to assist. They aren't her usual attendants. She'll squash 'em. No, they're managing, several on each side of a joint. Spread out, men, and let's see how many she has left of her hive. Miko, you're the shortest: check the waiting area down that right-hand tunnel.'

'Sir, I'm getting heavy concentrations of the selenaldehydes,' one of his team said.

'I'd expect that inside a collection facility. Wonder what they'll be in the queen's quarters.'

'Off the scale, prolly,' another remarked with a snort.

'Let's get to the queen's quarters. There may be some interesting variations of Hiver patterns on her main screen. You've got that recorder, don't you, Hickey?'

'Yes, sir, but even with the help she's getting, I don't see how she can make it back. She's oozing with every step.'

'As well for us. The left-hand tunnel leads to her quarters,

243

Hickey. Gallard, stay back and warn us should she get too close.'

'Not that she's an arm left to do anything with,' murmured Gallard.

'She's not the one who fights,' Hickey replied with disgust. 'She's got all them worker-warrior types we saw dead up above.'

'Fighter or not, someone mauled her good.'

The watchers on the ship could see Makako's team working further away from the landing site. They were some way from any other collective, stepping across sizeable vines which had been ripped from supporting posts, Hiver bodies caught in the tangles.

And so the search went. When Voorhees's team had exited from the facility, they returned to the shuttle and sent the first reports back to the *Asimov*. Then purged the portable GCs for their next stop. Voorhees took the shuttle up, cruising at a low level until they caught up with Makako's point. Then they veered slowly in another direction, landing on top of another facility. There weren't even any corpses about it. The queen's quarters were empty although Gallard thought he heard tiny scrabblings against one wall.

'The scuttlers, prolly.'

The screens were dead.

'They die when the queen does?' Hickey asked.

'Probably,' Voorhees said. 'Concentration in here is only parts per trillion, sir, much lighter.'

There were over two hundred and forty known hive facilities on the Main Continent and battles had been fought in every direction around them as queens led their warrior-workers out either to defend their hives or attack others. When the massed assaults ended, thirty-two facilities still had queens, some of them badly injured: two were combing through their egg reserves, beginning to fertilize eggs in a valiant attempt to repopulate their hives. The surface team did not have to physically inspect all of them. Life-form readings, set to queens and the large warrior-workers, showed which facilities

244

had queens and a rough assessment of their remaining minions. Recordings had been made of pheromones in a sufficient variety to give the scientists much to study.

Perry lifted the shuttle safely back to the Moon Base. The moment the shuttle doors opened, alarms on the boat deck went off.

'Do we stink that bad?' Gallard asked.

'You do,' was the response of the lieutenant who was on duty in the Base headquarters. 'You go through decontam until you register zero on the stinkometer and you guys are thoroughly deodorized. That OK with you, Commander?'

'If we reek enough to set off the alarms, we clean off before we undress,' Makako agreed and waved the troops towards the decontam facility. Since the unit held only one person at a time, there was a tedious wait.

'They still stink,' Gallard said, wrinkling his nose as the last man to hang his gear up in the storage closet. 'I'll never get rid of that reek.' He felt his hair, rubbed down his arms and legs. 'Yuck! Commander, can we use enough water to get really clean?'

'Permission granted,' Makako said, devoutly wishing she had enough cologne left to get rid of the residual smell. She lifted her arm to her nose.

'All in your mind,' Voorhees said, grinning.

'If it is, I'm in real trouble,' Makako murmured to him. 'And that shuttle still stinks. We'll have to moor it out in space for days. It's permeated the metal. Gods, those pheromones are pervasive.'

'All in your mind,' Voorhees repeated, enjoying his tease of the commander.

The com unit buzzed for Makako's attention. 'Prime Perry says he's moved the personnel carrier to the gym so you won't have to back through boat bay, sir, until it's been deodorized,' she reported.

'Thank him.' He held out his hand to Makako. 'Pleasure working with you.'

She shook his hand solemnly. 'And with you but gods, how I hope we don't have to do it again.'

'Sir,' and the com unit continued, 'Met says wind's picking up. What do we do about that? XO says all that smell moving to the eastern continent might be bad.'

Makako groaned. 'Get back to the *Asimov*. We'll have to do something . . . maybe seed some clouds and dilute those pheromones. Some of my readings were off the scale and most of 'em were subtly different.'

'I'll tell you what comes up in the analysis, soon's I know myself,' Voorhees said and then called for his four to come with him to catch their ride back to the *Asimov*.

Though the 'port was swift, the five men exuded enough residual pheromones to cause the ensign who opened the carrier to recoil with disgust written all over his face.

'Beg your pardon, sir,' he said sheepishly.

'Into the showers, all of you,' Voorhees said. 'Tell the captain I'm taking our readings up to the lab. I'll shower again there.'

'Yes, sir, but Captain Osullivan's orders were for you to contact him immediately,' and the ensign gestured to the boat bay's com unit on the upper level.

'All right,' Voorhees said, resettling the bag of data disks that contained the readings.

'What's this about a bad Met report, Voorhees?' asked Captain Osullivan.

'Winds have picked up. Can we do something about diluting the pheromones it's carrying to the east? I'm on my way to the lab, sir, but I really don't want to bring a pong to the bridge, if you don't mind.'

'Appreciate that, Mr Voorhees. Report when you're . . . deodorized.'

'Yes, sir.'

Voorhees then made it straight to the ship's well-equipped laboratory and started his technicians on a preliminary report on pheromones, levels and types. Either the ensign had warned them or constant proximity to lab smells had dulled their olfactory nerves, but none of them so much as wrinkled a nose when he came near them.

'Do a quick assessment and inform Prime Perry when it's

ready to be forwarded. We'll do the detailed chemical analyses later.' He caught one of the yeomen by the arm. 'Get me a clean shipsuit from my cabin, will you, Naves?'

'Yes, sir, right away, sir,' and the man jogged out of the lab.

*A cloud seeding is advisable, Prime,* Perry told Jeff Raven. *The consensus here is that we'd best dilute the pheromones with as much rain as possible before the stench spreads across the eastern continents. I wouldn't like to see such slaughter as the Main Continent again. The pheromones are diverse and powerful. There is some scuttlebutt that the personal carrier Commander Voorhees returned in is stinking up the boat deck. I believe he has taken four showers and applied to sick bay for a pungent skin lotion.*

*Does he really need it? Or is it all in his mind?* Jeff asked.

*I've a message tube ready for 'portation, sir.* There was an edge of amusement in Perry's voice. *See what* your *scientists think.*

*I'll ship you appropriate seeding materials. You've done it before, I believe, on Betelgeuse?*

*Yes, sir, I have and the meteorological conditions are fortunately favourable. Ah, sir? The science officer says we'd better check the eastern continents after the storm to be sure the rain dispersed the aggressive pheromones.*

*By all means, and my compliments to Commander Voorhees. Good thinking.*

# CHAPTER ELEVEN

The chromatograms, taken both in the open air and in the queens' quarters that were visited, with and without the occupants, compared with those taken by Prime Thian on the planet Arcadia, kept the lights burning in laboratories and offices all night long. A preliminary report – with many protestations of being a hurried summation and some speculations – was on Jeff Raven's desk by the time he arrived from Callisto at his office in Blundell Building. Copies had been sent to both High Councillors and Prime Elizara. Jeff glanced through the first few pages and 'pathed a call to Thian on the *Washington*.

*Thian, sorry to rouse you, but I need to have Lt Weiman and Grm here for an important meeting.*

*Sure, Grandfather,* Thian said, dragging himself from sleep and the comfort of Gravy's warm body. *Right away.*

*The queens on Xh-33 went to war on the Main Continent yesterday and damned near exterminated themselves.*

*WHAT?* That news brought Thian wide awake and he increased his efforts to get into his shipsuit.

*Please have Weiman and Grm bring all their data and visual records. 'Path me when they're ready and I'll assist in the 'port.*

*No need, sir. I can do it easily enough in gestalt with the* Washington's *generators.*

*It* is *urgent!*

*I believe it.*

Thian was at his com unit, tapping in Lt Weiman's quarters.

'A *war*?' Such news had as electric a shock on Sam as it had had on Thian.

'Grm is also needed and you're to bring everything you have on Arcadia's queens and any other research you two might have on the Hivers. Please go immediately to the boat bay and get into the personnel capsule. I'll alert the watch officer as soon as I've roused Grm.'

'He's here,' Sam said apologetically. 'We were correlating some data and . . .' His voice trailed off.

'Great. How long do you need?'

Thian could hear Sam's gulp. 'Ten minutes, sir?'

'You're a star,' Thian said with sincere appreciation.

Still groggy with insufficient sleep, Sam and Grm found themselves on Earth, in the Blundell Yard where the supervisor greeted them effusively and hurried them into the great blocky building and turned them over to Gollee Gren.

'Do you have any details about the war, sir?' Sam asked, stumbling along the corridors as the Prime's top assistant escorted them past security and to the high-speed elevator.

'Visual and data files,' Gren said, 'are awaiting you. I'd prefer you to see them first before I comment. Prime Raven has called for a meeting with the two High Councillors, the Rowan and other experts at two o'clock.'

'But . . . but . . . but . . .' Sam began and followed him into the elevator, absently keeping Grm's material from slipping out of the Mrdini's arms.

Gollee turned and grinned at him. 'Assimilate what you can in the time you have . . . and, if a correlation is obvious, make notes of it. We're all trying to absorb what happened yesterday.'

When the doors opened, he waved to the security guards who had come to attention.

'Lieutenant Weiman and the Mrdini Grm,' he said, looking up at the ceiling. 'From the *Washington*, at the request of Prime Raven. I am their escort.'

The guard relaxed. Another came forward with two scintillating disks, which she planted first on Sam's chest and then Grm's upper arm. As Sam looked down at it, the surface dulled.

'That admits you to this floor only, Lieutenant, Grm. If you need anything, use the com unit in the room,' she said, saluting as she stepped back and gestured down the short hall. 'It's set up with what we thought they might need,' she added to Gollee Gren.

'Grand, thanks, Monnie. This way, gentlemen.'

The room had the dead feeling of a high-security facility.

'Yes,' Gollee said with another grin, noticing Sam's happy reaction.

'It's a grand room,' the lieutenant said, glancing around a space that was quadruple the size of his office on the *Washington*. A full com unit with viewing screens above it occupied one wall, a wide sturdy round table with eight chairs was in the centre and comfortable chairs and a long couch stretched along the other wall. A serving unit was to the left of the entrance.

'You haven't had a chance to eat yet, have you?'

'We should get to work immediately,' Sam said, starting to arrange the files he had brought.

'I suggest you eat first, Lieutenant, Grm,' Gollee said with a grave bow. 'This will be a very busy day and you'll need to sustain yourself. Especially before you see the recording of the . . . queens' war on Xh-33.'

'That bad?' Sam asked softly.

Gollee nodded slowly.

'Coffee,' said Grm firmly, 'black, and porridge.'

'Good choice,' Gollee said and dialled it up.

'I'll have the same,' Sam said, his tone wary.

When they were served, Gollee left them to eat. 'There are other preparations to make for this afternoon's conference. If you'll excuse me?'

'Of course,' Sam replied and turned to his meal.

\*    \*    \*

250

Five minutes before the two o'clock meeting, Gollee collected the two xenbees. He saw the haunted look in Sam's eyes, the droop of Grm's poll and knew that the queens' war had affected them as deeply as it had everyone who had seen the recording. The viewers might have been spared the sounds and smells of the carnage but the omissions hardly mattered to the overall effect.

'It's nearly time, Lieutenant, Grm.'

'Yes, yes,' Sam said, hastily bundling up the scattered sheets of the hard copy, his files and notebook. Grm kept dropping files until Gollee gave it a helping hand.

'This way, please,' Gollee said and, to Sam's surprise, indicated the end of the corridor. 'Prime Raven will 'port you himself from this point.'

He nodded to them both and strode back to the elevators.

The next thing Sam knew he was in a huge office, facing a conference table that had individual units built into its surface. There were twelve conformable chairs, four of which were already occupied. He noticed the Chief Xenbee in charge of the Heinlein Base's queen installation and bowed to her, but he didn't recognize the others except that they were all Fleet officers. For a scared moment, Sam wondered if this was where the assassins had made their attempt on the lives of the Primes and the High Councillors.

'Actually, no,' and the quiet, slightly amused voice turned Weiman's attention to Prime Jeff Raven, whom he recognized from news-vids. He was talking to the equally recognizable High Councillors, Admiral Mekturian Tohl and Gktmglnt. 'Lieutenant Sam Weiman and Grm are from the *Washington*,' Jeff said to the others. 'Mr Weiman, perhaps you already know Lt Commander Whila Gallahue from the Heinlein Base,' and, when Weiman nodded, 'so I will make you known to Lt Commander Jan Voorhees of the *Asimov*, the *HGHL* xenbee, Stg, and Lieutenant Verla Mitab from the Xh-33 Moon Base.'

As they were acknowledging the introductions, a slender elegant woman seemed to glide into the room from nowhere, causing Sam some consternation as he was facing her point of entry.

251

Jeff smiled, holding out his hand. 'I'm sure you all must know my wife, Angharad, Callisto's Prime. No cause for alarm, Mr Weiman, the Rowan is the only person who can enter my sanctum sanctorum without invitation.' He guided her, with an air of conscious pride, to the nearest seat. 'Please, ladies and gentlemen, take your places. We have much to discuss.'

Soon they all had taken seats, the two minor 'Dinis slipping reverently into the Mrdini-suitable chairs on either side of the High Councillor, tilting their poll eyes deferentially away from such an august neighbour. Jeff Raven remained standing.

'This meeting was convened at the request of the High Councillors and in this room for security's sake. I turn it over to Admiral Tohl,' and with a courteous bow to the admiral, Raven sat down, beside the Rowan.

'I trust you all,' and the admiral glanced round the table needlessly for every eye was on him, 'have had time to assimilate the details of . . . the war.' He grimaced. 'Most unfortunate, especially as that sort of madness could spread to the other four continents of Xh-33.'

He noted that Verla Mitab of the Xh-33 Moon Base winced. 'My sentiments precisely, Mitab,' he remarked. 'And we must endeavour to formulate some solution. For in the solution for Xh-33, we may find the germs of a way to end the cyclic behaviour of the Hiver queens.

'I am given to understand,' and now he nodded to Commander Whila Gallahue, 'that the Hiver society exists in an oscillating equilibrium. This theory is borne out by the fact that, once the war was over and some of the surviving queens had returned to their hives, they immediately began to fertilize eggs to replace their losses. That is typical of such a society. It builds up population, overburdens resources and then forces the queens to set out aggressively to acquire enough land to support increased numbers. Since we confined the queens to their planet, destroying their spheres and preventing them from their usual modus operandi . . .'

252

'What else were we to do?' the Rowan interjected.

'Quite so . . . the need to expand could only result in more than mere border skirmishes.'

'You're not suggesting that we're responsible for their war?' asked the Rowan.

'Of course not. But we are certainly responsible for preventing them from leaving Xh-33 in a more orderly solution than war.'

'With respect, Admiral,' the Rowan went on, 'what's the difference? Their war solved their immediate problem. There's now plenty of unoccupied space available on Xh-33.'

'Not if the other continents erupt.'

'With so many queen hives vacant,' said Commander Gallahue in an unusually deep voice for a woman, 'couldn't we spread the queens and their followers about the planet, and relieve the crowding that led to the war on the Main Continent?'

'That possibility is currently being examined,' said Gktmglnt, turning its poll eye towards her. 'That is only a stop of the gap. We who have suffered much from the Hivers look to find a permanent solution to the problem of queen migration.' It turned its eye on Lt Weiman. 'Arcadia is much different, is it not, Lieutenant?'

'Ah? Oh, yes, indeed, honourable Gktmglnt,' Sam said. 'It is pacific, totally non-aggressive and, from what evidence we have, it has been so for centuries.'

Gallahue leaned slightly across the table in his direction. 'I have read your report on that Hiver colony with great interest,' she said sincerely. 'I must comment that, even though the Heinlein queen is quiescent, the pheromones she occasionally releases are unlike those you reported . . .' She held up her hand when Sam opened his mouth to defend his findings. 'I do not doubt the accuracy of your report. But if you compare Arcadia's ambience to the concentration of pheromones on Xh-33 . . .' She shook her head, leaving her sentence unfinished.

'That's it,' Sam said excitedly, 'there is no comparison but Arcadia has remained a pastoral, non-aggressive, almost underpopulated planet. So what happened to produce the warlike queens of Xh-33?' He spread his hands in puzzlement. 'And those who have plagued our Mrdini allies for two centuries?'

'If we could discover that, we could solve the problem,' said Admiral Tohl, also spreading his hands.

'It is on record,' Gallahue began, 'that the Heinlein queen did, on one occasion, emit pheromones similar, though not as intense or as concentrated, as those reported on Xh-33.'

'She did?' Jeff Raven asked. 'When?'

Only his wife knew him well enough to be wary of that tone in his voice: almost teasing and very knowing.

'I remember exactly,' Gallahue replied briskly. 'For it was the day when the Phobos Moon Base managed to activate the refugee Sphere they were examining.' She gave a shrug. 'There could not possibly have been a connection but she went into a state of frenzy, charging about her quarters. It was the most active she had ever been. She also started emitting what must be her mating pheromones for the two males, generally as languid as she, got quite excited – for them – and vied to stuff food into her maw and then to fertilize her by agitated stroking of her egg-bulb.'

'Yes, I vividly remember that report, Commander Gallahue,' Sam said. 'I've studied all you've had to say about the queen.'

'Thank you, Lieutenant. That was the only occasion when she was fed from vat six,' Whila Gallahue added thoughtfully. 'We were given supplies for her from the stored vats of that captured Sphere, you know. She usually accepted food from vats three and four.'

'We took samples from the foodstuffs stored on Arcadia but nothing there resembles the compound from vat six. Yet another anomaly.' Sam shook his head.

'Perhaps not,' Stg said, entering the conversation. 'Both Human and Mrdini require different food when engaged in martial activities. That has been noted. Why not Hiver queens?'

'If I may?' and Verla Mitab from the Xh-33 Moon Base raised a tentative finger.

'Go on,' Jeff said encouragingly.

'Well, sirs, ma'am, I think part of it is what they eat,' she said, 'because I've done two tours on the Xh-33 Moon Base and, by the time the Base was ready, they were growing a different main crop in their fields. I noticed that when I played back the probe recordings the young Prime, Rojer Lyon, made . . .' and she nodded half-apologetically at Rowan and Jeff '. . . and they also harvested more often. Another thing I noticed on my second tour,' and she was talking as fast as she could to prevent an interruption, 'was the way the workers started acting.'

'What way?' Admiral Tohl asked kindly, bouncing his fingertips together.

'Well, you know how the field workers march out in pairs?'

Sam was not the only one who nodded.

'Well, they stopped doing that. They started coming out one by one. They'd form pairs when they got enough space to do so. And it got worse.'

'How?' Jeff smiled encouragingly and she suddenly relaxed.

'It was like they had to push past . . . obstacles. Commander Makako sent a probe down but all we saw was more bodies. Only . . .' she paused again, and cocked her head in a puzzled fashion, 'what we saw was not too many workers trying to get out. It was many bodies moving around so the workers could actually exit. Then . . .' she blinked, 'when the workers came back in, it looked as if the others, who never came out of the hive, were taking the food from their backs before they could get it to the ramps or storage like they should have done.'

'Did you send another probe in to investigate the anomaly?' Admiral Tohl enquired.

She shrugged. 'Several more and in different hives but none had enough light to give us details beyond a sort of seething mass of bodies. And Commander Makako didn't want to send in a lighted probe.'

255

'Probably just as wise that she didn't,' Tohl said, 'though with hindsight I could wish that she had.'

'As I recall it,' the Rowan said quickly, 'remotes were installed in quite a few hives, weren't they?'

'Yes, ma'am,' Verla Mitab replied. 'Once the Base was established we were told to put remotes in fifty hives on each continent. But just in the queens' quarters. Those green boards of theirs gave us enough light to see what the queens were doing. And all they were doing was being fed and stroked to fertilize more eggs.'

'How many males did each queen have?' Stg asked, leaning forward. 'Where did the eggs go?'

'Oh, eight or nine. We could see that they were sort of . . . courting her, like. You know, trying to be the only one she'd take food from. We never did see what hatched from the eggs. The scurriers would take them out once they'd been . . . done.'

'That was standard behaviour in all the hives you could observe?' asked Gallahue.

'Yes, ma'am.'

'Undoubtedly the queens were building up their forces in secret,' Tohl suggested. 'I would hazard the guess that the . . . press of creatures that slowed the workers on their dutiful way to the fields . . . were the warrior mutations that followed the queen to war, having somehow been fitted with maces instead of shovels.'

'How did the queens mutate?' Gallahue asked. There was no immediate answer. Then she added, 'Diet? Only on that one occasion did the Heinlein queen eat from vat six.'

'How long did that last?' Tohl asked.

'Six days only, though the two males kept forcing food into her mouth. She'd let it dribble away from her maw,' Gallahue said.

'The males kept forcing her to eat?' Jeff asked, sitting upright. 'Maybe the queen isn't the guiding force in her hive that we thought she is. Could the males pressure her by feeding her a special diet . . . to produce the mutated warrior types?'

Glances were exchanged by the xenbees.

'Anything could happen with hive queens,' Gktmglnt said in a voice nearly as deep and dark as Gallahue's.

'Wait a minute,' Jeff said, putting his elbows on the conference table, 'how many males did you say the Xh-33 queens had?' he asked Verla Mitab.

'At least eight, sometimes nine.'

'Big ones?'

'Yes, sir, bigger certainly than any from Lt Weiman's Arcadia reports,' and Verla gave him a little smile.

'Big enough, then, to coerce an Xh-33 queen, big as they are,' Jeff said.

'But it was the queens that led the battles,' Verla said in protest. 'The males formed up like a sort of honour guard, to protect her. It was the mace-holders who did the actual fighting.'

'Until the queen was dead, or issued the "flee" pheromones,' Stg said.

'Flee pheromones?' Jeff asked.

'Yes, sir,' said Lt Commander Jan Voorhees, speaking for the first time. 'That suggests,' and he turned his gaze from Jeff to the other xenbees at the table, 'that the Hivers once did have natural enemies since flee pheromones imply an automatic stimulus-response behaviour.'

'Too bad we don't know what scares 'em,' said Admiral Tohl with a wicked grin.

Gktmglnt nodded agreement.

'A flee pheromone?' Gallahue repeated, pointing at Voorhees. 'I hadn't thought of that possibility in Hivers.'

'How could you, ma'am, with just a quiescent queen that has been separated from its normal society?' Voorhees said in a courteous tone.

'True,' she admitted, 'but a flee or danger pheromone is apparent in many Earth-type creatures like termites, ants and bees. That's not to suggest that Hive queens are hymenopterous, of course, merely that they also can produce flee pheromones.'

'Accepted,' Jan Voorhees said. 'However, Stg and I noticed distinctive variations in every site where a queen was killed.

257

We also noticed that a dead queen's remaining warrior types, as well as her males, ran away. Of course, some of them just ran into the forces from another Hive.'

'How did they tell who was friend or foe?' the Rowan asked.

'Each queen also generates her own specialized pheromone so her minions can identify her,' and Voorhees rolled his eyes. 'It was murder trying to differentiate but we did manage to identify quite a few of the hives of dead queens by the residuals.'

'Remarkable,' Sam said, remembering how many pheromones he'd had to log from the Arcadian queens. 'Arcadian queens are not quite as . . . intense, shall we say, as the readings you report on Xh-33.'

Jan Voorhees stared at Sam, pushing out his chin. 'What did you say?'

'I said the Arcadian queens do not emanate the type of pheromones that the Xh-33 queens do or did.'

He locked eyes with Voorhees as both evidently simultaneously made the shift to a conclusion.

'Can we substitute the pacific Arcadian pheromones for the aggressive ones of Xh-33?' Jan cried, almost hopping out of his seat.

'I would have thought that was an obvious solution,' the Rowan said, her chin propped in her left hand.

'Obvious, perhaps,' Sam said, shaking his head, 'but very difficult to implement. We would have to eliminate the identifying pheromones of an Arcadian queen and substitute the Xh-33 queen's. If that would even work.'

'Difficult to do,' Voorhees said, staring thoughtfully at Sam Weiman.

'But not impossible,' said Stg.

'This one agrees with Stg,' Grm said formally, its poll eye glistening. It turned almost apologetically to Sam sitting beside it.

'You would have to duplicate the pheromones exactly to get the required effect,' Gallahue said, shaking her head over that difficulty.

'Ma'am, with the practice Stg and I have just had, it's a case of accurately reading the GCs,' Voorhees said, almost boasting of his prowess.

'That is not simple,' Stg said, heaving a big sigh.

'Look, do I understand you correctly?' Jeff began. 'You are suggesting that, if we can accurately duplicate the Arcadian queen pheromones, we might pacify the Xh-33 queens? What's left of them?'

'The pacific pheromones could be sprayed on the surface and renewed frequently,' Voorhees was saying, more to the other xenbees than in answer to Jeff. 'It might just work. We could give it a try. What have we to lose?' He looked from Gallahue to Sam: he blinked at Gktmglnt and held Admiral Tohl's gaze.

The admiral swung his glance to Commander Gallahue.

'It is a possibility,' she said though she obviously still had reservations.

'In the meantime,' Jeff said, 'I have had an urgent message from Perry on the *Asimov*. The weather pattern is shifting. Captain Osullivan has asked for permission to seed the clouds for rain. I will need your approval, Admiral Tohl, honourable Gktmglnt. The aggressive pheromones must be diluted before reaching the other continents on Xh-33.'

The two High Councillors made eye contact. Gktmglnt inclined its poll permissively and the admiral gave a sharp nod of his head.

'By all means, seed the clouds and prevent more battles.'

'Then we have bought time to investigate the Arcadian possibility,' Jeff said.

'But not yet an answer to the main problem,' said Gktmglnt in a lugubrious tone. 'There are so many occupied Hiver worlds.'

'There is an Arcadia,' Sam ventured to say. 'Maybe there are more.'

'We can but hope,' the Rowan said pessimistically.

'Shall we then go a step further,' Admiral Tohl said, gesturing towards Commander Gallahue who had made the suggestion before he turned to Gktmglnt, 'and ask the *Asimov* to implement a clean sweep of the Main Continent's vacated premises?'

'To resettle the queens is a good idea,' the Mrdini agreed, nodding its head with great dignity. 'It will be interesting to note how long that expedient keeps Xh-33 peaceful.'

Jeff cocked his head, an attitude that suggested he was listening to a telepathed message. The others remained respectfully silent.

'The *Columbia* is just now entering the Ciudad Rodrigo system. Perhaps their examination of that Hiver-occupied planet will give us fresh insights, or confirm what we already know. Do we by any chance know whether or not one of the xenbees ever took GC readings on the big Sphere? Three of the escape pods were activated and those queens fled, so the Hivers must have known they weren't going to outrun the nova wave.'

Commander Gallahue smiled. 'I do believe the *Vadim* xenbee records show that GC readings were taken, along with every conceivable analytic material the Alliance specialists have.' She tapped rapidly on her notepad. 'I thought so. Yes, the readings, though faint, are available. Mostly of corrosion. Perhaps not enough to use for an additional point of reference.'

Jeff rose to his feet. 'Perhaps you would all care to continue discussing plans in a secure conference area?'

The xenbees certainly did.

'We have begun to control our destinies,' Gktmglnt said, lifting its large self to its feet, causing Grm to cower away from the mass. 'That is good. Our good fight continues.' It bowed to Jeff, and those assembled, the approving gaze of its poll eye lingering slightly longer on the two Mrdini participants. IF YOU WOULD BE SO GOOD, PRIME RAVEN, TO RETURN THIS PERSON TO ITS OFFICE, THERE IS MUCH TO BE DONE.

IT IS MY PLEASURE TO ASSIST YOU, HONOURABLE GKTMGLNT, and Jeff bowed formally. The Mrdini High Councillor disappeared. 'Anyone else? Admiral? To your office?' When the admiral nodded, he too disappeared and Jeff turned to the others. 'I believe that Gollee has secured a conference room for you, one with laboratory facilities attached,' and he smiled at the xenbees. 'You've been exceedingly helpful. My warm thanks and good day.'

'Very good of . . .' was all Commander Gallahue could say before she disappeared, along with the other six.

# CHAPTER TWELVE

Captain Osullivan ordered the Main Continent cleaned up, using teams from each of the nine ships in Fourth Fleet.

'That's so's we all smell as bad,' the com officer on the AS *Beijing* was heard to say to the com officer of the AS *Strongbow*. The comment was wisely ignored.

The removal of all the dead Hivers would require combined efforts, since the safest way to dispose of so much carnage was to vaporize it. While that left strong odours behind until the prevailing winds dispersed them, the pheromones matched none that might activate a queen's response.

'Not that many queens survived that horrendous battle,' Captain Osullivan remarked. 'What effect will that have on the real estate we'll be selling to queens we want to settle there, Mr Voorhees?'

'Some vegetation thrives on being burned out once in a while,' Voorhees replied. 'Whether that holds true for this planet I don't know, sir, but I do know that the longer we delay getting rid of the corpses, the longer it's going to take to prepare the vacant facilities for new residents.'

The battlegrounds had to be ploughed and decontaminated to remove the taint of the body fluids spilled so futilely. Not many viable crops remained unscathed but what there were were fertilized with the dung kept in the queens' facilities for that purpose. The stored eggs in each facility were vacuumed out of their repositories and those were flung into the seas and lakes for whatever denizens lurked there.

'Too bad the Hivers don't fancy fish,' one of the CPOs on that detail was heard to remark. 'Lots of aquatic types.'

The next job, preparing the vacated quarters for new residents, was made easier by Commander Makako's records of every queen facility on the entire planet. By pointing out the sites of the most recent 'boundary' skirmishes, she could show the xenbees where to find the most aggressive ones. These would be kept busy enough in their new quarters to forget about extending their holdings. Her observers had also identified several young queens who had only begun to lay eggs and develop an entourage.

The best job, according to the scuttlebutt of Fourth Fleet, was following the Nose around. Jeff had explained to Pierre Laney the urgency and importance of applying his unique Talent to the minute, but vital, differences of smell in queens' quarters. If the relocation were to work effectively, the queen must think she was still in her original quarters. Once Laney was assured that he was in no personal danger and how important it was to replicate the distinctive aura in each facility, he accepted the job, and the enormous fee that went with it.

A spare man in his forties, he had indeed a remarkable nose, in size and appearance, for it was, as Cyrano de Bergerac had described his, a veritable rock, a crag, a cape . . . a peninsula . . . of a nose, reddened, with capillaries fanning out on both cheeks. He totally ignored any stares it caused, evidently well accustomed to every kind of reaction, but, when he first came on board the *Asimov,* he had a habit of taking a quick sniff of each area he passed through.

'I can find my way about anywhere in total darkness entirely by scent,' Laney confided in Captain Osullivan, for he was naturally included in the captain's mess. His manner was always gracious and he was as good a listener as a Nose.

263

'Some places are more interesting . . .' and he tapped the tip of his thick nose, 'than others.'

'We're grateful for your willingness to serve,' Captain Osullivan said. 'A change is as good as a rest,' was Pierre's reply, smiling broadly. 'I've never been on a spaceship before. For that matter, I've never been off Earth.'

He never got tired, either, in his relentless tour of the deodorized facilities. He carried a wrist pad on which he made notations.

'Chemical formulas for the distinctive aromas,' he replied to Voorhees's query. 'However, I rarely forget one.'

'Never thought of these,' Voorhees murmured, gesturing around him at the empty queen quarters that they were currently evaluating, 'as aromatic.'

'Oh, they are, whether or not they are also pleasant to smell or so faint that only *I* can differentiate. Aroma does imply nice, as does scent. Aromatic suggests something stronger. But reek, smell, stink, pong, stench, fetor, redolence, all evoke memories in our minds of other times and places where our olfactory sense has met with that . . . flavour . . . on a previous occasion. Think on it,' Pierre Laney suggested. 'Aroma, smell, fragrance, whatever,' and he gave a Gallic twist of his hand, 'the mind . . .' and he tapped his proboscis, 'and the schnozzolla remembers.'

'Schnozzolla?' Voorhees echoed, his eyes protruding in astonishment.

'Schnozzolla,' Pierre echoed with a dignified nod of his head. 'An ancient comedian with a beak like mine,' and he caressed it with an affectionate finger, 'made an advantage out of what others would have called a disfigurement. Now, of course,' and another Gallic wave of his hand, 'physical perfection can be easily achieved.' He shrugged in a dismissal of physical perfection as the ideal. 'NOW do I get to see the occupied Hives?' he asked.

Voorhees respectfully gestured for Pierre to precede him out into the fresher air, wondering how the queens had turned on the air-circulation device that Thian had mentioned.

They moved more cautiously in their search and assessment of the quarters of the queens, scheduled to be relocated on the

Main Continent, to relieve the population pressure and the threat of more territorial battles on the other continents. Once Laney got over the initial shock of seeing a Hiver queen, propped up on her hind legs, watching the green wall screen and whatever messages it conveyed to her, he followed wherever Voorhees and his security team led him.

'I did review tapes taken of the queen at Heinlein Moon Base, you know,' he confided in Voorhees after the first investigation, 'when Prime Raven approached me for this assignment. Being in the same . . . ah . . . chamber with one is quite another matter.'

On his return to the *Asimov,* he would also concoct, as he called it, the essence of each live queen.

'There are so many to be remembered in such a short time, I should not like to put queen 13's scent where queen 33's should be. No, no, such a mistake would queer the entire operation,' he explained to the laboratory technicians who assisted him.

The concerned head technician informed Captain Osullivan that the Nose apparently took little sleep.

'Ah, but I need little sleep,' and Pierre beamed at such consideration when Etienne Osullivan expressed anxiety over his diligence. 'I only require four hours a night, you see. I love my work, you know,' and his brown eyes twinkled as he held a cautionary finger to his lips. 'I have even discovered several new fragrances from the musk of the queens.'

'Really?' Osullivan was surprised.

'Of course,' and a Gallic shrug. 'Many of the most popular perfumes are based on remarkable substances.' He held up his hand, bowing his head as one who is divulging an important fact. 'I have made up several quite passable colognes. Your female officers are kind enough to say they are enchanted.' He twinkled again.

'So am I!'

'If I recall correctly,' Captain Vestapia Soligen of the *Columbia* said, 'Ciudad Rodrigo had a Sphere which they sent up our tail end.' Her expression was unforgiving.

265

'No good did it do them,' Lt Rhodri Eagles remarked dryly, twiddling his thumbs. He had stretched out his long body in one of the comfortable chairs in the Talents' lounge aboard the Constellation class.

The captain gave him a long stare and, as if it had been his idea and not his captain's look, he straightened up and clasped his hands together.

'Do we know if it took its scout-ships with it?' Vestapia asked those in the room.

'No, sir, we don't,' said Commander Wayla Gregorian as the science officer.

'Mostly they do,' Rojer said, 'or they have no way of getting to and from the Sphere when they reach their destination.'

'Unless of course,' Roddie remarked, 'they've got ground-to-ship transports we've never seen.'

'A distinct possibility,' and Major Kwan Keiser-Tau frowned at the security risk that could pose.

'However, I've never seen any,' Rojer said from a position of more experience with Hivers than anyone else in the lounge, and looked at Captain Hptml of the *KMTM*. HAVE YOU, SIR?

The large bronze-coloured 'Dini shook its head. HAVE BEEN IN COMBAT WITH SCOUTS. NEVER BEEN TO AN OCCUPIED PLANET WITH LIVE QUEENS. THE POSSIBILITY EXISTS.

'Since your experts,' and Major Keiser-Tau inclined his head stiffly but respectfully in Hptml's direction, 'seem to think that the planet Prime Thian explored is a-typical and since you, Rojer, were at Xh-33 when its spaceworthy craft were demolished, we shall proceed with caution.'

*As ever,* Roddie said in a 'pathed aside to the Talents in the room.

*His hide gets skinned if we get hurt, Rhodri,* Flavia reminded him.

'Prime Raven is anxious for us to reconnoitre,' Captain Soligen said.

The world they were fast approaching had three big, sprawling continents as well as small islands that Wayla thought might once have been connected to the main continents. Icecaps glittered at both north and south poles. There

266

was little seismic activity anywhere so the planet was old, geologically speaking. The initial probes indicated it was well settled and most of the arable land had been laid out in typical Hiver field patterns. One of the continents narrowed on the equator so that, from space, looked like a tightly corseted caricature of a human figure. Soligen pointed to an area above the 'waist', a wide plain with a range of hills that separated it from the ocean.

'I propose we start with this one. There appears to be a large enough underground area to house scouts.'

'If they have any left,' Roddie said but he was paying close attention to the briefing.

'Certainly they have no Sphere, just the debris that suggests one was in geo-synchronous orbit to that field. Helm,' and Vestapia raised her wrist com to her mouth, 'how soon before we reach orbit?'

'Four hours twenty minutes, Captain.'

She rose. 'Very well then, Major,' and she turned to the security officer, 'assemble a small team to accompany our Primes. I shall be most interested in having a running commentary on your exploration.' She turned at the door leading to her bridge. 'The treated hazmat gear is to be worn.'

*And don't forget to brush your teeth and gargle away the garlic,* said the irreverent Roddie, though his expression was bland.

*I just hope I'm around when you forget and speak those mean thoughts out loud,* Flavia said, rising.

'Thank all the gods that I don't have to go with you. The temperature down there is like Clarf's,' she added, jerking her thumb at their target on the planet.

'I don't know about anyone else,' Roddie said, 'but my hazmat is able for any temperature.'

'Even the frost when you get cheeky with Vestapia?' Asia asked.

Roddie slowly brought his head around to look down at his youngest sister.

'Look who's talking about cheek!' he exclaimed, throwing up his hands as if in defence. He shot a quick glance at Rojer who merely smiled at Asia. 'I should never have encouraged him to court you.' He laid a hand flat on his chest and appeared wounded to the core. 'Serpent to my breast.'

Asia only laughed and, putting a hand on Rojer's arm, hauled him in the direction of their cabin off the Talents' lounge.

'Remember?' Roddie called after them, 'we have to report in four hours and . . . ten minutes.'

As the surface party's shuttle touched lightly down on the designated spot, Rojer could sense Asia's excitement as she darted glances out the porthole. Kwan Keiser-Tau gestured authoritatively at his sergeant to lead out the scouting party for a quick look round.

'Nothing's stirring, sir,' the sergeant said.

'Not even the dust,' came a low murmur.

'Can it!' the sergeant ordered. 'Found what seems to be a man-made . . . excuse me, unnatural formation. Spread out there, Monks, see how far it goes. Might be the opening to the underground.'

'Check for anything resembling a . . . manufactured remote or spotting device.'

Rojer peered past the wiry, shorter security major and then jumped to the ground . . . holding up his hand to silence Kwan's protest.

'Ain't no-one here but us chickens, Major,' Lt Rhodri Eagles observed as he dropped beside the Prime.

Rojer hunkered down to push a finger into the obviously manufactured seam, looking along its length until he saw the scout reach the end and hold up his arm. The man pointed south, indicating the perpendicular direction of the seam.

'This is it, then. There's enough space to send an optic down.' Rojer indicated the opening.

The major snorted but beckoned to one of his technicians, who promptly came forward, swinging the equipment pack from his back to a ready position. Kneeling by the crack, he inserted the optical wire, pushing it down, then kept his eyes on the dials and the small screen.

268

'Nothing down there but dust, and some sort of equipment stacked against the far wall. Over there, underneath us,' he said, pointing to well beyond the parked shuttle.

*Tell Captain Soligen, Flavia, that the stable's empty and the barn door's still locked,* Rojer said.

*Do I repeat exactly what you tell me, Rojer?* and there was a ripple of laughter in Flavia's tone.

*Whatever. She likes a good laugh now and then. We'll move out now, Kwan ever vigilant, to the nearest facility, about two kilometres from here, I'd say,* Rojer added, adjusting the glare by darkening his helmet's visor. 'Can we move out now, Major?' he asked politely.

'To the target area, Captain?'

'That's the idea, Major,' Rojer said, controlling his impatience with the methodical officer, and beckoned for Asia, Mialla Evshenk, Yakamasura and Wayla Gregorian to exit the shuttle.

*Nice touch that, though,* Asia said, grinning up at her spouse, *reminding you that you may be a captain in the Talents' lounge but he outranks you on the ground.*

Roddie carefully walked the very straight line of the hatch, did an abrupt right-hand turn with military precision, a hundred metres to another right turn, to the other end and around back to them . . . leaving a straight line of boot prints to mark out the underground garage.

The rest of the surface team exited the shuttle and, at Keiser-Tau's gesture, some trotted out to the perimeter, heads turning from side to side in careful survey. Others bracketed the specialists. When his scouts reported in that all was clear, the major signalled them to return. Once his team had reassembled, Tau raised his arm and led them at a jogtrot up the slight incline from what had been the queens' landing-field.

The terrain altered abruptly into lush green vegetation, obviously cultivated, neat tamped-down earth marking well-used paths.

'They sure do keep a tidy garden,' murmured one of the troopers.

'Maintain silence,' the major said, a scowl in his voice and probably on his face. He stopped at the edge of the cultivation, looking this way and that.

'The queens do not, I repeat, do not see or hear us, Major,' Rojer said. 'If they could hear, the patter of booted feet on an empty chamber would have roused some reaction,' Roddie added.

'As you say, Lieutenant,' and Kwan awarded the T-3 a bare turn of his head in acknowledgement.

'Nor should we trample down the fields of corn,' Mialla said, pointing to the neat, well-used paths. 'We can easily stick to them. There's certainly nothing else moving. Major,' she added deferentially.

'Keep to the paths. Sergeant, take the point.'

Mialla used his momentary distraction to snatch a leaf from the nearest plant and was stowing it away in a specimen container before Keiser-Tau could protest.

'Need to analyse everything cogent to the project, Major.' Her remark was not an apology. When that crop ended and a new feathery plant was visible, she also took samples of that variety.

Following the paths, they came to a T-junction.

'And leading directly to our target, too,' Yakamasura said.

The security officer grunted but, despite his scans of the surrounding fields, nothing moved save the top leaves in a light wind.

*So quiet you can hear the leaves growing,* Asia said to Rojer.

Another grunt from the major had the sergeant and two others jog up the track to a distant pyramidal structure, the slope to its open side plainly visible as a black maw.

'We can move out now,' and Keiser-Tau's raised arm gave them a needless direction.

Both Mialla Evshenk and Yakamasura paused long enough to gather botanical and soil samples on their way, a patient rear guard stopping as they did so.

*I didn't think a Hiver world would look so grand,* Asia confided to Rojer.

There was just enough room on the path for her to jog beside him.

*That's because you've only seen the ruined ones before. Xh-33 is . . . was like this,* he said, shaking his head. The *Columbia* had received copies of the Xh-33 massacre. Rojer had been particularly horrified by the slaughter since he remembered his probes across the orderly landscape that had been ruined by war.

Major Keiser-Tau halted them twenty metres from the slope into the facility. He sent the sergeant to the vantage point of the top of the pyramid and the man adjusted his visor for distance, turning slowly as he searched for movement. He paused, stiffened and pointed. The major adjusted his helmet but he had to join the taller sergeant on the structure to see what had alerted him.

'A group of inbound workers from the look of them,' he said. 'Up here, everyone. We'll let them precede us. Some appear to be carrying leaves and things.'

Without haste, the specialists joined the major and his troopers where they, too, could see the advance of swaying backs.

'All in step, too, looks like,' someone murmured.

'Worse'n boot-camp,' another anonymous voice added.

'Silence.'

Roddie twiddled with a setting on his helmet. 'MAYDAY! MAYDAY!'

*Cut out the nonsense,* Rojer said because the major had gone into a crouch and his troopers had drawn their weapons.

'I told you they wouldn't hear us.'

The major walked up to the T-3, his face contorted with rage. He was a full head shorter than Rhodri Eagles. 'You're on report, Lieutenant.'

'Yes, sir,' the lieutenant replied briskly replied, saluting.

*Roddie!* Asia said in exasperation. *One day one of these funny little things you think up is going to backfire on you.*

*So everyone tells me,* Rhodri said with a carefully 'pathed sigh.

The surface party watched the stalwart workers trundling along, their backs loaded with freshly plucked, wide, red-veined leaves.

271

'Like chard,' murmured Mialla Evshenk softly.

The burdens covered most of the creatures so that details of their appearance were obscured. They counted one hundred pairs of workers descending towards the facility. Still in impeccable files, they walked around to the entrance slope and disappeared into the maw. A mechanical rumble startled everyone.

'Sending the harvest to the processors,' Rojer said. 'Remember the data from Thian's downside visit?'

'Oh, yes, of course,' Yakamasura said, smiling with relief.

Keiser-Tau gestured to a technician who activated a hand-held device, turning it as it followed movement below.

'Life-forms are now in a short tunnel and proceeding into a low wide . . .' the technician reported, his sensor following the movement.

*Hole in the wall,* said Roddie Eagles, irrepressibly.

'. . . stable or some sort of holding place.' A long pause. 'No more movement there, sir.'

'Where is there movement, Corporal?' the major demanded.

The corporal walked, as if on eggs, across the top of the structure and then stopped at the edge of the roof. 'Further below, out in that direction, sir.'

'Laid out just as Thian's planet was,' Rojer said, 'and Xh-33, though I never got into the queens' quarters.' He gestured for the major to lead on.

*We need GC readings everywhere . . . and samples of any dirt,* Flavia said. *And keep talking. To me, if not to the major.*

So Rojer described everything as the ever-vigilant major led them cautiously down the slope. Yakamasura and Mialla took dirt samples, having to dig with their boot heels to loosen enough tamped earth to fill their containers.

Once inside the structure . . .

'Ooops. GC is picking up a high concentration of selenaldehydes and selenoketones, sir.'

Rojer reported that to Flavia.

'Night visor on,' the major ordered needlessly. Everyone had already adjusted their helmets to see in the underground darkness.

272

'The workers would have dumped their loads down a ramp directly in front of us and the moving belts are still taking the stuff wherever it needs to go,' Rojer said. 'The tunnel to the queen's quarters should be to our left.' He felt a vague sensation of uneasiness yet, with Thian's report to reassure him, he couldn't imagine what he need worry about.

The major grunted and signalled for advance scouts to go left.

'Tall narrow tunnels all right enough, sir,' was the report.

'D'you think we could have a look at where the workers went?' Yakamasura asked wistfully.

'Is that necessary?' Keiser-Tau asked.

'Well, if this report is to be as complete as Prime Thian's was, then we should,' he replied in his most conciliatory manner.

'Corporal, take four men and Dr Yakamasura . . .'

'Me, too, please,' Mialla said, putting up her hand.

'And Dr Evshenk . . .' The major's sigh was audible over the com.

When they had come to the end of the long narrow tunnel which Rojer described as well as he could – his apprehension still keen – their emergence into the queen's lair was almost anticlimactic. In fact, it was almost a duplicate of Thian's visuals. Scuttling things were running around on the floor and the queen, sitting among the attendants who were busy stroking and cleaning her many limbs, had her black eyes on the quivering, changing wall screen.

*I've been here before,* Rojer said to Asia who squeezed his hand and, ever so slightly, pulled him back the way they had just come. *Nothing new or any different.*

'We need GC readings, Prime,' the major said and held out something to Rojer. 'And this remote is to be placed . . .'

Rojer took the remote, removed the strip from the adhesive on the back of it, and 'ported it into place, exactly where Thian had positioned his.

*Now, let's get out of here,* Asia said. *Something is butting into me.*

'Could we be under attack, sir?' the sergeant asked, shifting

273

his weight and lifting first one leg and then the other, trying to look all around himself at the same time. Rounded beetles were buffeting him.

'Same thing happened to my brother, Sergeant,' Rojer said with as much reassurance as he could. 'Just more of the queen attendants.'

*I'll say one thing,* and there was an odd touch of pride in Rhodri Eagles's voice, *she isn't as big as MY queen at Heinlein Base.*

*She isn't?*

'We'll need to find scrapes, fragments, something metallic, Major, for carbon dating of this facility,' Rojer said.

'Sabin, can you find any metallic refuse in the workers' garage?' Major Keiser-Tau said over the com, but spoke softly as if he, too, were impressed by being in the presence of the queen.

'Yes, sir. Some sort of tool. Some broken bits just scattered about.'

'That may suffice. Now let's get out of here before they begin to smell us,' the security officer said.

If he had led the specialists to the chamber, he now rapidly led them all out again and into the wide-open spaces. There were many sighs of relief heard over the connected coms.

*How many of these do we have to go into, Rojer?* Asia asked.

*Oh, we have to do a fair number to make a valid report, honey.* Then he felt the least bit of a reluctance she was trying to hide from him, *but you don't have to go into another, if you don't want to.*

Asia stood up as tall as she could, which was not quite to Rojer's shoulder. *Where you go, I go. But it is spooky down there.*

*At least, in these hazmat suits, we don't have to endure sting-pzzt.*

*No,* and Asia brought her hands up to her suit, startled by his observation. *We don't. Trust you to remember that.*

*I kept waiting for it,* Rojer said, only just realizing that that was what he had been anticipating.

274

*Fooled me, too,* Roddie admitted with a sheepish grin which he allowed only the two Talents to see.

They felt the sting-pzzt, though, the moment they opened their helmets back in the shuttle. Sabin had draped a lumpy sack over his feet from which emanated the unique Hiver pheromones. The return 'portation took seconds and immediately the deck officer opened the shuttle door, the three Talents 'ported themselves to the lounge.

'What on earth . . .' Flavia began when she saw all three lifting an arm and smelling it.

'Well, it didn't stick to us,' Rojer said with an exaggerated sigh of relief.

'What didn't stick?'

Rojer explained on his way to his bedroom, Asia on his heels, both peeling down the hazmat suits as they walked.

'The sting-pzzt, for one thing,' Rojer said.

'Sweat and dust for another,' Asia said and waggled her fingers at Flavia before she palmed the door shut.

For comparisons . . . of which there weren't many, Rojer, Asia and Rhodri all agreed . . . they sampled twenty hives on the major land masses.

'There's still room for more hives,' Yakamasura agreed with Mialla Evshenk.

'But it would be better if there were fewer, rather than more, queens,' she said, giving a satisfied punch to the key that finished her personal evaluation of their efforts. 'So where do we go from here?'

'Doubtless, we'll be asked to accept a message tube with that information,' Roddie said, yawning hugely and settling his frame more comfortably on his couch.

A rap on the door from the bridge startled everyone just as an eerie chuckle touched the minds of the Talented.

'Come in, Captain,' Flavia called, having checked who was knocking. 'New orders seem to be on their way.'

*You guessed it, Flavia,* said Earth Prime. *Message tube coming in and, if the captain has her resupply list . . .*

*She actually has it in hand, sir.*

*Warn her,* and the flimsies in Captain Soligen's hand suddenly disappeared.

'How did that happen?' She looked around the room, glaring at Roddie.

'Earth Prime effected immediate acceptance of your supply list, Vestapia,' Flavia said, managing to keep a straight face. 'I didn't have time to warn you. And here . . .' she held out her hands, cocking one eyebrow briefly, as she 'ported a pillow into them. A message tube landed square on the pillow. '. . . are our orders, ma'am,' she added.

Vestapia looked down at her right hand, fingers still in a gripping position, then at the message tube and slowly walked over to it.

'I suppose just about the time I get used to the vagaries of Talent, I'll lose you.' She poked at the tube and jumped back when Rojer, using kinesis, opened it and the tightly packed data disks spilled onto the carpet.

'Not any time soon, I hope,' Rojer said, meaning it.

Vestapia picked up the packet with the Admiralty seal on it and broke it open, scanning the contents. 'Famous last words,' she said, clicking her tongue, and looked at Rojer. 'Earth Prime needs you, and Asia, to help with Operation Switch.'

'Operation Switch?' Rojer asked, confused.

Roddie, craning his head around to the data disks on the floor, read the titles and flipped one into Rojer's hand. 'Operation Switch! All the data you need for background on the new and spectacular Xh-33 real-estate program.' He clasped his hands behind his head and stretched out again. 'Better you than me.'

'I don't know about that,' Vestapia said ambiguously and returned to the bridge.

*Zara, any progress to report?* Elizara said, tapping lightly into the hospital generators for her contact with her namesake on Iota Aurigae.

*Yes, I was about to contact you.*

*Have you heard about Operation Switch?*

*Mother and Father pass the very latest bulletins on to me. Is*

276

*that progressing? Now that the Main Continent on Xh-33 has been cleansed, I believe they are going forward with the plan. So what is your good news for me?*

*If you have good news for me to pass on to the High Councillor Gktmglnt, it would be very grateful.*

Zara's tone brightened immediately. *I do.* She chuckled. *Using the principle that the last place you look is the right one, I started at Ward 19 . . .* She chuckled again. *There was considerable wagering . . .*

*Don't be difficult, Zara . . .*

*It was Ward 18, the second one. The chemical we need to delete to curb 'creation' is a valeric acid analogue . . . and we also need to reduce the quantity of phenol. We have now ascertained that a 'Dini bud starts to form, actually, before a 'Dini enters hibernation. It needs the hibernatory pheromones to be completed successfully. In essence, if the bud is nipped early enough to abort it before it has formed between the two 'Dini, reproduction will not take place. The keepers will remove the unformed buds so that the still-hibernating 'Dini pair will never realize. There are all kinds of reasons that can be given. At least this way, population can be regulated without any interference in cleansing the 'Dini bodies of dead cells and the restoration of their own bodies.*

*That is very good news. May I report this to Councillor Gktmglnt?*

*That's also why I was going to call you.* And Zara's tone turned grim. *The very honourable Gktmglnt is going to have to convince the older keepers that they must depart from tradition, by eliminating the valeric acid analogue and reducing the phenol content, to regulate reproduction. The younger ones, and I am blessed by having only one old fart flapping about in dismay over interrupting 'creation', see the sense of the process. Are quite willing to go along with it, although Iota Aurigae must be the only world where we could use all the 'Dinis that can be 'created'. At least while mining is in an intensive stage to supply more Washington-class ships. Pass the word along to Grandfather and Gollee Gren. They'll see that those who need to know will be informed. I'm tubing the formal stuff directly to you, Elizara.*

*You've done very well indeed, Zara. Very well.*

*Thanks!* And Elizara was aware of Zara's pride in having achieved such a notable success.

*My 'Dinis are real pleased, too. They helped me every step of the way, arguing with the old fart . . . its name IS Frtlmp, so that word fits it perfectly.* Elizara had no trouble imaging a malicious expression on Zara's face as she said that and the Medical Prime laughed. *It wouldn't know what I meant even if I spoke its nickname out loud.*

*Pal and Dis would,* Elizara said, still chuckling.

*Oh, they think it's apt enough but, of course, they are exceedingly formal in their encounters with Frtlmp. 'T any rate, it's up to the High Councillor and the various 'Dini leaders to settle how much they need to decrease 'creation' and enforce the orders at all hibernatories. Even on the shipboard ones.*

*Especially on those,* Elizara said. *Furthermore, it would be easier to explain the non-creation in the Fleets.*

*Yes, it would. Here comes your package.*

*Thanks, dear,* Elizara said as she heard the message tube rattle into the basket behind her. *Again, you've done very well.*

*Thank you.* And, if Elizara thought that Zara had responded in an unusually modest tone, she'd've been right. Her experience in the hibernatory, especially curing the victims of the Clarf disaster, had matured her as a healer and as a person. *We will have to do more field tests, as it were, to be sure it works on all 'Dini colour groups.*

278

# CHAPTER THIRTEEN

The acuity of Pierre Laney's Nose had never been put to such unusual usage. His infallible organ caught the subtle nuances of each queen's pheromone output, and the minor variations of the quarters, so that when the details were replicated in the hundred different sites that had been made available on the Main Continent, the queens were undisturbed. That is, until workers were sent out to cultivate the fields that had been left behind and found only raw turned earth instead of ready-to-harvest crops.

'We will add just a soupçon,' Pierre told Captain Osullivan, pinching thumb and forefinger together, 'of the essence so unique to the world Prime Thian explored. This ingredient may, in the long term, be what is needed to neutralize the aggressive ones and turn our . . . belligerent queens into tame pussy-cats, like yours.' He warily eyed the captain's tricolour barque cat, Tabitha, asleep on her pillow in the corner of Osullivan's ready room.

Osullivan snorted. 'You have only seen her asleep, Pierre,' he said.

'Which is what we want our queens to be, asleep. If my soupçon is successful, use it as a spray, dropping as a gentle rain upon the place below.' He smiled beatifically at Osullivan, who tried to remember the source of what was obviously a quote.

'Indeed,' he said ambiguously and gestured for Pierre to go on.

'A spray which can be applied when needed to the surface. And renewed as necessary. We will infect all Hiver-occupied worlds with the serenity of the most ancient hive in this part of the galaxy!' His vibrant voice roused Tab who looked sleepily at him for a moment, and then resumed her nap. His upraised hands indicated his exultation in discovering an answer to the vital question of how to keep the queens where they were.

'Excellent news, Pierre,' Osullivan said, realizing that praise for such a resolution – if it worked – was in order. 'Excellent!' He rose from his desk and came around, clapping Pierre on the back and accepting the Gallic embrace with his usual aplomb. 'Let's tell the good news to our team and have them forward it to Earth Prime and the High Council. I must tell you,' and he laid a hand on Pierre's back to guide him to the Talents' lounge, 'that I was dubious about so simple an answer to such an immense problem. But you've done it!'

'I live in hope,' Pierre said with a very Gallic shrug, a complete change from his previous exuberance.

To effect Operation Switch, Perry asked for more Primes and as many strong T-2 kinetics as could be spared for the several days the transfers would take. After all, it was not just the queens, but all their workers, attendants AND eggs that had to be moved. Damia allowed Afra as well as Kaltia and Morag to be nominated for the team.

*It'll be good experience and this won't take too long, will it?* Damia asked her father. *We're between loads and our apprentices can handle anything else that might come in with me as Merge.*

*I'm sending Gollee, too, by the way. He needs a break.*

*This will be a* break? Damia asked with some asperity.

Her father chuckled. *I'd borrow Zara, too, but Elizara has told me that her . . . work . . . is in its concluding phase. So*

*Elizara said she'd come. She can lend heft to a Merge and she's deeply interested in the project. She's volunteered her youngest, a strong kinetic T-2, for an unparalleled opportunity to meet so many of his peers.*

*How old is Pietro?*

*Old enough . . .* there was a brief pause. *Same age as Barry, your mother just tartly informed me. I'm borrowing Rojer and Asia from Second Fleet.*

*Oh, that'll be so nice for the children. We do miss them. And don't you dare say, 'only a thought apart',* she added in a fierce tone.

*Wouldn't dare,* her father replied.

*I almost wish I could join them. But I can't and that's that!* Damia said. *I do hope it's worth the effort.*

*We can wait and see. The Xh-33 at least allows us to try the theory that the alteration of the local pheromones will have the desired effect.*

*Are the militants giving you more trouble?*

*Oh, them! If we can prove we've got the queens planet-bound, and we release enough of the newly discovered M-type worlds, they'll find something else to complain about.*

Damia could almost see her father shrugging his shoulders. She wanted to remind him that he was not, as he sometimes assumed, invulnerable.

*I'm not, you know,* he replied. *But nearly. And I never make claims of being infallible.*

*Not with Mother to keep you on your toes.*

A chuckle trailed off into silence.


The Xh-33 planet was not at the other end of the galaxy but, with the help of the occupants and their Towers, the various personnel carriers landed in orderly fashion in the boat bays of the various ships of the Fourth Fleet that were to host them. Perry and Adela on the *Asimov* would host Elizara and her youngest son, Pietro. Gollee Gren and Barry Raven came into the *Beijing* to be greeted officially by a cheerful Captain Smelkoff. Afra, Morag and Kaltia went to the *Nova Scotia* and an enthusiastic welcome by Captain Ellen Hogarth while

Rojer, with his 'Dinis and Asia, graced the decks of the MS *HGHL* to the delight of Captain Ghl. Xahra was to be a guest of the Galaxy Class *Strongbow* and was instantly impressed by Captain Halsted who had given up his quarters as being the only ones suitable for a Prime on his smaller ship.

As soon as everyone had arrived and had had a chance to look through the schedule, the Primes and the T-2s assembled for a briefing session on the *Asimov* in the Talents' lounge.

*Not as big as the Washington's,* Rojer remarked to Asia.

*Bigger than the Columbia's, though,* Asia said and Rojer gave a quick look at her suddenly meek tone.

*Don't you dare go all modest and nervous on me.*

*Oh, I won't.* She grinned up at him, and reached for his hand, squeezing it. *But it is bigger. Oh, is that gorgeous woman Xahra?*

*Perry's sister. She's pouting. No, she's not. She's smirking. She looks haughty to me.*

*Oh, she is that, too,* Rojer agreed. And Xahra was certainly stunning in an exotic way. Odd that she was stolid Perry's sister. He much preferred Elizara's tranquil beauty.

*Why, thank you, Rojer,* Elizara said, nudging the lad beside her. 'Come, Pietro, I want to introduce you to Rojer and Asia Lyon.'

Pietro might be the same age as Barry Raven but he had a great deal more poise than the Denebian.

*The result of so much exposure to Talents at Blundell,* Elizara replied, smiling graciously, *and he's shortly to get a Tower assignment. Ah,* and her mental tone sighed. *They grow up so fast these days.*

Morag and Kaltia arrived, squealing with delight to see their brother with Asia, and rushed over to the couple.

*Not all of them do,* Rojer replied like any unimpressed older sibling, hugging first Morag and then Kaltia because he was glad to see them and they really couldn't be classed as 'kids' any more. Working on Clarf with Laria had subtly altered them despite their reversion to juvenile exuberance.

His father had a slight smile on his face as he looked over the Talents already present. Adela, assisted by Navy stewards, was serving hot canapés and looking slightly nervous.

'Never thought I'd be able to sneak up on you, Afra,' and Afra turned to grip Gollee Gren's extended hand, savouring once more the essence of the man who had been so much a part of his professional life.

*Looking your age finally, are you?* Afra said, noting the grizzle of silver in the T-2's dark hair and the crinkle of lines about the light green eyes.

*Actually, it's constant proximity to Gwyn-Raven offspring and the rigours of dealing with all those eager young Talents.*

*So this is work as well as play?* Afra asked.

Gollee rolled his eyes. *A bit of both and indeed a testing time for Barry, Pietro and . . .* he paused to grimace slightly *. . . Morag and Kaltia.*

*Morag's old enough,* Afra said with a slight nod of his head. *Did well at Clarf during the emergency.*

*They both did. You've a grand family to be proud of. Ah, and Rojer is still protecting Asia, I see.*

Afra chuckled. *She's well able for him to think so.*

The exchange had taken brief seconds for now they heard 'Dini voices behind them as Afra's Trpl and Rojer's Gil and Kat came down the passageway. Trpl was taller by a full head . . . Human head . . . than Rojer's two and was obviously regaling its juniors with the part it had played in nursing the four victims of the Clarf disaster. More muted Human voices echoed respectfully as the naval Talents who would form part of the whole Merge arrived.

*A goodly crew,* Gollee said, nodding as he was recognized by the Fleet Talents and accepting their salutes with a wave of his hand. One of the women looked apprehensive. 'They won't bite, Mimi, I'm here to protect you.'

'Then we've nothing to fear,' an ensign said, grinning.

'Asaf Katzir, isn't it?' Gollee replied. *A good kinetic T-3.*

'Do you know who we all are?' Asaf asked, stopping in surprise.

'He'd better or Prime Raven will replace him with one of

you,' Afra said, so solemn-faced that Ensign Katzir goggled slightly until Gollee's grin reassured him.

'But *you* wouldn't have had the chance to meet Afra Lyon of Iota Aurigae,' Gollee said.

'I think you can tell who's a Prime in there without naming names.'

'Don't listen to him,' Mimi advised her crewmate, winking coquettishly at Gren who winked right back.

'If we're all here,' Perry spoke up when they entered the room, 'I'd like to get on with the briefing. We're doing this in four teams, with a Prime as Merge, assisted by the naval Talents. Since we can all be in contact, we can each use the generators of our host ships. Xahra, I'm putting Gollee and Pietro with you on the *Strongbow*; Rojer will have Barry and Asia to back him up on the *HGHL*. Afra will be Merge with his daughters. I've spread out the stronger Talents from the *Asimov*,' and he deferentially nodded towards Captain Osullivan. 'Elizara and I will lead the *Asimov* team. We might need to do some switching around after our first day but that's to be expected when none of us have ever done anything even remotely like we are about to do.'

Even Xahra nodded agreement with that, slightly amused by her brother's instructions.

'I have data files for all the queens we are transferring and visuals for the Main Continent quarters they're to inhabit. Fortunately for us, the Hivers' unvarying patterns are of inordinate help to us.' He tapped his chest, grinning. 'According to our expert, Pierre Laney,' and he gestured to the Nose, who was listening avidly to the briefing, 'the quarters of any individual queen might smell slightly different . . .'

'Indubitably, they do,' Pierre said, tapping his nose with a sage expression on his face.

'Yes, but the layout for queen and workers is exactly the same. We have visuals on each separate facility but they're all much of a muchness. Our communications people have been able to transfer the wall screens. At least they hope so,' and Perry grimaced slightly, 'but they haven't found out how or where to turn them on or off.'

284

'They have very small creatures to do that,' Rojer said, 'as we discovered when we started up the Sphere at Phobos Moon Base.'

'How small?' Perry asked, blinking at Rojer in surprise.

Rojer indicated the first two joints of his index finger. 'Their tunnels ran everywhere on the Sphere. Doubt their holes would be visible.'

'They are but seemed to go nowhere,' Perry said, looking down at his notepad and checking something off. 'We'll see what happens.' Then he looked around at his audience. 'We're hoping that we've done our – renovations – so well that the queens won't notice. They will, however, notice the fields. We can't transfer the crops. We're good but not that good.' His chuckle was answered by smiles. Xahra rolled her eyes at her brother's attempt at humour. 'So, if there are any questions about procedures, I – and the staff officers – am at your disposal.'

'Body weights?' Afra asked.

'Good point, sir,' Perry said, pointing his stylus at the Capellan. 'We've estimated you will be lifting the equivalent of a large drone with the queens, likewise each stable of her workers.' He gave a shrug.

'But it's animate cargo,' Afra said.

'That's why we have designated teams. Watch your remotes and catch as many of the queen's attendants as possible in the first 'port and pick up the remainder on a second trip if necessary,' Perry replied. 'You can take the workers by rows . . .'

'They make it handy enough,' Rojer said, wondering if the creatures would even know they'd been lifted.

'Wouldn't the eggs be fragile?' Xahra asked.

'The ones in with the Heinlein queen have a thick outer coating,' Rojer said. 'Reasonable caution is all you'd need.'

'They are in a storage tube, at the back of the queen's quarters,' Perry said, and brought up the visual. 'Once you know the shape, 'port that. They won't crack.' His manner suggested that the Primes were more than capable of handling the transfer.

'You said there were little creatures, Rojer?' Gollee asked. 'What happens if some get left behind and come looking for momma?'

'You will, of course, check on each of the facilities to be sure that none are left behind,' Perry said, a bit on his dignity.

'The queen'll make more if we lose a few,' Rojer said.

'The wounded queens have been steadily replacing the attendants that were killed in the war,' Perry said. 'According to Thian's report, when he removed specimens for study, the queen would count . . .' He broke off and shot a glance at Pierre Laney who winked back when Perry did not finish the sentence.

'Noses, is what they count,' Pierre said blithely, arms folded over his chest where he sat beside Captain Osullivan.

'Noses it is then,' Perry said with a slight grin. 'They didn't appear to be concerned in any way that they were missing attendants and promptly replaced them.'

'It's the field and the crops that's going to throw them, isn't it?' Elizara said.

'Yes, but there's nothing we can do about that. And some of the fields they'll now possess will be in bad condition,' Perry went on. 'We're hoping that the queens will just . . .' he gave a shrug '. . . replant or harvest or whatever. Again, their adherence to tradition includes their plantings. The same crops appear time and again. Of course, not in the same order, because some of the vegetables require different soil and/or more watering. But that should be a challenge to each queen – to put her individual domain back in order as soon as possible.'

'Well, let's hope they take up the challenge in the spirit in which it is presented: and more space to expand,' said Captain Osullivan. 'Any more questions?' He looked around the room.

When there appeared to be none to be asked, Captain Osullivan rose. 'Then let us proceed to the main hangar. The *Asimov* is a grand big ship but we wish all of our Talents to be seated in the same chamber for tonight's feast. Or would it be easier to 'port yourselves down?'

'Those of us who can should do so,' Perry said, 'leaving the lifts for those who can't.'

286

He took Adela's hand in his and disappeared. Immediately half the assembly followed suit.

'I could take you, Captain Osullivan, if you don't mind that kind of transport,' Elizara said, 'and Pietro can convey you, Mr Laney.'

'Pierre, please, Elizara.' Then the Nose turned to Pietro and spread both hands. 'When you're rea . . .'

'Neatly done,' Osullivan said with a grin.

'Show-off,' she said but the next instant she was facing Osullivan on the deck of the main hangar where a long U-shaped formation had been set out, with white napery that glistened in the overhead lights, laid for the many diners. At one side, in a straight line, the captains and executive officers of the other ships awaited the arrival of the Talented guests. The hangar had been cleansed of its usual grease and oil and was redolent with aromas activating everyone's salivary glands.

'Ah, superb!' Pierre said, lifting his hand, forefinger and thumb meeting, and then he inhaled deeply. 'Magnificent! May I escort you to your seat, Elizara?'

And it was a magnificent meal. Several times the captain thanked the Primes for bringing in the raw materials, fresh meats, fish, vegetables, cheeses, fruits, and sweets which the *Asimov*'s galley had transformed into such an elegant repast.

Once the meal was completed and everyone sated with good food and wine, Perry stood and suggested that a night's rest would be essential for the morning's endeavour.

The guests were escorted to personnel carriers in the smaller boat bays and returned to the ships that accommodated them.

The next morning after a solid breakfast to sustain them in their labours, the Talents gathered in the cabins designated for their use: comfortable couches, screens, an expediter and engineer, as well as assistants to keep track of the progress on screen and in notations. To one side of the large screens were a big schematic of a queen's facility and the map of which queen was to be transferred to which place on the Main Continent. The targets of each of the four teams were different colours.

'Very organized,' was Xahra's comment when Captain Halsted led her into the messroom of the *Strongbow* that had been converted for this use.

'Very well done,' Gollee Gren agreed as he and Pietro followed her. 'As good as I have back in Blundell,' he added amiably and caught startled thoughts from both T-1s.

Xahra smiled as she checked on the other amenities. There was a courteous tap on the door before the five minor Talents on board the *Strongbow* reported themselves ready for duty and stood at attention by the padded chairs arranged behind the three major Talents.

'Shall I stand by?' Halsted asked politely.

'It won't bother us,' Xahra said and took her seat, gesturing for all to be seated. 'Do you have the order of . . . transfer, Expediter?'

'Yes, ma'am,' was the prompt reply.

'Engineer, prepare to effect the gestalt. Gollee, let's start Operation Switch . . . to number 54 green.'

The expediter highlighted number 54 on the map, and its destination on the Main Continent, and the two quarters came up on screen: the one with its occupants grooming their queen, the other empty and ready to receive its new tenants. The generator hum increased.

'Gollee, Merge. Pietro, Sam, Jennifer, Elias, Amos, Kathleen . . .' Xahra paused just a moment to gather the Merged minds to her and then 'NOW!'

A sudden deep noise in the generators and then the queen and every creature were transported from their original premises into their new domain.

'Let's wait for it,' Xahra said, eyes going from one screen to the next. 'Ooops. One just entered, stage right,' she said and flicked it to its new quarters.

A squeak was plainly heard.

For a long moment, the queen sat still, then slowly, majestically, she rose to her hind limbs, staring straight ahead of her.

'Ah ha,' Gollee said, 'she's noticed the screen isn't hers!'

From under her and around, movement could be seen but even with the remotes set up to receive images in the usual darkness of a hive, the watchers could not tell where and what was sent. Then, all of a sudden, a perceivable green glow bathed the queen. She sat back down.

'Suspects merely a power outage,' Gollee said, chuckling.

The queen had just settled back when she rose and scrambled with unexpected speed down her tunnel . . . beyond the remote's range.

'Can we get an outside fix on Transfer 54?' Xahra said.

'I'm working on screen transfer, ma'am,' said the expediter. 'On screen three.'

That showed the outside of the collection point. The queen, scuttling with breakneck speed and followed by her male attendants, raced to the top of her facility and stood, slowly turning to survey the fields. She moved her lower limbs.

'The queen of all she surveys,' Gollee remarked.

'I don't think she likes what she sees,' Pietro said.

'Not one little tiny bit,' Gollee agreed.

'Let's get her workers in place, shall we? She's going to be calling them and they'd better answer or we've blown the manoeuvre,' Xahra said, and the generators built up speed. 'Expediter, let's see the garages there.'

The screens split into several smaller sections. Quickly Xahra leaned into the Merge and from one stable after another, the workers were transferred to the new facility. Immediately the ranks began to move.

'We got that in time.'

*Thanks for the warning, Xahra,* Perry's voice came to them. *I think we caught #1 in her morning nap. Ah, now she's waking up to the switch. Damn it. Why couldn't we have transferred their screen designs, too?*

*Number 54 is sending her children out in their hordes,* Gollee said, as the ranks came trundling up out of the building, two by two, each file turning off and up into the fields. *If she's setting them to work, she seems to be settling in her . . . new quarters right enough.*

The trampled fields were further from the queens' quarters

as each had tried to protect their home grounds. The queen remained in position, slowly turning to be sure the workers were reaching the damaged fields before she came down on all legs and descended into the dark interior and back to her hive. She arrived, could be seen on the remote putting her face close to the screen, before she backed off and resumed the position in which she had first been seen.

'One down and fifty-three more to go,' Gollee said.

'We got the eggs to do first, you know,' Xahra said. 'Let's see if we can get them in the one basket.'

That was the trickiest part as they all admitted, trying to keep the ovoids from slipping away from their 'port. The first time they tried, half the eggs eluded their grasp. Some fell out onto the deserted floor of the queen's hive. These had to be gathered up.

*Get the sides, Gollee and Pietro, I'll get the top and bottom,* Xahra said.

*Why not . . .* Pietro said, *think a sleeve around them so they can't escape?*

*That's not a bad concept,* Gollee agreed.

*A stocking is better because it has a toe and nothing can slip out the bottom,* was Xahra's amendment.

*Better and better.*

*Then let's do it. Ready?* Xahra asked her crew.

'When you are, ma'am,' said Amos who was the receiving 'path.

This time the transfer worked smoothly.

'Whee, that's a 'port and a half,' Gollee said.

'You're just out of practice,' Xahra said with a teasing contempt in her voice. 'Expediter, may we have the co-ordinates for Number 53.'

'Yes, ma'am.'

*Let's not be so sloppy this time. On the double, queen and her gang first, the workers second and the eggs third. Then we can watch the queen react,* said Xahra.

*Now, now, we have to learn the tricks of doing these mass 'ports,* Gollee said cheerfully.

Xahra shot him a startled look. *What do you mean?*

*I mean that if this proves successful in preventing another war on Xh-33, we're likely to be doing it on other occupied planets where we need to prevent similar massacres.*

*We are?* Pietro looked delighted with the prospect even if Xahra didn't.

*Speak for yourself, Gollee,* she said rather tartly.

*Oh, I do. And we all obey Earth Prime.* A touch of reprimand coloured his tone but he had carefully spoken only to Xahra. He could see the flush on her cheeks. 'Let's handle number 53, shall we?'

And they did, with expedition and efficiency, missing not one egg or tiny scurrier.

*Sir,* said Prime Thian to Earth Prime from the *Washington,* in orbit around its second target, a Hiver-occupied planet. *This one has twelve empty facilities. It was one of those that sent its Sphere after us . . . or rather came out to join the Sphere heading towards the system with the right kind of primary.*

*Really?* replied Jeff Raven with suddenly active interest. *Just twelve? Been down on the surface yet?*

*We've done initial probes, sir, and can investigate if you wish. There seems to be a lot of arable land left for them to expand onto.*

*We need to have GC readings on at least twelve hives, to be certain of the basic . . . shall I say, health and welfare . . . of the queens. The more data we have for comparison, the better we can plan the Containment of the Hiver Queens.*

Thian chuckled. *As you wish. And, ah, how's Operation Switch doing?*

Jeff Raven laughed. *With the massed might of eight fine Primes, the switcheroo is going very well indeed. Got two more days of shifting to do. They average about ten a day. Bit tricky getting those eggs from one basket to another. Young Pietro thought of a sleeve and Xahra upped that notion to a stocking just about the time Elizara thought of a tube bandage.*

*Yes,* Thian replied, remembering how they had been stored on the Great Sphere, *that would be tricky. They don't make a neat package, like workers do.*

291

*However, the ones that fell out don't seem to have been harmed nor did their fallout concern the queens. They had more on their minds than wobbling eggs underfoot.* He sent Thian a flash of a report of the queens marshalling workers to the fields. *Your father, your brother and your two sisters have all performed very well, Gollee tells me.*

*You sent GOLLEE GREN out there?*

*Why not? A change is as good as a rest. Broaden his outlook on life.* There was a pause. *Your grandmother informs me that Gollee Gren's outlook is quite broad enough. Get me some GC readings and data for comparisons, will you, Thian? We want to try Pierre Laney's gentle rain from heaven on that planet and see if it is as effective as we hope it will be at Xh-33. Smell may be more powerful than a missile after all.* A chuckle. *The deterrent of the future – alter the outlook by altering the ambient smells. Wish I could apply that to certain elements on Earth.*

Then the touch of Jeff Raven's mind left Thian's.

'Anything wrong, Thian, honey?' Alison Ann Greevy asked him.

'More tunnel-crawling,' he said with a sigh, 'to get comparison stinks and all the data we can find.'

She laughed, rumpling his hair. 'You know you love it when you stand right in front of a queen and she doesn't so much as give two hoots 'n' a holler.'

'I do like that part,' and Thian smoothed back his hair. 'It's that damned hazmat suit . . . and decontam and deodorizing afterwards.'

'Yeah, but that suit keeps the sting-pzzt out, doesn't it?' Gravy said.

'It does.' He rose from the couch and took four long strides to the door into the bridge. 'I better tell the admiral. Oh, and honey, Operation Switch is going along well.'

'Wonders will never cease!'

'I hope not.'

Thian managed to shorten the time of the onerous assignment by organizing twelve teams, all eager for the chance to do a live inspection of a hive facility. There were enough T-2s and T-3s in the First Fleet to accompany each team in case of trouble. Not that one expected any from the aloof queens, but he wasn't about to have anyone under his guidance become a victim. He wondered what *could* provoke a Hiver queen to action. Aside from checking her fields. Surely there must have been some recognition among the queens on Xh-33 that they had been removed from their original quarters?

Gravy went with him this time, and she was rather more impressed than she had been by the visuals and all the reports he had made.

'Sure is one thing to hear about and another to see,' she remarked, having clung to his hand as they entered the queen's quarters.

With the familiarity of many such visits, his teams collected the samples of air and soil both inside and outside the facility, counted workers, checked to be sure none of them were sporting new mace-like accessories in their extendibles, and returned to the *Washington*. By mid-afternoon, Thian was able to send the carrier with the garnered samples and details back to Earth Prime. He received the formula of the pheromone 'gentle rain' that was being used on Xh-33. This was to be disseminated in a spray over the lands, to disperse through the soil and thus into the food and the hives.

'We'd have to check periodically,' the admiral said, shaking his head as if he didn't quite believe that such an expedient would suffice.

'I expect so, sir,' Thian agreed amiably. 'But that wouldn't take more than one of the fast scouts, with a T-2 aboard, instead of a Fleet.'

'True, true,' Ashiant said, still not truly convinced as Thian perceived from his body language.

'Your orders are now to leave this system and proceed to the next one that's been listed as Hiver-occupied.'

Ashiant tapped in the relevant report. 'Hmmm. Seven days away at top speed. Ah, well, one more on our way home. Thank you, Thian.'

'Thian, honey,' Gravy began that night as they made ready for bed. 'If we have to check out every single one of those suspect systems on our way back, there's no reason I can't ask for maternity leave now, is there? I mean, Laria's working her Tower and Nav regs allow me to work till I get too clumsy . . . and . . . well, would you mind being a father?'

Thian turned towards her, his face lighting up with his delight. He crossed the distance between them and held her fiercely to him.

'Mind? I've been hoping to persuade you to consider it!'

'I don't need much persuasion, Thian honey,' she said pertly, and reached up to brush back his white lock before framing his face in her hands. 'In fact, I stopped prevention just in case you were . . .'

His response showed her just how much he appreciated her willingness. Laria might have the first new generation of Lyons, but, with such obvious co-operation, he and Alison Ann would not be far behind. And a 'happy event' would certainly make the long Search worthwhile on a personal level as well as a professional one.

Operation Switch was completed two days later. In several of the now abandoned Hives tiny creatures had been found, running circles, and been 'ported to their new homes.

While an atmosphere of celebration marked the final evening meal on board the *Asimov,* attended by all the participating Talents and the captains, everyone involved was tacitly hoping that 'the gentle rain' *would* have a long-term effect. Certainly the potential for another queens' war on Xh-33 had been defused.

Captain Osullivan had orders from the High Council to leave the *Strongbow* and the MS *KLLM* in orbit, keeping a close watch, with Commander Makako in the Moon Base, on the Xh-33. They had sufficient quantities of the 'gentle rain' of Pierre Laney's compound to soak the ground: the pheromones it contained would permeate the atmosphere and drift down into the queens' quarters.

The report from Thian Lyon in the First Fleet had confirmed that the latest Hiver-occupied world he had investigated was in no danger of erupting into dispute, and the

294

pheromone spray saturating the soil should have the necessary calming effect. If the oldest Hiver-occupied world had never indulged in overproduction of workers so that colonization became necessary, perhaps that had been the original intent: not the constant emigrations and 'sterilization' of other planets and their indigenous life-forms. Yet there were many questions unanswered. Those worlds that the Hivers had occupied, or were occupying, had to be identified. In the course of that wide-ranging survey, more planets could be made available to Mrdinis and Humans.

'Our drives starward are not so different from the Hivers after all,' Pierre remarked *sotto voce* to Captain Osullivan.

'No, they're not,' Etienne Osullivan replied. He had entertained that thought on several occasions, with some private chagrin. 'Except that any world with an evolving proto-sentient life-form is off limits to us and our Mrdini allies.'

'True,' Pierre replied with a tight smile. 'But should we not also limit our aggrandizement when we have so criticized another's?'

'That is not for me to decide,' and Osullivan was extremely glad of that.

'Nor I. I merely make an observation. But this has been the most stimulating task of my entire career,' Pierre went on, idly turning his wineglass by its stem as he mused. Then he lifted it to Osullivan. 'This has been a marriage of the scientific and the psychic.'

'Indeed it has,' said Osullivan, lifting his glass to touch Pierre's. 'You might say God-sent.'

Pierre caught the pun and laughed appreciatively before he finished the fine wine in his glass. 'I am scarcely God or a god, Captain, but I do have the finest Nose in the galaxy. I never once expected that my Talent would prove of such worth to my profession.'

'We all serve, Pierre, each in our own way.'

Jeff Raven brought back to the Rowan in their Callisto quarters the news that Zara's research had borne fruit.

'You mean, don't you, that no fruit will be borne,' said the

Rowan, locked in her husband's home-coming embrace. She could feel the sense of accomplishment vibrating through his body without needing to touch his mind.

'Whatever,' he said, chuckling at her correction. He released her somewhat so that, with his arm draped around her slender waist, they could walk into the dining-room where dinner awaited him. He appreciated that his wife preferred to cook their meals. They enjoyed the peace and quiet of the evening hours together. Both were on call for emergencies but both had also trained their assistants in Blundell and Callisto Tower to distinguish a 'real' problem from something that could be solved by them or in the morning.

'Odd that the solution to both our major problems should be linked to pheromones.'

'They certainly play a larger part in interactions of all the known species than *I* ever realized,' Jeff Raven said as he drew out her chair and seated her at the table. 'Let's just hope that such simple remedies can be found to all our problems.'

He filled their wineglasses before he sat down. Then he inhaled deeply of the aromas wafting up from the covered dishes on the hotplates. 'This smells great!'

'It's the taste that really matters,' the Rowan said and then waggled a finger at him. 'Let's think no more about problems, love.'

Jeff smiled lovingly at her. 'A toast first, to Pierre and his Nose, to our children and their children, and to those who will take our places: may they have the sense . . . and the scents . . . to provide peace throughout the galaxy.'

'To peace!'

**THE END**

296